DELIVER ME

"Quirky humor and a charming hero make Rochon's debut novel attractive reading. Colorful characters create a down-home appeal that will make readers feel the warm welcome typically indicative of the South. This novel captures the true essence of a town struggling to get back on its feet."

—*Romantic Times BOOKreviews*

"This is a wonderful story with rich characters and tons of local history. It will definitely leave you wanting more of the hot Doctor Holmes and his equally hot brothers, who, by the way, deserve their own stories."

—Coffee Time Romance

"I look forward to more from this author. I sincerely hope we get stories for both of Eli's brothers and his niece as well; I just loved them."

—Romance Reviews Today

"Elementary, my dear readers, as Farrah Rochon captures the city inside her fabulous contemporary medical romance with hopefully more Holmesian sibling tales to follow."

—Romance in Color, Harriet Klausner

RELEASE ME

"Rochon presents a stellar story that thoroughly entertains. Her writing style is consistent and easy to follow from start to finish, and all the characters are memorable...*Release Me* is most definitely worth the exciting journey."

—*Romantic Times BOOKreviews*

"*Release Me* is written in a way that is intriguing and easy to follow. Ms. Rochon has a way with words that will hold your interest with each twist she adds at just the right time."

—*Romance Reviews Today*

"An enjoyable contemporary romance starring likable lead characters."

—*Midwest Book Review*

JUST BREATHE

She laid her pretty eyes on him and that heavy thumping thing started happening within Alex's chest at an accelerated rate.

"You look like you came out on the losing end of a fight with a Smurf," she said with a grin, pointing to his face.

Alex rubbed his cheek, hoping the paint wouldn't spread as it had on the table. "There was an accident in art class," he explained.

She just continued grinning. Her smile was mesmerizing,

"Here," Renee said. She reached up and wiped his cheek.

Alex's breathing stopped completely.

That answered one of the questions that had been floating around his brain since he'd seen her this morning. Her warm brown skin really was as soft as silk.

"That's better," she said, her fingers still lingering on his cheek. The air between them crackled and sizzled. There was something he should be doing, but for the life of him, Alex could not remember.

Oh, wait, breathing. Yeah. He should definitely breathe.

FARRAH ROCHON

Rescue Me

LEISURE BOOKS NEW YORK CITY

A LEISURE BOOK®

February 2009

Published by

Dorchester Publishing Co., Inc.
200 Madison Avenue
New York, NY 10016

ISBN 10: 0-8439-6224-0
ISBN 13: 978-0-8439-6224-6
E-ISBN: 1-4285-0608-X

Printed in the United States of America.

10 9 8 7 6 5 4 3 2 1

Visit us on the web at www.dorchesterpub.com.

For my mother and father.

Thank you for teaching me to never give up on my dreams and for letting me know you would always be there just in case they didn't work out as planned.

"Let us not become weary in doing good, for at the proper time we will reap a harvest if we do not give up."
—Galatians 6:9

ACKNOWLEDGMENTS

First and foremost, thanks be to God. Always.

Thanks to my sister, Tamara, for being my first reader, and my aunt Cathy, for always being ready and willing to help.

To my critique group, for reading my proposal at a moment's notice. Where would I be without you all?

Thanks to the many authors I've met online, who have also become my friends. Thank you for sharing your wisdom.

To the Dreadnaught husbands and that one brother-in-law with the great sense of humor. Thanks for helping with that very serious situation.

Lastly, many thanks to Cheryl Corson, for going above and beyond the call of friendship. Needless to say, this book would not have been done in time without you.

Rescue
Me

Chapter One

"Boss, watch out!"

He didn't see it coming, but he sure as hell felt it land.

Instant nausea gripped Alexander Holmes's stomach as pain sliced through his right shoulder, shooting to his fingertips. Searing in its intensity, the all-consuming agony roared throughout his bloodstream, wrenching an anguished gasp from Alex's lips.

He went down. Hard.

"Help me roll the beam off him!"

"Hurry up, man!"

Alex tried to distinguish the voices coming at him from every angle, knew they belonged to his men, the construction workers he'd handpicked to work this job. But his mind was quickly becoming numb to anything outside of the torturous pressure radiating from his shoulder.

He attempted a deep breath, but it was too hard. The effort to block out the debilitating pain sapped his energy.

"Come on! We need to get him from under the beam now!"

"Somebody call an ambulance!"

"No," Alex murmured, clenching his jaw as another rush of pain soldiered its way down his arm. "Jason." He called for his foreman, but the word came out weak, barely audible even to his own ears.

Alex cried out as the crushing weight was lifted from his shoulder, leaving even more pain in its wake.

"Don't move him." He heard Jason's voice. "Wait for the paramedics to get here."

"Jason," Alex tried again. It was no use, there was too much chaos surrounding him for his thready voice to be heard through the bustle of men scurrying around the construction site.

"Hold on, boss. The ambulance is on its way."

Alex gave a valiant attempt to remain conscious, but sinking into the unknown promised a relief that he craved. Registering the faint whirl of the ambulance sirens in the distance, Alex succumbed to the pain-induced darkness.

A streak of light pierced the blessed night. Alex clenched his eyes shut, determined to hold on to the tranquil obscurity for as long as he could. It had been years since he'd found such peaceful rest.

Wait, why was he resting?

The week of nonstop thunderstorms had Holmes Construction days behind on the Mahalia Jackson Middle School project and he had another crew scheduled to start on the renovations to the emergency wing at Children's Hospital tomorrow. Rest was not on this week's agenda.

Alex tried rising from the bed only to find his body immobilized. He struggled to lift his arms, but they wouldn't budge.

"Where are you trying to go now?" came a voice that Alex recognized, but his brain wouldn't allow him to assign an owner.

He tried lifting his arm again. Nothing.

"Alex, can you hear me?"

Alex opened his eyes. He finally remembered who the voice belonged to: his future sister-in-law, Monica Gardner.

"There you are," Monica said, appearing at his left side and leaning over him.

Alex groaned as he stared up at the unfamiliar white-tiled ceiling. He tried to move his head, but the brace encasing his neck made it all but impossible. Alex groaned again. He licked his lips, the dryness leaving a stale, nasty taste in his mouth.

"How are you feeling?" she asked as she raised one eyelid, then the other, shining a penlight into his eyes.

"At dinner last night," he started. Why was his voice so raspy? "You said you would be working today, didn't you?" Alex asked Monica, an ER physician at the same hospital where his brother Elijah had just been named head of obstetrics.

"Yes," Monica answered.

Alex winced. "That means I'm in the hospital," he determined.

"Yes."

"Why am I in the hospital?"

"Because you were injured."

Alex fisted a handful of scratchy, utilitarian hospital bedding. "I'll bet it was Jason who called the ambulance. That boy should have known better."

"If you're referring to Jason Deering, then you're right, he is the one who called the ambulance."

"I knew it," Alex ground out. As if he had time to waste laid up in some hospital. He attempted to rise from the bed again, and his brain finally registered the restraints tied to his wrists, holding him prisoner.

"Untie my wrists," Alex demanded. "And get this thing from around my neck."

"I'll take the restraints off if you promise not to try getting up from the bed," Monica answered. "I can't remove your neck brace. You'll have to wait for your doctor."

"Come on, Monica. I don't have time for this, and if anyone knows that, it's Jason. What was he thinking, having them take me away in an ambulance?"

"Exactly what did you expect him to do, Alex?"

"There's a temporary trailer on the work site. He could have just put me in there so I could rest for a couple of minutes until the pain subsided." Even as he said the words, a sharp pain shot through Alex's head, leaving a dull ache to throb at his right temple.

"You think so?" Monica asked, unbuckling one restraint from around his wrist.

"All that ambulance did was probably cause an unnecessary distraction at the site," Alex pointed out. "We're already behind on the job because of all the rain this week."

"And you think all you needed was to lie down on a sofa for a few minutes?" Monica asked.

"Some aspirin and an hour or so rest and I would be good to go."

Monica shook her head, the rueful grin on her lips setting him on edge.

Uncertainty tightened Alex's chest. A slight but definite pounding behind his eyes joined the throbbing at his temple. The painful onslaught created a nauseating swirl in the pit of his stomach.

Suddenly wary, he asked, "What time is it?"

"What time do you think it is?" Monica asked.

Suspicious of that knowing lift to Monica's brow, Alex thought back to what he remembered about this morning. It had been around 10:00 A.M. when Jason had pulled him aside to point out a discrepancy he'd found on the electrical wiring blueprints. That beam had rolled onto him from an above scaffold deck a few minutes later.

"Is it around lunchtime?" Alex tried.

Monica looked at her watch and said, "In about four hours."

That didn't make any sense. Unless . . .

"How long have I been here?"

"Since yesterday morning," Monica answered, confirming his suspicions.

"No way," Alex argued.

The door to the hospital room opened.

"You're awake!"

His mother's excited gasp caused Alex to attempt to whip his head to the left, but the motion was halted by that damn neck brace.

"He woke up a few minutes ago," Monica provided.

"Why didn't you call me?" Mama asked as she came charging to his hospital bed.

Margo Holmes was slight in stature, but made up for it in determination. She was easily one of the most formidable women to walk the planet. And she took fierce care of her family.

Mama pulled one of the metal chairs up to his bedside and captured his hand. "How are you feeling?" she crooned, the light touch of her fingers bringing Alex back to those days when he was a boy and she would nurse him back from the flu with one of the home remedies she'd learned from her mother.

"I'm okay. If I could remember where the past twenty-four hours went I'd be even better."

"Do you remember anything about what happened yesterday?" Monica looked up from the notes she was reading.

"You mean that beam falling on top of me? Yeah, I remember it." Alex was able to move his head just enough to see the bandages wrapped around his shoulder and upper arm through the corner of his eye. "I don't remember anything else, other than the guys at the site trying to lift the beam off me."

"And you remember nothing else about the accident or your surgery?" Monica asked.

"Surgery?"

"You had surgery yesterday," Mama said. "They just brought you from recovery to a private room a few hours ago."

"Let me get your doctor," Monica said.

"You're not my doctor?"

"I was when you first came through the ER," Monica answered. "But Dr. Lewis has taken over your care. He performed your surgery."

"What type of surgery did I have?"

"I'll let Dr. Lewis explain. He has a lot to go over with you, and I need to get back to the ER."

Mama rose from her seat and met Monica in front of his hospital bed, where the two hugged.

"You'll be at the house tonight?" Mama asked.

"I will. I'm not sure about Eli, though. The doctors in OB are taking turns covering for one of their colleagues who started her maternity leave this week. Tonight is Eli's turn." Monica stopped at the door. "I'm glad you're awake, Alex."

Alex smiled at his future sister-in-law, even though he couldn't look at her. He was grateful Eli had been lucky enough to find a woman like Monica to love him. She had a pure heart and a good head on her shoulders. That beautiful face didn't hurt, either.

Mama settled back in the chair and resumed caressing his hand.

"You scared us," she said.

"Sorry," Alex answered. "Where's Jasmine?"

"Mildred Collins's granddaughter is watching her."

He'd started paying Ebony Collins to watch his six-year-old daughter a few months ago—after Monica had pointed out that his relying on Mama as a babysitter was interfering with his mother's social life. Of course, Alex hadn't realized his mother even *had* a social life outside of working with her women's group at the church, but something was going on.

Earlier this year, Mama had picked up and left for three days without telling anyone. Six months had passed, and she still had not divulged the truth about where she'd been or who she'd gone with that week. Whenever Alex or his brothers brought it up, she said she was with a few friends and quickly changed the subject. Alex was getting tired of her evading the issue; he'd get a straight answer out of her soon. But not today. He had enough to worry about.

"How did Jazzy get home from school?" he asked.

"*I* picked her up," his mother answered with an exuberance that caused Alex to grit his teeth.

After years of relying on her sons to take her from point A to point B, Mama decided to get her license renewed a few months ago and bought herself a little used car. The last time he and his younger brothers, Eli and Toby, had gotten together for a game of pool, they'd all agreed they didn't like these new changes in Mama.

"Are you really feeling okay, honey?" Mama asked.

Alex tried to shrug his shoulder, but the zing that shot through his system was like a punch to his gut.

"Don't do that," his mother warned.

"What kind of surgery did I have?"

"Let the doctor explain," she said. Alex heard the door open. "And speak of the devil. Good morning, Dr. Lewis."

"Good morning, Mrs. Holmes."

A tall, slender man with gold-rimmed glasses and salt-and-pepper hair entered Alex's line of vision. He carried a magnetic clipboard in his hand and a large manila folder under his arm.

"How's the patient?"

"He's awake," Mama said enthusiastically, if unnecessarily.

"That's how I like to start my day." The doctor laughed at his own lame joke. "How are you feeling?" he asked as he read the printout from the machine that let out an intermittent beep.

"I'm a little sore," Alex answered. "Can you take this thing off my neck?"

"I'll bet that's uncomfortable."

Alex resisted an agitated eye roll as he lifted his upper body slightly so the doctor could get to the brace behind his neck.

"Okay, that's better. Are you feeling any pain anywhere?"

"It's nothing I can't deal with," Alex answered.

"Are you sure?" the doctor asked, peering at Alex over the rim of his glasses. "We can up the dosage of your morphine drip."

"No," Alex practically shouted. "I don't need any pain medication."

"Believe me, you want pain medication."

Alex knew it was Eli before he turned and spotted his brother leaning against the door jamb. He wore scrubs, which told Alex his brother probably had a round of deliveries scheduled for today. If he was just performing rounds, he would have been dressed in what Alex called his preppy doctor uniform, khaki pants and a polo shirt.

"How's he doing, Doc?" Eli asked, pushing from the door and coming into the hospital room.

"That's what I'm about to find out," Dr. Lewis answered.

Eli ambled over to the bed, giving their mother a kiss on the cheek before clasping Alex's left hand in a firm shake.

"How's it going, brother?"

"Just trying to figure out how I ended up in here," Alex answered.

"Dr. Gardner said you remember the accident at the work site," Dr. Lewis said.

"Yeah, a beam fell from the overhead scaffolding onto my shoulder. Now I've got to deal with OSHA and all that other crap."

Eli waved the thought off. "Jason is taking care of all of that."

"Do you remember anything else?" Dr. Lewis asked.

Alex shook his head, grateful that he could do so freely now that the neck brace was gone.

"Okay." The doctor slid an X-ray film from the folder he'd carried in with him. "Here's what we're dealing with." He held the film up to a lamp that extended over the center of the bed and, using a capped ink pen, pointed to a large white blob on the X-ray. "The beam caused severe trauma to the scapulohumeral muscle group, specifically the subscapularis."

"Uh, yeah, Doc?" Alex nodded toward Eli. "He's the one who went to medical school. You'll have to break this down for me in layman's terms."

"Sorry," Dr. Lewis said with a contrite murmur. "The subscapularis is the most frequently used of the rotator cuff muscles. When the beam came down it tore into it." He pointed the muscle out on the X-ray. "I'll be frank with you, Alex; a tear of this magnitude is pretty severe."

"Meaning what?" Alex asked.

"It means you're lucky Dr. Lewis happens to be one of the best orthopedic surgeons in the South," Eli answered.

Dr. Lewis accepted Eli's accolade with a nod. "It also means you have a long road ahead of you in terms of recovery."

"When you say 'long road' are we talking two, three weeks?"

The doctor shook his head. "Longer than that."

"How much longer?" Alex asked, impatience making his eye twitch.

With a shrug, the doctor said, "It all depends on how quickly the muscle heals, but it will definitely be more than a couple of weeks. I'd say you're looking at a minimum of six before you have any range of motion in that shoulder."

"*Six weeks*? You mean to tell me with all the strides being made in medicine people still have to wait a month and a half after surgery before they're back to normal?"

"Medical science must still bow down to the natural healing of the human body," Dr. Lewis answered. "There's only so much we can do."

Alex shut his eyes at the news. He did not need this, not with the work they were about to start on Children's Hospital, and the other jobs Holmes Construction had lined up. He couldn't afford a single minute away from his business, let alone a month and a half.

"You'll need to take it easy, Mr. Holmes."

"That phrase is relative," Alex said.

"He means no working on construction sites," Eli clarified. "You shouldn't have been out there yesterday."

"Your brother is right, Alex." His mother decided to chime in. "I thought you were supposed to be behind the desk from now on?"

"I am, Mama. I was just helping out since we were behind on the job. And I still have to supervise."

"Well, you're going to be sitting on the sidelines for a while," Eli said. "I don't know if I'll make dinner tonight," he added, leaning over to give their mother another kiss.

"Monica already explained. If you want, I can drive out here to the hospital and bring you some leftovers," she offered.

"No, thanks, Mrs. Roadrunner. You're going to tire out that car."

"I was just offering," Mama said.

"I'll suffer through the food here at the hospital." To Alex he said, "I'll try to stop in on you later."

"How long will I be in here?" Alex asked Dr. Lewis.

"I want to keep you for at least a week."

"No way." Alex shook his head.

"Alexander, listen to your doctor," his mother warned.

"Forget it. I'm not staying in the hospital for a week." He had a daughter to take care of, and a business to run. And he still had to turn in his test for his online macroeconomics class. He'd worked for two nights straight on that test.

"I need to get out of here," Alex said.

"I want to monitor the progress on that arm," Dr. Lewis said.

"I'll come in for a checkup. There are people way sicker than I am who can use this hospital bed."

"You suffered a serious injury, Mr. Holmes, and you just underwent major surgery. If you do not heed the recommended recovery regimen, the damage can be permanent."

"Don't worry, Dr. Lewis, he is going to follow your advice.

I'll make sure of it," Mama said in that voice that brooked no further argument.

Alex sighed, wishing he could bring both his hands up to rub his temples, but he had to settle for just his left one since his right shoulder was wrapped up tighter than King Tut's mummified body.

"Lay it out for me, Doc," Alex said. "What am I really looking at here?"

"How long since your last vacation?" the doctor asked.

Alex grimaced. "Long enough."

"I suggest you get ready for another one."

Chapter Two

Alex pressed the up button on the remote, skimming past soap operas and talk shows.

"Is there anything on TV during the day?" he asked the empty living room.

He settled on the Food Network and listened with half an ear as Emeril Lagasse whipped up some French dish Alex knew he wouldn't know how to pronounce if he ever saw it on a restaurant menu.

He rose from the recliner he'd spent most of his time in since arriving at Mama's house over a week ago. According to Dr. Lewis, he still had at least a couple more days of sleeping upright. He settled onto the sofa. Change was good.

"Alex, you want some iced tea? I just made a pitcher." His mother's voice carried from the kitchen.

"No, thanks."

She walked through the open doorway that led from the dining room to the living room in the shotgun-style house Alex's father had purchased more than forty years ago in Uptown New Orleans.

Alex had offered over the years to update the design, but Mama wouldn't hear of it. In a way, Alex was relieved she'd always turned down his suggestion to bring one of his construction crews over to renovate the structure. Some of the happiest memories of his thirty-eight years had occurred in this house. A sense of comfort and peace washed over him whenever he walked through the door.

These last two weeks, however, did not fall into the peaceful category. Mama's constant pampering was driving him crazy.

"You're out of your chair," she said.

"I'm tired of that recliner."

"Why did you sit on that end of the sofa?" Mama asked as she attacked the undetectable dust she swore had invaded the impeccably clean house.

"What's wrong with this part of the sofa?" Alex asked.

"You're putting pressure on your right arm."

"I've got a pillow under it."

"That doesn't matter. If you don't want to sit in the recliner, at least come on over to this side of the sofa."

"I can't see the television as good from there," Alex grumbled, and felt like a child for arguing.

Mama's lips thinned into a firm, familiar line. "Excuse me for trying to help you get better," she said, upping the stakes by crossing her arms over her chest.

She had that look—a mixture of disgust and disappointment—down to a science. She'd spent the last thirty-eight years perfecting it, and knew it was the one look that would make her three sons fall in line.

"Fine," Alex conceded, moving to the other end of the sofa. The woman was a master when it came to laying on a guilt trip.

He had to keep reminding himself that Mama had his best interests in mind. The coddling was bordering on unbearable, but Alex knew what he was getting into when he'd agreed to stay at Mama's after he'd been released from the hospital. When he'd revealed his intentions of recovering at his own house in Old Carrolton, Mama had looked at him as if he'd lost his mind.

She'd demanded he and Jasmine stay at her house until Alex was able to function, at least at a basic level, on his own. Jasmine had jumped up and down as if she'd won the lottery, which was almost the case with the way his mother spoiled her only granddaughter rotten.

Mama always fussed over her boys when they came over to the house, fixing their food, offering to do laundry; anything she thought would take away some of the burden. Alex could admit to going over to Mama's when he needed a little extra help, knowing the offer would be forthcoming. Heck, the majority of the time he counted on it.

As much as he boasted about being able to raise his six-year-old daughter on his own, Alex knew he'd be a burned-out waste if he didn't have his mother to turn to when he was in a bind. She was there for him whenever Alex needed her, and he was much more grateful than he ever told her.

But the past two weeks had been major overkill, even for Mama. From the moment Alex had been released from the hospital, she had been hovering like a bald eagle protecting her nest.

Alex had reluctantly accepted the invitation, knowing it was the most sensible option. How would he iron Jazzy's clothes and comb her hair for school with an immobile shoulder? He'd needed Mama's help.

What he didn't need was his mother breathing down his neck every five seconds and refusing to allow Alex to do anything for himself. His first day out of the hospital, he'd had to stop her from following him into the bathroom.

Most people would welcome someone waiting on them twenty-four-seven, but Alex had grown tired of the constant pampering by day two. If he didn't get out of this house soon, they would have to add a prescription for anxiety pills to the pain medication the doctor had him taking.

Alex used his left arm to push himself off the couch and silently cursed the slight wobble his unbalanced equilibrium caused. He knew it was all the pills in his system. They had his body out of whack.

"Where are you going?" Mama asked.

"To get dressed."

"Why?"

"Because it's eleven o'clock in the morning and I'm still in pajamas."

"What's wrong with that?" Mama asked, putting down the porcelain angel she'd been dusting.

"Pajamas are supposed to be worn at night, not in the middle of the day. I feel like a bum."

"You're recovering from surgery, Alexander. You need to be comfortable."

"Mama," Alex groaned. "I just want to change my clothes."

"Okay, baby. I'm sorry," his mother said. She came over to him and Alex put his good arm around her, bending down to give her a kiss on the cheek. "I don't mean to be such a nag," she said.

"You're not being a nag."

"I am," Mama admitted. "I just want to make sure you're okay, Alex. You don't take care of yourself."

"Of course I take care of myself."

"No, you don't. Not the way you should. You're too busy taking care of everybody else."

"Who, Jasmine? She's my responsibility," he pointed out.

"Yes, she is, but I'm not, and neither are your brothers, or the men and women who work for you. You put everyone before yourself. I just want to make sure you're taken care of for a change."

The sincerity in her eyes was a stark reminder of just how lucky he was to have someone like Mama in his corner. Alex leaned over and gave her another kiss. Thank God for this woman.

"I'm going to be okay, Mama," he reassured her.

"I know," she answered, giving him a squeeze. "Because I'm taking care of you."

Alex let out an I-give-up laugh. "Can I please get out of these clothes?"

"Fine," his mother answered.

Alex followed her into the kitchen, grabbed his favorite blue and white mug from the cabinet, and filled it with water from the tap.

"I'm going to drive over to the grocery store in a minute. Do you need anything?" Mama asked.

"Not really," he answered, draining the mug and setting it in the sink.

"You sure? I was thinking about picking up an oyster po' boy for lunch."

"Nah. I'll heat up some of that roast from last night."

"I can do that for you."

"I got it."

"Okay, honey," she said after a beat, though Alex could tell she was itching to grab the roast from the fridge and shove it in the microwave.

Mama picked up her purse from where it hung on the arm of a chair at the kitchen table. "I'll be back around one o'clock. I want to stop in on Oretha Borne. I haven't seen her since her hip surgery."

"Take your time," Alex said.

"Call my cell phone if you need anything," she called.

As soon as the door closed behind his mother, Alex hauled it to the other half of the house. The shotgun house had originally been two, but his father had bought the other half when their old next-door neighbors had moved to Mississippi. What used to be home to the Johnsons now housed three bedrooms and a bathroom.

Alex shuffled through the room his younger brothers shared on his way to the bathroom that separated the Holmes boys' childhood rooms.

He reached behind the shower curtain and turned on the hot water, then started to strip. It was hell trying to pull the button-down pajama top off with one arm. He managed to wrestle off the shirt, then pushed his cotton pajama bottoms and boxers down his legs, shoving them in the hamper.

Grabbing a washcloth from the neatly folded stack on the wooden shelving unit, Alex stepped into the shower, making sure to keep his right arm away from the spray as much as possible. He'd taken baths this past week since it was easier to avoid getting his postoperative dressing wet, but Alex didn't have time to wait for the tub to fill. He needed to get clean and get out of the house before Mama got back from the store.

He did a halfhearted job of showering, then quickly dried himself off and went in search of clothes. Any other day he would have ironed the jeans and button-down, even though he was going to a dusty construction site. Today, Alex could not have cared less if the image he projected was professional or not. His sole focus was to do something with his day that didn't include watching reruns of *Judge Joe Brown*. He had to find some semblance of his normal life.

Alex struggled through pulling on his jeans and donning the blue and white shirt Eli had bought him, two sizes too big. Thank goodness his brother had the ability to think ahead. The roomy shirt glided over his bandaged shoulder with ease.

The buttons, however, were another issue.

Alex fastened the four in the middle and said to hell with the two on the top and bottom. Mama had been gone fifteen minutes already. If Murphy's Law was up to par, traffic would be nonexistent, the ten-items-or-less line would be empty at the grocery store, and Mrs. Borne wouldn't be at home when Mama stopped in to visit.

He quickly passed a hairbrush over his close-cut hair, then hustled to the kitchen, where his keys hung on a nail next to the door. He locked up the kitchen and pulled the screen door to the porch tight.

His heart beat hard and fast in his chest as he climbed into his Ford F-150. He just knew Mama's little Toyota Corolla was going to pull into the driveway any second now.

Alex swore under his breath. He was a grown man. He could leave the house any time he wanted to leave.

That half-assed declaration of his manhood didn't stop him from heaving a bone-melting sigh of relief that Mama had not returned. His right arm immobile, Alex awkwardly reached across to start the truck and shift the gear into reverse. He backed out of the driveway, groaning in frustration as he reached over to shift the truck into drive. Maybe driving two weeks after shoulder surgery wasn't such a good idea.

Alex made his way up Amelia Street, taking a right onto St. Charles Avenue. He arrived at the construction site at Felicity and Orange streets less than ten minutes later. He parked just outside the newly constructed chain-link fence, noting one of the sections was leaning slightly.

"Boss?"

Alex looked up, finding his head foreman, Jason Deering, walking toward him, half his face covered by the safety shield attached to his hard hat.

"What happened to the fence?" Alex asked without preamble.

Jason looked from the top of the fence to the bottom, as if the piece of wobbly steel could speak for itself.

"Have somebody straighten this out," Alex said.

"I'm on it," Jason answered. "So, what you doing here, boss? I thought you weren't coming back for at least four more weeks?"

"I'm not back." Alex adjusted the hard hat he'd grabbed from the front seat of his truck. "I just stopped by to check out how things were going." He started for the group of guys carrying stacks of two-by-fours from a pallet just to the right of the newly poured concrete foundation.

"It's all good," Jason said. "We picked up a couple of the days we missed because of the rain."

"Oh yeah?" Alex's brow rose. "And how did you manage to do that?"

"A few of the guys on the Pennington Parking Lot job came over to help since they were ahead of schedule."

Alex nodded his approval that it was extra men, and not overeagerness, that accounted for their accelerated work schedule. His crews knew better than to compromise workmanship for the sake of timeliness. As much as he hated coming in behind schedule on a job, if it happened, so be it. It was better than shoddy work. Holmes Construction did not cut corners.

Alex surveyed the site and was startled at the annoyance building up inside him as he studied the superior work being accomplished.

Without him.

The reality of the construction site running like a well-oiled machine was a punch in the gut. It was counterproductive to hope that things would be at least a little chaotic since he had not been around for two weeks. Counterproductive and stupid. Anything that happened here, good or bad, was a reflection of the example he set as owner of the company. But if his foreman could elicit this level of production from the crew without Alex there to breathe down their necks, then maybe what Eli and Toby had been telling him these past few years really was true. Alex wasn't needed out in the field anymore.

The thought of cutting back his time at the work sites caused a chill to course through Alex's body. He'd tried doing the desk thing before. He'd lasted less than a week.

Alex admitted he had a problem with control when it came to Holmes Construction, but how could he not? He'd built this business from the ground up. Literally. He'd actually built the small building that had housed the company's first set of offices.

It was due to his blood, sweat, and tears that Holmes Construction was the fastest growing construction company in the Deep South, and one of the most successful African-American-owned small businesses in the region. He'd sacrificed nearly everything for this business. His time. His sleep. His marriage.

Alex briefly closed his eyes. Those were memories he didn't have the stomach to think about today.

"How's the arm?" Jason asked as he followed Alex on his perusal of the job site.

"It's healing," Alex answered.

"I swear, when that beam landed on you, I thought that was it, boss."

"It wasn't as bad as it seemed."

"Shoot, boss. From what your brother said after the surgery, it sounds like things were really bad."

Alex didn't have to ask which brother had stuck his nose where it didn't belong. "When did you talk to Eli?" he asked through clenched teeth.

"He came over to the site just after your surgery and briefed us all about what you'd been through. All the guys here felt so bad for you."

Alex made a mental note to beat the hell out of Eli when he saw him tonight at Mama's. As if he needed his brother to play spokesman for his injury. One thing he did not want was sympathy from the men who worked for him.

Alex toured the rest of the site and gave his employees the praise they deserved for a job well done. On the drive back to Mama's he tried to abate his sense of uselessness by going over all the work he'd accomplished in the past week. The time off had given him the opportunity to tackle the mountain of paperwork that had accumulated on his desk over the past few months. He'd had extensive safety investigations performed on two minor incidents that happened on a job over the summer. He'd spent the last couple of days studying the findings and had figured out measures he could implement to prevent the incidents from occurring again.

The extra time had also given him a chance to concentrate on school. No one in his family knew about the online classes he began taking last spring in an effort to finally earn the bachelor's degree he'd given up on after his father died and left Alex with two brothers and a mother to watch over. With running his business, taking care of Jasmine, and trying to finish up the paper he had to write for the European history class he'd foolishly chosen as an elective, Alex was on the verge of burnout.

He turned down Amelia Street and spotted Toby's Acura parked along the curb in front of his mother's house. His family usually got together for Sunday dinner, but his youngest brother, Toby, was leaving tomorrow to go on tour with the singing sensation he'd discovered, Aria Jordan. Six months ago, Aria had won the title of a reality-TV talent show and was now one of the hottest names in music.

Alex pulled up behind Toby's car and tried to get out of the truck as quickly as his aching shoulder would allow.

Mama was standing just inside the open front door.

Alex swore under his breath. He walked over to the gravel driveway, passing Eli's SUV and Mama's car. No one ever used the front door. Maybe he could pretend he didn't see her standing there with her arms crossed over her chest.

"Don't act as if you don't see me, Alexander."

His chin fell to his chest. Alex turned left and walked along the pathway up to the small front porch. "It's no big deal, Mama," he said as he approached.

"Then why did you have to sneak out of the house?" his mother asked.

He was about to argue that he didn't sneak out, but decided it was time he confront Mama about her constant hovering.

"I had to sneak out because someone has been keeping me in here like I'm in prison."

"I have not—"

"Yes, you have," he cut her off. "You've been smothering me and you know it. The fact that I had to wait until you were out of the house before I could leave says enough."

"I'm trying to help you follow your doctor's orders."

"Dinner is getting cold, Mama. Let's go inside."

"Where have you been?"

"Let's go inside," Alex insisted.

His mother turned and retreated into the living room. "I'm going to find out," she said.

"And just what are you going to do if you find out? You do remember I'm a thirty-eight-year-old man, right?" Alex asked.

"Since I'm the one who suffered through forty-one hours of labor with you, I guess I would remember," she answered. She was The Guilt Master. "Now tell me where you ran off to," she said.

"No." Alex followed her through the living room and into the dining room where his brothers and future sister-in-law, Monica, were already seated around the table.

"Oooh, you're in trouble," Eli said.

"I wouldn't want to be you," Toby followed.

"Shut up," Alex told the both of them.

"Hey there, Alex." Monica rose from her seat and greeted him with a kiss on the cheek. "Don't pay attention to your brothers."

"I never do," Alex said.

"Daddy!" Jasmine flew in from the kitchen, her arms opened wide. Her light brown eyes, so much like her mother's, were bright with excitement.

"Hey there, Jazzy Bean." Alex smiled, stooping down to give her a one-armed hug. One of her two thick braids was missing a barrette on the end and had started to unravel. "How was school?"

"I killed a turtle," she answered matter-of-factly.

"On purpose?" Toby asked.

"No, Uncle Toby." Jasmine gave him an exaggerated eye roll only a six-year-old girl who watched more television than she should could pull off.

Alex tapped her on the shoulder to draw her attention back to him. "What happened to the turtle, Pumpkin?"

"I don't know." Jasmine hunched her shoulders. "Mrs. Overland brought the turtle in for everybody to see, and we all got to hold it. When it was my turn, it just died."

"Well, did you do anything to it?" Monica asked.

Jasmine shook her head, guilt gleaming through her round eyes.

"You sure, Water Lily?" Eli asked, using one of the many nicknames Jasmine pretended she didn't like, but secretly loved. Eli always called her a different type of flower.

"I didn't do nothing to that turtle," Jazzy persisted.

"You didn't do anything," Eli corrected.

"I didn't do *anything*," Jasmine reiterated, again with the eye roll. It was time Alex broke her of that habit. "I just tried making the turtle better, that's all."

The adults at the table all looked at each other. Alex turned his daughter to face him again and asked, "How?"

"I gave him a cough drop."

"Why?"

"He looked sick, and when I put him up to my ear, I didn't hear him breathing. When I couldn't breathe, Grandma gave me cough drops to help clear up the mussus."

"Mucus," Alex corrected.

"Yeah, the mussus. I thought the turtle had mussus, so I gave him one of my cough drops to help him breath better."

"She murdered the turtle," Eli deadpanned.

"Stop it," Monica said under her breath. "It was a mistake."

"Let's hope," Toby added.

Mama came into the dining room carrying a glass dish with baked pork chops covered in gravy.

"Grandma, did you see the towels?" Jasmine asked. "I put them all away."

"I saw, baby."

"So, can I go?"

"Your plate is on the kitchen table."

"Yes!" Jasmine cheered. She disentangled herself from Alex's hold and ran to the kitchen. In a matter of seconds, she ran back from the kitchen holding a plate of something Alex couldn't identify, and went straight through the dining room into the living room. The sound of the television firing on soon followed.

"What was that about?" Alex asked his mother as he rounded the table and took the seat at the opposite end.

"I told her she could have chicken nuggets and watch TV if she helped me with the laundry. She put the towels away."

"That's part of her chores at home, Mama. She shouldn't get special treats for doing something she already has to do."

There was a pregnant pause; then Eli said, "We didn't think Jasmine should be in here for the conversation we're about to have."

The hairs on the back of Alex's neck stood at attention as his eyes roamed over the faces at the table. Faces that were focused on him.

"What's wrong?" His heartbeat automatically escalated.

"Jasmine's principal called while you were away," Mama answered.

Trepidation slithered down his spine. "What did she say?"

"Apparently, Jasmine has been acting out in class," Monica said.

"Acting out how?"

"The teacher says she's been bullying some of the other students," Eli answered. "And any time they try to discipline her, she starts screaming uncontrollably and crying about not having a mother anymore."

"Pretty smart, if you asked me," Toby said, stabbing a pork chop with his fork and plopping it on his plate. "I tried milking Pop's death my entire seventh-grade year."

"Tobias Anthony!" their mother screeched.

"Could you try not being an ass once in a while?" Eli grumbled.

"No language at the dinner table, Elijah," Mama warned. She turned to Alex. "The principal wants to speak with you tomorrow."

If he were not so upset, Alex would have laughed at the irony. He'd gone through twelve years of school without ever being called to the principal's office for discipline problems. Jasmine was only in the first grade and was already making a name for herself as a troublemaker.

"What am I supposed to do?" Alex asked.

"Talk to the principal. Then you'll need to talk to that little diva in there," Mama said. "She has to learn she cannot use Chantal's death as an excuse to behave however she wants."

"This from the woman who's allowing her to eat junk and watch TV during dinner," he snorted. A flash of hurt stalked across Mama's face, and Alex immediately felt like a jerk. "Sorry, Mama."

"We are all guilty of spoiling her," his mother argued. "I can admit to giving her more than I probably should. She's my only grandchild, and it is hard to think about her having to grow up without her mother."

"Yeah, but she's not the only kid that's ever had to grow up without a mother," Eli rationalized.

Mama nodded. "We've got to stop making excuses for her."

"Did the principal suggest a time we should meet?" Alex asked.

"She asked that you call her office tomorrow morning so you two could set up a time that works for the both of you."

"Well, any time works for me. It's not like I'm doing anything with my day."

"Except for sneaking out like a teenager," Mama said.

Alex swallowed his retort as they settled in to eat. Dishes piled high with succulent sides made their way around the table as everyone took turns filling the rest of the family in on what was happening in their lives.

"Where's Sienna?" Monica asked Toby.

Sienna Culpepper was Toby's fiancée. The two had been best friends since childhood. However, Toby had never pursued a real relationship with Sienna until earlier this year when Sienna worked on the promotion for the TV show that also solidified Toby's career in the music business.

"She's having dinner with Ivana. She said she would try to stop in tomorrow to see you before we leave," Toby said between bites.

"Well, Monica and I have some news," Eli interrupted.

Alex, Toby and Margo looked at them expectantly.

"We've set a date for the wedding," Monica answered, her smile stretching from ear to ear.

"It's about time," Toby said.

"Congratulations." Mama jumped out of her seat and came around to the other side of the table, lavishing both Monica and Eli with kisses. "I can finally start buying all the wedding favors and decorations I've found on the Internet."

"Only if you plan on bringing all that stuff to St. Martin," Eli said.

"What?" Mama asked.

"We've decided to have a small ceremony in the Virgin Islands," Monica explained. "We're thinking of St. Martin, since that's where Eli's father's ancestors came from."

"Oh yeah, baby," Toby said, rubbing his hands together. "I'm up for a little fun in the sun. When are ya'll gonna do this thing?"

"We were hoping to get married later this fall. The weather is really mild around that time."

"But all the ladies from the church can't go to the Virgin Islands," Mama argued as she returned to her seat.

"That's a good thing, since they're not invited," Eli said.

"Eli." Monica slapped his hand. "We just want a small ceremony with family, Margo."

"But—"

"No buts, Mama."

"I hope I can get away," Toby said.

"You'd better," Monica threatened. "We'd love for Aria to perform at the ceremony."

"I wonder if Sienna would go for a double wedding on the beach," Toby mused, reaching for the last dinner roll.

A high-pitched sound chimed throughout the kitchen.

"That's me." Eli pulled his BlackBerry from its leather sheath and stared at the screen. "I've got to get to the hospital."

"I thought you were off tonight," Mama complained.

"Not for this patient," Eli said as he rose from the table, taking one last bite from his pork chop. "I promised Amanda Daniels I would deliver her baby boy, no matter what."

"Wait, I've got pecan pie in the kitchen. Let me get you a piece."

"Send it home with Monica," Eli said. He kissed his fiancée, then went over to Mama's side of the table and kissed her.

"I should probably get going, too," Toby said. "I left one last batch of clothes in the dryer. I need to get my laundry done so I can finish packing."

Everyone started rising from the table at the same time. Mama went around and gave Toby a long, hard squeeze. "Love you, baby."

"Love you, too, Mama," Toby said, returning her hug.

He said good-bye to Monica before making his way to Alex. Alex captured the hand Toby held out and brought his brother in for a hug.

"Take care of yourself," Alex ordered.

"You, too. Don't push it too hard. You need to give yourself time to heal."

"You sound like the doctor," Alex said.

"No, I sound like someone who knows a little about injuries."

If anyone knew about debilitating injuries, it was Toby. His spine had been crushed in a head-on collision just before his rookie season in the NBA began. Toby had endured a long recovery, but he'd gotten through it.

"Good luck with that meeting with Jazzy's principal tomorrow. Call and let me know what happens," Toby said. "Let me go in and give her a kiss good-bye."

"Give Sienna my best, just in case she doesn't make it here tomorrow," Mama said, giving Toby one last squeeze.

"I will, Mama," he answered, then went into the living room to say good-bye to Jasmine.

"I'll clear the table," Monica offered.

"Don't worry about that," Mama said, going for the dish with the squash and shrimp casserole.

"I've got it, Margo," Monica insisted. "Go in the living room and give Toby one last kiss good-bye. You know you're dying to."

"Oh, all right," Mama said. She headed for the living room without another word.

Alex reached for his empty plate and received a slap on the hand.

"Don't you dare," Monica warned.

"I am capable of removing a few dishes from the table."

"Not when I said I would do it," Monica replied. "Save your energy for when no one is here to help."

Alex followed her into the kitchen. He picked up the empty bread basket on the way.

"Your head is as hard as a rock," Monica chastised, grabbing the basket out of his hand.

Looking back to make sure his mother was still in the living room, Alex sidled up next to Monica, and whispered, "How are the plans coming along for Mama's party?"

Monica had pretty much taken over the plans they were making for the sixtieth birthday party he, Eli, and Toby had decided to throw for their mother. Ever since she'd put together a charity banquet for the hospital where she and Eli worked, Monica had turned into the ultimate social planner. Alex had been more than happy to hand the preparations over to his future sister-in-law, since anything without a *Dora the Explorer* theme was outside his realm of knowledge when it came to parties.

"You should see the cake!" Monica's eyes lit up. "It's going to be gorgeous."

"Just let me know if there's anything you need."

Monica waved off his concern. "Let me worry about the party. You've got enough on your plate. Speaking of which, what are you going to do about Jasmine?"

Alex's entire body sagged under the weight of this new problem. He expelled a deep sigh and ran his left hand down his face. "I need to find out exactly what's going on first. She hasn't been acting any differently at home. I had no idea what she was up to at school."

"That's because she's the only six-year-old at home and it's easy for her to get whatever she wants. At school, she has to compete with twenty classmates for attention."

"That's no reason for her to throw tantrums. And using her mother's death as an excuse? Jasmine knows better than that."

"Maybe she doesn't, Alex," Monica said. She dropped the stopper into the sink and started running hot water. Mama did not believe in automatic dishwashers. "It's obvious she's seeking something, or else she wouldn't be acting out."

"You just said it yourself; she gets practically anything she wants. I'm guilty of spoiling her too much as it is, but when you add in her grandmother, uncles, and you, Jasmine wants for nothing."

"I'm not an expert in child psychology but I have seen enough cases in the ER where kids have acted out against their own bodies as a call for attention. It sounds like Jasmine's aggression is being projected onto her classmates, instead of herself."

"So you're saying I should be happy she's beating up her

classmates as opposed to slicing at her skin with razor blades?"

"I'm not saying you should be *happy* about any of this, but you need to get a handle on it before things get out of hand. I don't want to see her in my ER in five years."

Alex leaned back against the kitchen counter, closed his eyes, and kneaded his temple. "Sometimes I doubt whether I'm cut out for this parenting stuff."

"Alex, you are one of the best parents I've ever met," Monica said.

He cocked one eye open.

"Seriously," Monica insisted. "You shouldn't automatically assume this has anything to do with you as a parent. There's no telling what goes through the mind of a little girl Jasmine's age." She patted him on his good arm. "Wait until you hear what the principal has to say about her behavior before jumping to any conclusions."

"Wait until the morning before trying to figure out why my daughter has turned into a demon child who kills innocent turtles with over-the-counter medication, *and* beats up her classmates? Oh yeah, I can do that," Alex snorted.

Monica burst out laughing. "The turtle death should be under investigation. I think it was an accident."

"As far as the turtle's concerned, that doesn't really matter, does it?"

Sobering, Monica stared at him with sympathetic eyes. "It's going to be okay," she reassured him.

Alex could only hope she was right.

Chapter Three

"It's a good thing I'm not vain," Renee Moore said after the shower of plaster rained down on her head, sending up another cloud of white dust when it landed at her feet.

"Well, I am," her aunt Lorna complained, shaking bits of crushed Sheetrock out of her peppered gray and black hair. "I'm going to get a bottle of water. You want one?"

"In a minute. I want to finish tearing down this section first." Renee heaved the bulky sledgehammer over her shoulder, cringing at the ping of pain that shot through her arm as the tool connected with the drywall. She and Aunt Lorna deserved a massage after the work they'd done today.

Renee mentally reviewed the bank statement she'd pulled up online earlier this morning. There had been enough money for a couple of massages, but not nearly enough to pay for a demolition team to come in and finish tearing down these walls. Of course, the forty thousand dollars her aunt had given the man who'd promised to demolish her house would have gotten the job done. Too bad the lowlife had run off with the money without unscrewing a single lightbulb.

Of course, if she were wishing for things she could not change, she'd just as well wish that Hurricane Katrina had not blown in and wreaked all this havoc in the first place. It had been three years since the storm and eventual levee breach had flooded her aunt Lorna's house, and this entire neighborhood still looked like a ghost town. The closest living soul was more than three blocks away.

Renee had tried to convince her aunt to pack up and move with her to Florida. She winced just thinking about how Aunt Lorna had cursed her out over the phone for suggesting she leave. Renee should have known better than to utter such nonsense.

Her aunt adored New Orleans. Renee felt the same way. She'd spent every summer here since she was nine years old. Wonderful, glorious summers lived without fear of her father's belt leaving lash marks on her arms and legs, or hearing her mother scream as that maniacal bastard pounded her with his fists.

Renee pulled in a deep breath, sucking in the paper mask covering her mouth. Even after all this time, those memories still had the power to panic her.

"Renee, come on out of there," she heard Aunt Lorna's voice call from the front of the house. Renee propped the sledgehammer's handle against the wall and traipsed over the pile of broken Sheetrock littering the floor. She found her aunt on the porch fishing through a small Styrofoam ice chest.

"You've been in there since you came home from work. Here." Aunt Lorna shoved a bottle of water at Renee. "It's time to take a break."

Renee pulled the dust mask from her mouth and let it hang just under her chin. "I was going to stop in a minute, anyway," Renee said. She took a drink from the water bottle, her body sighing in relief as the cold liquid cascaded down her parched throat. Maybe she had gone a little longer than she should have without resting, but it was hard to justify taking a break. There was just so much to do.

Renee geared up for another battle, already aware of the response she would receive. But the pain in her right arm prompted her to try at least one more time to talk a little sense into her aunt's head.

"You do realize we can't do this on our own, don't you?" she asked, lowering herself onto the step next to her aunt.

"I can't afford to pay anybody to do it for me and I am not taking out a loan on a house that is already paid for."

"You don't have to—"

"And don't you even suggest that you take out the loan."

Renee gripped the water bottle tighter to stop herself from grabbing her aunt's shoulders and shaking some sense into her.

"Do you want to be in this house before the year 2020?" Renee asked. "Because at the rate we're going, that's how long it will take to get it back into livable condition."

"We're doing just fine on our own." Lorna sipped her water.

"I hate to break the news to you, but we are in way over our heads."

Her aunt stared straight ahead. She brought the water bottle to her mouth and took a deep, long pull. "You have to go to work tomorrow," Lorna finally said. "Go on in the trailer. I'll finish up for today. "

Renee rolled her eyes at Lorna's obstinance. She glanced over at the small pop-up camper sitting in the front right corner of her aunt's huge front yard. The trailer, issued by the Federal Emergency Management Agency to the thousands of people who'd lost their homes during Katrina, had been her home since she'd moved to New Orleans. She was tired of living in the cramped quarters, and she knew Aunt Lorna was fed up with living in there, too. But Lorna's stubbornness trumped comfort every day of the week. She would not take a cent from Renee, even though no amount of money in the world would suffice in paying Lorna back for all she'd done over the years.

Renee looked over at her aunt, sitting beside her on the dilapidated house's front step, her shoulders erect with mulish pride. She could talk until she was blue in the face, and it would not do one bit of good where Aunt Lorna was concerned.

"Come on," Renee said. She pushed herself up from the

step and held her hand out for her aunt. "I can handle another hour. Maybe we can finish tearing down the kitchen today."

So *this* was what being called to the principal's office felt like.

Alex tapped a nervous rhythm on his thigh as he waited for Principal Green to enter her office. The only time he had ever been called to the principal's office was to receive a certificate for having the highest grade point average in the tenth grade. He had never been a troublemaker. But, apparently, he was raising one.

"Mr. Holmes?"

Alex jumped out of his seat. "Mrs. Green." He nodded.

"Thanks for coming. Is everything okay?" she asked, motioning to his bandaged shoulder.

Alex waved off her concern. "I had an accident on the job a few weeks ago."

"Oh, I'm sorry."

"Recovery is going well. It wasn't a big deal."

"Please, have a seat," she said as she rounded her desk. "Would you like any water? Coffee?"

"I'm fine," Alex declined her offer. He took the seat he'd occupied for the past ten minutes.

"Give me just a moment to jot down a few things before I forget them," she said as she made notes on a desk calendar like the one on his desk at Holmes Construction.

Principal Green was probably in her late fifties. From the numerous awards and certificates on the wall behind her, she was dedicated to educating children, and had been for a very long time. Alex had only met her briefly at the parent/teacher conference that kicked off the new school year last month.

She capped her pen and returned it to the *Teachers Deserve an A+* coffee mug that held a dozen or so writing utensils. She folded her hands on the desk and smiled.

"So, we're here to discuss ways we can help Jasmine," Principal Green opened.

"I need to know exactly what she needs help with," Alex answered. "What's been going on?"

"Mrs. Overland will be joining us in just a few minutes," the principal said. "Her preparation hour starts at the next bell."

Almost as if she'd planned it, a high-pitched whirling sounded throughout the office.

The principal pulled out a folder. *Jasmine Holmes* was printed in bold letters on the label. Principal Green flipped through a few sheets, then stopped at a yellow carbon copy.

"This incident happened this past Wednesday," she said. "It's what prompted her teacher to call this conference." She handed the paper to Alex.

As he read over the report, Alex was convinced the teacher had mistakenly called in the wrong parent. There was no way his daughter had engaged in such behavior.

As Alex continued his study of the incident report, disbelief mingled with growing anger at the thought of Jasmine calling her teacher a fat cow and throwing a chalkboard eraser across the classroom. If this turned out to be true, she was punished until next year.

There was a knock on the door. Jasmine's teacher, Mrs. Overland, entered the office.

Alex rose again and awkwardly offered up his left hand to shake. He'd met the slightly plump woman with gray sprinkled throughout her red hair at the parent/teacher conference, too. Alex had meant to make the first PTO meeting of the year and the other meeting that was held to discuss the first grade class's scheduled field trips, but something had come up at work both times.

A sour taste settled in his mouth as he swallowed the familiar excuse. He was falling back into the same behavior that had cost him so much already, putting the business before his family. It had been Chantal's biggest complaint.

She'd constantly accused Alex of paying more attention to Holmes Construction than he did to her. She'd told him, point-blank, that the time he spent at Holmes Construction was the reason she'd gone out and found herself someone who appreciated her as a woman.

But, damn it, she and Jasmine were the reasons he worked so hard in the first place. It was a catch-22. How else could he provide for his family if he didn't work so hard?

"I see Principal Green shared what happened on Wednesday." Mrs. Overland pointed to the incident report as she took the other seat that faced the principal's desk.

"I'm sorry she said those things," Alex apologized.

"It wasn't what she said. She's said those things before. It was throwing the eraser that I could not tolerate. Another student could have been injured."

"Wait, what do you mean she's said those things before?" Alex asked.

"Jasmine has said quite a few mean things during her outbursts."

Alex turned his full attention to Mrs. Overland. "How often has this happened?"

"Several times over the past couple of weeks," the teacher answered.

"How many times is several?"

The principal pulled three more yellow carbon copies out of the file. "These document what has occurred since the end of the month."

Alex flipped through the pages, his anger escalating by the millisecond. "Why am I just hearing about this?"

"In most disciplinary situations, we encourage our teachers to handle as much as they can without resorting to parental involvement," Principal Green began. "It's part of our conflict resolution initiative. Students are taught how to manage disagreements on their own instead of constantly running to mommy and daddy. We find it fosters a sense of independence in the students."

"We also want to be sensitive to your current circumstances," Mrs. Overland interjected. "We know you've been dealing with your wife's death as well."

"I do not use my wife's death as an excuse and Jasmine is not allowed to do so, either."

"Jasmine is not alone in her behavior. So many of our students have been under added mental stress dealing with the aftereffects of Hurricane Katrina."

"Jasmine didn't lose her home or any of her millions of possessions in Katrina. There's no excuse for this."

Principal Green clasped her hands together over her desk. "Mr. Holmes, we'd like permission to send Jasmine to the school psychologist. That's the customary first step when we suspect a child is undergoing some type of mental trauma."

She would undergo some serious mental trauma when she got home and found the television and computer off-limits.

"When would she meet with the psychologist?" Alex asked.

"Actually, two of the students who were set up to meet with him are absent, so Dr. Powell would be able to see Jasmine this afternoon."

"That's fine with me," Alex said. "Should I join them?"

"No, the initial meeting will be with Jasmine and Dr. Powell. If he feels there should be further counseling, he will write a referral to an outside mental health professional, and you would be included in that dialogue."

"Okay, so she meets with the psychologist today. Does she have detention or something for throwing the eraser?"

"No, no, we don't send first graders to detention," Mrs. Overland said.

"Maybe you should, that would nip the bad behavior in the bud," Alex suggested.

"We know this is frustrating, Mr. Holmes," the principal continued. "Once Jasmine is done with Dr. Powell, we'll call you in to discuss what came out in her session."

Alex nodded. "You should have contacted me as soon as she began acting up. You can always call if something is happening with Jasmine, no matter how small. If I'm not available, my mother is always there."

"Well, I'm happy we were able to get you in today," Mrs. Overland said. To the principal she said, "I need to get some things done for my next class period."

"Of course," Principal Green said. "This is about all we can discuss at this stage, anyway." She rose from the chair behind the desk. Alex and Mrs. Overland followed suit.

"Thank you for coming, Mr. Holmes," Principal Green said. "I'll give you a call later this afternoon."

"Thanks for letting me know about all of this," Alex said. "I'm sorry Jasmine has been causing so many problems."

"It really isn't anything we haven't seen before," she assured him. "My main concern is finding out what is at the root of her behavior."

"That's what I'd like to know," Alex said.

"Don't worry yourself too much over this, Mr. Holmes."

Why did everyone keep telling him that? As if he wouldn't worry about his daughter turning into a menace. "I just want to make sure Jasmine is okay," Alex said.

After all, she was all he had.

This was not his cup of tea. Not at all.

Seated on a high stool at the curved bar that occupied the left wall of the Hard Court, Alex studied the social scene before him. Things had changed since the days when he used to go out. Not that he'd ever been big into clubs, but he'd visited a few back in the day. Back then, couples actually danced together. Here, the women danced in groups of five or six while most of the men in the club stood to the side and ogled. A few young bucks were brave enough to step up to the women; the lucky ones actually got to join in on the dancing.

The Hard Court was the brainchild of Toby's former

college basketball teammate Jonathan Campbell. In the six months since its doors first opened, the Hard Court had become one of the most popular nightclubs in New Orleans. Alex had to admit, the place was class with a capital C, and its clientele were the type of people he would probably choose to hang out with—if he ever had the time or the inclination to hang out. Personally, at the end of the day, Alex preferred to wind down on his couch with a banana smoothie and the History Channel.

Damn. *Secrets of the Egyptian Pyramids* was on tonight. He'd forgotten all about it.

Alex spotted Eli as he entered the club. He caught his brother's attention and waved him over.

"What's up, man?" Eli said, patting Alex on his uninjured shoulder. "You want to go upstairs and get a bite to eat?"

The Hard Court's second level sported a full-service bistro that had just received top honors in a local restaurant guide, and had added to the club's astonishing success.

"Nah, I'm good," Alex answered. "They'll bring us an appetizer to the booth down here, right?"

"That's if we can get a booth," Eli said, his eyes roaming over the steadily thickening crowd.

"Jonathan said we could have the one over there." Alex pointed to the corner. "He said he'd join us a little later." He motioned Eli to follow him. "I'll signal for one of the waitresses to bring some of those breaded cheese sticks I had the last time I was here."

"That sounds good," Eli said. "And I think the correct term is hostess, not waitress."

The twelve booths that rimmed the interior wall of the Hard Court's bottom floor were partially curtained, allowing occupants a measure of privacy, yet still a view of the dance floor and raised stage where they could take in performances by some of New Orleans's hottest acts. A hostess came up to their booth less than a minute after they had taken their seats.

"Hi there, Eli," she said.

"Tamika, how's it going?" Eli scooted from the booth and stood, giving the hostess a hug and a peck on the cheek.

"Where's Monica?"

"Work. I dragged my brother here tonight instead."

"Oh, this is your brother?" The woman's eyes glistened with instant interest, and Alex's guard went on full alert. "I'd heard there were three of you." She smiled.

"This is Alex," Eli introduced him. "He's the oldest."

"Hi."

"Hello." Alex nodded. "We want some of those cheese sticks. They still serve those?"

"The breaded mozzarella sticks? We sure do." She inclined her head, still smiling.

"Yeah, and can we have an extra cup of sauce?"

"Mozzarella sticks with an extra side of marinara. Anything else?" she asked, that smile even wider. Alex turned his attention to the glossy card advertising the Hard Court's upcoming music acts.

"We'll order drinks a little later," Eli said. Alex's head rose at the irritation he heard in his brother's voice.

The hostess mumbled something into the microphone extending from her headset. "I just put in your order. It should be out in a few minutes."

"Thanks, Tamika," Eli said.

"Yeah, thanks," Alex said.

As soon as she left their table, Eli fired at him, "What in the hell is wrong with you, man?"

"You didn't want the cheese sticks?" Alex asked.

"Forget the cheese sticks," Eli spat. "Alex, can't you tell when a woman is flirting with you?"

"Who?"

"Who?" Eli's eyes bucked. "Weren't you sitting right here? You didn't realize Tamika was flirting with you?"

"She took our order, E, that's all. Why are you always reading more into stuff than you should?"

"She couldn't have been more obvious if she'd ripped her clothes off and sat in your lap."

"She wasn't flirting," Alex stated.

"Yes, she was, just like half the other women you meet. And I'm sure there would be a lot more who flirted if you would get rid of that damn ring."

Alex fingered the simple gold band around the fourth finger on his left hand. He'd contemplated taking it off a couple of times, but as Eli had just pointed out, his wedding ring did a good job of keeping women at bay. Most of the time.

"Forget about her," Alex said, demanding a subject change. He wasn't in the mood for this tonight. Sure, he'd known the hostess had been coming onto him. He wasn't *that* blind, despite what his brothers believed. He just had no plans to act on any of the passes women threw at him with insufferable regularity. "Now why don't you explain why you asked me to come here?"

Still shaking his head, Eli said, "I thought maybe you'd want to get out of the house."

"That's it?"

"Honest, man." Eli raised his hands. "I felt bad for you yesterday, having to sneak away from Mama. You know you were never good at that."

"Because I didn't get as much practice as you and Toby," Alex snorted. "What's up with you? Yesterday was the first time you'd stopped in at Mama's since I've been out of the hospital."

"I've been working a lot," Eli answered. "Between the responsibilities that come with the head of OB position and putting in time at the Parenting Center, I'm lucky if I get time to sleep and eat."

"How *is* the parenting center? It sounds like you're spending just as much time there as you spend at the hospital."

"Feels like it, too. Monica has taken ownership over the

center. That's where she spends all her free time, so naturally, that's where I'm spending mine."

Alex laughed, shaking his head. "I never thought I'd see the day when a woman ran your life the way Monica does."

"She doesn't run my life," Eli protested. He glanced up at Alex and they both laughed. "Yeah, okay, fine. She runs my life. But I've never been happier."

"She's a good woman."

"I thank God for her every hour of the day," his younger brother admitted.

"You should, it's rare to find someone who makes you happy."

"Rare, but not impossible," Eli said. He shifted in the booth. "All right, enough of this relationship crap. I feel like I'm in the middle of a movie on the Lifetime Network."

Alex tried not to take offense. Sometimes, when he couldn't find anything interesting on the History Channel, he switched to Lifetime. Those movies were pretty good.

Eli signaled for another hostess. "How did things go at the school?"

"You don't want to know"

The hostess stepped up to the booth to take their drink order, and Alex had to stop himself from asking her to add a little vodka to his standard cranberry juice on the rocks. Once she'd left with their order, Eli returned to his question.

"Okay, what's going on with Jazzy?"

Alex gave his brother the abbreviated version of the meeting he'd had with Jasmine's teacher and the school principal earlier in the day. Eli was just as shocked at the name-calling and other behavior that was so out of character.

"Does she have detention?" Eli asked.

"They don't put first graders in detention."

"Since when?"

"That's what I wanted to know," Alex answered. "Anyway,

she had a session with the school psychologist earlier this afternoon."

"And?"

Alex took a gulp of the juice the hostess had just placed on the table, seriously regretting the lack of alcohol.

"Let's just say Jazzy's having some issues," he grunted. Alex pounded the table with his good hand. "Damn it, E. I've been trying so hard to do the right thing with her."

"C'mon, man. Don't do this to yourself," Eli said after sipping his drink. "It's the biggest double standard in the world, but it's the truth. Single fathers have a harder time raising children on their own, and you have a daughter. That's tough, Alex. The job you've done with Jazz over the past two years has been amazing. Hell, over the past six years. It's not as if Chantal was the most stellar mother figure when she was alive."

Alex tended to defend his dead wife when his brothers tried to discredit her, but he wasn't up to it tonight. More than ever, he was pissed at Chantal for the pain she was causing Jasmine.

"So what did the psychologist say?" Eli asked.

"He thinks Jasmine still isn't over Chantal's death."

"It's only been two years. Of course it's going to take her longer than that to get over losing her mother, if she ever gets over it. You didn't need some psychologist to tell you that."

"I know, but he also has a theory as to why she's been acting up in class lately." Eli looked at him expectantly. "Her bad behavior started the day after I got hurt," Alex said.

Eli's eyes widened with understanding. "I'll be damned."

Tamika arrived with their mozzarella sticks, but her smile had dimmed. Good, at least she'd taken the hint. Alex placed three of the fried cheese sticks on one of the saucers she'd left on the table and drenched them in red sauce.

"According to the psychologist, Jazzy is convinced I'm going to be killed, and she'll be without both parents."

"That didn't even occur to me. She must have been scared

out of her mind when she heard about your accident," Eli said, cutting one of the cheese sticks with a fork. He pointed at Alex with the fork, a line of mozzarella stretching from the plate. "Now that I think about it, that's probably why she didn't want to see you when you were in the hospital. Mama tried to get her to come along, but she never wanted to. I can't believe we didn't consider this," he said around a mouthful of mozzarella.

"Probably because she hasn't been acting all that differently at home," Alex rationalized.

"What does the psychologist suggest we do about it?"

Relief settled over Alex at the effortless way Eli automatically included himself in on whatever had to be done to help Jasmine. Alex accepted his role as a single father, but he was never totally alone in his task. His entire family had a hand in raising his daughter.

"Jasmine and I are long overdue for this conversation," Alex admitted. "If I can't get her to open up, the psychologist suggested I seek outside help. It's not that he thinks she's crazy," Alex added quickly. "He just thinks it would be a good idea to have her talk about what she's feeling."

"Seeing a mental health professional doesn't automatically mean you're crazy," Eli said. "She's been through a lot for a six-year-old. I can't believe none of us thought about how your accident would affect her."

"The school psychologist also said it would be beneficial if I spent a little extra time with Jazzy, sort of like a reassurance that I'm here and I'm not going anywhere."

"That makes sense."

"Yeah, well, I've decided to volunteer at her school."

A surprised smile drew across Eli's face. "That's cool, Alex."

"It's something I've been meaning to do, but never could find the time. I've got the time now." Alex smothered another cheese stick in marinara sauce. "Besides, it'll get Mama out of my hair."

"Mama's got you ready to climb the walls, huh?" Eli laughed. "I knew she would eat this up, having somebody to take care of again."

"It's worse than I ever imagined it would be. That's one of the reasons I moved back into my house earlier this afternoon."

Eli's brow converged in an arrow of concern. "You think that's wise, Alex? You really should lay off the arm as much as possible," his brother warned.

"I'll be fine," Alex said. "Even though the school doesn't believe in punishing first graders, I do. Jazz is not getting away with what she did. It's time for her to learn that she can't go around acting this way and not face any consequences."

"And if you leave her around Mama, she'll get whatever she wants." Eli nodded his understanding.

"Exactly. No more spoiling her. From now on, she has to earn every present she gets."

"That's going to be a shock to her system. Hell, it's going to be a shock to mine. I pick something up for her every time I go to the store."

"Not anymore," Alex stated firmly. "I'm sorry I went so over the top with her birthday party. If I had known about this a few weeks ago, I never would have called in that favor with the guy at Audubon Zoo."

"There's Jonathan," Eli said. They both stood to greet the owner of the Hard Court, who had also become a good friend to both Alex and Eli.

"What's up, E?" Jonathan shook Eli's hand. "I didn't get a chance to ask earlier how the arm was healing," he said to Alex as he took a seat and motioned for the hostess. She arrived minutes later with refills for both Alex and Eli, and something clear in a highball glass that she placed in front of Jonathan.

"My shoulder's fine," Alex answered. "It looks like things haven't stopped hopping here since your opening."

"It's been pretty steady ever since Aria put my club on the map."

"You should be able to quit the law practice soon with all the money this place must be pulling in," Eli said.

"Ivana would love that," Jonathan answered, speaking of his fiancée, Sienna's sister, Ivana Culpepper. "I have been spending less time at the office. In a few years, depending on how the club fares, I may do just pro bono work at the law practice."

"Ivana's altruism is rubbing off on you already," Eli joked.

Jonathan laughed. "She is a force of nature. It's hard not to just fall in line."

"Ivana's a good woman, if a little scary," Eli said.

"She's a lot scary, but I like that," Jonathan said. "Hey, I need to finish making my rounds. You guys feel like a little pool when I'm done?"

Alex shook his head. "Of course, I could beat the both of you even with only one good arm."

"Whatever, man," Jonathan said with a laugh.

"We'll probably be out of here in a few, anyway," Eli said. "I've got to be at the Parenting Center early tomorrow morning."

"And I have to get ready to go back to school," Alex said.

Jonathan gave him a confused look.

"Don't ask," Eli said.

"I'll catch the two of you later," Jonathan said.

Alex pulled out his wallet and dropped two twenties on the table.

"I got this," Eli said. "I'm the one who invited you, remember?"

"Don't worry about it," Alex said.

"Come on, Alex. Use the money to buy Jazzy—" Eli stopped short. He shook his head, a contrite grin at the edge of his lips. "It's going to be hard breaking that habit, won't it? I don't want to be around when you lay down the law," Eli said. "I hate to see my Jazzy cry."

"Yeah," Alex said. "This is definitely one of the not so fun parts of this parenthood thing."

Alex sat at his kitchen table, leaning against the high-backed chair's wooden slates, his thumb rolling the gold wedding band around his finger. Wisps of steam swirled from the mug of hot chocolate he'd made in an attempt to lull himself to sleep.

After church this morning, he and Jazzy had spent most of the day at Mama's, as was their typical Sunday afternoon ritual. But Alex had left earlier than usual today, figuring he could get a jump start on getting Jasmine's things ready for school, and then get to bed early himself.

That wasn't happening. The clock above the stove showed it to be just past two in the morning, but the weight of what he was to embark upon tomorrow taxed his brain to the point of making sleep impossible.

Alex studied the ring on his finger. It had been an effective means of keeping women at bay. Just the thought of jumping back into the dating scene triggered a sick feeling in his gut. The ring was a constant reminder to never open himself up to the kind of pain Chantal had put him through.

But every second it remained on his finger was a mockery of the sanctity of marriage. A mockery of the love his parents had shared, the love he saw when his brothers looked at their wives-to-be.

Alex ran his thumbnail under the edge of the ring. If the ease at which it shifted on his finger was any indication, he'd lost weight these past few weeks since the surgery. He'd been afraid the lack of physical activity would put on the pounds, but Alex had to admit his appetite had not been up to par. He had too much on his mind to think about food, especially these past couple of days.

His eyes focused on the porcelain teapots lined along the

ledge above the upper kitchen cabinets. Chantal had found one of the ornate teapots at a flea market and had gotten it in her head that she should own every antique teapot in southeastern Louisiana. For months they had spent every Sunday afternoon taking long drives, scouring the region for flea markets and antique shops. They would find a little out-of-the-way place for lunch, and then find an even more obscure place to park the car and make love.

They were happy back then.

Alex could pinpoint the exact day their marriage had started its downward spiral. It was the same day Chantal had gone to the doctor's to see about the stomach flu she couldn't seem to shake, a flu that had turned out to be Jasmine. They had never really talked about having children. Alex had always known he wanted to be a father, and had just assumed his wife had the same views on family that he did. He'd been stunned at Chantal's outrage over her pregnancy, and devastated when she'd threatened to have an abortion.

He'd begged, promising Chantal everything under the moon if she went through with having their child. He would have been better off making a deal with the devil.

Alex shook his head, a derisive laugh escaping his lips as he thought back on his naiveté.

Where she had been just a little spoiled and demanding before, Chantal had become more callous and selfish than he could ever have anticipated. She had demanded the impossible, insisting Alex lavish her with gifts she knew he could not afford. She'd played the fragile life of their unborn child like a pawn. And when the time had passed for her to safely have an abortion, she'd changed her tactic to guilt, accusing Alex of forcing her to give up her freedom in return for having his baby.

He'd worked like a man possessed, executing sixteen-hour days, working right along with his men on the construction sites during normal working hours, then spending most of the nights in the office poring over the books.

In the midst of chaos a silver lining had emerged. His business had started to grow exponentially as a result of the constant pressure Chantal had put on him to provide. But that success had not come without a cost. Alex had spent less and less time focusing on his marriage, and soon after Jasmine's birth, his wife had turned to other men.

She'd been blatant in her infidelity, threatening to take Jasmine away if Alex so much as uttered a word about her affairs. It was at that moment Alex had considered his marriage over. Instead, he'd chosen to devote his energy to making sure his daughter wanted for nothing. Jasmine's well-being had become his reason for living. His own happiness was a nonissue.

As his eyes fell on the ring again, a bitterness he'd suppressed for years stirred in his gut. He'd been a good husband to Chantal, but she had not been a good wife. And now—because of his injury, because of Jasmine—he refused to cling to this symbol of a marriage that had lost his respect long before his wife's death had ended it.

Alex hooked his thumb under the ridge of the gold band and gave it a push. He inched it up a few centimeters more, a weight gradually lifting off his shoulders with each shift of the ring. It fell to the table with a soft ping, rimming around a few times before finally falling still. Alex lifted the gold band from the table and stuck it in his pocket. He brought his mug up to his lips and took a drink.

Chapter Four

"I want everyone to record their quiz score in their booklets before logging off the computer. You all remember how to properly log off, right?"

The laconically sung chorus of "Yes, Ms. Moore" that resounded from the group of second graders brought a grin to Renee's lips. She strolled around the computer lab, assisting those students who needed a little extra help logging out of the computer program while the others gathered their belongings. She had only a few minutes before she had to get this group back to their regular class and retrieve a set of fourth graders. It was test day for the fourth grade children enrolled in Accelerated Reader, just one of the programs that fell under her supervision as Special Projects Coordinator.

"Ms. Moore?"

Renee felt a tap on her knee. She looked down and grinned at the huge brown eyes staring up at her. She already knew what would come next, so Renee halted the student's request before she had a chance to voice it.

"No, Mariah, you cannot stay in the computer lab. The next session is for fourth graders. Second graders have to go back to Mrs. Pitts."

"I promise to be good," Mariah said, laying on the puppy dog eyes with amazing effect. It's a good thing a few of the teachers had already schooled Renee in refusal techniques.

She was not used to students who didn't reach her waist. Coming from the community college ranks, she had needed a few weeks to adjust to her much younger student base.

Not surprisingly, the maturity levels were not all that different from some of the freshmen she'd dealt with in her last
position teaching European history at a community college
in Tampa.

Renee took Mariah by the hand and guided her to the
colorful chart taped to the door of the computer lab.

"Look at the schedule," Renee said. "When will you be
back in the lab?"

Mariah studied the chart with such concentration Renee
had to bite back a laugh.

"There it is." Mariah pointed. "Thursday."

"That's right. Your class will be back in the lab on Thursday." Renee raised her voice for the rest of the students to
hear. "Will everyone have their stories read by then?"

A cacophony of "Yeah, Yes, ma'am, and Uh-huh," flitted
across the room.

"Very good." Renee nodded. "Now let's get you all back
to Ms. Pitts's classroom. I'm sure she misses her little angels." Renee's wink garnered the giggles she'd anticipated.

By the time her preparation period rolled around, Renee
was more than ready for a break from her classes. The third
and fourth grade students were not nearly as sweet as her
first and second graders. The bad manners some of these
students possessed were unreal.

Renee entered the teachers' lounge and went straight for
the coffeepot. She poured a cup and took a much needed
sip of the strong, chicory-laced blend that was the brew of
choice in her new home of New Orleans. Renee took another sip and settled into a well-worn recliner.

The teachers' lounge at St. Katherine's Episcopal School
wasn't in the running for a spread in *Architectural Digest*, but
the school had done the best it could to make the space
comfortable. Two round tables sat in the middle of the large
room, providing a place for those teachers who did not have
to accompany students to the cafeteria to enjoy their lunch.
There were three separate seating areas with comfy chairs

and mismatched recliners, and an array of old magazines and teacher supply catalogs strewn across battered coffee tables. The entire left wall housed the copy center, with four copy machines Renee tried to steer clear of at all cost. She caused a paper jam every time she touched one of those machines.

Penelope Gaines came through the door and mimicked Renee's exact steps as she headed for the coffeemaker.

"Caffeine is a gift from God," Penelope said as she refilled her ceramic mug and added cream and a packet of sweetener.

"You look like you've had a rough morning," Renee commented.

"You, too." She gestured to the bandage Renee had placed on her forehead after her run-in with a wayward curling iron.

"The price of beauty," Renee answered her friend's unspoken query.

Penelope tested her coffee, added another pack of sweetener, and came around to the recliner at a right angle to Renee's. Penelope taught fourth grade math and science. With both of them single and about the same age, it hadn't surprised Renee that she and Penelope had gravitated toward each other. There was a snarky sense of humor hidden behind the teacher's fresh, freckled face and red hair that never failed to lift Renee's spirits even on her worst day.

One of the copy machines made that annoyingly loud beep Renee usually elicited from it. She looked over and grinned in commiserating amusement as the guy bending over the machine poked at the computerized screen. The view was a pleasant surprise on a Monday morning. Thank God for both caffeine and well-fitting jeans.

Renee glanced over at Penelope and caught her admiring the view.

"So." Renee snapped her fingers, causing Penelope's head to jerk. "What happened this morning?"

"What didn't happen?" Penelope sighed. "I accidentally flushed one of my contacts down the toilet."

"I noticed you were wearing your glasses," Renee commented. "They're cute."

"I hate having to wear these glasses." Penelope grimaced. "Anyway, I get in my car, and it won't start. Thankfully, Mr. Miller was still at home and was able to give my dead battery a jump. Now if only Mrs. Miller would meet an untimely death, he could give my other battery a jump."

Renee nearly choked on her coffee.

"What?" her friend protested. "You've seen him. Mr. Miller is hot."

"Hot and married. Happily married as far as I can tell."

"Yeah, they're happy," Penelope griped.

The copy machine beeped again.

"Is that all?" Renee asked, trying to keep her eyes averted from the scene at the copy machine. "A lost contact and a dead battery?"

"And a message from my contractor telling me it's going to cost more to fix my house than what's on the estimate. I'm nearly at my breaking point," Penelope said.

The copy machine beeped again.

"It looks like someone needs rescuing," Penelope said, placing her mug on the coffee table and pushing herself out of the chair.

"If you don't mind, I'll just watch," Renee said, rising from the recliner. "That copier hates me." She followed Penelope to the other side of the lounge.

"Having a little trouble?" Penelope asked. The man on the other end of a losing battle with the copy machine looked up from where he was crouched over the open paper drawer.

He was built like a linebacker, solid without an ounce of flab, as far as Renee could tell. She'd already observed the fabulous image from behind, and had to admit the front view was just as breathtaking. His eyes were the color of warm maple syrup, and even though it was set in a frown, his mouth was strong, with full, supple lips.

"Whatever happened to a simple start button?" he asked, eyeing the copier as if he were ready to tackle it.

Penelope waved him off. "That went out in the early nineties. Now you need a Ph.D. in computer technology in order to make a copy. Let me see what you have here," she said, shooing him away from the machine. "So, any luck finding another contractor?"

It took Renee a second to realize Penelope was talking to her. "No, I think Aunt Lorna is afraid to trust anyone just yet."

"Any word from the police about locating the other guy?" Penelope asked.

"There have been so many counts of fake contractors robbing people blind, the police department said it would take years before they could get through the backlog." A quick shot of anger speared through Renee's gut at just the thought of the crooked contractor who had made off with most of her aunt's life savings.

"That sucks, Renee. Here's the problem. The paper jammed." Penelope gently pulled a small stack of copy paper that had lodged in the automatic feeder.

"Did I break the machine?" the guy asked.

"No, it does this a lot." Penelope took the sheaf of paper from his hand and placed them in the feeder. "How many copies?"

"Eighteen."

Penelope punched the number into the computer screen and started the machine to rolling. "You should probably use the one down there." She pointed to the last copier tucked into the corner. "It's an older model, so it's a bit slower, but it's easier to use. It actually has a start button." She smiled.

"So." Renee took a sip of her coffee. "Are you a new teacher?" she asked. He was studying the copies as they shot out of the machine.

"No, just volunteering," he answered.

He had a really nice voice. Deep, but with a softness that was unexpected given his outward appearance. Not that there was anything wrong with how he looked on the outside. The way his shoulders and chest filled out his gray polo shirt would be considered a work of art in some sectors of the world. But there was a hint of roughness around his nicely defined edges that told Renee he was more a T-shirt and jeans man than a Brooks Brothers suit-wearer.

"My daughter is in Mrs. Overland's first grade class. I'm helping out while I recuperate." He gestured to his shoulder, where a square gauze bandage peeked from under the collar of his shirt.

"Good for you," Penelope commented, handing him his copies. "We don't get nearly as many parents to volunteer as we'd like, and you're definitely the first father I've seen in the three years I've been here."

He shrugged, the motion causing the shirt to pull slightly across his chest. The outline of the pectoral muscles that appeared caused Renee's eyes to automatically widen.

"I heard you mention a problem with a contractor," he said.

Renee snapped to attention. Had she been staring at him?

"Yes," she said, shaking her head. She noticed the grin on Penelope's face. Oh Lord, she *had* been staring. "Uh, yes," Renee said again. "We've been having contractor issues. The one my aunt hired sort of skipped town without completing the job."

"You've got to be careful who you hire," the guy said. "For every legitimate contractor, there are ten shady ones out there ripping people off."

"And, unfortunately, the legitimate ones cost an arm and a leg," Penelope snorted. "I swear, if my contractor raises my estimate one more time, I'm going to kill him."

"Just be grateful he hasn't made off with forty thousand

dollars of your hard-earned money," Renee said. "And at least you know what needs to get done. I'm not sure the guy my aunt hired even knew what he was talking about. She was just so desperate to get *someone* to start rebuilding."

"And you haven't found another contractor?" Volunteer Dad asked.

"Not yet." Rene shook her head. "Why, you know someone?" she asked jokingly.

"Actually, I own a construction company," he said. "We focus more on commercial developments, but since the storm, my guys have been volunteering to help rebuild homes on the weekends. I can take a look at your house and see if there's anything we can do."

"Are you serious?"

He nodded. "Sure."

"That's very generous of you," Renee said. Who knew God sent down such handsome angels to answer prayers?

"It's no problem." The bell rang, signaling the end of third period. "I need to get these math worksheets to Mrs. Overland. I'll be helping out in her class for at least the next month, so just let me know when's a good time for me to come out and take a look at your house." He turned to Penelope. "Thanks for the help with the copy machine."

"Anytime," she answered.

"I can take a look at your house, too. Let you know if your contractor is padding the rebuild cost."

"That would be awesome," Penelope answered. The coy smile lifting the edge of her lips was more invitation than anything else. Renee fought the urge to roll her eyes.

"Time to get to class," Renee said.

Volunteer Dad exited the teachers' lounge ahead of them and headed down the corridor, dodging the munchkin-high students making their way to class.

Penelope grabbed Renee by the arm and pulled her close. "Oh. My. *God*."

"Don't I know it?" Renee agreed.

"Hey, hands off. You already have a man."

"Who? Rashad?" Renee asked. "I wouldn't call him my man. We've only been out a few times."

"That's a few times more than I've been out over the past year. I want that one."

Renee laughed. "Did it occur to you that maybe *that* one is married?"

"No ring," Penelope answered. "I checked."

"So did I, and I noticed a ring line."

"But not a ring, which means, technically, he's up for grabs," Penelope reasoned.

"Come on before you're tardy to your own class."

Renee followed her coworker to her class, then walked two doors down to Rashad Richards's classroom. The fourth grade teacher had been helping inventory the library when Renee had come to St. Katherine's to interview for the special projects coordinator position this past summer. He'd asked her out then, but she'd declined since she'd had to head back to Florida that same night to finish packing up her things.

When she returned for the start of the school year, Renee had given Rashad Richards the chance he'd missed over the summer, figuring she could use a friend native to the area since most of those she'd made over the summers she'd visited her aunt had left after Hurricane Katrina. To her disappointment, Rashad was having trouble with the whole *just friends* concept.

He was four years younger than her thirty-four years, but he was very mature for his age. Sometimes, he was a little *too* mature.

Renee's personal motto was live every day as if it were your last. She loved getting outside and getting her hands dirty. Give her a mountainside to climb, or a muddy hill to conquer on her dirt bike, and she was a happy camper. Rashad's idea of fun was attending a poetry reading, or watching a movie with subtitles.

And he hated football.

If that wasn't a glaring sign that this so-called relationship was going to go nowhere, nothing was.

Knocking lightly on the door, Renee entered the classroom. "Hello, hello," she said to the group of fourth graders and their teacher.

"Look who's here," Rashad said. "I hope everyone finished reading their stories this weekend."

"I'm sure they did," Renee said. "Students, get your backpacks and line up at the door. Make sure you bring your booklets to record your quiz scores." She had to remind the older kids more often than the little ones.

"I'll have them back to you before the end of the period, Mr. Richards."

"Thank you, Ms. Moore," Rashad answered. He winked, and Renee hoped he was sufficiently chastised with the look she shot him over the heads of the fourth graders. He knew better than to wink at her in class, and if he didn't, she would tell him when she returned the students at the end of the class period.

"Have fun, class," Rashad called out to his students. "Behave for Ms. Moore."

"We will," the students answered in unison.

"Behave for my students, Ms. Moore," he said, winking again. Some of the students giggled.

"I will," Renee answered through clenched teeth.

He was *so* going to hear about this.

Alex wiped the table with a damp cloth, scrubbing the splatter of blue paint that continued to spread with each pass of the washcloth.

"Oh, wait a minute, Mr. Holmes. I have a special cleaner that works better with this paint." Mrs. Overland sprayed a pale green solution onto the table, plucked the towel from Alex's fingers, and had the table looking brand-new with a couple of swipes. "Art time is the kids' favorite, but in all honesty, I could do without it. There will be at least one accident, guaranteed."

"At least they had fun," Alex said.

"You'll soon learn that more mess equals more fun with this group. They definitely keep me on my toes," Mrs. Overland said with a good-natured laugh.

Alex chuckled along with her. He'd had a good time today. The kids were attentive, and for the most part, well behaved. Although Alex quickly learned the little angels could turn into devils in an instant. When Mrs. Overland had to step out of the class to take an important phone call, the students had gone wild.

Alex was completely dumbfounded. On a construction site, dozens of men followed his orders without the least bit of resistance, but give him a roomful of six-year-olds and he lost all control. No matter how loud he bellowed, clapped his hands, or banged on the table, the little critters had paid him no mind whatsoever.

Yet when the soft-spoken Mrs. Overland had returned to the room, the rowdy students had quieted immediately.

"You did really well," Mrs. Overland complimented him. "Most parents would not have lasted the morning."

"Thanks," Alex answered. Even though he didn't believe he'd done a good job, he appreciated her attempt to make him feel like less of a fool for being overrun by the little heathens. "It did become a bit overwhelming. I'm not sure how you handle them day in and day out. I have a hard enough time dealing with just one."

"It's not always easy managing all those little personalities, but it's worth it when they come back years later as successful young men and women."

"I'm convinced people are born to be teachers. Not everyone can do what you all do," Alex said.

"Well, thank you, Mr. Holmes. Now, will I see you tomorrow?" she asked.

"Oh yeah, I'll be back."

"Good, because I think this is going to do a world of good for Jasmine."

"Mr. Powell recommended I gradually back out of the picture. So I figure I'll stick around full days for the next couple of weeks. Maybe start leaving after lunch the week after next, and the week after that I'll come for just a couple of hours in the mornings."

"That sounds like an excellent plan. She really is a sweet child, Mr. Holmes. I hope you don't mind my saying so, but I am so very impressed with the way you are raising your daughter. I know it must be difficult."

Alex shrugged, and simply answered, "She's mine."

The fact that people were so awed that he was raising Jasmine on his own continued to baffle him. Who else was going to raise his daughter? It was a double standard that irked Alex to no end. Millions of single mothers raised their children without praise. Hell, after his father died, his own mother had become a part of that group. Why did people feel the need to constantly pat him on the back for fulfilling his responsibility?

"The kids have another twenty minutes in music class, and then I'll walk them to the bus loading zone. Is Jasmine riding home with you this afternoon?"

Alex shook his head. "When we talked about my helping out in her class, I explained that she would get no special treatment, which included being chauffeured to and from school. She'll take the bus home just like all the other students."

"Well, if you want to, you can leave. When they get back from music class they'll only have time to pack up their backpacks and head out to the bus loading zone."

"Is there anything you need me to do to help prepare for tomorrow?" Alex asked.

"No, I—oh, wait. Are you up to wrestling with the copy machine again? I want to start the morning with a few penmanship exercises." Mrs. Overland shuffled through a few papers on her desk. "Here they are. Eighteen copies of these."

Alex tried to hide his unease behind a smile. "No problem," he lied.

Alex headed back for the room that housed the copiers. Maybe those two teachers from this morning would be there to bail him out just in case he broke the machine. He'd break the copier on purpose to get the one with the Band-Aid on her forehead to come to his rescue.

The admission blew his mind. Just the fact that he was still thinking about her shocked the hell out of him.

These days, Alex rarely allowed himself to give an attractive woman a second glance. It's not that he didn't notice them. He *was* human, after all, and one hundred percent hetero. He simply didn't have the energy getting involved with a woman would require.

His lack of interest in the opposite sex had been a constant battle between Alex and his brothers, who were of the mind-set that a life without sex was a life not worth living. They thought the fact that Alex had gone two years without getting any was more tragic than a Greek play. If they only knew just how long it *really* had been since he'd been with a woman, both Toby and Eli would drop dead.

His wife had been dead for two years, but the intimacy between them had died long before Chantal had perished in that car accident. Of course, *she* hadn't gone all that long without sex. She'd probably had some in the backseat of the car before she'd cracked it up against that tree.

Alex wrapped up the thought and shoved it in that little compartment in his mind that held all his "bad wife" memories. He usually had more control over when he allowed those to surface. His mind must still be weak from dealing with all those first graders. That's probably why the teacher with the Band-Aid had gotten to him, too. Weariness had his defenses down.

Alex pushed through the door to the teachers' lounge,

finding it more crowded than it was earlier today. Unfortunately, neither the pretty teacher with the deep brown eyes, nor her friend who had the ability to save him from another copying fiasco were among the room's occupants.

Alex walked over to the last copy machine. He stared at the array of colorful buttons for a minute, trying to make sense of it all. Why did they have to make these things so complicated? His assistant, Jennie Marconi, handled all the copying at Holmes Construction. She would probably laugh her butt off to see him trying to work a Xerox machine.

He inserted the two worksheets into the automatic feeder on the top of the machine, punched in a one and an eight, and pressed the green start button. The copier quickly swallowed the originals and started spitting out collated copies, and Alex sent up a small prayer of thanks.

He retrieved the copies from the tray and made his way around the two circular tables. The door to the lounge opened and the pretty teacher with the Band-Aid on her forehead walked through it, followed by a male teacher.

She stopped short. "Hi again," she said.

"Hello," Alex answered.

She gestured to the man standing next to her. "Rashad, this is . . . you know, I didn't get your name this morning."

"Alexander Holmes," Alex provided.

"Rashad, this is Mr. Holmes."

"Alex," he corrected her.

"Alex," she said, his name rolling slowly from her lips. Time stopped for a moment as their gazes locked. Her generous, full lips parted in a slight smile, revealing a dimple and accentuating high, delicate cheekbones. Her eyes softened just a bit around the edges and a quickness Alex hadn't felt in years began to pump through his blood.

"Renee?" the guy standing next to her said.

"Oh, gosh, I'm sorry. Alex, this is Rashad Richards," she continued. "He teaches fourth grade here at St. Katherine's. Rashad, Alex is volunteering in Mrs. Overland's class, right?"

Alex nodded. "I didn't get your full name this morning, either."

"Sorry about that. It's Renee Moore."

"Ms. Moore." Alex paused slightly, hoping she'd give him permission to call her Renee. When she didn't, he continued. "The offer still stands to check out your house if you'd like."

"You know about houses?" Richards asked.

"He owns a construction company," Renee answered. "He offered to have some of his workers look over my aunt's house and Penelope's."

"That's pretty decent of you," Richards put in. To Renee he said, "Let me grab my leftovers from the fridge, and then we can go."

"Okay," she answered Richards, and then turned back to Alex. She laid her pretty eyes on him and that heavy thumping thing started happening within Alex's chest at an accelerated rate.

"You look like you came out on the losing end of a fight with a Smurf," she said with a grin, pointing to his face.

Alex rubbed his cheek, hoping the paint wouldn't spread as it had on the table. "There was an accident in art class," he explained.

She just continued grinning. Her smile was mesmerizing.

"Here," Renee said. She reached up and wiped his cheek.

Alex's breathing stopped completely.

That answered one of the questions that had been floating around his brain since he'd first seen her this morning. Her warm brown skin really *was* soft as silk.

"That's better," she said, her fingers still lingering on his cheek. The air between them crackled and sizzled. There was something he should be doing, but for the life of him, Alex could not remember.

Oh, wait, breathing. Yeah. He should definitely breathe.

She removed her hand, but her eyes creased at the corners

and a sexy, secretive smile curled her delicately plumped lips.

"I've got my stuff." Richards sidled up next to her.

"What's that?" Renee asked, her eyes still on Alex.

Alex was the first to break eye contact. He glanced over at Richards, who was looking back and forth between Alex and Renee. After his assessment of the situation, Richards apparently felt the need to stake his territory. He draped his arm around Renee's shoulder, and gave her a squeeze. Alex was convinced chest thumping and caveman grunts were next.

The guy could check that possessiveness crap at the door, because he didn't have a thing to worry about where Alex was concerned. Renee Moore might be prettier than just about any woman he'd ever seen in his life, but Alex could not afford to be interested in her, despite his heart rate's continued escalation every second she was near. With physical therapy, work, his online classes, and the added stress of having to deal with Jasmine's behavioral problems, now more than ever, Alex didn't have time to deal with the complications a woman would bring to his life.

"Let me talk to my aunt about the house," Renee said. "It's ultimately her decision what happens with it. I'm sure she'll be grateful for whatever help you can provide, but I want to run it by her before men show up and start poking around."

"Of course," Alex said. "I'm putting in full days here at St. Katherine's for the rest of the week, so just let me know what you decide."

"I will," she answered.

"Have a good night," Alex said.

She turned. "You, too," she said before following Rashad Richards out of the lounge.

Alex stared at the door for several moments as he tried to figure out just what the heck was going on with him. He was turned on. *Really* turned on. After years of believing the need for a woman didn't exist in his world, he found it strange to have such feelings stirring in his gut.

Alex cursed under his breath as he pushed through the door of the teachers' lounge. Without his permission, his libido had ended its hiatus.

Chapter Five

"I was thinking we could catch the viewing of *A Clockwork Orange* at the Zeitgeist Theater on Friday," Rashad said as they walked across Claiborne Avenue to the teachers' parking lot that sat directly across the street from St. Katherine's.

"I'm not really up to seeing something that deep," Renee said.

"But it's a classic."

"One you've probably seen five times."

"Oh, I've seen it more times than that."

"Then it won't hurt if you miss it on Friday," she reasoned. "Why don't we go to a regular movie?"

"That crap Hollywood puts out there isn't worth the ten bucks they make you pay," Rashad complained. He draped his arm over her shoulders and gave her a squeeze. He dipped his head, and with his mouth close to her ear, said, "Come on, Renee, you know you want to be alone with me in that nice, cozy theater."

Renee pushed him away, halting her steps. "Okay, stop that."

"What's the problem?"

"Look, Rashad, when I agreed to go out with you that first time, I told you things would have to go extremely slow. And if anything more were to develop between us—

which I have not agreed to—it would be strictly after hours."

"And I've respected that."

"You just tried to kiss me!"

"What's wrong with that? This *is* after hours. The school is over there," he said, pointing to the building across the street.

"So what was that wink about when I came to get your students?"

"Oh, that." He waved her off as if it was some insignificant joke. His nonchalance only irritated her more.

"That's the type of stuff I'm talking about, Rashad. Some of the students saw you."

"You're biting my head off because some of the students noticed a harmless wink?"

"What you fail to realize is that I didn't see it as harmless. I saw it as inappropriate in front of my students, and I don't want it to happen again."

He spread his hands wide in surrender. "Fine, I won't wink at you ever again. In fact, I'll close my eyes and turn my back whenever you come to get the kids for Accelerated Reader."

Renee saw the smile tugging at the corner of his mouth, and couldn't help laughing. Maybe she was blowing this out of proportion. Rashad was a nice guy, and to be honest, she didn't want to lose him as a friend.

What would be the harm in hanging out with him Friday night, even if it meant watching a movie she didn't particularly want to see? Friends sacrificed for their friends, right?

"What time does the movie start?" she asked.

"Seven o'clock," Rashad answered with a triumphant smile. "Why don't I pick you up at your aunt's at six? We can have an early dinner."

"That sounds good," Renee answered. He leaned over as

if he was going to kiss her, then jerked back and stuck out his hand instead.

Renee burst out laughing. She captured his outstretched hand and gave it a hearty shake.

"Have a good night, Ms. Moore," Rashad said. He plucked the keys from her fingers and unlocked and opened her car door.

"Thank you," Renee told him. She noticed the black folding case on the floor of the front passenger side of the car. It was the teaching manual kit she'd forgotten to return to the fifth grade science teacher, Mrs. Payne.

"Shoot," Renee said, reaching over for the case. "I need to bring this to Mrs. Payne. She let me borrow it two weeks ago."

Rashad shrugged. "Give it to her tomorrow."

"It's been in my car since last Tuesday. I need to bring it now before I forget again. I'll stick it in the reading lab. At least it'll be one step closer to Mrs. Payne's class."

"Okay, I'll see you tomorrow." Rashad took her hand and placed a slight kiss on the back of it. "That's gallantry, and nothing else."

"Good night, Rashad," Renee laughed.

She tucked the folding case under her arm and walked to the end of the block so she could cross the street with the assistance of the cross guard. Traffic was heavy around this time of the day, and she had no desire to meet with the front bumper of a car.

She entered through the side door that was closer to her reading lab. One of the custodial workers was emptying the trash bin when Renee walked into the classroom.

"Hi there," she said.

"Hi, Ms. Moore. Working late?"

"No, just bringing this in before it spends yet another day in my car." Renee deposited the teaching kit on her desk. "Have a good night," she called to the custodian. As she exited the lab, Renee spotted Alex Holmes coming up the hallway. Hot anticipation gripped her. Should she pretend she didn't see him and head out of the building?

Yeah, right. It took only a few seconds for his long stride to eat up the distance of the corridor.

"Hello again," Renee said as he approached.

"Hi, Ms. Moore."

"Are you trying to earn extra credit?" she asked. "School let out a half hour ago."

He looked down from the seven or so inches he had on her. He had incredibly beautiful lashes for a man. They hooded his eyes, like a delicate awning over a secret door.

He held up a white sweater with pink and yellow flowers edging the collar. "My daughter left her sweater."

His voice was as rich as the slow-churned Belgian chocolate ice cream she occasionally treated herself to after a bad day.

"Are you on your way out?" he asked.

Renee nodded. Speaking wasn't really high on her list of priorities at the moment. She was perfectly content to just look.

He held the side door open for her, and Renee slipped past him. They walked along the sidewalk, the towering oak trees that lined Claiborne Avenue shading them from the sun.

Renee chanced a glance at the man strolling beside her. He had a presence about him, as if he was used to being in charge. But he did say he owned that construction company, didn't he?

Given those muscles rippling under the cover of his sleeves, Renee presumed he put in his fair share of hours on those construction jobs. His body was taut and fit. She'd always had a thing for shoulders, and he had been blessed with a gorgeous set, even though one was covered in a bandage.

"What happened to your shoulder?" she asked.

He glanced over to his injured arm. "A beam fell on it."

"Ouch." Renee grimaced. "I'll bet that hurt."

He shrugged with his undamaged shoulder. "I could

pretend the pain was nothing, but truth is, I passed out after it happened. I hardly remember anything about it."

"Did it require surgery?

He nodded. "Along with a lot of physical therapy. I can't return to the job for at least another few weeks."

"That must be frustrating."

Another shrug. "It's over and done. Can't do anything about it now other than keep up with the PT. And it hasn't been all bad. I've been meaning to help out here since my daughter entered the preschool. This gives me the chance."

"Who is your daughter?" Renee asked.

"Jasmine Holmes," he answered. "She's in Mrs. Overland's first grade class."

Renee nodded. She knew Jasmine Holmes. She'd also heard the little girl had lost her mother two years ago and was being raised by her widowed father. Her apparently *still single* widowed father. Penelope would be happy to know she was right in her assumption.

"So, if my aunt agrees, does this mean you'll be able to check out the house once you're well?"

"No," he said, taking her hand as they crossed to the median. His hand was rough, almost like sandpaper against her skin, but it felt good. "I can still come over and inspect the house," he continued. "Once I get a clear picture of what needs to be done, one of the volunteer crews can start working."

He looked down at their clasped hands and quickly let go.

"I'm sorry," he said, "I'm so used to taking Jasmine's or my mother's hand whenever we cross the street."

"That's okay," Renee said, a slight smile tipping up the corners of her mouth. "I didn't mind."

He stared at her for a beat before averting his eyes. Renee could sense he was a bit flustered. Unsure. She also sensed the sweetness she'd perceived in him was genuine. She wondered what else she would find if she looked past Alex

Holmes's set of spectacular shoulders and amazingly soft brown eyes.

"You know, Jasmine is one of my best readers," Renee commented as they entered the gated teachers' parking lot.

"You're one of Jasmine's teachers? I thought Mrs. Overland and Mr. Hebert were the only ones who taught first grade?"

"I'm not a teacher in the traditional sense. I'm the special projects coordinator, which includes the Accelerated Reader program here at St. Katherine's. Jasmine comes to me twice a week. I'm also filling in for the librarian, Mrs. Johnson, while she recovers from gallstone surgery."

"I'm surprised Jasmine hasn't mentioned there was a new librarian. She loves the library."

"I can tell." Renee nodded. "She actually reads at a third grade level."

"She's always loved books. I've been reading to her since she was a baby."

"It's paid off."

They came upon her car and Renee felt a pang of disappointment that their conversation would soon be over. "Well, this is my car," she said.

He stopped, stared. At her.

Renee stared back, completely taken in by his intense gaze.

"Ms. Moore?"

"It's Renee."

"Renee," he said slowly as if he wasn't sure how her name would sound on his lips. It sounded pretty good to her.

He shook his head with a start, snapping the connection between them. "Have you noticed a difference in Jasmine over the past couple of weeks?" he asked.

Renee forced herself to get a grip, which would probably be easier if she didn't stare at those eyes that had the ability to put her in a trance. Instead, she focused on unlocking her car door.

"What kind of difference are you talking about?" she asked.

"Has she been acting strange in class?"

Renee tried to remember if anything little Jasmine Holmes had done over the past few weeks stood out in her mind.

"I only have her for forty minutes, twice a week. I can't recall anything out of the ordinary. Is something wrong?" Renee asked.

After a significant pause, he shook his head. "No. She's okay."

If everything was okay, why would he have asked about Jasmine's behavior in the first place? But Renee resisted the urge to question him further. He didn't seem all that interested in playing the sharing game.

"Well, thanks for walking me to my car," Renee said in an attempt to fill in the awkward silence.

"Have a good evening, Renee." He gazed down at her for another long moment, then continued on to a huge black and chrome truck two spots down.

Renee opened her car door and slid behind the wheel. She looked in her rearview mirror and stared as the shiny pickup passed behind her car and exited the parking lot.

Renee thought about Friday night and her date with Rashad and Stanley Kubrick at his most symbolic. She wondered what Alex Holmes had planned for this Friday night. She couldn't imagine him out clubbing, especially with a six-year-old to take care of, and definitely not with that injured shoulder he had to nurse back to health.

And just why are you thinking about him, anyway? Renee thought to herself.

"Because he is fine as hell," she answered aloud.

Margo poked her head out of Alex's kitchen pantry. "Are you sure you don't want to come back to the house? Even if it's just another week?" She grabbed the aluminum foil from the pantry, tore a piece from the roll, and used it to wrap up the remaining apple pie.

"One week won't make much difference," Alex answered.

"Of course it would. It's an additional week of healing time for your arm."

"I can handle it, Mama. Stop worrying."

"That's not going to happen no matter what you tell me," Mama said as she rinsed suds off a dish and wiped it dry. Not only had she brought dinner and dessert, but she'd insisted on cleaning up, too.

"I was going to wash those dishes," Alex said.

"You were going to put them in the dishwasher. I've told you that you can't count on those machines to get your dishes clean." She lowered the pot that had held the chicken stew into the soapy water. "So, things went well at the school today, huh?"

They'd talked a little over dinner about his and Jasmine's day at school, but now that Jazzy had gone into her room to work on her penmanship, he could fill Mama in on everything he'd observed, which actually wasn't much. Of course, Jasmine had not engaged in any of the behavior that had caused Principal Green to originally call him in, not with him in the classroom. The psychologist still thought his volunteering was the best way to allay Jasmine's irrational—albeit understandable—fears of him dying.

"Everything went well, but I'm not sure that's a good thing." He walked over to the sink and leaned against the counter. "Both Mrs. Overland and the school psychologist said they don't expect her to misbehave while I'm there. It's when I start to gradually back away that the psychologist thinks she may start to rebel again."

"The fact that she's using Chantal's death as an excuse concerns me. She seemed to be coping so well over the last year."

Alex shook his head. "Maybe she's trying to get attention, and she thinks reminding them that her mother is dead will get her sympathy from her teachers. According to Toby, it worked for him."

Mama looked back at him with a disgusted eye roll. "Toby needs a good smacking," she grunted. "What did Jasmine say when you talked to her about acting out at school?"

Alex ran a hand over his head. "We haven't really talked about it. I told her she was punished because I was called to the principal's office for her, but that's about it."

"Alex." She turned and perched a hand on her hip. "What good is punishing her if you don't discuss *why* she's being punished?" she asked, the words thick with chastisement.

"I know that won't cut it," Alex sighed. He attempted to cross his arms over his chest, then realized he couldn't with his right shoulder's limited range of motion. "But I have to psyche myself up for this conversation, Mama. I've been avoiding it for over two years."

"You need to sit her down and really talk to her, Alex. Jasmine has been through a lot for a little girl. That's something we all have to remember. Just because she no longer cries every day, it doesn't mean she's over Chantal's death."

"I know," Alex admitted.

"Think of how hard it was for you boys when your dad died," Mama said, wiping her hands with a dishcloth as she made her way to his side. She cradled his jaw in her palm, which was still moist and slightly wrinkled from the water. "Your daughter needs you, Alex. You need to be there for her. Find a way to make her open up to you."

He nodded, covering her hand. "I'm going to talk to her." *Eventually.*

After Mama left, Alex poked his head into Jasmine's room. She sat up in her bed, her back against the headboard, a book opened in her lap.

"How's it going, Pumpkin?"

She looked up. "Okay, I guess."

Alex stepped into the room. "Something wrong?"

She shrugged.

"What is it, Jazz?"

"I'm missing *The Suite Life of Zack and Cody*," she answered. Alex's mind drew a blank; then he remembered it was one of those shows on the Disney Channel she couldn't live without.

"No television for the rest of the week is part of your punishment," Alex reminded her.

"I don't like being punished," she huffed, crossing her arms.

"That's the point." He stepped farther into the room. This was the perfect time to bring up the topic he and Mama had just discussed, but after such a long day, Alex didn't have the mental strength for such a heavy conversation.

Or maybe he was just being a coward.

"What are you reading?" he asked.

Jasmine held up the book.

"*The Hundred Dresses* by Eleanor Estes. Is it any good?" Alex asked.

"Yes," Jasmine said with an emphatic nod. "All the people at school make fun of Wanda because she wears the same dress to school every day, so she lied and told them she has a hundred dresses. But, Daddy, they shouldn't make fun of Wanda just because she's poor."

"No, baby. You should never make fun of anyone." He sat on the edge of the bed. "That sounds like a really good book for you to read."

"Ms. Moore said it was her favorite book when she was a little girl."

Alex's stomach tilted just at the mention of Renee Moore. "So, you like Ms. Moore's class?" he asked Jasmine.

"Yes." Jasmine's eyes lit up. "If I get all the questions right on my next quiz, I get an eraser that looks like an apple and *smells* like an apple. I want that eraser, Daddy."

Alex chuckled at the seriousness in her voice. "Well, you need to get to reading."

"I know. And I like the book, too. It's good."

"Wow, an eraser that smells like an apple and a good book. School is a lot more fun these days then it was when I was a little boy."

"You didn't read good books?"

"Sometimes," Alex said. "But we didn't get to pick them ourselves. The teacher picked the books and we all had to read the same one. And we did not get prizes."

Jasmine shook her head. "Daddy, I am so happy I'm not old like you."

"Hey, I'm not that old."

"You're a little old."

"That's better," Alex said. He leaned over and placed a kiss on his daughter's forehead. "I'm going to get your clothes ready for school tomorrow, okay, Pumpkin?"

She nodded.

Alex pointed to the clock on her nightstand. "Ten more minutes; then it's time for you to go to bed. I'll come back so we can say our prayers together."

A half hour later, after he'd tucked Jasmine into bed, Alex sat at the desk in the spare bedroom he'd converted into an office. He stared at the computer screen, contemplating the wisdom of picking it up and tossing the machine out the window. His professor had granted him an extension after he explained about his accident, but with the way he had to peck at the keyboard with one hand, he probably still wouldn't get his paper done on time.

If only he could go back to the days when his required reading was *The Adventures of Tom Sawyer* and *Huckleberry Finn*. These days, his reading time was consumed by European history. What in the hell had he been thinking when he'd signed up for this class?

Alex clicked the disk icon at the top of the computer screen to save what little he'd been able to write on his paper, then shut down the word processing program. He would have to get to bed earlier if he was going to make it to St. Katherine's on time tomorrow. Jasmine had nearly missed her bus this morning. He hadn't expected it to take so much longer to get ready, but when trying to operate with only one functional arm he couldn't expect things to work as smoothly as they usually did.

Alex stripped out of his clothes and covered his bandage with the stretchy, plastic covering Eli had brought him from the hospital to prevent the dressing from getting wet.

He stepped into the separate glass shower and dipped his head under the spray, expelling a contented sigh as the water flowed over his head and down his torso. The stress of the past few days had the muscles in his back rigid, the tension overwhelming. Alex turned the knob on the jets he'd installed—possibly the best decision he'd made when renovating this bathroom. The barrage of high-powered water shot out of the stone-laid shower wall, attacking his aching muscles with nearly painful force.

God, it felt good.

Alex let the powerful stream beat upon his body. As his muscles began to relax, he allowed his mind to wander. He wasn't surprised when Renee Moore's image popped to the forefront of his brain.

Thoughts of her had hovered around the edges of his mind most of the day, and now that he had the time to really concentrate on her, Alex could not banish the onslaught of enticing pictures his mind conjured.

There was something about her that captured his attention as no other woman had in years. That playful smile that tilted her lips and lit up her amazing eyes called to him. She'd been so easy to talk to the first day they'd met, when he'd walked her to her car and held her hand inside his own.

His fingers tingled at the memory.

He soaped his chest, using the heel of his hand to massage

the aching muscles. His hand traveled down his stomach, then moved lower.

Alex closed his eyes as his fist wrapped around the erection he'd become accustomed to taming in his nightly shower. But tonight his hand didn't move with the detachment he usually employed to bring about the physical release his body demanded. For the first time in years, his self-gratification ritual was accompanied by a full-blown fantasy.

As he focused on the image of Renee's face, his hand moved in slow, measured strokes. His breathing slowed, becoming labored with each pump of his fist. Alex thought about her smile, and his hand stroked faster. His memory summoned her sexy voice, and he pumped harder. He clenched his eyes tight; his pace frenetic as his fist moved faster and faster, squeezing tighter and tighter, pain mixing with pleasure. In his mind it wasn't his own hand bringing about this rush of bliss; it was Renee's.

His release erupted in an explosion of pleasure. Alex braced himself against the shower wall; his knees weakened, his body shuddering as ripples of expended desire reverberated throughout his being.

"Damn," he whispered on a ragged breath.

He opened his eyes and wiped at the water that flowed down his face in steaming waves. He tried to push himself from the shower wall, but after a slight wobble, realized his muscles didn't have the strength. Alex sagged against the dripping wet tile, his body slowly recovering from the torrent of erotic sensations still coursing through his veins.

"Have you given up on Mrs. Overland already?"

Alex looked up from the list of students still waiting to see the nurse, finding Renee Moore's enticing brown eyes staring back at him, a pretty smile gracing her lips.

"Today is the hearing and sight screening for kindergarten through second grade," he explained, gesturing to the clipboard with his pen. "I'm splitting my time between helping out in the classroom and giving Nurse Juliana a hand."

"I didn't know you went out on loans." She smiled. "Does this mean I can steal you for the library when I need extra help?"

Was she flirting with him? "Um, I guess," Alex answered. Her eyes always tended to have that sparkle to them whenever he saw her. He wasn't sure if the smile in her eyes was just for him, or if everyone was afforded that sexy look.

"I'm only kidding," she laughed. She gazed over the array of colorful health brochures that had been laid out for the students. She picked up the one with the huge grinning tooth holding a toothbrush.

"Are you sure?" Alex asked. "I wouldn't mind joining you in the library. Just say the word, and I'm there." Okay, was *he* flirting now? It had been a long time since he'd played the game.

"Really, that was just a joke," Renee said. "I've been doing a pretty good job holding down the fort in Mrs. Johnson's absence. The library isn't in danger of collapsing. Yet." She smiled. "However, on the subject of needing a little extra help, my aunt nearly did cartwheels when I told her about your offer to check out the house."

"Good," Alex said.

"Whenever you're able to stop by, you will be more than welcome."

"I can stop by tomorrow after school lets out, if that's okay."

She hesitated for just a minute before nodding. "That's fine."

"I promise not to take too long," Alex said, sensing it wasn't really fine. "I just want to get an idea of the work that still needs to be done so I can give my foreman a heads-up. It should take a half hour, tops."

"Of course, of course" she said. "Let me give you the address."

She flipped over the smiling tooth pamphlet, took the pen out of Alex's hand, and jotted an address on it.

"I'll have Aunt Lorna leave the front door to the house unlocked, just in case no one's home. It's not as if there's anything inside worth stealing."

"I'll be there between five thirty and six o'clock."

"That works for me," she said. "Thank you so much, Alex."

"My pleasure," he said with his own smile.

"I'll see you later," she said, and headed down the corridor.

Alex still wasn't sure if he would admit to actively flirting, but seriously, how long had it been since he'd deliberately smiled at a woman, hoping to elicit a reaction from her? He *was* flirting with Renee Moore.

And he was enjoying it.

Chapter Six

Alex spooned two scoops of mashed potatoes from the microwavable dish and brought Jasmine's plate to the kitchen table where she sat with her chin resting in her hands.

"Are we supposed to have our elbows on the table?" Alex asked.

She slowly dragged her hands away from her face and let them fall into her lap. It would be one of those nights.

"What do you want to drink, apple or cranberry juice?" he asked.

"Can I have Sprite?"

"No. Apple or cranberry?" Alex asked again.

"Cranberry," Jasmine said with that resignation that had become her signature when she knew she could not get her way.

Alex retrieved two glasses and filled them with cranberry

juice from the refrigerator. He picked up one glass and automatically reached for the other with his right hand, grimacing at the pain that shot through his arm.

He was getting tired of this one-handed crap.

It had been nearly a week since he'd left his mama's house and moved himself and Jasmine back into their home. Alex wondered for about the hundredth time if he'd made a mistake. He had to wake up an hour earlier in the mornings because it took him twice as long to do everything with one arm still incapacitated.

Alex brought Jasmine's juice to the table, then went back for his own. Taking his seat, he reached out his hand and Jasmine laid her tiny hand in his palm.

She bowed her head and prayed. "Father God, bless this food, my family, and my mommy in heaven. Amen."

"Amen," Alex reiterated. He gave her hand a squeeze before letting it go.

His chest tightened at just the thought of this little girl. Her mere existence was such a source of wonder; he could stare at her for hours on end and still marvel at the gift God had given him when He'd blessed him and Chantal with their daughter. Jasmine was the one thing that prevented Alex from completely regretting his ill-fated marriage.

It wasn't until Jasmine asked, "What, Daddy?" that Alex realized he was still staring at her.

"Nothing," he answered. "How was your music class?" he asked, using his fork to break off a chunk of meat loaf.

"I got to play the cymbals," Jazz answered around a mouthful of potatoes. He couldn't fault her for this slip in manners. He *had* asked the question just as she was stuffing the potatoes into her mouth.

Alex wished they could sit and talk cymbals throughout dinner, but that would be avoiding the issue. Dr. Powell had recommended Alex broach the subject of Jasmine's behavior since he had already been at the school for nearly a week.

"How do you feel about me hanging out at the school?" Alex asked.

She scrunched up her mouth and shrugged.

"What's that face supposed to mean?"

"I don't know," Jazz mumbled.

"Well, do you like me being at the school, or do you want me to start staying home?"

Another shrug.

This was going well. "Jazz, do you know why I've been helping out at the school lately?" Alex asked.

"Because Grandma and the doctor said you can't pick up big stuff at your job," she answered.

Alex chuckled. Of course, Grandma's orders rated higher than the doctor's.

"That's true," he said, "but that's not the only reason I've been at your school this week. You know why Daddy had to put you on punishment, right? Because you called Mrs. Overland nasty names and threw the chalkboard eraser at her."

She slumped her head, burying her chin in her chest.

"Why did you do that?" Alex asked.

She hitched her shoulders, but said nothing as she pushed the remaining potatoes around her plate.

"Jasmine, look at me."

She raised her head and her eyes were bright with unshed tears, her bottom lip quivering.

Alex clenched his fist against the urge to pull her into his arms and tell her all was forgiven, but that wouldn't solve this problem. She needed to admit to what she had done.

"Why did you throw the eraser and call Mrs. Overland names, Jasmine?"

"I don't know," came a tremulous reply.

"You know it was wrong, don't you?"

She nodded.

"So, why did you do it?" he asked again.

Another shrug and a huge snuffle, followed by a single tear that trailed down her cheek and landed on the edge of her plate.

He couldn't do this. One of the hardest things for him to endure was seeing his little girl cry, and he could not stomach being the cause of her tears.

"Come here, baby." Alex pushed back from the table and held out his hand. Jasmine leaped out of her chair and onto his lap.

He knew he would have to get to the root of her discipline problem soon, but Alex wasn't up for that discussion today. She'd admitted the name calling was wrong. That was a start.

"I'm sorry, Daddy," came her soft, muffled voice.

"I know, baby," Alex answered. He wrapped his good arm around her and pressed a kiss to the top of her head. "I know."

Alex pulled up to the curb at the address Renee had written on the pamphlet and shifted his truck into park. He was finally getting the hang of one-handed driving. He walked up the cemented walkway that led to a classic Creole-style cottage with a wide wraparound porch. Even though the house was on pillars, the faint water line that still rimmed the exterior siding suggested the house had taken in a good four feet of water. The homes in this neighborhood had remained submerged in floodwaters for nearly two weeks after Hurricane Katrina. Whatever the actual water had not destroyed had probably been ruined by toxic mold.

Alex spotted the small pop-up camper off to the side. The trailers issued to residents by the Federal Emergency Management Agency had become a part of the landscape of post-Katrina New Orleans.

He climbed the steps of the house, noting the superior workmanship. He tried the doorknob, but it wouldn't budge. He walked along the wraparound porch to the side door, taking in the warped wooden boards under his feet. If these bloated floorboards were any indication of what he'd find inside the house, Alex figured they were looking at total demolition and rebuild. Sometimes, it was easier to just bring in a wrecking ball and start out with a clean slate.

Alex jiggled the handle to the side door, but it, too, was locked. He walked back around to the front of the house. The car Renee had gotten into earlier that week when he'd accompanied her to the parking lot at St. Katherine's was parked next to the FEMA trailer.

Alex walked over to the trailer and up the three wooden steps. He knocked. There was no answer. He knocked again.

He tried the handle on the trailer and was surprised and a little confused when it turned. Did she say the trailer would be open and not the house? Maybe he'd misheard her instructions.

Alex pushed the door open and felt his stomach drop as a glisteningly naked Renee screamed at him to get out.

For several interminable moments, Alex was rooted where he stood, incapable of doing anything but stare at the amazing body that was quickly being wrapped into a towel. In that millisecond he noticed high, firm breasts, a small waist, curvy hips, and deliciously smooth, toned thighs.

"Get. Out!" she screamed.

Alex snapped to attention, his brain registering where he was and what he was doing. He shut the door and clumsily made his way down the steps. Leaning against the outside of the trailer, Alex took several deep breaths. This was bad. Really bad. Should he go back and apologize? Should he just leave?

He'd embarrassed the hell out of himself, and would be lucky if Renee didn't come running out of the trailer wielding a butcher knife.

He should definitely leave.

Yet what he really wanted to do was break the door off that trailer and get another eyeful of the heavenly, dripping wet creature standing just on the other side of it. She could not have been as perfect as she had appeared. But it was his shoulder that was banged up; not a damn thing was wrong with his eyes.

The door to the trailer opened, and Renee stepped out wrapped in a yellow bathrobe. Alex had a feeling he was more the cause of the red tinge to her cheeks than the shower she had apparently taken minutes before he barged in on her. He could *not* believe he'd just done that.

"I'm sorry," Alex said. Because, really, what else did you say after walking in on a woman when she was naked?

Renee held up her hand. "Let's put the awkwardness behind us right now. We'll just pretend you didn't see anything, even though I know you did."

"Yeah, I did," Alex admitted. He was sure he would see her in his dreams every night for at least the next year, if not forever.

"Okay, stop staring at my chest," she said, and pulled the collar of the robe tighter.

Alex knew he was staring. He knew it was rude. He knew it only added to both their embarrassment.

But he could *not* stop.

"Alex!" she said, her voice hitting a new level of agitation.

"What?" Alex looked up into a face that was seriously pissed off. "I'm sorry," he said again. He needed to pull his head together and stop thinking about what was underneath that robe.

"I'm assuming you needed something," Renee said. She clenched the bathrobe so tight at her throat her knuckles were white.

"Uh, yeah," Alex answered. "I need to get into the house."

"The door should be open."

"That's what I thought you'd said, but it's not. I tried both the front and side doors; they're locked."

She blew out an aggravated breath. "Aunt Lorna was supposed to unlock the house. I'm sorry."

"No, I'm sorry," Alex said, for what, the third time?

It was those FEMA trailers. If they were equipped with bigger bathrooms, she would have been in there instead of drying off in the middle of her kitchen/living room/second bedroom.

"It was a mistake," Renee said. "Stop apologizing."

"Do you have a key for the house?" Alex asked, anxious to think of anything else but her body.

"Give me a minute." She stepped back into the camper and, seconds later, returned with a single key on a plain metal key ring. "This is for the side door."

Alex took the key from her outstretched fingers and had to swallow back the groan that nearly escaped his throat when their fingers touched.

"I'll, uh, get to work," he said.

This bordered on ridiculous. He was as aroused as a teenager who had just discovered girls. Although, after six years without a woman, what did he expect? He was impressed as hell that he'd refrained from dropping to his knees and begging Renee Moore to get naked for him again.

"Let me get dressed. I'll show you what the other contractor *didn't* do before he skipped town with Aunt Lorna's money."

"Okay," Alex answered, and quickly headed for the safety of the dilapidated house. He was way more at ease surrounded by lumber and insulation than a nearly naked woman. It hadn't always been that way, but life had a funny way of changing on you.

Alex entered the house, the stale, mildew stench assaulting him as soon as he opened the side door. He hadn't even thought to bring a mask when he'd left the house. He might have one in the glove compartment in the truck, but Alex figured his cursory inspection of the partially gutted home wouldn't take long to complete. The proverbial writing was on the torn-down walls.

He pulled the memo tablet out of his back pocket, along with the short, stubby carpenter's pencil he'd lifted from his desk before he left home. Being left-handed, Alex was grateful that beam had fallen on his right shoulder. This way, at least he wasn't completely useless.

He slowly made his way around the hollowed house. Some of the walls had been torn down to the studs, but much of the mold-ridden Sheetrock remained. Patches of black and green mold dotted the ceiling tiles.

Alex turned at the sound of the door opening. He spotted Renee entering the side door with a hospital mask covering half her face, and another dangling from her hand. She was also fully clothed in a dress that was pretty inappropriate given all the dust on the construction site.

"I forgot to tell you that you'd need a mask," she said, handing him the mask she carried.

Alex put it over his nose. He tried to bring the elastic bands around his head with his good arm, and nearly dropped it.

"Bend your head," Renee said, plucking the mask from his fingers and fitting it around his head. As he leaned over, his face was just inches from the exposed cleavage beautifully displayed by the V-neck collar of her wraparound dress. Alex was convinced his weakened knees would give out in the next sixty seconds.

The deep pink dress clung to her subtle curves. She wasn't nearly as voluptuous as Chantal had been, but that was a good thing. Alex had a particular repulsion for women who even slightly resembled his late wife.

Renee was Chantal's complete opposite. Where Chantal had been vanilla light, Renee's skin tone was a rich walnut brown. She had deep brown eyes, and wore her hair straight, just past her chin, unlike Chantal's long, bouncy curls.

"What do you think?" Renee asked. It took Alex a moment to realize she was talking about the house and not the way she looked in that dress. Replying that it was a nice view would definitely have gotten him slapped.

It *was* a nice view, though.

"It looks like the contractor only got through half the demolition," Alex answered. "And he wasn't very thorough." He pointed to the patches of dirty pink insulation still attached to some of the studs. "How much did your aunt pay him?" Alex asked, moving toward the back of the house to inspect the sturdiness of the remaining studs there.

"Forty thousand," Renee answered.

Alex whipped around. "You're kidding, right?"

"I wish I were," she answered. "He gave her an estimate of eighty-five thousand for both demo and construction, but told her she had to pay half as a down payment before he could start working. She emptied her savings."

Her aunt had been ripped off, big time. "Let me guess," Alex said. "Verbal contract?"

Renee nodded.

That money was gone.

"She called me after the guy didn't show up after three weeks. I swear if I ever find him I'm going to take joy in killing him."

Alex shook his head, sharing her anger. The number of fake contractors out there ripping people off was staggering. The demand was so high, all a criminal needed was a pickup truck and a sign on the door advertising his fake business.

"We've been trying to do as much as we can on our own, but it's been slow," Renee said. "We don't have the proper tools. Just that old sledgehammer and our hands."

"Wait? You and your aunt have been working in this house?"

She nodded.

"What did the contractor do?"

"That's it. He didn't do anything. He wouldn't start the work until my aunt gave him half, and when she did, he took off. I'm just sorry she waited so long to call me. By the time I moved here from Florida, all of this had already happened. There was nothing more for me to do but to help her out as much as I could with the demolition."

A car horn blew.

"That must be Rashad," Renee said. She walked over to the side door and poked out her head. A minute later, Rashad Richards came through the door.

"What are you doing in here?" Alex heard him ask.

"We're checking out the house," Renee answered.

Richards turned, spotting Alex for the first time. "Mr. Holmes, how's it going?" he said, reaching out to shake Alex's hand. Alex returned the gesture, unnerved by the surge of jealousy that shot through his system at the realization that Rashad Richards was the reason behind Renee's knockout dress. Alex had figured they were a couple when he first saw them together in the teachers' lounge at St. Katherine's, but having it confirmed, especially after catching a full-frontal view of a naked Renee, was way past disappointing.

"Are you ready?" Richards asked, covering his mouth and nose with his sleeve.

"We still have a few minutes, don't we? I want to show Alex the copper piping in the bathroom and kitchen."

"We're going to smell like mold. They'll put us out of the theater."

"I can check the piping on my own," Alex said. "You want to try saving it, right?"

"If at all possible," Renee answered.

"I've got a pretty clear picture of what needs to be done already," Alex said.

"Yeah, everything," Richards said with an insensitive snort.

"Basically," Alex agreed. "But most of the framework is

still in good shape. This cedar is from the swamp, so it can hold up to the waters from the flood without encountering too much damage. We'd have to get rid of the warped ones, but most of it can be saved."

"Renee? The smell," Richards whined like a schoolboy. What was she doing with a guy like this?

"Why don't we get out of here," Alex suggested, "so you don't get put out for stinking up the theater?" He hoped Richards caught his sarcasm.

Renee did. Alex could see the smile in her eyes, and couldn't help but return it. He wondered if Richards realized just how lucky he was to have *that* woman, with *that* smile, wearing *that* dress, on his arm tonight.

Richards was first out of the house, followed by Renee, then Alex. Once they were on the porch, Renee pulled the mask over her head, and shook her hair out.

"So, what do you think?" she asked Alex.

That she had the prettiest brown eyes he'd ever seen. That her legs looked amazing in that dress. That they looked even more amazing out of it.

"Mr. Richards summed it up," Alex answered. "Everything needs to be overhauled."

Her eyelids slid closed and she brought her hands up to rub her temples. "I know there's a lot of work ahead of us."

"Don't worry about any of it right now," Alex said. "I'll have a crew out here tomorrow to tear out these walls and the ceiling. Once they're done, they'll wash down the studs with a mold-killing solution and set up dehumidifiers throughout the house. I want to make sure we save as much of that cedar as possible. That wood probably goes for twenty times as much as it did when the house was built."

"I know this is early, but can you give me a ballpark figure of what this is going to cost?" Renee asked.

Alex hunched his good shoulder and shook his head. "I can't be sure. Give me the weekend to work on it. Once my foreman gets a look, he and I can get a clearer picture of exactly what we need and I can give you a few numbers."

"Renee, we need to get going," Richards said. "The movie starts in an hour and we have to eat first."

God forbid the woman worry about putting a solid roof over her head, not when there was a movie to watch. This was just another reason not to like Richards, in addition to the fact that the insensitive bastard was dating Renee.

"Give me just a minute, Rashad." Renee turned back to Alex. "Thank you so much for doing this. Keep the key, just in case no one is here tomorrow when your crew comes."

Great. Just what he needed to think about tonight, Renee Moore not being at home because she'd spent the night at Richards's place.

She took his left hand and squeezed it. "Thank you so much."

"My pleasure," Alex answered. He stood on the front lawn long after Richards's blue Mustang had pulled out of the drive.

Chapter Seven

"I can't do this anymore."

Margo took a sip of her dry white wine and waited for a reaction from the man sitting across the table. There was none, just as she'd expected. Gerald Mitchell brought the linen napkin to his mouth and dabbed at both sides. He folded it, returning the napkin to his lap.

"Gerald, did you hear me?"

"Yes, I did," he answered with a calmness that was the complete opposite of the anxiety coursing through her bloodstream. "What exactly do you mean by that?"

"Just what I said. I can't do this anymore. I cannot continue lying to my boys."

"Then don't."

"That's your solution?"

"Yes, Margo. I'm still not sure why you had to lie to your sons in the first place."

"Gerald, you don't know my boys. They would have a fit if they knew I was seeing you."

"They're grown men. They can handle it."

Margo pushed her plate of half-eaten pecan-crusted flounder to the side and finished off her glass of wine, her hand shaking slightly as she set the glass on the table. She knew it was time to tell her sons about Gerald. She was growing weary of coming up with excuses about her whereabouts.

It had never been her intention to deliberately keep Gerald a secret, but the more serious their relationship had become, the more Margo had to consider how news of her seeing a man would affect other aspects of her life. After so many years alone, it had taken *her* a few months to get used to the idea of dating again. She couldn't just spring Gerald on her family.

Thank goodness she had her future daughter-in-law to confide in. Monica was the only one she'd told about Gerald. And even though she thought Margo was being too considerate of her boys' feelings, Monica had proven to be a wonderful ally.

But the subterfuge had gone on too long. After their six months of seeing each other several times a week and talking on the phone nightly, it was obvious Gerald had become an integral part of her life. She just had to figure out how to integrate him into the rest of her life.

Gerald reached over and covered her hand with his. Margo looked up and smiled at him. He was a handsome man who looked much younger than his sixty-three years. His black hair had only a sprinkling of gray around his ears, which were a bit darker than his walnut-colored skin. He'd probably gone out on his boat without any sunscreen on his ears.

Margo tamped down the urge to chide him. She'd spent so many years mothering her boys; it was hard for her to switch hats. But Gerald didn't need a mother. He needed a companion, a lover.

Just the thought caused Margo's pulse to quicken.

It had been years since she had felt this way about another human being. Gerald Mitchell elicited emotions Margo thought she had buried when she'd laid Wesley to rest nearly seventeen years ago.

She thought about what Wesley would think of her dating again after all these years. Knowing Wes, his biggest complaint would probably be that she'd never allowed him to take her to an expensive restaurant.

With three boys to raise and a house to pay for, an expensive night on the town was something they could not afford in those days. There were times Margo thought she would have to choose between paying the electric bill and putting food in her sons' bellies.

Price was not something that concerned Gerald. With the money he pulled in as a corporate attorney, the man sitting across from her could buy this restaurant and everyone in it.

"Are you done with dinner?" Gerald asked.

"I am. It was delicious," she said. "This restaurant is amazing. I've always wanted to dine here," she said, marveling at the elegantly dressed dining room, with its impressive chandeliers and silk-covered walls.

"It brings me great pleasure to show you a good time, Margo. You're so busy making sure everyone else is okay that you don't take time to do anything for yourself."

Hadn't she accused Alex of doing the very same thing?

Margo had never considered the support she provided to her family a burden. She cherished every moment she spent helping her boys, and don't get her started on her grand-child. They were what she lived for.

But what about when they were all gone?

Both Eli and Toby would be getting married soon, and Jasmine was becoming more independent by the day. Before she knew it, her grandbaby would be out of the way, and Margo wouldn't be needed anymore. In fact, it had already started. The fact that Alex had left her house so soon after his surgery was extremely telling. What would happen when her family didn't need her anymore?

"If you're done with dinner, I thought we could go to this little jazz club that just reopened," Gerald said.

Margo thought about what she originally had on tap for the rest of the night. She had planned to start the base for her special bread pudding that had to stand for twenty-four hours. Eli had requested she make the dessert for Sunday dinner. A dinner he wasn't even sure he would be able to attend because of his schedule at the hospital. A few months ago, Margo would not have considered taking time for herself at the expense of preparing one of her son's favorite desserts.

But now . . .

Maybe it was time she start thinking about herself.

Margo placed her hand in Gerald's. "I would love to accompany you to that club, Gerald. I'm in the mood for a little jazz."

Renee broke off a piece of graham cracker crust and smashed it with the tines of her fork, creating a mess on the edge of her dessert plate. It had occurred to her less than a half hour into this date that she was bored stiff, and that was before the movie nearly put her to sleep.

This wasn't the first time she'd been out with Rashad and found herself thinking about the million other things she could be doing with her time. Yet it had never occurred to her to just tell him that she wanted to leave. She hated the thought of being rude after he'd been such a friend these few months since she'd moved from Florida. He didn't deserve to be treated that way.

But she wasn't feeling this. Not at all. She had a choice in how she spent her Friday night, so why was she sitting here halfway engaged in boring conversation with a guy she was becoming less and less interested in by the minute? They would never be more than friends.

"Is everything all right?"

Renee's head popped up at Rashad's inquiry. Should she be honest? That usually wasn't even a question, except when it came to hurting someone's feelings.

"I'm fine," she lied. *Coward.*

"Is the cheesecake okay?"

"It is." She nodded. "I guess I'm still a little full from dinner earlier."

"What are you doing tomorrow?" Rashad asked.

"It's the Florida versus Tennessee game," she answered.

Rashad rolled his eyes. "Sorry, I forgot. Can't you miss just one?" he asked. "There's an exhibit at this gallery on Julia Street I've been wanting to check out."

"I said it's Florida versus Tennessee," she said, figuring that should be enough. "Two of the top teams in the Southeastern Conference going head-to-head," she continued, when he still didn't seem to get it.

Rashad shook his head and sighed. "Fine, what about after the game?"

"Another SEC matchup: LSU versus Alabama."

"But you didn't go to either of those schools."

"The game still has major implications for the rest of the conference," she argued.

"I don't understand how you can sit in front of the TV for hours and watch game after game," Rashad said.

The same way he could stare at painting after painting for

hours on end. At least the people on the TV moved. It was just her luck to pick a guy friend who wasn't into sports, while she was the poster child for the outdoors. "Rashad, I'm really tired. Can we call it a night?"

"You sure? You've hardly touched your cheesecake."

"I'm going to get it to go. It'll be my breakfast tomorrow." She might be athletic, but she wasn't a complete health nut.

Rashad pushed from the table and came around to pull out her chair. One thing he had going for him was the gentleman quality.

"Do you want to get another slice of cheesecake to take home for your aunt?"

And thoughtfulness, too.

But that didn't make up for having nothing in common. It was time to end this. "No, thanks," Renee answered.

Even keeping up the small talk on the short drive from the restaurant had become increasingly difficult, which solidified Renee's decision to make this her last official "date" with Rashad. She would break it off with him on Monday.

She hated to think how this would affect things at work, but she could not continue with this pretense. Tonight would have been better spent doing her laundry than watching a movie she didn't want to watch and engaging in conversation she couldn't remember.

When Rashad pulled his Mustang into her aunt's driveway, Renee didn't give him a chance to get out of the car. She gave him a slight peck on the cheek, thanked him for dinner, and quickly made her way out of the car and into the trailer. Aunt Lorna was sitting on the sofa with the remote in her hand.

"You're home earlier than I thought you would be," Aunt Lorna said. "I'm disappointed."

"Good to see you, too," Renee laughed, bending over to give her aunt a kiss on the cheek.

Aunt Lorna was her mother's only sibling. Never married, she'd been the rebel of the family, moving out at the tender age of seventeen and making her way to New York City, where she spent years performing off Broadway. Even though her preacher father had not agreed with her career choice, he'd still supported her. It was Aunt Lorna's decision to pose for *Playboy* that had been the proverbial straw that broke the camel's back.

Although it completely alienated her from her parents, Aunt Lorna maintained that the day the magazine hit news-stands was one of her proudest moments. Renee had seen a copy of the photo layout. She had the right to be proud. Her aunt had possessed a body to die for, and it had been shown to full advantage on the glossy pages of the magazine.

Despite the riff her unconventional lifestyle had caused between Aunt Lorna and her parents, there had never been a break in the relationship between her and her sister, Doreen, Renee's mother.

When Renee finally broke free from the abuse of her childhood, she had turned to her aunt, who welcomed her with open arms. That's why when Katrina hit, it had not been a question where Lorna would evacuate. Renee even gave up the bed in her one-room apartment, sleeping on the sofa so Aunt Lorna would be as comfortable as possible dur-ing the weeks she remained with her in Tampa after the storm. When Lorna was scammed by that contractor, Renee hadn't thought twice about leaving her job and moving to New Orleans to aid her aunt in whatever way she could.

"Do you want a slice of cheesecake?" Renee offered.

"I have a figure to maintain, thank you very much. It's not as easy to keep those pounds off once you pass fifty. You'd better enjoy those sweets while you can."

"Thanks for the warning," Renee laughed.

"What happened with the construction worker from the school?" Aunt Lorna asked. "Did he show up to check out the house?"

"Yeah," Renee answered. He'd had the chance to check

out a lot more than the house. Heat rushed through her just at the thought of the look on Alex Holmes's face when he'd accidentally walked in on her stark naked.

"What did he say?"

"That you were ripped off." Renee opened the miniscule refrigerator and retrieved a carton of milk.

"Did he say anything I don't know already?"

Renee rested her hip against the kitchen counter while she poured milk into a glass. "He thinks we can save most of the wood from the frame."

"Oh, thank God. I'd hate to throw that cedar away. It was one of the reasons I bought this house. What about the copper piping?" Aunt Lorna asked.

"He's sending a crew tomorrow morning to look everything over and start taking down the walls and ceiling."

"How much will it all cost?"

"That's one thing he didn't say."

Lorna sighed. "I guess it doesn't really matter. It has to get done, no matter the cost."

"And it's not as if you have to worry about taking care of it by yourself."

"I told you I'm not taking money from you, little girl." Aunt Lorna's stern warning drew another laugh from Renee.

"And I told you that you don't have a choice."

Renee still remembered waiting in line at Western Unions along the East Coast as her mother received emergency wire transfers from her big sister. Aunt Lorna's financial support had kept them afloat those times her mother had tried to leave her father. It was throwing good money after wasted intentions, of course. After a few weeks, her mother would always find her way back to her abusive husband.

"Will you be here tomorrow when the work crew arrives?" Lorna asked.

"I can be," Renee answered. "I was going over to Penelope's to watch football, but I can do that here."

"I agreed to teach an acting class at the Boys and Girls Club, so I'll be gone early tomorrow. I should be back before noon." Aunt Lorna rose from the sofa and extended her arms in a generous stretch, her hands reaching the low ceiling of the trailer. "Well, since I don't have to worry about waiting up for you, I'm going to bed."

"As if you had to wait up," Renee said, giving her aunt another kiss on the cheek.

"I promised myself I would take care of you," Lorna reminded her.

"I'm perfectly capable of taking care of myself, but I appreciate it anyway. Have a good night's sleep."

"I will, baby. I'll try not to wake you when I get up in the morning."

Renee flopped down on the sofa, picking up the remote and muting the volume as she flipped through the channels, settling on ESPN to catch the eleven o'clock *SportsCenter*.

She thought about the past few hours she'd spent with Rashad, and wondered if she was being too hard on him. Rashad had been a good friend these past few months. Sure, he'd tried to take things a little faster than she had been willing to allow, but as she'd just told Aunt Lorna, she was a big girl. She could definitely take care of herself. The first time Rashad's hand had traveled where it shouldn't have, he'd found his arm bent up behind his back, and her knee primed to turn him into a soprano. Renee hadn't had much of a problem dealing with him after that. It was only in the last couple of weeks that he'd started coming on strong again, but all it would take is another lesson in manners to nip that behavior in the bud.

But was it even worth it?

Their friendship would go no further than where it was right now. She'd already established that in her mind, and her boredom with their date tonight had confirmed it. If Rashad could not handle being strictly friends, then Renee would have to cut all ties. It was as simple as that.

She'd never been one of those women who needed a man on her arm to feel complete, but she was careful about not pushing guys away, either. She knew she had her share of daddy issues, but she refused to let her abusive father color her judgment of men in general.

She'd only had a couple of serious boyfriends in her life, and they had always started out as friends. In the beginning she'd sort of hoped she and Rashad could develop the same type of friendship. But that wasn't going to happen. Whenever she finally decided to enter a relationship again, she needed to have at least one thing in common with the guy.

"And he should definitely love football," Renee whispered as she raised the volume on the television a couple of notches. Stuart Scott was about to lay out the matches for tomorrow's games.

Chapter Eight

"Why do I let you get me into these situations, especially at this time of the morning?" Penelope huffed. "Normal people choose to sleep in on a Saturday, you know."

"This is more fun than wasting away your Saturday morning in bed." Renee said as she grabbed hold of the brown peg above her head and heaved, scaling up another foot of the rock wall.

"As cold and lonely as my bed is, I'd still rather be there than hanging off the side of this stupid wall," Penelope said.

"C'mon, it's not that bad."

"I'm guessing this harness thingy doesn't have your underwear riding up your butt," Penelope deadpanned.

Renee laughed so hard she nearly lost her footing. "I am so going to get you for that," she warned, still laughing.

"We only have a few feet to go before we're done. You can take the stairs down."

They made it up the rock wall. Renee held back just a bit so Penelope could climb onto the ledge ahead of her. Her friend was waiting with her hands on her hips when Renee finally pulled herself up into a standing position.

"You do realize only insane people engage in these types of activities for 'fun,' don't you?" Penelope made air quotes after the word *fun*.

"In addition to being great exercise," Renee said, taking off her helmet and shaking out her hair, "it's also an excellent stress reducer."

"Ah, you see, hon, that's where we differ. For a girl like me, hanging off the side of a rock *causes* stress, even if it's a fake rock with a padded floor at the bottom. Besides, there is not enough stress in the world that will send me to doing some of the things you do to relieve stress."

"Please, with all the stuff going on these days, I'd have to go skydiving to release the adrenaline stored up in these muscles. Come on." She motioned for Penelope to follow her down the staircase that ran along the backside of the rock wall.

"What's going on?" Penelope followed close on her heels.

"Don't worry about it," Renee said.

"You know me better than to think I'd let you brush me off," Penelope snorted. When they arrived at the bottom of the stairs, her coworker grabbed her by the arm and pulled Renee around to face her. "You dragged me out of bed at six in the morning; the least you can do is bare your soul."

"Such a small price to pay," Renee chuckled.

"Spill it."

"Really, it isn't anything serious."

Penelope just stared, her expression unrelenting.

"Oh, all right," Renee said. "Can we at least talk about this over a round of kickboxing?"

"Uh-oh, this must be big."

"You asked for it," Renee reminded her. Grabbing a couple of padded gloves from the rack that ran the length of the gym's wall, she dragged Penelope to the center of the floor.

Fashioned in kneepads and protective headgear, Penelope held up her gloved hands. "Come on, talk to Mama."

Debating the wisdom of *baring her soul*, Renee asked, "Remember the copy machine guy from the other day?"

"Oh yeah. I found out he's little Jasmine Holmes's father. The one who lost his wife in an accident a few years back."

"Yeah, I know," Renee said.

"And I found out he is still single."

"Yeah." Renee executed a roundhouse kick. "I know."

Penelope gave her a hard look, her eyes in an accusing squint. "What did you do?"

"Nothing," Renee said.

"Renee." Penelope sounded like a mother who knew her guilty two-year-old was lying about stealing a cookie before dinner.

"I swear, nothing happened."

"But you want something to happen."

"Oh yeah," Renee answered. She threw three successive punches into Penelope's gloved hand.

"Take it easy," Penelope said. "Why don't we just talk before you kill me?"

"I'm sorry." Renee wiped sweat from her brow. She took a swig of water from the bottle she'd placed a few feet away from them on the floor. "I kind of ended things with Rashad," she confessed.

"When?" Penelope tore the cushioned helmet from her head.

"Last night. I didn't exactly end it, but I'm going to."

"Why?"

Renee sent her a blunt look.

Penelope sucked in a breath. "Copier guy? You gave it up to copier guy? When?"

"Please," Renee snorted. "When was the last time I gave *anything* up? But I wanted to," she admitted. "I still want to. Really, *really* bad."

"I'm trying to decide whether I should be upset since I specifically told you I wanted him, or if I should do a little happy dance for you."

"He is so not the type of man a girl would just hand over to her friend. So if you want to fight over him, be my guest. Just remember I'm in much better shape than you are."

"Who are you telling? You'd kick my butt from here to Thursday."

"Yes, I would," Renee laughed.

"When did you get all possessive over this man you just met?"

"Since he saw me naked."

Penelope's eyes widened to the size of dinner plates. "It was an accident," Renee explained. "He came by yesterday to look over the damage to the house, and he walked in on me as I was getting dressed for my date with Rashad."

"Oh my God, I would have died."

"I know!"

"*I* would have died. You have no reason to. If I had your body I would have given him a tour of the house completely naked. I, on the other hand, have this muffin top to hide."

"You do not have a muffin top," Renee chided.

"Thanks to you. I guess I shouldn't complain about these six a.m. workouts anymore, just in case some hot guy decides to barge in on me when I'm naked. What am I talking about?" Penelope snorted. "That stuff never happens to me."

"I'm starting to regret that it happened to me," Renee said. "I can't stop thinking about him. My body has been in that hot, just-ask-me-to-strip-and-I'd-do-it-in-an-instant mode ever since he walked in on me."

"Oh, all hot and tingly. I remember that feeling," Penelope said with a wistful sigh. "It's been a long time since I felt that way."

"Me, too, which is what scares me. Granted, I only went out with Rashad a few times, but I wasn't tempted to so much as take off my shoes around him. Alex Holmes comes over to assess Aunt Lorna's house, and I'm ready to drag him on the sofa and rip his clothes off. It's crazy."

"It's not crazy, it's instant attraction, baby. Don't fight it."

"I can't allow anything to happen with him. He's the parent of one of my students."

"You're his daughter's librarian. What kind of favoritism can you show?"

"Not the point. It's unethical."

"Whatever." Penelope waved her off. "If you want him, you'd better go after him because a horny single gal like me will be waiting to scoop him up."

"Keep your hands off," Renee laughed. "He's coming over again this morning, along with a crew from his construction company."

"Wow, he works fast, doesn't he?"

"Yeah, they're going to start with demo."

"Well, this is what I suggest." Penelope clasped her hands around Renee's. "Bypass the showers here, invite him in the trailer for his morning coffee, and do a little innocent striptease."

"You are no help at all."

"Oh, come on. You have to do this. For both of us, because I expect you to give me the play-by-play when you're done."

"You are worse than a guy," Renee laughed. "Are you coming over to watch football?"

"It depends on what time I finish with the meeting with *my* contractor. How did I get stuck with a sixty-year-old grandpa with a beer belly for a contractor, and you get Alex Holmes? Life is so unfair."

"Don't envy me just yet. I'll most likely end up making a fool of myself. Let's get our stuff together. I want to make sure I'm home before the work crew arrives."

"Take my advice," Penelope said. "Wait to shower."

Alex stopped Jasmine as she came up the hallway from her bedroom. He pointed to her feet. "Where are the pink socks I laid out for you?"

"I don't want to wear the pink socks," Jasmine said in that whiny voice Alex had heard more than he had the patience for this morning.

"Jasmine, get the pink socks."

"But I want to wear my SpongeBob socks."

"You're the one who said you wanted to wear your pink jumpsuit. Those SpongeBob socks are yellow and blue. Now, if you want to wear SpongeBob, go in the closet and get your jeans and that yellow shirt Uncle Eli bought you."

"But I want to wear my jumpsuit." She stomped her feet.

"Jasmine!" Alex tried hard to keep his voice at a tolerable level. His shoulder had been hurting the hell out of him since yesterday, and had kept him up most of the night, along with that stupid European history paper he'd been working on for a week. He wasn't up for dealing with a tantrum.

"I'm putting an end to this right now. I've already ironed the jumpsuit. Put on your pink socks." She started to speak, but Alex stopped her. "I don't want to hear it. Get the socks."

Her bottom lip poked out and her eyes welled with tears, but Alex held his ground. His daughter had inherited her mother's manipulative streak, along with her light brown eyes and naturally curly hair. Jasmine could turn those tears on and off like a faucet, and had learned to use them to her advantage. As hard it was to see his little girl cry, Alex was learning to refrain from giving in to her demands. The battle over the socks would probably be just the tip of today's iceberg.

A car horn blew.

"Jasmine," he called. "That's Kayla and her mom. You're going to be late for Campfire Girls."

Jasmine trudged up the hallway, her pink and white backpack hanging over one arm. Alex captured her by the ponytail and slipped the backpack from her arm. He unzipped it, took out the SpongeBob socks, and stuffed them in the front pocket of his jeans.

Sneakiness. Another trait she'd inherited from Chantal.

Alex shook his head. The girl was only six years old. If she was already trying to pull the wool over his eyes, how would he get through the teenage years?

He followed Jasmine as she stomped out of the house to the silver SUV in his driveway. Leslie Morgan sat behind the wheel, her daughter, Kayla, in the front seat.

Alex took a deep breath, gearing up for this morning's encounter with the Queen of Horny. The newly divorced Mrs. Morgan had made her feelings more than clear when she'd come up to him at Jasmine and Kayla's first softball game and not so innocently brushed her hand across his fly while handing him this season's game schedule. If he ever had the urge to engage in a little casual sex, Alex knew of at least one willing participant.

"Thanks for picking Jasmine up for the meeting," Alex said by way of greeting as he walked up to the SUV. He looked over to the passenger side and gave Kayla a wave.

"My pleasure," Leslie Morgan said. Her eyes traveled from the top of his head to his slipper-clad feet in a slow, blatantly sexual perusal. He needed a shower after that dirty look.

"I'll pick Jasmine up around four?" Alex confirmed.

"That's fine. These girls have no problem keeping themselves occupied for hours on end," she said. In a lowered voice, she continued. "If you want to come by a little earlier, I have ways to keep you occupied, too." She ran her tongue along her lips.

Alex backed up a step. "Uh, yeah. Okay, then. I guess you

all better get going before you're late for the meeting." He
peered at Jasmine sitting in the back of the SUV. "You have
on your seat belt, Pumpkin?"

"Yes, Daddy," came her reply.

Leslie put the SUV in reverse. "See you later, Daddy."
She whispered the last word, her mouth tipping up in a sensual smile as she backed out of the driveway.

"Lord, have mercy," Alex said under his breath.

This celibacy thing wasn't easy, and women like Leslie
Morgan made it a hundred times more difficult. Just because he'd chosen to abstain from sex didn't mean it wasn't
on his mind a hell of a lot. And after yesterday, it was about
the *only* thing on his mind. The thought of Renee's wet,
naked body wrestled a groan from deep in Alex's throat. He
ran his hand down his face, clenching his eyes shut as the
image of her incredible body assaulted him.

"Just stop thinking about her," Alex pleaded with his
brain.

As if that would happen any time soon. He needed to
head back in and get ready to meet the twelve-man crew
that would be at her aunt's house in another half hour. If
everyone who'd signed on to volunteer showed up, it
wouldn't take his men long to get through the demolition.
They could possibly start the washing-down process and de-
humidifying the house to rid it of the toxic mold by next
weekend.

The phone was ringing when Alex reentered the house.
He picked up the cordless in the kitchen, grabbing an apple
from the bowl on the counter.

"This is Alex," he answered.

"Hey, man, have you heard from Mama?" came Eli's
voice over the line.

"Not since yesterday. Why? What's up?"

"I called her a couple of times last night, and then again
this morning, but she's not answering the house phone or
her cell phone. She asked me to check the hot water heater."

The apple was arrested halfway to Alex's mouth. "What do you know about hot water heaters?"

"I've helped you on enough home repair jobs. And you shouldn't be doing that kind of work."

"I'll stop by there on my way home later today," Alex said, cradling the phone between his ear and left shoulder. "I can look at a hot water heater without injuring myself," he snorted before taking a bite out of his apple.

"Where are you going today?" Eli asked, and Alex realized he'd said too much.

"Nowhere," he answered.

"Alex." Eli's voice was filled with accusation.

Alex emitted a long-suffering sigh. He was not up for hearing his brother's mouth this morning, but Eli wouldn't stop until he got the information he sought.

"I've got a crew going out to look at a house today," Alex said. "One of the teachers at Jazzy's school got ripped off by a crooked contractor. I offered to put one of the volunteer crews on it to help her and her aunt rebuild."

"What happened to taking it easy? You're still recovering from major surgery."

"I'm supervising, E, that's all."

"And I'm supposed to believe that?" Eli muttered.

"I'm hanging up," Alex said, and pressed the end button on the phone. He immediately dialed his mother's number.

She picked up on the fourth ring with a groggy "Hello?"

"Mama? What's wrong? You sound sick."

"I'm sleeping," she said. "And I think I have a hangover."

Alex took the receiver from his ear and stared at it, certain he hadn't heard what he thought he'd just heard.

"Mama, what's going on with you? Eli said he's been calling you since last night about the hot water heater, which I could have fixed, by the way."

"Alex, please. I can't think about the hot water heater. I'm going back to bed."

The line went dead.

Alex listened to the dial tone for a full ten seconds, until the recorded voice came through the line telling him to try his call again.

What had happened to his neat little world? First he nearly got killed on the job; then his daughter decided to turn into a demon child. And now his fifty-nine-year-old, upstanding, churchgoing mother had just hung up in his face after admitting she had a hangover?

Alex didn't know what to make of his mother's behavior these days. Ever since that weekend she'd mysteriously taken off about six months ago, she'd been acting strange.

He noticed the time illuminated on the microwave. He had to be over at Renee's house in twenty minutes. Not enough time to go over to Mama's this morning, but he *would* be there later today. It was time for whatever was going on with Mama to come to an end.

Alex showered as quickly as he could. With the help of the plastic covering Eli had brought him, he'd finally mastered the art of not getting his bandages wet. Putting on his clothes was a little more difficult, but he still managed to dress himself in under six minutes. He filled his travel coffee mug and left the house.

When Alex pulled up to Lorna Davis's home, his crew was already there, surveying the outside of the structure. Even though it shouldn't have mattered, relief rushed through his veins when he spotted Renee's car parked next to the trailer. Sure, she could still have spent the night with Richards and just come home early this morning, but Alex wouldn't know either way. He'd rather believe she'd slept the night away in the tiny little FEMA trailer.

Alex walked along the outer fence to the back of the property.

"Boss." Jason Deering waved and started toward Alex. He shoved out his right hand, but took it back as if he thought Alex couldn't return the handshake. "How's the recovery going?"

"According to the doctor's schedule," Alex answered, stretching out his hand. It hurt like hell, and stung even more when Jason pumped their clasped fists two times. "I'd hoped the recovery wouldn't take as long as predicted, but it looks like the doc knew what he was talking about."

"But you will recover, right?"

"It'll take a while, but with physical therapy, I'll eventually get back to normal."

"You don't have to worry about the business while you're out, Alex. It's going to do just fine."

"I know it will," Alex answered. "That's why I put you in charge."

Jason had worked for Holmes Construction since its inception nearly twelve years ago. If Alex could not be there himself, Jason was the only man he would trust in running his business.

"What do you think about the house?" Alex asked. He and Jason started a slow perusal of the perimeter of the property.

"It isn't as bad as it could have been," Jason said. "The house was solidly built. Did you see that cedar?"

"Beautiful, isn't it?"

"Man." Jason shook his head. "What I wouldn't give to have a steady supply of that wood."

"Hey, boss, you're looking good," Cory Williams, one of his best carpenters, called as he strode up to where Jason and Alex stood. "We're ready to get started," he said.

Alex flipped him the key. Cory let out a loud whistle, and the rest of the crew descended on the house, carrying sledgehammers, crowbars, and hammer drills. In a matter of minutes, they were in full work mode.

"Are they rebuilding the interior as is, or are they looking to do a little redesign?" Jason asked.

"I'm not sure," Alex answered. "I haven't discussed anything other than demo with the owner's niece. We're going to go over the house plans a little later today. I promised I would come up with a ballpark figure of what this is going to cost them."

"How's it going, boss?" a worker called as he carried a load of mold-laden ceiling tiles and dumped them into a waiting wheelbarrow.

Alex patted the guy's back when he passed on his way back to the house.

"Too bad Lance couldn't make it," Jason said. "He would have a better idea of what the materials would run for a house this size."

"I'll get with him later. His daughter's volleyball team is in the state semifinals, and I wouldn't let him miss her match."

Lance Poche was another who had been with Alex since the early years. After Hurricane Katrina, he had put Lance in charge of the special volunteer rebuilding project.

The storm had been a financial windfall for his company, and it didn't sit well with Alex to reap benefits from something that had been so devastating for so many. The crews that worked on the weekends helping to rebuild homes did so on a volunteer basis, but Alex provided as much incentive as he could to get his workers to give a little of their time. A raffle for a pair of New Orleans Saints tickets would be given away on Monday for the guys who'd showed up to help today. Alex had wanted to make sure he had a good turnout.

"Hi there."

Alex turned to find Renee in running shorts and a workout shirt made of a meshed, breathable material. She had an iPod strapped to her upper arm, her skin covered in a fine sheen of moisture.

"Look at all of this," she said, turning in a full circle. Exertion lent a breathy quality to her voice that set Alex's heart on a familiar, accelerated pace. It happened whenever he was around her. "Sorry I wasn't here when the crew arrived," Renee continued. "I hadn't expected so much activity so soon."

"I asked the guys to show up a bit earlier than usual this morning. I wanted to get a head start on the interior demo," Alex answered.

"You have a great house," Jason said. "They don't build them like this anymore."

"Well, it's my aunt's house, but thanks on her behalf. She loves this place. I love it, too."

"Is your aunt here?" Alex asked.

"No. She left early this morning to head on over to the West Bank. She's teaching an acting class at a community center out there. She's picking up a set of plans from the architect and should be back here around noon."

"Once your aunt returns we can go over exactly what she's looking to do with the house. After going over the house plans I can possibly give an estimate on what the materials will cost for the rebuild," Alex said.

"Is she looking at just renovating?" Jason asked.

"She wanted to change a few things about the inside," Renee said. "But since being ripped off by that contractor, she's convinced she won't be able to afford it."

"What did she have in mind?" Alex asked.

"It was just a few things here and there, like making the living room a little bigger, and adding a walk-in pantry to the kitchen. She's going to tell you those things aren't important, but don't listen to her," Renee said. "I'll cover the extra cost."

"It may not be as expensive as you think," Jason said. "It'll depend on how much has to be revamped."

"Aunt Lorna just wants her house back. That's the most important thing, to get her back in the house."

"Yeah, that trailer can get pretty cramped," Jason said. "My family and I were in one for eleven months while we rebuilt the house."

"The trailer is a bit cozy," Renee answered with a light little laugh that had Alex's skin getting hot. "It's not bad with just the two of us," she continued, "but I know how much Lorna loves that house. The sooner she gets back in it, the happier she'll be. I'm going to shower; then I'll be back out to help," she said.

"No." Alex stopped her.

"Excuse me?"

"There's nothing for you to help with," Alex said. "My guys have it under control."

"I can't expect you all to come in and help us and not even lend a hand."

"That's what we do," Jason said with a happy-go-lucky shrug. "Listen to the boss man." He patted Alex on his good shoulder. "Let us take care of this."

Jason headed toward where the crew was mixing the solution to wash down the interior of the house.

Renee captured Alex's hand and squeezed it. "Thank you," she said. "When you said you would have a few of your workers come by to help out, I never expected this." She didn't let go of his hand, and Alex wasn't sure he would be able to speak.

"I've got some good guys." Good. His voice was still in operational mode. "They know how much work still needs to be done in the city. They're happy to help."

"They are very much needed, and appreciated. Thank you, Alex. If there's anything you need, please let me know."

If only this was a different time and he at a different place in his life, he would have had a very perverse answer to her offer.

"It's our pleasure," he said, and she granted him one of those smiles as she let his hand go and headed for the trailer.

It would be pathetic to smell his hand.

So he was pathetic, Alex thought as he discreetly brought his hand up to his nose and inhaled her scent deep into his lungs. God, she smelled good, even after running.

"Hey, boss, come take a look at this," Jason called from the porch.

Alex looked over one last time as the door to the trailer

closed behind Renee; then he headed over to hear what his foreman had to say.

A loud crash caused Renee to jerk up from the sofa. She checked the time on the DVD player, and realized she'd been asleep for nearly an hour and a half, still wearing the sticky clothes she'd worn rock climbing and on her run.

"That'll teach you to push yourself to exhaustion," she said.

As she waited for the propane that heated the water for the trailer's shower to do its thing, Renee grabbed a handful of pistachios and settled in to watch the show taking place outside the small kitchen window. The construction crew worked with amazing precision. As two guys pulled insulation from the house, another waited with a wheelbarrow to haul it away. Another set of workers used those industrial-size brooms to push debris from the house, onto the porch, and from the porch into plastic catch bins they had brought with them.

The crew Alex had provided had done more this morning than she and her aunt had been able to accomplish in months. The insistence that she not help didn't sit well with Renee. The least she could do was offer them some water. But just as that thought occurred, the guy Alex had introduced as Jason wheeled a cooler to the edge of the porch and started passing out bottled water to the crew. She really didn't have anything else she could do to offer help.

Renee capped the can of pistachios and returned it to the cabinet. She drew her shirt over her head, but a knock on the trailer's door halted her progress. She pulled the shirt back on and opened the door.

"I knocked this time," Alex said with a slight grin that bordered on adorable. This man was dangerous, especially since he seemed to have this sixth sense about when she was in a state of undress.

"Knocking is good," she returned his grin. "Come in." She stepped out of the doorway to make room for him, but he declined with a shake of his head.

"That's okay. I just wanted to let you know the guys will be wrapping up in a few minutes. They'll come back early tomorrow morning to finish up demo and start the wash-down process."

"Of course," Renee answered. "You all are helping us out. Aunt Lorna and I will take whatever you're willing to give. Will you still be able to meet with us to go over the plans, or do you want to wait until tomorrow?"

"We can still meet today. Jason gave me the price list from the last job we did, so as we go through what your aunt is looking to include in the house, we can come up with a rough estimate."

"That sounds great," Renee said. "She's going to make herself sick worrying about what all of this is going to cost, but we both know it has to get done."

"Don't worry too much about the cost," Alex said. "It won't be as bad as you're probably expecting. We have a good relationship with our supplier; they give us a decent discount."

"Which you're going to pass on to us?"

"Of course," he answered.

Renee shook her head. "I can't believe you're doing all of this."

"Look, Renee, I'll be honest. Katrina has brought a lot of work to my company. I'm just giving back a little. Your aunt is just as worthy as any of the other families we've volunteered to help." He gestured toward the house where the work crew was gathering up the array of tools they'd brought in for demolition. "I would have rather the guys finish up the scope of work we'd laid out for today, but they volunteer on their off time and there are some pretty big college football matchups on TV today."

Renee pointed to the chips, dip, and the bag of oatmeal-raisin cookies on the counter. "I've got my mini party ready for the Florida/Tennessee game." Alex peered through the door, his big frame filling the entire space. "I'm a Gator," Renee explained. "I've got my blue and orange face paint in the back."

His grin widened and Renee's breath hitched in her throat. Lord, this man was fine.

"Well, I'll make sure I'm done before the game starts. I need to be home for kickoff, though I'm waiting for the LSU game myself."

"That should be a good one." Renee nodded. He continued smiling, and Renee decided to throw caution to the wind. The worst he could do was turn her down. "You know, if you want to join me, I've got enough snacks here for an entire army."

A blanket of surprise crowded his face. He looked from the snacks, to her, and back to the snacks.

Renee knew she was taking a risk extending the invitation, but something about this just felt right. Alex was attracted to her. He was trying hard not to show it, but he'd done a poor job of hiding his interest, especially after he'd walked in on her yesterday. Still, there was no mistaking his discomfort at her suggestion.

To set his mind at ease, Renee added, "Penelope, the teacher who rescued you from the copy machine the other day, will be here in a few. She's a Georgia Bulldog fan, but I try not to hold that against her."

Alex's face visibly relaxed. "Well, I'll be here meeting with your aunt, anyway, right?" he said with a smidge of reluctance.

"That's right." Renee nodded, fighting the urge to smile. "Aunt Lorna will be here, too." Maybe it was better they have a chaperone.

"Okay, then, let me get things straight with the guys," Alex said.

Renee stood at the door, watching him walk toward his crew. They would have to take things slowly, but for the chance to know Alex better, Renee was willing to slow things down a bit.

Chapter Nine

Margo heard the rhythmic thumping coming from the living room, but it took several minutes for it to register that the sound was of someone knocking.

It must be a solicitor trying to sell something if they were knocking at the front door. If it was anyone she knew, they would have known to go around to the back door. Whoever was out there would eventually get the picture and leave.

But they didn't. The knocking continued.

Margo groaned. If her mother hadn't instilled the principles of being a good, southern Christian woman in her, she would curse whoever had interrupted her morning and slam the door in their face. Margo rolled over in the bed and stared at the ceiling for a moment, willing her legs to work. Only marginally confident they would keep her upright, she planted her feet on the floor and felt around for her slippers.

"Margo!" The call came from just outside her window.

Gerald?

Margo jumped from her perch on the bed, slipping on the floor in her dash for the window. She caught her toe on the edge of the nightstand and one of those unladylike words slipped from her mouth, anyway. Margo hobbled the rest of the way to the window and spread the curtains wide. Gerald stood right below, crushing her begonias.

"Gerald, what are you doing here?" Margo choked out.

"Checking on you," he yelled. "Let me in."

What on earth was he thinking, showing up here?

"Go around the back," she yelled at him through the pane of glass. Margo winced at the pounding in her head, courtesy of the hangover and the thumping of her own heart.

She snatched her robe from where it draped over the back of the rocking chair and stuffed her arms through the sleeves as she made her way from her room to the kitchen. She opened the kitchen door, and jumped when she saw Gerald standing right in front of her.

"You should keep that porch door locked," he said. "Any old crazy from the street can get in here." He leaned over and touched his lips to hers. Margo took a millisecond to savor it. She loved his kisses. She stepped onto the porch and closed the kitchen door behind her.

Gerald's brow rose. "You're not going to invite me into your house?"

"Gerald," Margo sighed. "We talked about this. I told you we had to follow certain rules if we were going to see each other, and you said you understood them."

"I said I would follow them, I never said I understood them." He took both her hands in his. "I was worried about you. I called to check on you, but you wouldn't answer your cell phone. I wanted to make sure you were okay after last night."

"I'm sorry." She felt like an ungrateful witch for biting his head off after he was only calling to check on her. "I thought it was Eli calling my cell phone."

"You're avoiding your sons now?"

Margo nodded. "With the way he and Alex have been hounding me today, I'm starting to suspect they know about you."

"You make it seem as if I'm this terrible disease you're trying to keep the world from knowing you've caught, Margo."

She looked up at the hurt she heard in his voice, and saw

it in his eyes as well. "Oh, Gerald." Margo brought her hand up to his face and rubbed his cheek. "I'm sorry."

He covered her hand and pressed his cheek more firmly against it. "There's nothing wrong with what we're doing."

"I know," she whispered.

He didn't deserve this. He treated her as if she was the most precious human being on the face of the earth. And she treated him as if she was ashamed of him.

He took her hand and brought it to his lips, kissing each finger. "Margo, I wasn't sure if I should say this yet, but I need you to know something." He paused, taking a deep breath. "I'm falling in love with you."

Margo's stomach dropped. Her heart clenched in her chest.

"I am," he said. "I think about you every minute of every day."

"Gerald," she whispered.

"You don't have to love me. Not yet. I know you're still unsure about me for some reason."

"It's not you, it's—"

It's that she had worn the mantle of the respectable widow for so long it had come to define her. What would her boys think of her being someone's girlfriend? She'd been loyal to their father's memory all these years. She knew her boys well enough to know the thought of another man in her life would not go over well.

And what about the ladies at the church? She herself had been guilty of joining in the gossip when Josephine Johnson brought her gentleman friend to church last year. Would her friends say the same things about her if they found out about Gerald? The image she'd built and protected for all these years was in jeopardy of crumbling around her. Was it worth it?

Margo looked into Gerald's handsome, understanding face and a fervent *yes* soared through her blood.

He was worth it. She just had to figure out a way to introduce him to the other people in her life.

"Whatever your reason is for resisting me," Gerald was saying, "it's not going to keep me away. I will not let anything, including your sons, come between me and the most special person I've found in a long time."

Margo couldn't speak past the lump in her throat.

"I haven't felt this way about someone since my wife. When she died, I thought that was it, Margo. I'd had my one true love. But God has brought me another one, and I'm not letting you go. We'll keep up this pretense for now if you're still not ready to tell your boys about us, but the time will come when you'll have to shatter this illusion they have of you. They need to accept that you are still a healthy, sexy, vibrant woman, with the *needs* of a healthy, sexy, vibrant woman."

She gave him a wry grin. "You don't know my sons."

"And whose fault is that?" he asked with a grin of his own.

"They're so overprotective. I'm not sure how to even broach the subject with them."

"You're a smart lady," Gerald said. "You'll figure it out." He gave her another slight peck, this time on the tip of her nose. Then he turned and headed for the screen door, but before he walked through it, he turned around. "And don't think I'm letting you off the hook. I'm eventually going to see the inside of that house." He winked, and walked out the door.

Margo clutched her hand to her chest, slumping against the door with a wistful sigh. The past six months with Gerald had been incredible. She'd had more fun last night than she'd had in years. Even though she was paying for it this morning, she thought with a wince as pain sliced behind her eye.

How freeing it would be not to worry about the boys'

reaction to her newfound relationship, or what the deaconess board would have to say if they saw her walking hand in hand with Gerald.

Margo leaned her head back against the door with a sigh.

"One day," she whispered. "One day."

Alex stuffed the envelope containing the bid for a project Holmes Construction was vying for in the glove compartment of his truck. He grabbed the price list Jason had left for him to use as a guide in estimating what the materials for Lorna Davis's renovations would cost.

Alex looked over at the FEMA trailer and his breathing escalated.

When Renee had extended the offer to watch football with her, Alex's first instinct had been to decline. Over these past couple of years, he'd been attracted to his fair share of beautiful women, but he'd always been able to rationalize his way out of feeling anything more than a slight attraction.

Not with this woman. When he tried to counter his reaction to Renee with his usual refusal tactics, his mind had a rebuttal each and every time.

He told himself he was too busy with work to be concerned with a woman, but over the past couple of weeks, Alex had come to the harsh reality that he really wasn't as essential to the running of Holmes Construction as he wanted to believe. The place had not imploded upon itself just because he wasn't in the office or with his men on the construction site every day. In fact, just before he'd left to catch the games with some of the plumbers, Jason had fed Alex a pill he was still having difficulty swallowing. Turned out his guys were working even more efficiently without him. According to his lead foreman, most of the workers had admitted to being more comfortable over the past couple of weeks without Alex around. Apparently, they thought he was intimidating.

Even if the work excuse was shot to hell, Alex could always count on Jasmine to be his shield against diving back into the dating pool and opening himself up to all the potential crap that could come out of it. But Jasmine loved Renee. This morning, when Alex told her over breakfast that he would be helping Ms. Moore rebuild her house, Jazzy couldn't have been more excited. She'd gone on and on about how much she loved her Accelerated Reader class, and how she wished she could go more than two days a week because Ms. Moore was her favorite teacher.

He was out of excuses.

Well, except for the fact that Renee had a boyfriend.

Yet, she'd said it was the other female teacher coming over to watch the game, not Richards. Maybe they'd had a fight last night, and she'd kicked Richards's butt to the curb. Alex figured since he was fantasizing, he might as well add that scenario to the mix.

He knocked on the trailer door and a second later, it opened. Renee had changed into a blue University of Florida T-shirt and a pair of well-worn jeans. She was still sporting the ponytail. Give her a backpack and she could be a student walking the quad. She said she'd taught at the community college level, which meant she had to at least have some graduate work under her belt. If she was in her thirties, she wore it well.

"You can have a seat on the couch," Renee said. "We only have a nineteen-inch TV but this place is so small, it's really all we need."

"This is fine," Alex said, taking the time to survey the small trailer. He'd been in a few and still wasn't sure how families had been able to survive in such close quarters. The living room, kitchen, and dining areas were no more than six by ten feet, and some families were living five and six to a trailer. It was better than nothing, but Alex said another quick prayer of thanks that his home had been spared during Katrina.

"Can I get you a drink?" Renee asked. "I've got Coke,

Sprite, and iced tea. Sorry I don't have anything stronger, but I'm not too big on alcohol."

"Neither am I," Alex said. "Iced tea is fine."

She poured a glass and took the seat next to him on the sofa, popping the top on a can of Sprite for herself.

"Have I thanked you for all that you and your guys are doing?" she asked.

"Uh, yeah, about a hundred times," Alex said. Dang, she smelled good, like City Park when the flowers were in bloom. She must use one of those fancy women soaps you could buy only in a department store.

"I've apologized for walking in on you yesterday, right?" Alex asked.

"About a hundred times," she laughed. "And I swear, if you do it again, I'm going to be deeply offended."

He laughed, too. "Honestly, I was only being polite. I'm really not all that sorry."

Renee's shocked gasp was filled with humor. "I should have charged you for the show."

"I would have paid any price," he said before he could stop himself.

Awareness, bold and all-consuming, surrounded them. Alex stared in fascination at the pulse that beat at the base of her throat. His gaze traveled from that spot, down to her breasts that heaved with each breath she took.

"Alex?" His name came out of her mouth on a soft moan. Alex's eyes shot back up to her face, enthralled by the desire staring back at him.

The front door opened.

Alex and Renee jumped up from the sofa as if they had been caught kissing.

"Aunt Lorna," Renee said. She grabbed a roll of blueprints from an older woman dressed in a long, flowing dress with bright flowers printed on it. Even with her graying hair and the slight wrinkles around her eyes, she was nearly as beautiful as her niece.

"Hello there." Renee's aunt extended her hand. "I'm Lorna."

"Alex," he returned.

"Thank you so much for offering to help with all of this." She gestured toward the house. "I can't believe how much they've already done out there."

"Isn't it amazing?" Renee said. "They worked all morning."

"As I told your niece, it's no problem," Alex said. "My guys will be back tomorrow to continue gutting the house, but I stuck around so we could get a jump start on coming up with an estimate."

"Let's clear off the table so you can get a look at the house plans," Lorna said.

She took the two steps to the table and moved a napkin holder and a few pieces of mail from the table to the counter. Renee unrolled the blueprints, and Alex picked up a jar of salsa and a jar of queso dip, using them to hold down opposite corners of the sheets.

"It's not all that different from the original layout," Lorna explained. "I just figured since I had to rebuild, I may as well put in some of the changes I've always wanted."

"Show me what's changed," Alex said.

"Little things, like this coat closet off the front door, and a separate shower in the bathroom."

Peering over her aunt's shoulder, Renee asked, "What happened to the plans for your master bedroom?"

"I've decided not to do them."

"What do you mean? You had your heart set on that bay window."

"I can't afford to do those things now," Lorna explained.

"What did you have in mind?" Alex asked.

"It was nothing."

"It was not nothing," Renee argued. "She wanted one of those bay picture windows with the bench and storage space underneath. And she wanted to add a walk-in closet with lots of drawers and storage."

"None of which I can afford after that contractor made away with my life savings." Lorna turned to him. "I just want my house back. I don't care if it has to be the same layout as the original floor plan, as long as I can get out of this trailer and back into my home."

"You're going to be back in your house soon," he reassured her.

Renee was shaking her head, her arms crossed over her chest. "It doesn't make sense not to build this house exactly the way you want it built," she said. "You're essentially starting off with a clean slate. Just get what you want. I told you I'll help you pay for it."

"And I told you I'm not taking one red cent from you. This little girl has always been hardheaded," Lorna said in a stage whisper.

"I can hear you," Renee sang.

Suppressing a smile, Alex said, "From what you've explained, I don't think it would cost all that much to incorporate those changes. In fact, I just redid my daughter's room with a huge walk-in closet and storage unit I designed myself. We could drive over there right now and take a look at it if you want to. I'm only about fifteen minutes from here."

"Really?" Lorna mused. She turned to Renee. "Honey, why don't you go with Alex and check out the closet? You know exactly what I want."

Renee frowned. "You know what you want more than I do."

"Not really. You're the one who suggested I put in the closet. I was just going to make do with what I already had."

"No—"

"Don't argue, Renee," Lorna managed to snap while still smiling.

It didn't take Alex long to understand the situation as he

looked back and forth between aunt and niece. He had witnessed his mother, the unofficial president of Matchmakers of America, operate long enough to spot another of her cohorts at work.

"Why don't I just take pictures and bring them back for you both to see?" Alex suggested, though he already knew the opposition that was about to surface.

"Oh no. I think Renee needs to get a firsthand account. Pictures won't do at all."

The glare Renee shot her aunt should have scorched the ends of her hair, but Lorna Davis handled the situation with aplomb reminiscent of the great Margo Holmes. She steamrolled right over her niece.

"Go on, now," Lorna said, ushering both Alex and Renee toward the door. "I'll have your little football party ready when you get back, Renee. Alex, do you like football?"

"Yes, I do," Alex answered.

"Renee loves football. She's such a tomboy. But she can be a lady when the occasion calls," Lorna quickly added. Renee's eyes turned to fire, but her aunt forged ahead. "Go, go. I'll see you two in about an hour."

"I am so sorry about that," Renee said as she walked alongside Alex on the way to his truck.

"Sorry about what?" he asked.

"As if you couldn't tell what she was doing?" Renee said.

"Don't worry about it," Alex said as he opened the passenger door of his Ford F-150 and stepped back so Renee could get in. "My mother's matchmaking would put your aunt's attempts to shame."

"That's scary," Renee said, buckling her seat belt.

Alex climbed into the driver's seat and buckled up. "Actually, as I think about it, my mom's pretty good at it," he said. He put the truck in reverse and backed out of the driveway. "Both of my brothers have found the loves of their lives in the past year."

"Are you the only one left?" Renee asked. "Or had you already found the love of your life?"

Alex glanced over at her, his muscles tightening up like the strings on a guitar.

"Your wife?" Renee prompted. "Jasmine's mother? I heard she was killed in a car accident."

"Uh, yeah," Alex replied.

"I'm sorry, it's none of my business," Renee quickly apologized. "I had no reason to ask that."

"No, no, it's okay," Alex said, even though he wasn't sure how to answer, or even if he should. Chantal had been the love of his life when they were first married, but that love had vanished far too soon. He hoped God had someone else in store for him, but only when he was ready to open himself up to the possibility, which he was not right now. Or that's what he thought.

"Chantal was killed about two years ago," he began. "It hasn't been easy."

"I'm so sorry," Renee said with genuine sincerity. "That must have been so hard for Jasmine. For you, too."

"It was," he answered, but wasn't sure if he meant it. He hadn't shed a tear over Chantal since the night of her funeral, and that was only because he'd spent that night holding Jasmine as she'd cried for her mother.

"What about you?" he asked, pushing away the emotions. "Is your aunt your only family?"

"You can say that," she said. She looked out the window, but turned back to him a moment later. "My parents live in Georgia. Right outside Savannah. I don't talk to them much."

"I'm sorry," Alex said. He couldn't wrap his head around the concept of estranged families. He talked to his mother and brothers at least once a day, oftentimes more.

"Is it just you and your two brothers?" Renee asked. "No sisters?"

"Just the three of us."

"I always wanted brothers and sisters," she said.

"No, you don't. They're a pain in the ass," Alex said.

"I'm sure they can be," Renee laughed. "But I was lonely as an only child. My parents were . . . overprotective. They were always afraid I'd fall in with the wrong crowd. I wasn't allowed to have friends over or anything. That's why I loved visiting my aunt Lorna here in New Orleans when I was growing up. At least she would let me hang out with the neighborhood kids."

Alex had to ask the question that had been lingering in the back of his mind. "You said you moved to New Orleans to help your aunt rebuild. Does that mean once the house is completed you're moving back to . . . where did you say you were from? Florida?"

"I was teaching in Tampa," she answered. "I'm still up in the air about whether or not I'll go back any time soon. I enjoy working with the younger kids much more than I thought I would. After teaching college-aged students, I wasn't sure I would be able to adjust, but I've been pleasantly surprised."

"What did you teach before coming to St. Katherine's?"

"European history."

Alex whipped his head around. "Are you serious?"

"Yeah, what's wrong with European history?"

Nothing, other than the fact that it was the one class he was close to flunking the hell out of in school. A germ of an idea started to bloom in Alex's brain, but he was unsure if he should allow it to grow. Although he *had* considered hiring a tutor to help him get past this European history hurdle.

"How would you feel about doing a little tutoring?" he asked.

Even the puzzled glance she sent his way looked good on her.

"I'm working on my business degree through this online school," Alex explained. "This quarter, I'm taking European history, and I'm having a much harder time than I thought I would. I usually eat that stuff up, but Europe has a long history, and—"

"I find it all fascinating," Renee interrupted. "But some parts are more interesting than others."

"Would you mind looking over a paper I have to turn in tomorrow?" Alex asked.

"Of course not," she said. "I think it's wonderful that you've gone back to school."

"No one knows about it," Alex said.

"As in your family?"

"As in everyone in the world except for myself, my professors, and the eight other participants in the online class."

He'd kept the fact that he was working on his degree from his family. He'd thought about coming clean, but Alex remembered how upset his mother had been when he'd dropped out of school to help support the family after his dad's death. He'd always told her it never bothered him that he'd never gotten his degree, but it had. He didn't want Mama to feel any of the guilt she'd felt after he left school.

They pulled up to a stoplight.

"I respect your privacy, and I'll be more than happy to help, especially after everything you're doing for my aunt."

"That's not why I asked," Alex said. "Don't think I wouldn't continue to help your aunt if you'd said no. You don't have to—"

"Alex." She put her hand on his forearm. Alex looked from the soft brown hand resting on his arm to her soft brown eyes. "I'd love to help you," she said.

Her touch was warm and delicate and light as a feather, but it had the effect of a three-hundred-pound weight pushing down on his chest. Air became a precious commodity that seemed to be escaping his lungs at an alarming rate.

"Uh, okay," he said. "Thank you."

"You're welcome," she answered. "Are you going to drive?"

"What?" Several horns blared from the cars behind them. "Oh, damn. Sorry," he apologized for his language. "I'm only a couple of blocks away," Alex said. A minute later he turned into the driveway of the huge wood-frame home he'd bought a year after he and Chantal had been married. Alex had completed so many renovations on the house that it hardly resembled the original.

He got out of the truck and walked over to open her door, but she'd already gotten out.

"This is beautiful," Renee exclaimed as she rounded the front of the truck.

"Thanks," Alex said. "It's probably bigger than we need, being just the two of us."

"It looks like the perfect house to raise a child."

"Jazzy loves it here, especially since I added her own suite."

"Her own suite? We should all be so lucky." Renee smirked.

"I figured she was growing up and needed a bigger space," Alex explained with a shrug. "That's where the closet is. "C'mon." He motioned for her to follow. "I'll show you the design. You can determine if it's close to what your aunt was thinking of doing in her room."

Renee grabbed his forearm again. "Alex, I think I should warn you about something before we go any further. The minute my aunt saw you, her agenda changed. She couldn't care less about the closet."

"I recognized what she was up to," he confided. "I told you about my mother. I can spot a matchmaker from a mile away."

That grin on her was *so* sexy. Alex should just accept defeat. The struggle to keep his attraction at bay was too much to withstand.

"I just didn't want you to feel uncomfortable," she said.

"I've become a pro at handling meddling family members," Alex reassured her. "But since we're here you might as well have a look at the closet, right?"

"Of course, let's go in," Renee said, holding her hand out for him. "I would love to see your home."

Renee barely contained her gasp. The structure was gorgeous from the outside, but when she entered through the seven-foot, double oak doors, Renee was blown away. The entry opened to a massive family room with high ceilings and a bank of tall windows along the right wall. The sun streaming through them cast a honeyed glow on the richly polished hardwood floors.

"Jazzy's room is this way." Alex motioned for her to follow him through the family room and down a hallway. Renee halted at a picture of a young, petite woman with model-quality features that hung next to a mirror. She had long, curly jet-black hair that stood out starkly against her creamy skin. Her light, hazel eyes seemed to hold a secret, along with the slightly curved smile.

"Is this your wife?" Renee asked.

Alex looked back. Renee noticed the surprise on his face when he realized she wasn't directly behind him. She pointed to the picture on the wall.

"Your wife?" she repeated.

Alex nodded. "That's Chantal." He walked back up the hallway and stopped beside her, staring at the portrait.

"Jasmine looks just like her," Renee commented. "She was beautiful."

"Yes, she was."

"Do you miss her?" she asked. His brow drew downward in a frown. "I'm sorry," Renee said, shaking her head. "I usually don't bombard people with nosy questions. And the fact that I hardly know you makes it even more improper."

"I wouldn't say we hardly know each other," Alex said. "I have seen you naked."

Renee burst out laughing, then sobered the instant she remembered that she was standing in front of a picture of the man's dead wife. "I'm sorry. Can we please take a look at that closet?"

"Follow me." He led her down the hallway toward the back of the house. They passed the open door of a room that had a definite masculine feel to it with its shades of brown, blue, and green, and Renee realized it was most likely his room.

A pool of something warm and tingly settled into her stomach at the sight of the rumpled linens. The image of a sleeping Alex wrapped up in those sheets filled her mind's eye.

"Here we are." Alex opened a door directly across from his bedroom.

This time Renee could not contain her gasp. It was as if she'd walked into the pages of a fairy tale. The room was magical, adorned in pink and cream with shimmering gold and iridescent accents. A huge canopied bed took up the far corner of the room, which was made to look like a castle, with towering Grecian columns flanking either side of the bedposts. Catty-corner to the bed was a vast sitting area with the bay window that was straight out of the design Renee had envisioned for her aunt's master bedroom, but Jasmine's seating area also held a padded rocker, and a dainty chaise made of the same pattern as the comforter set on the bed and the curtains.

She stepped farther into the room, her amazement increasing tenfold.

The other half of the suite was straight out of every little girl's dream. An arched entryway, with *Jasmine's Play Land* stenciled in dramatic script across the top, led to a deep alcove filled with every toy one could imagine. A huge wooden dollhouse, big enough for the six-year-old to step into, took up the back wall of the alcove. Dolls, stuffed animals, princess costumes, tiaras, and child-size furniture filled the area.

"I'm in awe," Renee admitted as she stood in the center of the room and turned in a circle. "This is absolutely amazing."

"It was my project this year."

"So this is all new?"

"Yeah, it added another seven hundred square feet to the house. It came out pretty good."

"Pretty good?" Renee turned to him. "If you call this pretty good, I'd hate to see what you call spectacular. It's every little girl's dream room."

"I only built it. My cousin, Indina, decorated it. C'mon, I'll show you the closet."

They walked over to double beveled doors that opened into a walk-in closet that rivaled the size of Renee's entire apartment in Florida. The pungent fragrance of fresh cedar imbued the air. Shelves lined either side, followed by deep drawers with brushed gold knobs. As they forayed deeper into the closet, Renee marveled at the racks of shoes, and hair ribbons hanging from a specially made spool holder. The entire back wall of the closet was compartmentalized for hanging shirts, pants, and dresses.

"Amazing," Renee whispered. She could not think of another word to describe the workmanship and ingenious design.

"I figured if I ever sell the house, I would present this room as the master suite."

"You did a fabulous job," Renee said. She turned to him, grateful the huge closet afforded them some space, even though it wasn't as much as she would like. Being in such close proximity to Alex, she could feel him all over.

"My aunt's right, you know," Renee continued. "I doubt she could afford something this elaborate, even with me helping her pay for it."

"Don't worry about the cost."

"That's easy to do in theory, but I've got to be practical," Renee reasoned. "The money that contractor stole was most of the money from my aunt's savings. I'm going to help her as much as I can to pay for the renovations, but it's not like I'm rolling in dough. My aunt paid off the house years ago; she's trying not to go too much deeper into debt.

"Even with your guys volunteering to perform the labor you know better than I do what it would cost in materials alone to add something like this to Aunt Lorna's house plans."

He shrugged with his good shoulder. "I've still got a lot of stuff left over from when I did these renovations."

Renee shook her head. "Don't even suggest it. You are already going way beyond the call of duty. I would never think about taking anything more from you."

"You're not taking, I'm giving."

"No, Alex."

"Renee?" She looked up to find him staring at her with an almost needy look, as if he was dying to do this for her.

"Why?" she asked. "Why would you want to do this?"

"Because it's the right thing to do," he said simply.

"But why me? You could do this for so many others."

"Which the company has done."

"But—"

"Look, you could just call it an even trade for the help I'll need to pass that European history class."

Renee shook her head again. She could not allow him to give her any more than he and his men were already giving. They were saving her and her aunt tens of thousands of dollars by performing demolition and agreeing to do the labor on the rebuild for free.

"Alex, I don't know about this," Renee said.

"Actually, it's not your call. It's your aunt Lorna's house."

"Sorry, but she's just as stubborn as I am," Renee said.

"I can be stubborn when I need to be," Alex countered. A smile tipped up one corner of his mouth. The effect was overwhelming. Did this man have any idea how incredibly gorgeous he was?

"It won't happen," Renee said.

He sighed. "Would you just let me clear my conscience?"

"What does any of this have to do with your conscience?"

"I already explained this to you. Hurricane Katrina has brought a huge amount of business to Holmes Construction. The company has made more money this past year than it has in the past four years combined."

"You say that as if it's a bad thing," Renee said. "You should be grateful."

"I am," he was quick to say. "Don't get me wrong, I thank God every day for all He's blessed my company with, but it's still hard to reap the benefits from something that caused so much devastation for so many people. I didn't even have a broken window on my house as a result of the storm," he said.

"You're feeling guilty, but I really don't understand why, Alex. If anything, the city is grateful to have Holmes Construction here to help with the rebuild. You're running an honest business. You're not ripping people off. Your guys are volunteering their time every weekend to help out. It's like you're an angel."

"You telling me this won't stop me from feeling as if I'm making out like a bandit," he said.

Renee realized any words she told him would not change his mind. She could tell Alex was one of those people who believed in fairness, and for some reason, he didn't believe it fair that he should benefit from his years of hard work. As Renee saw it, it was simply God's blessing for living a good life.

"It's not my call," she said. "But I have to warn you that you'll have a hard time convincing my Aunt Lorna." At least Renee thought he would. Lorna had been quick to agree to the help his men were providing.

Taking one last look at the closet's fabulous design as she followed him out, Renee secretly hoped her aunt would take Alex up on his offer. Renee *so* wanted this closet for Lorna's house.

"I'm still going to take a few pictures of the window and the closet so your aunt can see what I'd like to build."

"Pictures will not do this closet justice," she said.

"They'll give her an idea," Alex said. "And maybe while I'm taking the pictures you can read over something for me? Something about the Polish-Lithuanian Commonwealth?"

"Sure," Renee laughed.

"I'll be back in a second," he said before heading out of Jasmine's room.

Renee strolled around, simply awed by the attention to detail that was evident in every aspect of the room. From the elaborate eight-inch, intricately carved crown molding, to the polished honey-colored hardwood floors dotted with rich throw rugs, the space screamed *opulence*, yet had just enough of a little girl's feel to make it appropriate for a child Jasmine's age. The little girl should feel like a princess in this room. It was obvious to Renee just how much her father loved her in order to put this much love and care into her room.

Her own father hadn't given a crap about her, but Renee had come to terms with that aspect of her life a long time ago. One result of growing up with a deadbeat, abusive father was a keen ability to spot a good one. Alex Holmes was, by all accounts, a spectacular father. The fact that he was raising his daughter on his own just added to his appeal.

"Oh Lord. You've got something on your hands with this one," Renee whispered to herself. She was definitely into this man.

Renee stopped short when she came upon another photograph of Alex's dead wife, which sat on the nightstand next to the huge canopy bed. She had been a beautiful woman. Jasmine had acquired many of her mother's features: those gorgeous light brown eyes and the high cheekbones. Not to mention the head of curly jet-black hair.

Renee swallowed the pang of sadness that lodged in her

throat at the thought of that little girl waking up one morning to find her mother gone. How hard must it have been for Alex to lose his wife that way? What courage he'd had to display in order to continue on the way he had, raising his daughter, running his business. A lesser man would have allowed such circumstances to break him, but Alex had faced his lot in life and persevered.

No wonder she was attracted to him, Renee thought. How could she not be?

"I apologize for the grammatical errors," he said, reentering the room with a digital camera in one hand and a sheaf of papers in the other. "What?" he asked, and Renee figured her face must have still held that look of wonderment that had been seeping into her bones as she roamed around this gorgeous room he'd so selflessly built for his daughter.

"Nothing," she answered. She stretched out her hand for the papers. "What's the topic?"

"The governing rules of the Polish-Lithuanian Commonwealth," he said with about as much enthusiasm as a little boy waiting for a spanking.

"Not one of your favorite topics, I assume."

"If I had a list of a thousand favorite topics, this one would be nine hundred, ninety-nine," he answered.

A crack of laughter escaped her mouth. "What would be number one thousand?" Renee asked.

"Women's fashion during the time of the Polish-Lithuanian Commonwealth," he answered.

Renee burst out laughing. She was toast where Alex Holmes was concerned. Her first order of business was to tell Penelope hands off, because this one was hers.

"Have a seat," Alex said, taking her by the hand and guiding her to the rocking chair nestled in the corner and surrounded by two bookshelves loaded with books.

After the first couple of paragraphs, Renee knew the entire paper would have to be rewritten, so instead of reading further she took the time to discreetly study Alex as he made his way around the room. He snapped pictures of the bay window from every angle, checking the picture on the small LCD screen each time. Deleting a few, and retaking the shots. When he moved to the interior of the closet, Renee was tempted to follow him.

A few moments later, he exited the closet. "You want to take a look at them before we head back?" he asked, holding the camera out to her.

"I'm sure you snapped enough to give her a good idea of what you're capable of," Renee answered.

"What do you think about the paper?" Alex asked.

Renee avoided eye contact, trying to think of a nice way to say what she had to say.

"It's crap," Alex said. "You don't have to be afraid to tell me," he said. "But do you think there's potential?"

"Uh, possibly," she answered.

The theme song from *Cinderella* began to chime throughout the house.

"It's the doorbell," Alex explained. "Jasmine begged me to put that in."

Renee bit back a smile.

"Alex, you in there?" a voice called from the front of the house.

Annoyance flashed across Alex's face. "Excuse me," he said.

Before he broke the plane of Jasmine's door frame, another man, this one nearly as gorgeous as Alex, and no doubt related to him, appeared in the doorway. "What are you doing in here? Oh, hello," the other man said when he noticed Renee. He wore hospital scrubs. He also looked really familiar.

"Renee Moore, this is my brother Elijah."

"Wait a minute." Renee pointed at him. "Aren't you the doctor who delivered the baby during that huge traffic jam on the interstate a couple of weeks ago? I saw it on the news."

"Super Doc to the rescue," Alex said with a sufficient amount of sarcasm, but the hint of pride Renee heard in his voice was undeniable.

"That was amazing," Renee said.

"Just a part of the job," Eli answered. "So, Renee—" He looked from her to Alex and back, his mouth tipping up at the corners. Goodness. It was not fair that one family be blessed with two gorgeous men.

"So, Eli," Alex interrupted his brother. "What do you want?"

"I had a break between patients. My next C-section isn't scheduled to start for another couple of hours." He looked to Renee. "Look, man, if I'd known you weren't alone, believe me, I never would have stopped by. In fact, I'll leave right now," he said, turning.

Alex caught his brother by the shoulder, and turned him around. "I'm helping Ms. Moore, who happens to be one of Jasmine's teachers, to rebuild her house," Alex said. "I brought her here to see the walk-in closet I designed."

"I should have known," Eli grumbled with obvious disappointment.

The look Alex shot his brother was deadly. "What the hell did you want, E?"

"It's about Mama," Eli answered. He did the triple look again, from Alex to Renee, then back to Alex.

"I can step out," Renee offered. This was clearly something they didn't want to discuss in front of a stranger.

"I won't be long," Alex told her. "Help yourself to anything in the kitchen. I promise to have you back home before kickoff."

Chapter Ten

"It's about time you brought a woman up in here." Eli punched Alex on his good shoulder. "I was starting to think you were trying to recapture your virginity or something."

For years Alex had thought the eldest sibling should be given at least one free shot at killing a younger sibling. Of course, he would have the hardest time trying to figure out which brother to use the privilege on.

Alex leaned against the doorjamb leading to Jasmine's closet. "Get to the point. What's up with Mama?"

Eli propped a hip on the short bureau, and rubbed his hands together before letting them rest on his thighs. "Well, according to an unnamed, but very reliable source—"

"Monica," Alex provided.

"Monica," Eli confirmed. "Your mother has up and found herself a boyfriend."

"That's bull," Alex said, refusing to believe such a thing about his mother. "Monica told you this?"

Eli nodded. "I had to coax it out of her, but I'm inclined to believe her. I knew Monica had an idea of what was going on."

"Who's this boyfriend?"

"Monica claims she doesn't know the guy's name."

"I don't believe her," Alex said. His mother tended to tell her future daughter-in-law more than she ever told her sons, which was starting to annoy him, especially if this was the type of stuff she was keeping secret.

"As Monica's soon-to-be husband, I'm supposed to believe her, but I don't think she's giving me the entire story, either," Eli said.

"How did you get her to give up information on the boyfriend in the first place?" Alex asked.

Eli's lips broke into a telling smile, and Alex was sorry he'd asked. "Yeah, whatever," Alex said.

"I'm perfectly willing to try and get this guy's name out of her."

"I'm sure you are," Alex retorted.

"I don't like the thought of Mama with some man," Eli said. "Who knows who this guy is, Alex? He might be some con artist who preys on unsuspecting widows."

"I can't believe Mama would be taken in by someone like that."

"Yeah, but can you be sure? You told me yourself Mama admitted she had a hangover. You can't be comfortable with her hanging out with some guy who gets her drunk."

No, he wasn't. And he'd be damned if he let some slick-talking con take advantage of his mother. "I'm going to stop in on Mama after I drop Renee back to her house," Alex said.

"Good. Call me as soon as you find out anything. So"— Eli nodded toward the front of the house—"is she married?"

"Don't start," Alex warned.

"Aw, man, come on. Tell me something, do you even remember what sex feels like? It's good, Alex. Really, really good."

"I'm not having this conversation again." Alex pushed away from the doorjamb. "I promised to have Renee back at her house before the Florida/Tennessee game kicks off."

"Hold up. Are you saying she watches football?"

"Yeah. And?"

"You're kidding me, right? She has a face like that, *and* she's into football? Find out if she can put together a decent meal and you've got the perfect woman."

"Are you following me?" Alex asked as he headed out of the room. He refused to entertain his brother another minute.

Alex had thought Chantal was perfect, too, and look how that had turned out. He could not afford to go through that amount of suffering again. Even if it meant he was missing out on a good thing with Renee, it was worth it not to endure the possible pain he'd been subjected to by the last "perfect" woman he'd fallen for.

When they entered the kitchen, Alex found Renee staring up at the ceiling.

"Sorry that took so long," he said.

"Don't worry about it." She waved him off. "I was just admiring this crown molding. The attention to detail in this house is absolutely amazing," she said.

"That's Alex for you," Eli joined in. "Though sometimes, he gets so mired down in the details he forgets to look at the whole picture. He'll miss a good thing even when it's standing right in front of him, ain't that right, Alex?" He clamped a hand on Alex's good shoulder.

"Remind me to kick your ass later," Alex said under his breath. "Are you ready?" he asked Renee.

"If you are," she answered. "Are you still going to watch the game with me?"

"Heck yeah, he's going to watch the game with you," Eli piped up. "Alex eats and breathes football. He played at LSU for a few years."

"Really?" Renee's eyes lit up in surprise.

"Until I quit school," Alex said.

Her eyes softened with understanding.

"He still cheers for the Tigers, though," Eli said.

"Well, I invited your brother to watch the key SEC matchups on television today. I'm pulling for LSU to win but only because it'll help out my Florida Gators."

Renee stared with huge, expectant eyes, and Alex realized that he couldn't say no. Despite the warning signals going off in his brain, warning signals born from years of suffering at the hands of Chantal, something just as strong warred with his conscience. His brain told him to hold back, but his gut was all for going for it. Alex could picture himself enjoying an afternoon of watching football with Renee. He felt comfortable around her. It felt strange, but it also, in a way, felt right.

"Since Jasmine will be busy with Campfire Girls and a trip to the museum with Monica," Alex said, remembering his daughter's schedule. "Besides, it'll give us time to go over the rest of the rebuilding plan."

"Of course," Renee said. "Penelope just called to say she can't make it, so we'll have more space to spread things out in the trailer's little kitchen."

They headed for the front door. Alex gestured for Renee to walk ahead, with Eli following behind. Eli tugged on his good arm and pulled him back.

"Look," he said in a low voice. "I know it's been a long time since you've been out with a woman, so let me give you a few tips. Start out with just a regular kiss, no tongue. You don't want to freak her out."

"Shut up," Alex said with a harsh whisper, pulling his arm away.

"And don't put your hand on her butt unless she asks you to," Eli continued. "That'll get you slapped every time."

Alex blasted his brother with a fierce scowl, but Eli only chuckled as he made his way to his Range Rover.

As they drove the short distance back to her aunt's house, Alex explained how he had come up with the design for the walk-in closet, and how he went about building it without the help of his work crews.

Alex brought his left hand up to the back of his neck and rubbed.

"Alex, are you okay?" Renee asked.

He sighed, still massaging his neck. "Eli thinks my mom has a boyfriend, and I'm starting to suspect it may be true."

"And that's a problem?"

"Well, yeah," Alex answered.

"Why?"

Alex just stared at her, partly because the answer was obvious, and partly because he couldn't pinpoint his exact problem. He just knew there was something wrong with his mother dating.

"Because she's my mother," he said.

"Oh, come on, Alex. She's a grown woman who's raised three sons. What's wrong with her dating?"

"I'm just concerned about her," Alex said. "Somebody has to take care of her."

"Even though she's a grown woman?" Renee reiterated.

He was quiet for a moment, but only a moment. Alex shook his head. "You don't understand."

"I do," Renee answered. "More than you can imagine. I took on the job of taking care of my mom when I was still a kid. I thought it was my job to protect her." She shrugged. "Sometimes, you have to let go. Especially if your mom is starting to assert her independence."

Alex didn't want to hear this, particularly because Renee was making total sense.

They pulled up to her aunt's home. Alex noticed Lorna Davis's car was no longer parked beside the trailer.

"Your aunt's gone." He pointed out the obvious.

"She probably just ran to the grocery store," Renee said. "Come on, we only have a few minutes before kickoff."

There was a note taped to the front of the trailer door. *Gone to Baton Rouge.*

"Your aunt reminds me of my mom," Alex said. "Since she bought her car, she's always on the road."

"Aunt Lorna never stays put for long. She's into everything," Renee said. She led the way into the trailer.

"She was true to her word," Alex said , looking over the food laid out on a narrow table that sat next to the sofa. Tortilla chips and salsa, Buffalo-style chicken wings with celery sticks and a dipping sauce, and a bowl of mixed nuts. "This is a lot more than I would have had at my house," Alex said.

"Well, it's a good thing I convinced you to join me, isn't it?" Renee called from inside the refrigerator. She returned with two cans of soda in her hands. "Is this okay?"

"That's fine," Alex said.

"And now for the pièce de la résistance," Renee said as she came into the living room and set a platter of marshmallow squares on the narrow table. She looked over at him. "What? Rice Krispies treats are the quintessential football-watching snack," she explained.

"Of course they are," Alex agreed with a chuckle.

She reached across to grab a handful of mixed nuts and her breast brushed against his arm. Alex sucked in a breath.

"Excuse me," Renee said.

"Not a problem," he assured her. His heart was pounding within his chest so hard Alex was convinced she could hear it.

On the small television, the opposing players lined up for the kickoff.

Renee's face was intense as she watched the kick returner run the ball to midfield. "Good job." She clapped. "I've got ten bucks on this game."

"You're a gambling woman," Alex laughed.

"When it comes to Florida Gator football, I sure am. I always take the bets I know I can win. So, you played ball in college?"

Alex nodded. "I had a scholarship."

"What position did you play? No, wait, let me guess. Linebacker, right?"

He shook his head.

"Offensive tackle?"

He shook his head again.

"Okay, I give up."

"Center," Alex answered.

"Really?" Her eyes were just as beautiful with a look of surprise. "That's a tall order."

"You think so?"

"Of course," she answered. She paused to watch the play unfold, cursing as the Gators failed to convert on third down. "Not good to start the game with a three and out on the first possession," she commented. "Anyway." She turned her attention back to Alex. "People usually think of the quarterback as controlling the game, but I think the center position is the most important."

He lifted an inquiring brow.

"If the quarterback doesn't have a reliable center to snap the ball to him, the quarterback can't do his job," she explained.

Alex chuckled, impressed with her assessment of the game. "You know your football," he said.

"I've always loved football. I wanted to play *so* bad when I was little."

"What position would you have played?"

"Definitely not center." She grinned. "I would have been a good wide receiver," she mused. "I've always had good hand/eye coordination, and back in high school, I could run a four-eight."

"Whoa, that's almost unheard of."

The roar of the crowd interrupted their conversation. Renee's eyes darted back to the television. "Interception! Go! Go," she yelled so loud Alex figured the player racing down the football field could surely hear her.

"Touchdown!" She shot her fist in the air and wiggled her hips in a silly, sexy little victory dance.

"I have a feeling this isn't just for show," Alex laughed. "You would have had the same reaction even if you were by yourself, wouldn't you?"

"Heck no. I'm toning it down because you're here. If I was alone, I would be jumping on the sofa cushions and high-fiving myself."

Alex laughed again. He was doing that a lot today.

Eli's words rang in his mind. With a face like that and a mind for football, Renee was possibly the perfect woman. She didn't even have to know how to cook. His mama had taught him how to find his way around the kitchen.

For the next hour, they watched in relative relaxation as the Florida Gators made three more touchdowns in the first half.

"Can you breathe easier with a twenty-eight-to-zero score?" Alex asked.

"Not really. Tennessee is a second-half team. We can't get too comfortable," she warned. The Tennessee Marching Band took to the field; then the programing switched to a panel of four sports commentators giving a rundown of other game highlights and previewing upcoming matchups.

"Did you have prospects of going pro?" Renee asked. She stuffed a cheese-slathered nacho chip in her mouth and followed it with a swig of Coke.

"There was some talk early on, but I quit school at the beginning of my senior year," he answered.

"I still don't understand why you had to quit altogether. You were right there in Baton Rouge. You weren't that far away from your family."

"My mom needed someone here with her all the time," Alex answered.

"Did she ask you to quit?"

He shook his head. "Mama never would have done that. She raised enough hell when I told her I was dropping out."

"Then why did you?"

"I told you, Mama needed me."

She gave him an assessing look that did nothing for his comfort level. "You know what I've discovered about you?"

Alex raised his brow, waiting.

"You like being in charge."

Not what he'd expected to hear. "What makes you say that?"

"Maybe being in charge isn't the right way to say it. It's more that you're a caretaker."

"I wouldn't say that," Alex said.

"How could you not? From the little I know about you so far, I can tell that you take it upon yourself to care for your family. Plus, you own your own business," she continued. "But, unlike most people, you put the needs of others above profit. Heck, you played at the center position on your football squad, which is essentially like carrying the entire team on your back. You thrive at taking care of people."

"I never thought about it that way," Alex said.

"Those people who do it automatically never think about what they're doing, they just do it."

"Just the other day, my mom told me that I don't take care of myself because I'm too busy taking care of everyone else," he admitted. "I always thought the same thing about her."

"It's sweet that you look out for your family. The fact that you're so involved in Jasmine's life is just amazing."

He shook his head. "I haven't been as involved as I should have been. If so, she wouldn't have been acting up in school."

"Jasmine was misbehaving?"

"Yeah, in Mrs. Overland's class. That's one of the reasons I'm volunteering at the school. Mr. Powell, the psychologist . . ." He waited until Renee nodded. "He thinks Jasmine may be going through abandonment issues. Sort of a delayed reaction to Chantal's death."

"I'm not sure how long it would take a child Jasmine's age to grieve over the lost of a parent. I can only imagine how hard it must have been for her."

"I haven't been paying attention," Alex said softly. He was too busy feeling guilty over his own lack of grief.

He would never have wished death on the mother of his child, but in a way Alex had felt vindicated after Chantal's fatal accident. She had flaunted her lovers in his face, hell-bent on hurting him. When he'd stared down at her body lying on the cold metal table in the morgue, Alex had not been able to summon even an ounce of love for his wife.

"Are things getting better?" Renee asked.

Alex shook his head. "I'm not sure. She hasn't been disruptive with me in the classroom, of course."

"At least you've taken a step forward in helping her cope. Eventually, things will work themselves out," Renee reassured him.

Halftime ended and they settled back in to watch the rest of the game. Tennessee scored two quick touchdowns, slicing the Gator's lead in half. When Tennessee intercepted the ball, halting Florida's march to the end zone, Renee started to pace.

"Are you going to be okay?" Alex asked, trying to hide his amusement. He enjoyed football as much as the next red-blooded American, but Renee took it to a whole new level. She was on the verge of a conniption.

"I told you Tennessee is a second-half team," she said, still pacing.

"There's still a lot of game left to play," Alex said. "Why don't you sit down?" He patted the seat next to him and she sat.

Renee buried her face in her hands and growled when Florida failed to stop Tennessee on third down, but a Gator interception that was run back for a touchdown had her off the sofa in an instant, jumping up and down and causing the flimsy trailer to shake.

"Yes, yes, yes!" she said, plopping to her seat once again. "You have *got* to love this game," she said.

"More than life itself," Alex laughed.

"You are not making fun of me, are you?"

"Never," he said, his chuckle belying his answer.

"You can laugh all you want, all I know is my Gators are up by three touchdowns and we're about to reach the two-minute warning. There is no coming back for those Volunteers."

"I'll bet you were the most obnoxious fan in the stadium when you were in college," Alex said.

"You'd win that bet, buddy. I was put out of the student section twice for disorderly conduct. I yelled cusswords at the refs," she explained.

"You, Ms. Moore, are my kind of woman," Alex said. The instant the words left his mouth, Alex wished he could take them back. The atmosphere in the trailer changed; the playful camaraderie of just a few moments ago morphing into an undisputable mutual desire. The air in Alex's lungs seemed to solidify, making his next breath an uncertainty.

A smile curled up the corner of Renee's lips. "That's encouraging," she said, her seductive gaze drawing him in like a siren. Alex tried to break eye contact, but her eyes held him captive.

She leaned in an inch. He followed.

"Alex—" His name came out of her mouth on a breathy sigh.

"How's Richards?" Alex asked, jerking back, breaking the spell. Thank God.

The momentary shock that flashed across Renee's face was quickly replaced with resignation. "Rashad is fine," she answered. "You know, Alex, you can be straight with me."

"What do you mean?"

"Just tell me, 'Renee, I'm not interested' and that would be the end of it. You don't have to bring Rashad—who, by the way, isn't my boyfriend, in case you were wondering—into the picture. I'm a big girl. I can handle it."

Eli was right, he was out of practice. It had been so long since he'd dealt with all of this, he wasn't sure how to act around a woman he wanted to get to know better. Alex wished they could just skip all of this "getting to know you" crap and go straight to being comfortable around each other.

But he *was* already comfortable with Renee. They'd just spent the past few hours watching football. She knew the game just as well as he did. Hell, she'd had to explain some of the new officiating rules that had been implemented last season.

Chantal had hated anything to do with sports, and wouldn't have known a wing-T formation from a chicken wing. Renee was different, and *that's* what drew him in. And scared the hell out of him.

"Can I be honest with you?" Alex asked.

"As opposed to lying to my face?"

"As opposed to handing you a load of bull instead of explaining what my hang-up is," Alex answered.

"Okay," she said, "be honest with me."

Alex stalled for a moment, debating whether he should tell the truth. He had to be honest with her; she deserved that much. "I haven't been out with a woman since my wife died," he said.

She was silent for several long moments. Alex could see her mind working through that. "She's been dead for two years, right?"

He nodded.

She took a long, deep breath. "Wow. So, you, um, haven't been . . . *out* with a woman for about two years?"

Actually, he hadn't been *out* with a woman in about six years, if *out* was the current euphemism for sex.

"If you don't mind, I think I'm going to be a little more honest," Alex said.

"Go for it," Renee answered.

He settled his elbows on his thighs and rubbed his hands together, feeling the sting in his right shoulder. "You're the first woman I've wanted to go out with in the past two years," Alex revealed.

Her eyes widened a fraction and her chest heaved as she took another deep breath. "Um, okay."

"I don't mean to make you uncomfortable, or pressured in any way," Alex said. "We don't have to go out."

She straightened and placed her feet flat on the floor. She spread her palms out flat and tapped her fingers on her jean-clad thighs. "Well, since we're being honest here, you should know that I've been thinking about going out with you, too."

"You have." It was more statement than question.

"Yes," Renee admitted.

"Oh God," Alex said under his breath. The arousal clenching his gut had the blood thrumming through his body on a direct route to his groin.

"Alex." Renee's soft voice pierced through the haze of desire clouding his brain. "If it's okay, I'm going to kiss you right now," she said.

Alex turned toward her voice and opened his eyes, finding her mere inches from his face.

"Is that okay with you?" she asked.

Alex gave a short nod.

Renee captured his jaw in her palm and pulled his face inches closer. She leaned forward and Alex feared his heart would hammer completely out of his chest. That's just how hard it was beating.

With her eyes locked with his, Renee touched her sweet, succulent lips to his. The moment their mouths connected, an indescribable tightness grabbed hold of Alex's body. She was so soft, like a pillow sent down from heaven.

Alex tried to heed Eli's warning about being aggressive, but the urge to invade her mouth was too hard to resist. He prodded her lips open, gently at first, but when they willingly parted, he plunged, slipping his hand in her hair and finding a firm grip. He didn't want to let her go; knew he couldn't any time soon.

Alex lost it. Slow and steady became fast and furious. He turned, bracketing her between his body and the sofa. He needed to touch her.

But she touched him first; placing her delicate fingers against his chest and squeezing. The sensation burned through his shirt, through his skin, straight to his soul.

She pushed him. Alex cursed in frustration as he realize

she must want to stop, but when he pulled away, she went with him, pushing him down on the sofa and flattening herself against his chest. She settled her body in the V of his legs, fitting herself against the massive erection raging out of control behind his zipper.

He was close to losing it. Thoughts of what he had been denying himself all these years flooded Alex's brain. Sensations he had forgotten about; how good it felt to have a woman's breasts cushioning his chest. How soft a woman felt cradled against his body. It was all coming back to him, but the remembered sensations were heightened now that he was here with Renee.

"Alex, are you ready to start going out again?" Renee asked.

"Yes," he answered on a ragged breath.

"Are you prepared to go out right now?"

"Oh yeah," he growled. *Wait. No.* "Are you asking if I have a condom?"

She nodded.

"I don't," Alex said, disappointment assaulting him. And how strange was that? He was disappointed that he wouldn't be able to sleep with a woman he'd known less than two weeks, his daughter's teacher?

"I guess that would have been asking too much," Renee said. "Condoms probably aren't high on your shopping list." Renee looked up at him from where her head lay on his chest. "You're doubting this, aren't you?"

"Just a little," Alex admitted.

She pushed up from him and settled back on the sofa. Her lips were a delicate crimson after their kissing. "So which *this* are you doubting?" she asked. "That we couldn't continue or that we started this in the first place?"

"Both." Alex laughed a little. "Stupid, huh?"

"Not stupid," Renee said. "I understand where you're coming from."

"I'm happy you do, because I don't."

"This is a big step for you, Alex. I don't want you to think I'm one of those fast little girls your mother probably warned you about," she said with a sly smile. "Can I ask you something?" she asked, completely serious now.

"Okay," Alex answered, unsure he wanted to hear the question after noting the gravity in her voice.

"You can tell me this is none of my business, or to shut up, or whatever," Renee said.

He definitely did not want to hear this. "What is it you want to know?" he asked anyway.

"Why haven't you gone *out* since your wife's death?"

He wasn't shocked by the question, but Alex still didn't know how to answer it.

"Does it feel like you're being unfaithful?" Renee asked when he remained silent.

Alex really laughed this time. It started deep in his stomach and continued rolling until he could hardly breathe.

"Alex," Renee said. "Alex, stop that."

"You have no idea how funny that is," Alex said, trying to contain himself.

"None of this is funny," she protested.

"If anyone has the right to be unfaithful, it's me," Alex said. He would probably question the wisdom of divulging what he was about to share, especially to someone he'd known for such a short period of time, but it felt right. Something in his gut told him Renee would understand.

"When my wife was killed in that car accident, the man she had been cheating on me with died with her," Alex said. That familiar mixture of pain, regret, and anger began to churn in his stomach.

"Oh, Alex," she said on a short rasp of breath.

"He wasn't the first, but I think she was with him the longest."

"I'm so sorry."

"You know what's funny?" He ran his fingers along the fringe of the sofa's lone throw pillow. "I'm not sure how I feel about it anymore. Not sure how I feel about her, except for that underlying hate I can't seem to get rid of."

Had he actually said that aloud? He looked down at Renee. She didn't seem disgusted, which was the reaction he would have expected her to have after he'd just admitted to hating his dead wife.

"Your animosity toward her doesn't make you a horrible person, Alex," she said.

"Doesn't keep me in the running for Widower of the Year, either," he said. How had they found themselves on this subject, anyway?

"You know what?" She traced her finger in circles on his chest. "We've had a good day, and I have a feeling talking about this will ruin it."

Had she read his mind, or what? "Yes, it would," Alex said.

She looked up at him. "If and when you're ready to talk, I want you to know that I will listen, Alex. If you ever need an understanding ear, I'm here."

Alex ran his hand along her hair and down her arm, settling it at her waist. "I've spent the last two years convincing myself that I could handle all the crap Chantal put me through," he said with a mirthless laugh. "What makes me think I can help my mom or my brothers with their problems if I can't deal with my own?"

"If you asked them, I'll bet your family would offer to help, too," she said.

"They would," Alex agreed. "I just don't want to burden any of them."

"It wouldn't be a burden for me. My offer stands. Please, when you're ready to talk, let me be here for you."

He dipped his head and gave her a peck on the nose. "I thought we decided we weren't going to talk about this anymore," he said.

"Yes, we did." She smiled up at him.

"So, what do you want to do?"

"We could kiss a little while longer," she said.

"A few hours, at least," Alex agreed, but even as his lips connected with Renee's, Alex knew he would soon have to leave this fantasy world of football watching and making out on an uncomfortable couch. There were too many issues waiting for him to tackle in the real world, like a daughter who had yet to open up to him, a business that still needed a leader, and a shoulder that had to be rehabilitated. Not to mention Mama and whatever was going on with her.

But he could stay just a few minutes longer, Alex rationalized as he dipped his tongue past Renee's lips and teeth and into the warm heaven of her mouth. The art of kissing had come back to him with incredible ease. He had always loved the intimacy involved, the trust a woman put in him when she really allowed herself to be kissed. He could go on like this for hours, which told Alex it was time to bring it to an end.

"Renee," he said at the first break in their kiss.

"You have to go," she said with a mournful sigh.

"Jasmine will be home soon," he said before capturing her lips once again for a swift kiss. "I'll see you tomorrow."

When the door to the trailer shut behind him, Alex was more than a little shocked at the ache that settled into his bones. How had he been satisfied with the status quo just a few short weeks ago? Now the thought of being without Renee until tomorrow afternoon was almost too hard to comprehend.

He tried to put a name to what she made him feel and finally settled on one. It was laughable in its simplicity. For the first time in a long time, what he felt was happiness.

Chapter Eleven

Margo held the top of the blue silk suit up to her chin and studied the image looking back at her in the mirror. It was nice, but not right for dinner with Gerald and his youngest daughter, Raquel.

She'd met both Raquel and her older sister at a company picnic given by Gerald's law firm, but conversation that afternoon had been pretty impersonal. They'd talked about New Orleans's resurgence after Katrina, a stock conversation piece just about anywhere you went in the city. She had not sensed animosity from either of Gerald's daughters. Things had been . . . pleasant.

Margo wanted more than just pleasant and impersonal. Like her boys, Gerald's daughters were a huge part of his life. If she was going to continue seeing him, Margo knew she had to develop a good relationship with his daughters.

Yet she wasn't giving Gerald a chance to establish any type of relationship with her sons. Margo swallowed back her guilt.

"Mama?"

Margo jumped at the sound of Alex's voice. She pitched the suit on the bed and pulled the comforter over the half dozen outfits she'd been mulling over.

"Mama?" he asked as he knocked on her bedroom door.

"Come on in, Alex," she called.

He opened the door a crack. "You okay in there?" he asked.

"Yes, of course," Margo said, moving to intercept him

before he could step into the room. "Come on in the kitchen. I was just going to get something to drink."

Before she could make it past the threshold of her bedroom door, Alex captured her arm, halting her attempt at a retreat.

"We need to talk," he said.

"About what?" Margo asked. She'd lived long enough to learn the finer points of playing dumb when the occasion called.

"Let's see, there's the issue of you having a hangover this morning," he said.

She waved him off. "I was joking."

"I can't believe this! You're standing here lying to my face."

"Don't you come into my house and accuse me of lying, Alexander Wesley Holmes."

"Well, don't lie," he retorted.

"I will not stand here and listen to this," Margo huffed. She brushed past him, bumping him into the opposite wall.

Alex grabbed his injured shoulder. "Son of a——"

"Oh my God!" Her stomach dropped. Margo reached for him, but he shooed her away.

"No. I'm fine," he strained through clenched teeth.

"Do you need to go to the hospital? Yes, you need to get to the hospital."

"My arm is fine, Mama. Don't worry about it."

"Alex, I'm sorry. I wasn't thinking," Margo said.

Lord, what had she done? What if she'd set back his recovery with her stubborn behavior?

He motioned with his head. "Let's go in the kitchen," Alex said.

Margo sucked in a silent cry, shaking her head at her foolishness. Alex sat her at the table, and she felt the light pressure of the kiss he planted on her head. She'd hurt him, and he was trying to comfort her. It should be the other way around.

Margo shot up from the table. "You sit," she said. "Let me look at that arm."

"Really, Mama, I've banged it up more getting out of bed in the morning," he said with that lopsided smile he always brought up when trying to soothe her.

"I'm sorry," she said again.

He pulled out the chair next to hers and sat.

"What's going on, Mama?" Alex asked.

Margo flinched under his intense gaze. "I was with your aunt, Lynda. One of her girlfriends had a birthday party, and she invited me to come along."

Lord, the lies were coming out way too easily.

"Eli thinks you have a boyfriend," Alex said.

Margo's heart stopped for three good beats. "What?" she laughed, praying it didn't sound as tremulous to Alex's ears as it did to hers.

"That's what he told me when he stopped at the house earlier today. He drove over here after he left my house this morning, but you were gone."

"I had errands to run," Margo sputtered. "I don't know what Eli is talking about."

"It would explain why you've been acting so strange lately," Alex said.

"How have I been acting strange? Because I bought myself a car? Well excuse me if I want to get up and go when *I* want to and not when one of you boys have time to step away from your busy lives to come and drive me around."

"That's not fair, Mama. If ever you need anything, I try to get here as quickly as possible."

"No, Alex, what's not fair is me depending on you boys for everything."

"But that's how it should be. We're a team. We all take care of each other."

Margo reached across the small, square kitchen table and covered her son's hand. He was so much like his father; his hands even felt like Wesley's, rough after working so hard.

"Your brothers are both getting married soon. And I pray every day that you will find someone to make you happy again."

His head reared back in surprise. "You do?"

"Of course I do. You're still so young, and you are such a good man, Alex. I don't tell you this nearly enough, but I am so proud of you, and I know your father is, too."

He gave her that smile, so like Wesley's. "Thanks," he said.

"There's a woman out there who has done something remarkable enough that God is going to bless her by giving her *you*. And when the two of you find each other, I have to be prepared to go on without my boys."

"Mama, you will never have to worry about us not being here for you."

"I know," she said. "But I have to start doing things for myself. And that's all I'm doing, Alex."

"I told Eli it was a stupid idea. You wouldn't have a boyfriend after all those years with Pop," he said.

"Of course not," Margo said, her heart breaking. A small part of her had held on to this foolish hope that her boys would surprise her and actually encourage her relationship with Gerald. "Now, do you want me to fix you something to eat?" She pushed herself up from her chair. "There's leftover spaghetti and meatballs."

"Can I get it to go? I'm picking Jasmine up from the hospital. Monica took her to the museum today."

"Grab a plastic container out of the cabinet," Margo said, opening the refrigerator and coming out with two containers. "I'll give you enough for both you and Jasmine," she said.

Alex placed another kiss on the top of her head. "Whoever the woman is you think God has in store for me, she'd better know how to cook."

"If she doesn't, you can teach her," Margo returned.

"Well, I did learn from the best," he said.

She held his gaze, and really looked him in the eye.

"You're going to be okay, Alex," she said. "All of this, the arm, Jasmine, it's going to work out."

"I know it will," he said. He pulled a plastic grocery bag from the drawer where she kept them. "And I will tell Eli he'd better get his facts straight before he starts spouting foolishness about you having some boyfriend," he said.

"You do that," Margo said with a strained laugh. She held the smile until Alex walked out the back door, then fell back into her chair and covered her face with her hands.

Oh Lord. How would she ever tell her boys about Gerald?

"How did I get roped into doing this?" Renee sighed. She pulled at the gauzy synthetic spiderweb, stretching it thin.

"Blame that fancy title of yours. As special projects coordinator you can be stuck just about anywhere," Penelope answered.

"The question was rhetorical," Renee deadpanned.

"I know, I just like to bug you." Her friend smiled. She gestured toward the spiderweb with her chin. "That stuff looks way too real." Penelope unloaded two intricately carved pumpkins on a nearby folding table.

"Those came out great." Renee motioned to the pumpkin with a graveyard scene carved into the front.

"Thank the gifted and talented art class. They work on these every year. There's another twenty or so in the back. At the end of the Halloween Bazaar, they're sold to the teachers and parents to help fund art activities."

"That's a neat idea. I may have to buy one to put in the window of the trailer," Renee quipped.

"It doesn't need it. Those trailers are scary enough as it is." They both burst out laughing. "Honestly, I thought you and your aunt would be in the house by now," Penelope continued. "From the way you described it, Alex's construction crew is working at lightning speed."

"It's coming along much faster than what Aunt Lorna and I were able to do, that's for sure."

"My goodness, girl. Do you realize how lucky you are? All that free help *and* a gorgeous man to ogle."

"He is fine," Renee agreed with a smile.

"You're going to kill me for asking this," Penelope said.

"Then don't ask."

"Oh, come on, Renee. You know I had my eye on him since day one. The least you can do is let me know what I'm missing out on."

"Alex is incredibly sweet."

"That's not what I want to know."

"But that's all you're going to get," Rene laughed.

"Just give me a hint of how big he is," Penelope whispered. "That's all I want to know."

Renee's eyes widened. "You did not just go there."

"I'm trying to find out if *you* went there."

"I do not kiss and tell."

"So you've at least kissed him. Is he any good at it?"

"That would be telling," Renee sang as she attached plastic spiders to the spiderweb she'd just hung.

"I'll bet he's really good," Penelope said with a faraway look. "He's got the lips for it."

"What are you doing looking at his lips?"

"I won't touch, but don't ask me not to look."

Renee leaned in close. "I'll give you this one, itsy-bitsy detail. He has both the lips and tongue for kissing."

Penelope gasped in fake rapture, clutching a swath of black felt to her chest. "I knew it," she sighed. "I really need a boyfriend."

Renee swatted at Penelope with a bag of fake moss, but hearing her friend's words gave Renee pause. She wasn't sure if she would call Alex her boyfriend just yet.

Things had undeniably changed between them that Saturday they watched football at the trailer. In the weeks that had followed, as she saw him at school, then later in the evenings when he stopped in to check on the progress of the house, Renee had grown more and more comfortable around

Alex. They kissed every time they were together. Still, that didn't mean they were seeing each other.

Or did it?

It had been a long time since she'd allowed a man to kiss her so freely, and Renee had to admit she was ready to go even further. If either of them had had protection that Saturday when they'd watched the Florida/Tennessee game, there was no doubt she would have slept with Alex right there on the miniscule FEMA trailer couch. The condoms she'd purchased the next day had been burning a hole through her favorite leather Coach bag these past few weeks.

In all of her thirty-four years, she'd only slept with two men, and they'd both waited a heck of a lot longer than a month before she allowed them anywhere near her. What was it about Alex that made her let her guard down?

"Here, help me drape this stuff over the basketball goal." Penelope interrupted her thoughts. "Since you're the adventure junkie you can climb the ladder, and I'll hand it to you."

"I'm in heels and a skirt," Renee said.

"Oh, whatever." Penelope pushed her to the side. "You make me climb a huge rock wall, but I can't get you to go up a four-foot ladder." Penelope started her ascent, then looked back at Renee. "Catch me if I fall, please."

"I don't know. Think of how cool it would be to have a real dead body for the Halloween Bazaar."

A surprised gasp escaped Penelope's lips. "I cannot believe they allow you around small children. Okay, pass me the felt," she called.

Renee tried handing it to her, but Penelope was too high up. "I still have to climb this darn ladder," she said. She kicked her shoes off and climbed the first two rungs.

"Anything I can do to help?" came a low-pitched voice just behind her.

She would recognize Alex's deep voice out of a cast of thousands. She looked down. "Hi, Alex," she said. "You broke out of class?"

"The second graders are in an assembly with a guest speaker from the fire department," he explained. "Mrs. Overland let me off the hook for the rest of the class period. I thought maybe I could help out with the bazaar."

"You most certainly can," Penelope said. "You want to drape the felt over this basketball goal?"

Alex gestured to his shoulder. "Probably should have mentioned that my ability to help is limited," he said.

"Great." Penelope rolled her eyes and went back to covering the basketball goal.

"Ms. Moore." Bianca Lewis, one of her third graders, came running up to her. "Mrs. Johnson said she can't find the plastic skeletons," Bianca said with more drama than the situation warranted.

"Tell her to look in the old reading lab," Penelope called from atop the ladder.

"Where?" Renee asked.

"It's the room next to the teachers' lounge." Penelope heaved the felt over the backboard. "They turned the reading lab into storage after they instituted Accelerated Reader and had to move to a bigger room. That's probably where the rest of the Halloween decorations are."

"I can go and take a look," Alex offered.

"That would be wonderful," Renee said. She turned to Bianca. "Tell Mrs. Johnson it is taken care of."

Bianca's little shoulders sagged with relief now that the skeleton crisis had been averted. She took off to tell Mrs. Johnson the good news.

"To have the threat of no plastic skeletons at the Halloween Bazaar be the most pressing problem in your life," she laughed.

"What's Halloween without skeletons?" Alex asked. "Let me take a look in that storage room. I'll be back in a few minutes."

Renee got so caught up in decorating that twenty minutes had passed before she realized Alex had not returned.

She sought out Penelope, and found her emptying apples into an aluminum washtub.

"Have you seen Alex?"

Penelope stood and looked around. "Not since he went in search of the skeletons," she said. "Maybe they carried him over to the dark side?"

"I don't know why you're wasting your time teaching when you could make so much more money as a stand-up comedian," Renee said.

"I tell myself that all the time," Penelope said, returning to her apples.

Renee deposited the orange and black streamers she'd been about to drape along the snack tables, and headed out of the school gymnasium. She entered the main building through the second set of double doors that were closer to the teachers' lounge. The door to the storage room was closed.

Renee knocked. "Alex?" She didn't hear anything, so she turned the knob and pushed. The room was tiny and dark, with only one bulb burning dimly in an old-fashioned light fixture. Renee was happy they'd changed the reading lab. She would become claustrophobic cooped up in this little room all day.

"Alex?" she called again, foraying deeper into the room.

"Hey," he said from behind her.

Renee jumped and screamed. Clasping her hand to her chest, she turned around. "Are you trying to kill me?"

"What?" he asked, holding up a beady-eyed bat with a two-foot-long wingspan.

"What's been taking you so long?" she asked, stepping over to where he stood among dusty cardboard boxes.

"Sorry," he said. "I found the skeletons, but there's a bunch of other stuff, too. I'm still going through boxes." He handed her the plastic bat, a ghost that would look great hanging from the rim of the basketball goal Penelope had covered, and a thick wad of fake spiderweb.

"Oh, this is cool." Alex held up a fat gray rat, and Renee screamed so loud she knew someone would come running from the halls in a minute. She held her chest again, breathing hard.

"I'm guessing you don't like rats," Alex said, a smile tugging at the corners of his mouth.

"Who does?" she asked.

He shrugged. "Michael Jackson. He dedicated an entire song to a rat."

"That is so not funny," Renee said.

"Sorry, I've never been known for my sense of humor," Alex said.

"It's a good thing you have other qualities going for you," she said.

He set the rat on the box behind him and stared at her. "You think I've got other stuff going for me?" Alex asked, all traces of humor gone from his face.

"I would have thought that was obvious," Renee answered.

He took a step toward her. "What kind of qualities?" he asked. His stare was so intense it caused her breath to stall in her lungs. "What is it, Renee?" he urged when she didn't speak.

"I'm not sure," she answered honestly, breathlessly.

"I'm having the same problem," Alex said. "Trying to figure out just what it is about you that causes this reaction in me," he whispered just before his lips touched hers. His kiss was soft, sensual. His lips brushed hers only a few times before his tongue stepped in, invading her mouth with warm, insistent thrusts.

Renee moaned against his mouth, running her tongue along his teeth. Alex wrapped one arm around her, pulling her body against the full length of his. They reclined against the cardboard boxes, the boxes crushing beneath their shared weight.

"Should we be doing this here?" Renee asked.

"Probably not," Alex replied. He snaked his hand down her stomach and thigh, stopping where her skirt hem met bare skin.

"I don't care," Renee said, relaxing her legs, opening them a bit wider to allow him better access.

Alex accepted her invitation, moving his hand to her inner thigh and pushing it under her skirt. "Neither do I," he said. His fingers brushed across her center, and Renee widened her stance even more, that part of her aching for his attention.

"Alex," she breathed as he dipped his head between her breasts.

"Yeah?" Alex asked between gentle nips.

"We really should stop," Renee warned, even though she wanted nothing more than to strip both their clothes off and fulfill the fantasy she'd started having since the day she met him.

"Just a few more minutes," Alex breathed into the valley of her breasts.

He pushed her skirt to her waist and brought his hands around to grip her butt. His fingers felt *so* good sinking into her flesh.

He was scary hard, his body like a length of steel against her stomach. He pulled her tighter and his pulsing erection pushed up against that place that was crying out for him. Renee whimpered, gripping his back and cursing the modest layers of clothing that separated her from him.

Alex moved her underwear to the side and slid a finger inside her. Renee exploded, coming hard and fast, her body shuddering as she bit down on her lip to prevent her screams from escaping. Blinking through the sparks of white light shooting behind her closed lids, she opened her eyes and stared up at the water-stained ceiling. She didn't want to think about moving for at least the next five minutes. She heard Alex suck in a breath and saw him wince.

"Is it your shoulder?" she asked.

He nodded, but when she tried to slide from under him, he stopped her with a hand on her spine.

"Just a few more minutes like this," Alex said. "I just need to feel you against me."

"You'll hurt yourself, Alex."

"No, I won't," he replied. "If I do, it would be worth it."

Shaking her head, she said, "We just made out in the storage room. How clichéd is that?"

"Just because it's clichéd doesn't mean it wasn't fun, does it?" he asked.

"Fun? It was amazing." She smiled. "But what's even more clichéd than making out in a storage room is being *caught* making out in a storage room."

"I suspect it wouldn't sit well with Principal Green, either," Alex said, pushing himself up.

Renee moved her underwear back into place and pushed her skirt down, grateful the soft rayon/polyester blend didn't wrinkle easily. She accepted Alex's outstretched hand, then turned to examine the damage they'd done to the boxed-up books and manuals they'd used as an impromptu bed.

"Are we going to eventually finish this?" Renee asked.

"I want to," came his hesitant response. "But there are other things I need to consider," he said.

"We're not on any set timetable, Alex. I'm willing to slow it down if that's what you want."

"Eventually," he said, pulling her close for another kiss. "Now that I've gotten a taste of you, I won't settle for anything less than everything."

Chapter Twelve

Margo added another pinch of salt to the mustard greens simmering atop the stove. She tried to keep her mind occupied by transferring the rest of today's meal from pots into serving dishes, but at the sound of a car pulling up the drive, she nearly dropped the small casserole dish of buttered corn.

She ran to the kitchen window, her entire body sighing with relief when she saw Jasmine running up the driveway toward the back door.

That Gerald Mitchell was going to give her a heart attack. Before ending their hour-long phone conversation last night, he'd told her he would show up for Sunday dinner.

Most of their discussion had centered upon her resistance in taking their relationship public. Gerald had been more than accommodating, understanding that she had other things to consider, like a family and friends who might not be as accepting of him as his daughters were of her, but after six months, he was becoming frustrated. It did seem as if she was ashamed of him, even though nothing could be further from the truth. In fact, Margo was pretty sure she was falling in love with him.

"Lord, help me," she said under her breath.

Margo heard the screen door slap shut. A second later the kitchen door flew open and Jasmine came barreling through it.

"Grandma." Her grandbaby ran up to her, arms wide open.

"Hello, my angel."

"You didn't go to church, Grandma."

"No, Grandma was feeling a little tired this morning," she said, giving Jasmine's soft hair a kiss.

"Hey, Mama." Alex walked through the door. "What happened to you this morning?"

"She was sick," Jasmine provided.

"What's wrong?" Instant concern clouded Alex's eyes.

"It's nothing. Probably just a stomach virus," she said, jumping on Jasmine's erroneous excuse.

"Where's Eli? Maybe he needs to check you out."

"Nonsense." She waved him off.

Eli and Monica picked that moment to walk through the kitchen door. Margo had not even heard their car approach.

"Hey, y'all." Eli entered after Monica, carrying a brown bag that Margo suspected held vanilla ice cream. He'd said he would bring some when she told him she was making peach cobbler for dessert.

"Mama's sick," Alex said.

"What's wrong?" Eli asked, his eyes darting to her.

Margo's shoulder sagged with a sigh. "I'm fine," she said.

"Do you have a fever?"

She slapped Eli's hand as it approached her forehead.

"Goodness, a person can't have a little stomachache around you people." Margo picked up the cooking spoon and turned back to her mustard greens.

Monica approached her at the stove. "Why don't you go lie down, Margo? I can finish up dinner."

"Really, I'm fine," Margo insisted. A car door slammed, and her heart nearly stopped beating.

"Somebody else coming to dinner?" Eli asked.

"I—" Fear knotted in her gut as panic held her rooted where she stood. There was a knock at the back door.

"I'll get it," Jasmine called.

"No," Margo yelled, but it was too late. Jasmine had already run onto the porch.

"It's Uncle Jonathan and Auntie Ivana," her granddaughter called.

Margo felt her knees go weak with relief. She forgot she'd invited Jonathan and Ivana to dinner to celebrate their engagement.

"Hi, everyone," Ivana said, her long, flowing sundress hanging perfectly on her willowy frame. "Thanks so much for inviting us to dinner, Margo." She leaned over and planted a kiss on Margo's cheek.

Jonathan picked Jasmine up and twirled her around. He planted a loud, sloppy kiss on her cheek that had her giggling and squirming like a worm.

"Come on, Ivana, we can talk about wedding plans," Monica said.

Carrying bowls and platters filled with the food Margo had spent the morning preparing, Monica and Ivana went into the dining room.

"Mama, are you sure you're okay?" Eli asked.

"I'm fine, Elijah."

Her cell phone started dancing on the kitchen table. She dashed over to the table and grabbed the cell phone. It was Gerald. Margo opened and shut the phone to stop the ringing.

"Who was that?" Alex asked.

"Wrong number," she lied. "I want to change out of these clothes before we sit down to eat. You boys go into the dining room and get settled. I'll be back in a minute."

Margo closed the door to her bedroom and sank onto the bed. She flipped the cell phone open and dialed Gerald's number.

"What are you doing?" Margo whispered into the phone as soon as he answered.

"I can't call you now?"

"Gerald." She dropped her head into her hand. "I can't take this much longer."

A hushed static filled the air before Gerald replied. "Just what does that mean, Margo? Are you saying we're over?"

"No." The word rushed out of her.

"Then what?"

"I don't know." She rubbed her temple. "I just don't know."

"You already know where I stand," he said.

Yes, she did. Last night, Margo was sure he was going to give her an ultimatum. Even though he didn't, she was pretty sure it wasn't far away.

"I just need more time," she said.

"How much time?"

"Gerald, please don't ask me that."

"It's a legitimate question, Margo. How long am I supposed to remain your dirty little secret?"

"You're not . . . I'm just . . . I don't know what to do," she whispered into the phone.

"Margo?"

"Yes?"

"I love you."

The sweetly whispered words washed over her like a soothing balm over a long-aching sore. Margo covered her mouth with her fist, trying to absorb the sob on the verge of escaping her lips. "Oh, Gerald," she said.

"I'm not trying to pressure you, sweetheart. But I need you to know how I feel. This isn't some halfhearted fling to me. I'm in this. Every part of me."

"Gerald, you know I don't think of you as a fling," she said.

"Mama." Margo jumped at the loud knock on the door. "Mama, we're ready to start dinner."

"I'll . . . uh, be out in a minute," she said. "Gerald, I have to go," Margo whispered into the phone. "I'm just asking that you give me a little more time," she said.

"Go and have dinner with your family," Gerald said. "I'll see you later this afternoon."

"Okay," Margo said. She shut the cellular phone and pressed it to her chest. She feared nothing would appease the ache that had seemed a permanent residence for the six months.

He loved her.

Margo allowed the reality of his words to settle over her; they warmed her from the inside out. She thought about her family just beyond the door, and cold dread stole into her bones again. There was a man out there who loved her, and the people closest to her had no idea he existed.

How would she bring her two worlds together?

"Ms. Moore, can I have a minute?"

Renee's eyelids slid shut. She turned. The harsh scowl on Rashad's face clashed with the cheerful painting taped outside Mrs. Kelly's kindergarten classroom.

"What is it, Mr. Richards?" she asked.

He grabbed her wrist and guided her a few steps down the hall to an alcove that housed a bank of water fountains. "What's the deal, Renee? Why haven't you returned any of my calls?"

"Rashad, please don't do this," Renee pleaded. "I told you the last time we talked that I'd rather we just be friends."

"After everything we've been through, you want us to just be friends?"

After everything they'd been through?

"We only went out a few times, Rashad. I even paid my own way. If you consider that dating, then I'm also dating my aunt Lorna, Penelope, and a couple of the girls from my book club. Oh, wait, I'm more than dating them, because a few of them actually picked up the tab once or twice."

He winced.

"Look, Rashad, I still consider you a friend, and I don't want to lose your friendship, but we have so little in common."

"That's not true."

"It is." He wanted her to be blunt? She could do blunt.

"Truthfully, I find most of the things you like to do boring." His head reared back as if she'd slapped him. "You feel the same way about me. You hate outdoor sports, and watching football, and Eddie Murphy movies."

"Fine. We don't match. Does that mean you have to cut me off altogether? I can't call to say hi?"

Chastised, she apologized. "I'm sorry about that. I got your messages, but I've had a busy couple of weeks."

"Well, do you want to grab some dinner Friday night? As friends." He smiled. "We both love Thai food."

She hated to do this, but she needed to be straight with him.

"Rashad, I don't think it would be appropriate for us to go out anymore, even as friends. I'm seeing someone."

He laughed, a cynical, condescending snort. "So that's why you didn't answer my calls. I should have known."

The bell ranged.

"I have a class," Renee said. "So do you."

"Who is he?" Rashad asked.

"That's none of your business."

"It's the guy working on your aunt's house, isn't it? The one who's volunteering here."

"Look, Rashad, things don't have to be awkward between us."

He snorted. "You really are a cold bitch, aren't you? I hope that Holmes guy knows what he's getting himself into."

Well, that sufficiently put an end to her goodwill. She leveled him with a glare. "Don't talk to me again, Rashad."

"I wasn't planning to," he said. He turned and headed up the hall.

Renee took several deep, cleansing breaths before continuing in the opposite direction. She closed her eyes and tried to calm herself down as she stood just outside Mrs. Overland's door. Rashad Richard's bitterness would not ruin the rest of her day.

Renee gave two solid raps on the door. As she entered the

classroom, her spirits were instantly buoyed by the bright colors and finger paintings decorating the walls. Her day got even brighter at the sight of Alex tacking a long sheet of white paper on the wall in the far corner of the room. She'd driven to the Mississippi Gulf Coast with Aunt Lorna this past weekend, and had not seen him since Friday afternoon. She'd dreamed about what had almost happened in the storage room way too much while lounging poolside this weekend.

"Good morning, Ms. Moore," the class sang.

"Good morning, students," Renee answered.

Alex turned, his surprised smile reaching his eyes. "Hello, Ms. Moore."

"Mr. Holmes." She nodded toward the paper he'd just hung on the wall. "You look rather busy."

"Just getting ready for art class," he answered. "We're doing profiles." He pointed to the overhead projector. "The students have to sit in the chair here and another student will trace their profile."

"That sounds like fun. I'm sure everyone will be itching to get out of Accelerated Reader today."

The students giggled.

Mrs. Overland entered the classroom. "Ms. Moore, is it that time already?"

"Almost, I'm a little early."

"Give the students a minute to put away their math supplies," Mrs. Overland said. "My class knows they cannot go anywhere if they have not taken care of their work space."

"Then they better get to it. We just received a huge shipment of new books, and I think a few of them are about pirates," Renee tempted the students with a smile.

"Mr. Holmes was just telling me about today's art project," Renee said. She stepped a few feet over to where Alex was struggling with another sheet of paper. He should have known better than to attempt this with only one good arm.

"You look like you could use a little help," she said to Alex. "Why don't I hold and you staple?"

"Thank you, Ms. Moore," he returned with a grateful smile.

Renee crouched a little as he stretched above her head to tack the strip of freezer paper to the wall.

"I have a few texture designs for the walls in your aunt's house," Alex said with a lowered voice. "Do you mind if I stop over this afternoon?"

"Not at all," Renee answered. "Will you be stopping over around dinnertime?"

"I can," he said.

"I can cook dinner. Why don't you bring Jasmine?" she suggested.

His face went grim. He shook his head, and was about to speak when Mrs. Overland called, "Ms. Moore, they're ready to go and read about pirates."

"Wonderful," Renee answered. She looked back at Alex, disconcerted by the perplexing expression still crowding his face. "I'll make sure everyone is back in time for today's art project. I know they wouldn't want to miss this fun. I'll see you later this afternoon," she said in a voice low enough just for Alex to hear.

By the end of the day, Renee was tempted to stop over at the KFC for a bucket of chicken, but she wasn't sure if she needed to buy for two or three since Alex had never confirmed whether he would bring Jasmine tonight. Aunt Lorna's social calendar was once again full. She was teaching dance at an after-school program, then had a meeting at her church, then was helping out at a shelter for battered women. Renee didn't know how Aunt Lorna did it, but then again, her aunt said her activities were what kept her young.

Opting for a home-cooked meal, Renee stopped at a grocery store on the drive from school and picked up the makings for spaghetti and meatballs. It was quick and easy, and she didn't have to fire up the oven, which usually turned the FEMA trailer into a hot box. As the spaghetti boiled and her meat sauce simmered, Renee changed out of her slacks and blouse and into a pair of yoga pants and her favorite cotton shirt.

That was one of the things that was different about whatever this was she had going with Alex. Her appearance wasn't an issue. She didn't have to constantly be *on*. She could just be herself, and he was cool with that.

However, that didn't mean she couldn't primp. Renee dragged a hairbrush through her hair and touched up her soft pink lip gloss.

There was a knock on the door, and she shivered at the ripple of excitement that skittered across her skin. She had just seen him a few hours ago, but that didn't matter. He still caused a reaction.

"Hi." Renee opened the door with a smile.

"Hi," Alex answered.

She looked around him. "Where's Jasmine?" she asked.

He shuffled from one foot to the other, his big body taking up the entire doorway. "I didn't bring her," Alex answered. "That's what I was trying to tell you earlier today." He looked past her into the trailer. "Can I come in?"

"Of course. I'm sorry," Renee said. "Come in." She stepped back, giving him access to the trailer. He motioned for her to go ahead of him.

He placed the three-ring binder he'd carried with him on the counter. "I was trying to tell you this earlier when you came to Mrs. Overland's class."

"What?" she prompted when he hesitated.

"I'm not sure what we have going on here, Renee."

Oh God. Was he already dumping her?

"I like you," he said.

Her spirits started to lift just a smidge.

"I like you, too, Alex."

"This is strange territory for me," he said. Renee could

feel the unease flowing off him in waves. "I've felt attracted to women—wait, is your aunt here?"

Renee shook her head. "She won't be back for a few hours."

"Busy woman." The edge of his mouth tipped up in a crooked smile.

"She is," Renee answered with a smile of her own. "You were saying?" She couldn't take much more of this evading the issue. He had her nerves on edge.

"Yeah." He looked around the trailer, wiping his hands on his thighs. Stalling.

"Alex," Renee said with a pleading voice.

"I'm sorry." He looked up at her, contrite. "I haven't felt this way in a long time. I've been attracted to women since Chantal died, but not like this. This is different. I've been able to fight off those feelings, but I can't fight this."

She shook her head. All those words, and she was still as confused as when he'd first opened his mouth.

"I still don't get it, Alex."

"I'm not sure what to do about you," he admitted. "What am I supposed to tell my family? And Jasmine? What am I supposed to say to her? We've never talked about me dating anyone."

"She knows you can't remain single for the rest of your life," Renee said. "Oh, wait, I get your point now. How is a six-year-old supposed to accept that her widowed father is dating again, when you, at your age, can't accept that your widowed mother is doing the same thing?"

His brow pulled together in an affronted frown.

"Does this mean you want us to stop seeing each other?" Renee asked.

"*Are* we seeing each other?" he asked.

Renee was so taken aback by his question that she literally took a step back. Did he think she let just anyone feel her up while watching football, not to mention what they'd done in the storage closet on Friday?

"That didn't come out right," Alex said.

"Whew, that's a good thing, because I was about to punch you in the stomach," she said, wrangling a smile from him. "I understand where you're coming from, Alex, but I don't necessarily agree with your stance. It may not be my place to say this, but I think you're sheltering Jasmine."

"What makes you say that?"

"What is she allowed to do on her own?"

"Nothing, she's six."

"At six years old, I got myself dressed for school in the morning and made my own breakfast. Don't get me wrong, Alex. I think it's amazing the way you take care of her, but you have to let her grow up. You can't shelter her from the world, and a part of her world should be seeing her single father with a woman."

"I just don't know if she's ready for that."

"You seem to use that excuse an awful lot, Alex. What about the reason you're volunteering at the school in the first place? Have you addressed Jasmine's behavior with her yet?"

"I'm working on it," Alex said. "I caught her bullying one of the other students when she thought I wasn't in the classroom. Instead of going out for recess, we stayed in and talked about what she'd done. When I asked her why she's been acting up she said the kids who act bad get to sit at the front of the class, and Mrs. Overland calls on them more."

"She's looking for attention." Renee nodded.

"Mr. Powell thinks it goes even deeper," Alex said, referring to the school's psychologist. "He thinks Jasmine is acting out specifically in Mrs. Overland's class because Mrs. Overland uses more of a mothering approach when disciplining her students."

"Of course," Renee said with a gentle whisper. "That makes perfect sense."

Alex expelled a frustrated breath. "We've spent the last two years spoiling her rotten, trying to make up for her not having a mother, but I think we missed what was most important."

"A girl Jasmine's age needs her mother," Renee said.

"But I don't want her to think I'm trying to replace her mother with someone else, that's why I haven't wanted to bring another woman into her life so soon."

"I can understand where you're coming from," Renee said. "Will it make you start hyperventilating if I suggest that we are possibly more than just friends?"

He took a deep, extremely pronounced breath.

"Seriously, Alex. We were seconds from *going out* in the storage room at St. Katherine's; we may have to up the status. You're not the kind of guy who goes out with someone who's just a friend. And I'm certainly not that type of girl."

His body visibly relaxed. "Does that mean you never went *out* with Richards?"

"None of your business," Renee returned, "but yes."

"That shouldn't make me feel as good as it does," Alex said.

"It really shouldn't," she said. "But I'm happy it does." She leaned in close, her lips an inch from his. "That means I'm a lot more than just your friend."

"I'm ready for you to be more than just a friend," Alex said. He stopped her before she could close the gap between them, his face serious. "I just want to make sure you know what that means."

"What?" Renee asked, uneasy with the gravity she heard in his voice.

"Eventually, I'm going to have to introduce you to my family," he said.

Renee slapped his chest. "Don't scare me like that," she said.

"You should be scared," Alex warned.

"Stop it. I already met your brother, and he seemed perfectly fine."

"You don't get it; these people have been pressuring me to start dating again for nearly two years. My mother? She's going to bug the hell out of you."

"I think I can handle it," Renee answered, feeling no small amount of excitement at the thought of meeting Alex's family. "Now, are you going to kiss me, or what?"

"Hmm, I guess kissing is one of the nice perks that comes with the more-than-friends territory," he said.

"Oh, we're just getting started," Renee said.

"Daddy, do you like Ms. Moore?"

Alex froze, the hand holding the hairbrush arrested above his daughter's tangled head of curls he'd spent the last fifteen minutes trying to tame.

"What was that?" Alex asked, stalling for time. Had his infatuation with Renee been so transparent that even a six-year-old could see it?

"Do you like Ms. Moore?" she repeated.

"I don't dislike her," Alex answered. He resumed the hair brushing, which was no easy feat with the limited range of motion in his shoulder; even though it showed progress that he was able to comb her hair again. "Why are you asking about Ms. Moore?" Alex asked.

"Because I like her." Jasmine shrugged her answer.

"That's good. You should like your teachers. You like Mrs. Overland, don't you?"

"Yes," Jasmine answered. "But she's old."

"She's not old, Jasmine."

"She's too old for you to marry her." Alex stopped brushing again. "And Mrs. Overland is already married anyway," Jasmine continued. "But Ms. Moore don't have a husband and you don't have a wife."

"I didn't know you wanted me to get married," Alex said. They had never even discussed him dating. There had been no one—until now—who'd captured his interest.

"Well, Uncle Eli and Auntie Monica are getting married, and Uncle Toby and Auntie Cee Cee are getting married. You're going to be lonely if you don't get a wife, too."

"Why do you think I need a new wife? I thought I had you," Alex teased, pinching her cheek.

"What about when I leave for doctor school?"

Alex's brow rose. "You're going to doctor school?"

"Yeah. I'm going to deliver babies like Uncle Eli," she said matter-of-factly. "And if you don't marry Ms. Moore, you're going to be by yourself when I leave."

"Grandma's by herself," Alex said.

"But Grandma's old, she's not afraid to be by herself."

"We probably shouldn't mention this conversation to Grandma."

"Okay." Jasmine shrugged again.

"Scoot this way so I can brush the other side of your hair," Alex said. She turned around on the pillow she'd placed on the floor, and Alex took the brush to the other mess of tangles and curls. When he'd sat here to comb Jasmine's hair after washing it, he had not anticipated having the conversation he had been avoiding for the past two years. He'd always assumed Jasmine wasn't ready for this discussion, but if he were honest with himself, Alex could admit that maybe he was the one who wasn't ready.

"You know, Pumpkin," Alex started. "I've been afraid you would be upset if I started seeing someone else."

"But you need somebody to keep you company like Kayla's mommy. She has a new boyfriend."

Kayla's mommy probably had several new boyfriends.

"That's a little different," Alex said. "Kayla's mommy and daddy got a divorce. Remember we talked about what happens between two people who get divorced?"

Jasmine nodded. "I still think you should get another wife," she said.

"Maybe one of these days," he said. "Maybe once you leave me and head to doctor school."

"Okay," she grumbled, and pouted.

"Wait, what's the face about? You just told me you wanted me to get a new wife, and when I say I will, you get that sad look?"

"You don't have to wait until I go to doctor school, Daddy. You can get a new wife now, and I can have another Mommy," she said.

Alex stared down at his daughter. How had he missed cues that Jasmine had been yearning for a mother figure? "I didn't know you wanted a new mommy," he said.

"I miss Mommy," she said with a melancholy gaze that forced a lump in Alex's throat.

"I know you do, Pumpkin."

"Why was she driving so fast, Daddy?"

"I don't know, baby. But you remember what we talked about, right? How Mommy is sorry she had to leave you, and that she's still watching over you?"

"And that she's my angel in heaven." Jasmine recited the words Alex had tried to instill in her since Chantal's death.

"Yes, she is." Alex put his fingers under her chin and turned her to face him. "You know that another mommy won't replace your real mommy, right?"

"I know."

"But you would be okay if Daddy started seeing someone else?"

She nodded.

"Come here, Pumpkin." Alex helped her rise from the floor, then enveloped her in a bear hug. "Daddy loves you so much."

"I love you, too. And I really like Ms. Moore, Daddy. She's better than Mrs. Johnson. I hate Mrs. Johnson," Jasmine said with feeling.

"Jasmine, that's not nice."

"But I do hate her, Daddy. She used to always tell us to shhhhhhh, even when we didn't make noise. I hope Miss Johnson stays sick."

"Jasmine, you know it's not nice to say things like that."

"But Grandma says I'm supposed to tell the truth."

"Yeah, but . . ." This was one of those parenting dilemmas that continued to stump him. Which lesson should he teach today, honesty or politeness? "That's true," Alex said, "but sometimes being honest can hurt people."

"So I should lie?"

"No, not really."

Jasmine hunched her shoulders. "So what should I do?"

Alex pondered the question for a moment and realized he didn't have a sufficient answer. "Ask Grandma when we go over there tomorrow."

"Okay." Jasmine shrugged.

"So, are you having fun playing softball?" he asked. He snapped the last barrette on the end of her ponytail.

"Yes," Jasmine affirmed with such enthusiasm Alex had to laugh. "Coach said I'm good at sneaking bases."

His brows arched in humorous surprise. "You know how to sneak bases?"

"Yep. You have to wait until the pitcher is almost ready to throw the ball. Then you run, run, run. I can run *so* fast. I'm the fastest one on the team. You coming to the game tomorrow?"

"Of course I am."

"You promise, Daddy?"

"Hey, what's up all the questions? You don't believe me?"

"You might have to go to work," she said. "You couldn't go to my games last year because you always had to work."

Instant regret washed over Alex. How many times had he missed her softball games, assuming having Mama there in his place was enough? How many times did he say to people that Jasmine was his daughter, his responsibility? Well, fulfilling his responsibility meant more than plying her with toys she didn't need and signing her up for a bunch of after-school activities. He needed to be there. He needed to give her his time.

Tying a satin head wrap over her combed hair, Alex squeezed her shoulders. "Stand up for me."

She scooted off the floor and turned to him, her wide, bright eyes vulnerable, and filled with uncertainty.

"I missed out on a lot of the things you did last year, didn't I?"

"You came to my recital," she said. "Well, to the big recital. You missed the one with just my class, but Grandma was there. Grandma said you have to work a lot because you're the boss."

"That's true, but the boss doesn't have to be there all the time. Look, I'm not there now, am I?"

"No, but that's because you hurt your arm."

"My arm will still be hurt tomorrow, which means I will definitely be at your softball game, and even when my arm is better and I go back to work, I'll still be at your games."

"Really, Daddy? You promise?"

"I promise, baby. Now hop into bed."

"Daddy, guess what?" she said as she shuffled under the thick, down comforter. "Grandma said if I'm good she's gonna take me to buy a new bathing suit because there's a big swimming pool at the house where Auntie Monica and Uncle Eli are getting married. I'm getting a pink bathing suit." She smiled.

"You already have a pink bathing suit," Alex said.

"But that one has strawberries on it. I want one with flowers."

An idea Alex had began to mull over in his mind started taking shape.

"Jazz, what do you think about Ms. Moore coming with us to Uncle Eli's wedding?"

"For real?" Her bright eyes doubled in size.

"Maybe," Alex said. "If she wants to. I was thinking about asking her to come along."

Jasmine threw off the covers, hopped out of the bed, and started jumping up and down and clapping her hands.

Sitting back as Jasmine carried on as if she'd just won a shopping spree at Toys "R" Us, Alex couldn't help but laugh at his cluelessness. Here he'd thought his getting involved with another woman would be upsetting for his daughter, and all the while she'd been thinking that he should marry the one woman who had been driving him insane with desire. Life had a funny way of making an ass out of him.

"I haven't asked Ms. Moore to come along with us, so you can't say anything, especially to Uncle Eli or Uncle Toby. Not even to Grandma, okay?"

"You want me to lie," she stated.

"It's not lying." At least not in the traditional, six-year-old sense of the word. Lying by omission surely didn't count for first graders.

"When you gonna tell Ms. Moore she's coming with us to the beach to see Uncle Eli get married?"

"I'm not going to *tell* her that she's coming; I'm going to *ask* her if she wants to come."

"But she has to, and she can come with me and Grandma to buy a new bathing suit. I don't want her to have a pink one with flowers on it, though. I want to be the only one with that bathing suit."

"I don't think Ms. Moore can shop for a bathing suit at the same store where Grandma is taking you."

"No, I think the biggest size there is seventh grade."

The image of Renee in a bathing suit jumped to the forefront of Alex's mind. God, please let him summon the nerve to ask her to come on this trip. They'd had some pretty close encounters these past few weeks, but that didn't mean she was ready to pack up and come with him to the islands.

In fact, the more he thought about it, the more Alex realized Renee would probably look at him as if he was crazy. They hadn't even been on an official date. Other than that afternoon they spent watching football and making out on her aunt's couch, all their time together had been spent at the school. Granted, they had gotten to know each other really well, especially in that storage room, but they still didn't *know* each other.

And that was the craziest part of it all. He really wanted to get to know her. Even more than he wanted that next kiss, Alex wanted to know more about *her*. What was she like as a child? What did she want out of life? Was she ready to settle down, start a family?

"Daddy?" Jasmine's voice knocked him from his musing.

"Yeah, baby?"

"I think Ms. Moore likes you, too," she said, a smile tipping up the corners of her mouth.

Alex barked a laugh. "Good night, Pumpkin."

Chapter Thirteen

Renee stood just beyond the front porch, her hands on her hips, her mind sufficiently blown by the unfailing precision in which the men from Holmes Construction did their jobs. Two workers carried in sheets of Sheetrock, one after the other. Another group used a huge mixer to mix the texture that would be blown on the walls. Alex said it would add depth and character that you wouldn't get with just paint. Renee had learned over the past weeks that when it came to the house, she should just put her trust in Alex.

She still wasn't sure if she could put her trust in him with regards to other aspects of her life—namely her heart. Something deep inside told her she should. It was obvious he had a strong sense of family, something she'd always longed for growing up.

Renee still could not completely grasp how a man could lavish so much love on one child. Until she'd met Alex, she didn't believe such love could exist between a father and daughter. Even the friends she'd envied back in grade school didn't have fathers who treated them as if they were princesses. It was enough that they were not beaten every night.

She was used to belt lashings and humiliation. To lying in bed at night, afraid her door would open and her father would unleash his fury on her or her mother.

The thought of Alex bringing his fist to Jasmine's face was preposterous. He just was not that kind of man. He was warm, and gentle, and sweeter than just about anyone Renee had ever encountered.

"Hi there."

Renee jumped. Turning, she felt her heart skip a beat at the sight of Alex in a soft yellow polo shirt, khaki cargo shorts, and sandals. He wore a pair of sunshades, and looked even more gorgeous than usual.

"Good morning," Renee said, her hand still over her heart. "I'm guessing you're not here to supervise," she said.

"The guys can handle it. I have a prior engagement, one I was hoping you could join me at."

Renee looked at him curiously; then she heard a car door slam.

"Hey, Ms. Moore." Jasmine came running toward her from Alex's truck. She wore a softball uniform and had a ponytail bouncing from the back of her cap.

"Hi, Jasmine, you look like you're ready to hit a home run."

"Daddy said you could come and watch me play."

"I—" Renee looked from Jasmine to Alex.

"Hold on, Jazz, remember what Daddy said?"

"Oh yeah, we have to ask first." She turned to Renee. "Can you come and watch me play, Ms. Moore? Please? I'm really, really fast, and I know how to steal second base."

"You do?" Renee looked to Alex. The slight, apologetic smile tipping his lips spiked his yum factor up to one hundred.

"Sorry to just show up like this, but I thought—"

"Daddy!"

"*We* thought maybe you would like to catch a softball game."

"Please, Ms. Moore," Jasmine begged.

Alex tapped Jasmine's shoulder to stop her from jumping up and down. "We understand if you already had something planned. I know this is last minute," Alex said. "But Jasmine and I were talking last night, and I asked if she would mind if I brought someone to her softball game. When she found out you were the person I wanted to ask, she couldn't have been more excited. Neither could I."

The breath caught in Renee's throat. He'd discussed her with Jasmine. Finally.

But did Jasmine see her as his date, or as one of her favorite teachers coming to her game? Even though she'd just started working with younger children, Renee already had a sense of how their minds worked. She knew Jasmine enjoyed her Accelerated Reader and Library Skills class. Just because she wanted Renee at her game, it did not mean she wanted Renee dating her father. She wondered if Alex considered the difference in the way a six-year-old would interpret this situation when they'd discussed her last night.

"Well, Ms. Moore?"

"Of course I'm coming to the ballpark," Renee said. "I've got to see just how good you are at stealing those bases," she said to Jasmine.

Thank you, Alex mouthed.

Renee looked down at her baggy T-shirt and cutoff shorts. "Give me a minute to change," she said.

"You look fine," Alex insisted.

"I look like I'm—"

"Going to a ballpark." Alex spoke over her.

"Come on, Daddy. We gotta get to the game."

"At least let me grab my purse," Renee said. She ran over to the trailer and picked up her purse and her favorite Florida Gators cap. Alex was giving Jasmine a boost into the double-cab truck when she returned.

"Come on, Ms. Moore," Jasmine called, sticking her head out of the backseat area.

"I'm here," Renee said. Alex held out his hand, and she grabbed hold of it and allowed him to help her into the truck. Renee tracked him with her eyes as he rounded the front of the truck. He got in, strapped on his seat belt, and reached over with his left hand to start the truck. He pulled the gear shift into reverse, and backed out of the driveway. He did a credible job of steering the car with one hand.

"Ms. Moore, do you have a swimsuit?" Jasmine asked from the backseat.

"Jasmine," Alex said in a warning tone.

"Oh, I forgot. I'm sorry, Daddy."

Renee looked over at Alex, raising her brow in question. He shook his head, dismissing Jasmine's comment.

The park where Jasmine's peewee softball team played ball wasn't all that far from her aunt's house. The four- and five-year-old team was just finishing their game when they arrived. Jasmine bounded out of the truck, gave Alex a kiss on the cheek, and ran to where her teammates were warming up.

"She looks so cute in her little uniform," Renee said as they walked from the makeshift parking lot to the baseball diamond.

"I rather her in softball than dance. That was last year."

"Oh, I'll bet that was cute."

"Jazzy is cute in just about anything she does."

"She takes after her father," Renee teased.

"You think I'm cute?" he asked, the smile on his face far surpassing cute. It was heart-stopping.

"You're okay," Renee answered.

"I'll take that," Alex laughed.

They made their way to the bleachers. Alex sat her down and walked off, returning a few minutes later with two hot dogs and two cans of soda.

When Jasmine's team took to the field, Renee's heart filled at the love and pride she saw on Alex's face. He explained that in peewee softball, each child gets a chance to hit the ball at least twice. Even so, the first inning lasted less than ten minutes, with both teams garnering lightning-quick outs. The second inning went just as quickly.

"Well, it looks like we won't take up too much of your Saturday," Alex said.

"I don't mind," Renee laughed. "This is more exciting than what I had planned to do."

Alex raised a questioning brow.

"Cleaning out the cabinets in the trailer," she answered. "They're so small it would have taken about as long as that last inning. So why did Jasmine ask if I had a bathing suit?" Renee asked.

He shifted uneasily on the bleacher. "One thing I don't have to worry about is my daughter keeping secrets from me," Alex said.

"Alex, what's going on?"

He turned to her. "I was going to wait a few more days before asking you this, but I guess it doesn't matter now." He took a deep, fortifying breath. "My brother is getting married at the end of the month. I was hoping you could join me, be my date at the wedding."

"Really?" Renee asked, a warm giddiness seeping into her bones.

"The wedding is in St. Martin," Alex said.

"St. Martin? As in the Virgin Islands?" Renee nearly choked. "You want me to go to the Virgin Islands with you?"

He looked as if he was having just as much trouble catching his breath as she was at the moment. "I would understand if you didn't want to," he said. "We haven't known each other all that long, and I wouldn't blame you if you would feel uncomfortable going off to the islands with me and my family, whom you haven't even met yet," he rambled. "God, what was I thinking to ask you to come away with me? I'm sorry."

"Don't apologize," Renee said. "I haven't given you an answer yet."

"You would go?"

"Alex, being with you in the Virgin Islands sounds wonderful."

"You really mean that?"

She nodded. "I know we haven't known each other all that long, but there's something happening between us."

"You feel it, too, huh?"

"I just want to make sure you're okay with this attraction, Alex. I know you have this guilt thing going."

"I'm working on that," he said. "Asking you to come away with me seemed like a pretty big step in the right direction. So, will you consider it?" he asked.

"When do you need my answer?"

"I've already bought Jazz and my plane tickets. As long as I have time to add you to our flight . . ." He trailed off.

"I'll let you know soon. I just need to think this over a bit," she finished, although her mind was already heady at the thought of being with Alex in a lush, tropical setting.

"That's fair," he said. "I don't want you to feel pressured, but I really want you there, Renee."

"Thank you," she said, wiping a spot of chili sauce from the side of his mouth, and placing a light peck in its place. "Look." She turned her attention to the diamond. "Jasmine's up to bat."

"I shouldn't be nervous," Alex said, rubbing his left hand on his thigh.

"Are you kidding me? I'm nervous and she's not even my child."

The pitcher threw the ball. Jasmine swung at it about three seconds after the ball had already crossed the plate.

"Strike one," the umpire called.

Jasmine turned their way and hunched her shoulders.

"That's okay," Alex called. "You'll get the next one."

Jasmine grinned, then turned back to the pitcher. She pulled her helmet down, wiggled her hips, and swung at the next pitch. A soft *thwack* sounded, and the ball went puttering along the ground. Jasmine took off running. Three members of the opposing team went after the ball, all of them missing it.

Jasmine's little legs flew around the diamond. When she slid into home plate, Alex took off. He pummeled down the bleachers and ran out to home base, snatching Jasmine up in one arm and twirling her around.

Renee felt the tears forming, but could do nothing to stop them from trailing down her cheek. The open display of love and true affection was priceless, and so unlike anything she'd ever experienced from her own father as a child.

The coaches were finally able to tear Alex from his daughter. He gave her one final kiss on the cheek and headed back to the bleachers.

"Sorry," Alex said to the crowd after holding up the game for three minutes. "I let my excitement get the best of me."

Renee laughed, wishing she could throw her arms around him, but she wasn't sure how much of their relationship he had discussed with Jasmine, and she didn't want to cause him to rush that significant conversation. It was up to him to decide when the time was right to tell his daughter that he was ready to start seeing a woman after her mother's death. Renee wondered if she should offer to be there whenever he did decide to talk to Jasmine.

"That was awesome, wasn't it?" he asked.

"It was pretty amazing," Renee answered.

The next three innings went by with no hits; then in the bottom of the seventh, two hitters on the opposing team scored, and the game ended two to one.

The teams walked in straight lines, shaking hands in the

middle of the diamond. When they were done, the two coaches gathered their players in their respective dugouts for a postgame pep talk.

Renee stood to the side with Alex, waiting for Jasmine to come out. She didn't notice the woman who sidled up next to them until she spoke.

"Hello, Alex," she said.

"Leslie. Hello," Alex said. He turned to Renee. "Renee, this is Leslie. Her daughter and Jasmine are best friends."

The woman looked Renee up and down and turned to Alex without acknowledging Renee. "Exciting game," she said; then her voice turned sultry. "I would love to see you swing your bat one of these days."

Alex's eyes widened. "Okay, then," he sputtered. "The girls are done. We need to get going." He grabbed Renee's arm and practically dragged her toward the dugout where Jasmine's team had just begun to disperse.

"She was about as subtle as a tornado," Renee said.

"She's a pariah," Alex snorted. "A recent divorcee," he explained.

"And she has her sights set on you."

"That was evident even before she got divorced. Now it's as if she's got the green light to go for it." Alex turned to her. "That will probably happen a lot," he warned. "And not just with Leslie."

"Are you trying to tell me women come on to you on a regular basis?"

"Sometimes," he said.

"It's a good thing I'm not a jealous person."

"You shouldn't be. I've always been a one-woman man, Renee, even when some would argue I had the right to stray."

She placed a hand on his chest. "I'm not worried."

"Daddy." Jasmine came running over to them. "Can I get a frozen lemonade with Kayla?"

Alex fished a five out of his pocket. "Do you want one?" he asked Renee.

She declined with a shake of her head. When they were once again alone, Renee asked, "So how have you been able to fight the women off?"

Alex shrugged. "It's easy when you're not interested. That doesn't seem to stop them, though."

"And apparently, neither does having a woman on your arm."

"Hopefully, that will curb it for most women, but I knew having you standing right next to me would mean nothing to Leslie."

Renee knew one thing, that Leslie chick had better keep her hands off. She'd finally gotten Alex to open up and acknowledge that he felt something for her. She was not letting some horny divorcee mess with her good thing.

Jasmine ran up to them, another little girl with pigtails trailing behind.

"Ms. Moore, did you see me hit the ball?"

"I did. You were both spectacular," Renee said.

"And fast, too. I told you I was fast."

"I almost hit the ball," the other little girl said.

"Yes, you did. If you two practice, you're going to start hitting the ball more and more. That's how I got better when I played softball."

"Can you practice with us?" Jasmine asked, her eyes bright as Fourth of July sparklers.

"I, uh, sure," Renee answered, looking to Alex.

"We can practice at my house, in the backyard, huh, Daddy?" She turned to Alex.

"I'm sure Ms. Moore is busy, Pumpkin."

"Not too busy," Renee said. Seeing the girls play today had brought back some of the few happy memories she had from childhood when she'd belonged to a biddy baseball team. It would be fun to help the girls learn the game. Not to mention the opportunity she would have to get closer to Alex.

"Kayla, I thought I told you to meet me at the car," that Leslie woman said as she stalked up to them.

"Mom, guess what? Mr. Holmes's girlfriend is going to help us practice hitting balls."

"Ms. Moore's not Daddy's girlfriend," Jasmine said. "Are you, Ms. Moore?"

Alex looked to Renee. She looked right back at him. Leslie stared at them both, her arms crossed over her surgically altered breasts, a catty smile tipping up the corners of her mouth.

"Yes," Alex answered. If Jasmine's inquiry had not already rendered Renee speechless, Alex's answer would have. "Ms. Moore is my girlfriend," he continued. "Kayla, Jasmine will call you later to let you know when Ms. Moore will be by the house to help you practice."

The look in Leslie's eyes could stop a freight train. "Come on, Kayla," she bit out.

"Bye, Jasmine," Kayla said as her mother dragged her toward a blue SUV.

When Renee looked down at Jasmine, the little girl was staring at her with excitement and awe dancing in her eyes. "Are you and Daddy getting married?" Jasmine asked.

"No—"

"No!"

"But you're Daddy's girlfriend," Jasmine stated, as if she was trying to get things clear in her mind.

"Uh, yes," Renee answered. Maybe Alex should have waited until he had the chance to discuss things with Jasmine before just blurting out their new relationship status. Renee could have used a heads-up herself.

"Why don't we go for ice cream to celebrate the game?" Renee suggested.

"But we lost," Jasmine said.

"But you scored a run," Renee reasoned. "That's cause for celebration. And while we're there, your dad and I can talk over a few things with you. How does that sound?"

Jasmine shrugged. "Okay. I can get two scoops?"

Renee looked to Alex.

"Sure," he said, his expression confounded.

"Good, then let's get out of here. We'll all get two scoops and have a nice, long talk," Renee said.

"So Ms. Moore is your girlfriend, but you don't want to tell anybody?" Jasmine licked along the side of the cone, catching the rivulet of chocolate cookie dough ice cream that had escaped.

"It's not that we don't want anyone to know," Alex said. "I just want to make sure you're okay with Ms. Moore and me being more than friends."

"Your dad wants to make sure you know that I'm not trying to take your mother's place or anything," Renee added.

"My mommy is dead," she said slowly, as if she were explaining this to a set of six-year-olds, instead of the other way around.

"So you're okay with Daddy and Ms. Moore seeing each other?" Alex asked again.

"Yes," Jasmine answered. "I told you that already."

Well, that was easy enough. After their conversation last night, he had not expected kicking and screaming, but he was still surprised at Jasmine's acceptance of the situation. Maybe it was simpler in a six-year-old's black-and-white way of looking at the world. Maybe he should take a hint from his daughter.

"Is Ms. Moore coming to Uncle Eli and Auntie Monica's wedding?" Jasmine asked.

"Maybe you should ask Ms. Moore that," Alex said, looking pointedly at Renee.

"I'm not sure, but I'm thinking about it," Renee answered, spearing Alex a look that told him she knew exactly what he was doing.

Alex decided to press harder. "We have to convince her," he said.

"Daddy will pay for everything," Jasmine offered as incentive. "Right, Daddy?"

"Of course I will."

"See?" Jasmine said, as if that should settle it.

"I'm thinking about it," Renee said again. "Give me a few days to think some things over."

Alex leaned over to whisper loudly in Jasmine's ear, "I think she's going to say yes."

"Me, too," Jazz returned in that same loud whisper.

Renee looked at them both and burst out laughing. "I have to be careful around you two. I've got the feeling you're trying to tag-team me."

"You've got that right," Alex said.

Margo wet the tips of her fingers with the muddy water and brought them back to the base of the rapidly spinning lump of clay. She pulled in a breath, letting the now familiar mixture of wet and baking clay smells soak into her lungs. The pottery wheel moved at lightning speed, the makings of a bowl or vase or pitcher forming before her eyes. She still wasn't sure where she wanted to go with this piece. It was the story of her life these days, not knowing which direction she should take.

"I'm worried about Alex," Margo said. "He's been volunteering at Jasmine's school for weeks, but we haven't really discussed how things have been going."

"Maybe he wants to handle things on his own, without your input," Gerald answered.

"What's that supposed to mean?" She tried to keep the defensiveness out of her voice.

"Just what I said, maybe your son wants to handle his own business without your input."

Margo opened her mouth, then shut it, not all that certain she could control what would come out if she chose to speak.

"Say it," Gerald encouraged with an indulgent sigh.

"I have nothing to say," she answered, focusing on her pottery wheel.

The hourglass-shaped vase on his wheel was nearly complete. He'd never veered from his course. Using the sketch he'd drawn at the beginning of the class, Gerald had efficiently and methodically created a thing of beauty from the fat lump of clay the teacher had plopped on the base of the pottery wheel.

"Fine, I'll say it," Gerald continued. "It's none of my business."

"That is not what I was going to say, for your information."

"Yes, it is," he laughed.

"You think you know me so well."

He nodded. "I might not know everything, but I think I've gotten to know you pretty well over the past year."

"We've only been seeing each other a little over seven months," Margo argued.

"But it's been a year since we met," Gerald reminded her.

"Goodness, you're right," Margo answered. "It was Halloween."

"I was trick-or-treating with my granddaughter, and you let her use your bathroom."

"And the poor thing nearly peed on the floor, trying to wrestle out of that Tinkerbell costume."

His head flew back and his rich laugh turned the heads of some of the other students in the pottery class. He had a wonderful laugh, deep and full of humor. And sexy.

Margo looked on with wonderment as his strong fingers gently worked the wet clay. His touch was so light, so tender, coaxing the clay into shape.

"You never finished telling me about your surprise party," he said.

"It was just as Monica and I had planned, we were even able to get the second line brass band I wanted."

"Did your boys buy your surprised look?"

"Oh yeah. They have no idea I helped to plan the entire thing," she laughed.

"I wish I could have been there," he said.

Margo sobered. Gerald's absence was the only disappointment with her surprise party, and it had affected her enjoyment of the event more than she thought it would. She'd spent most of the party thinking about how she couldn't wait to tell Gerald about it. She shouldn't have had to go back and tell him. He should have been there by her side, sharing in the celebration.

"How are your grandbabies doing?" she asked, turning her attention back to her wheel, and away from the guilt that continued to mount within her.

"They're doing fine. A'naire is being honored at a banquet next month because of some state test. Her scores were the highest in the county."

"That's wonderful, Gerald. You should be proud of how they've adjusted to living out there." Gerald's oldest daughter, Layla, and her husband had moved their children to Atlanta after Hurricane Katrina. Margo knew it was hard for him to be so far away; he'd adjusted pretty well, too.

"I am, but I'd rather have them here," Gerald replied. "How would you feel if Alex moved Jasmine to Georgia?"

Anxiety tightened Margo's chest just at the thought of her grandbaby living four states away. "I get your point," she said.

"Financially, they're better off," he reasoned. "Still, it's hard not having family around all the time."

"You've got me," Margo said. "And, eventually, you'll have my family."

"Will I?" he asked.

"Yes," Margo said. "I've put off telling my family about us for far too long. I want to tell them after Eli's wedding."

Gerald reached across his wheel and covered her mud-splattered fingers with his equally dirty hand.

"Thank you for being so patient with me," Margo continued. "Most men wouldn't put up with me the way you have."

"I know a good thing when I see one," Gerald answered. "You're worth it."

Margo's heart melted right then and there. She was dangerously close to falling in love with this man. As smothering as the guilt had been when she'd first starting seeing him, Margo could no longer deny the multitude of sensations that rumbled through her bloodstream every time she was around him. Not just when she was around him, but all the time. Whenever she thought about Gerald, which was nearly every minute of the day, her entire being sang. She'd felt this way only one other time in her life. Years ago, with Wesley.

Wes, please don't be angry with me, Margo silently pleaded with her husband. In a lot of ways he was still her best friend, the one she turned to when she needed to talk to someone. His spirit was always there.

Margo wasn't surprised at the sense of peace that washed over her. Wesley wanted her happy. And that's how Gerald made her feel. Happy.

The instructor walked up to their station. "You've got great technique," she said. She had to have been talking to Gerald because the misshapen mound of wet clay sitting on Margo's wheel required no technique at all.

"Thank you." Gerald accepted the teacher's praise with his usual grace. She was probably a couple of years younger than Margo, with a long braid of graying hair that hung down the middle of her back. If she were not already so sure about the depth of Gerald's feelings, Margo would have been jealous of the looks the teacher continued to throw his way.

It happened often when they were out. It was expected. Gerald was phenomenally handsome. His tailored suits and ridiculously expensive car only added to his appeal for most women. Those things didn't mean much to Margo. It was the way he made her feel that continued to draw her in. He made her feel wanted again. With Gerald she was more than just a mother, or a grandmother. She was a woman.

She was a *woman*. She had a right to share her life with a man who loved her. Nothing else mattered—not whether her boys were ready to face the thought of her dating again or the way the women at the church would view her if she introduced them to her new boyfriend. The only thing that mattered was that Gerald loved her, and she loved him.

"I'm not sure how I'll survive an entire week without seeing you," she said once the teacher had floated over to another set of students.

"Tell me about it," Gerald answered. "You'd better make sure you pack the battery charger for your cell phone, because I'm going to call you like crazy."

"Do you know how much international calls cost?" Margo said.

"I don't care. I'm calling you every single day, and I don't want to hear another word about it."

She smiled at him across the wheel. "I wish you could come to Eli and Monica's wedding," she said. "I really do."

"You're just saying that because you know I can't go," he laughed.

"That's not true."

"Don't tease me. Remember, I'm the boss. I can say to hell with the case I'm working on and hand it off to one of the associates."

"You wouldn't do that," Margo reasoned.

"Don't be so sure," he said. "It's going to be hell knowing you're so far away."

She felt the same way. The realization hit Margo right in the center of her chest. She craved this man. It had become harder and harder to hide their relationship because Margo found herself wanting to be with him more and more.

"It's only five days," Margo said. "We're flying down there on a Friday evening. I'll be back home by that next Wednesday morning."

The teacher came back, carrying a flat spatula. "I think

this one is ready for the kiln," she said. She slipped the spatula under the vase and lifted it, carrying Gerald's creation to the small open oven that would fire it solid.

"It's still a long time for you to be away," Gerald said. "That good-bye kiss will have to be something else if it's going to carry me for five days."

Margo laughed at her good fortune. There were so many women who would be more than willing to hand their bodies over to him. Younger women. More beautiful women. Women who wouldn't have a problem introducing him to their families.

"Why do you put up with me?" Margo decided to ask.

"What kind of question is that?"

"A legitimate one," she answered. "You have to admit I haven't been the ideal . . . companion," she said. Look, she still had a problem thinking of herself as his girlfriend. "I refuse to tell my children about you, and the furthest you've gotten with me is kissing. There are dozens of women who would give you so much more. Several in this room," Margo said, thinking about the teacher.

"Are you trying to tell me that I should look for another woman?"

"Of course not," she said with more force than she'd anticipated. The thought of him with another woman made her crazy. "I just want to know why, Gerald. Why do you put up with me?"

He leaned over the wheel. With his mouth mere inches from hers, he whispered, "I put up with you because I'm in love with you, Margo Holmes."

Her breath caught in her throat, just as it had the first time he'd said those words to her.

"I love hearing you say that," she said. "Although I still find it hard to believe."

"I wouldn't lie about the way I feel about you, Margo. It's not something I take lightly, and I know you don't, either."

"I haven't loved another man since my husband died," she admitted.

"And you don't have to love me yet, either, but I'm determined to make you love me, Margo."

She stared at his face, so handsome, so understanding.

"I think I already do," she whispered.

Chapter Fourteen

"Do you think I'm a tramp?"

"What kind of question is that?" Aunt Lorna's surprised laugh made Renee feel marginally better.

"Well, I just told you I'm contemplating going away with a man I've only known a few weeks, when I've been going out with another man for several months now."

"First of all, I think you're forgetting just who you're talking to, little girl. *I'm* the family tramp, and you'd do best to remember that," Aunt Lorna said with a wink. "Secondly, you were not serious about that Rashad boy."

"I think he'd take exception to you calling him a boy." Renee set the basket of folded laundry on the kitchen table.

"I couldn't care less about what he'd take exception to," Lorna answered. "The two of you dated for several months, yet never once did he bother to even walk you to the door."

"Because it wasn't necessary," Renee said.

"Of course it was necessary. If he really wanted to impress you, he would have gotten out of his car and walked you to the door every time he dropped you off. But it doesn't matter." Lorna waved the subject of Rashad away. "You didn't really like him, you only tolerated him."

"I did like Rashad," Renee answered. "As a friend."

"You feel a lot more than just friendship for Alex," Lorna said, in a voice that dared Renee to contradict her. Her aunt always thought she knew so much, but she was right this time.

"Yes, I do," Renee admitted. "He's such a good man, Lorna. I never knew men like Alex existed."

"Not to mention his nice butt," Lorna said. Renee burst out laughing. "Oh, come on now. You know you've checked out his butt." Her aunt smiled.

"On occasion," Renee answered, handing Lorna a set of dish towels that her aunt slipped into the small kitchen's only drawer. "Regardless of his nice . . . posterior, I'm still not sure I know him well enough to fly away with him to the Virgin Islands. What if I'm wrong about Alex?" Renee asked.

"You're a better judge of character than that," Aunt Lorna said with a dismissive wave.

"Remember who you're talking to. For the longest time, I thought any man who didn't bash me in the head was a prince. Didn't matter that he treated me like crap."

Lorna leaned a hip against the kitchen counter and folded her arms over her chest. "So you haven't had the best judgment when it comes to men. Don't let a few mistakes dictate the rest of your love life, Renee. And you can't allow what your father did to control you, either."

Renee shook her head. "It took me a long time to get over everything I went through with that man," she said, refusing to call him a father, not after seeing how a *real* father like Alex treated his daughter.

"I wonder if you're really over it," Lorna said.

"I am," Renee asserted. "It took a few years and thousands of dollars in counseling, but I'm finally in a place where I can let it go. I refuse to be like your sister. I'd rather be strong, like you," she said, giving her aunt's shoulders a squeeze.

"Of the two of us, who would have ever thought *I* would be the one you would look up to?"

"Well, I do. So, help me make a decision about this trip."

"I don't see what the big deal is." Aunt Lorna shrugged. "You like him, and you're having fun. There's no reason you shouldn't go."

Her aunt was right. She did like Alex, and she could hardly put into words the fun she had when she was with him. When she'd called to get Penelope's input, her friend had used the same line of reasoning. But something in the back of Renee's mind told her to watch herself. It was starting to feel like more than just a strong liking where Alex was concerned. That could be a dangerous thing.

But could a few days in paradise hurt?

"Mama's sixtieth birthday party was off the chain," Toby said as he motored the golf cart past a bunker on their way up the course.

"We did good," Eli agreed. "Remind me to e-mail ya'll the pictures I took Saturday night. I caught a great one of her when she came through the door. Mama didn't have a clue."

"She had a good time, though. Everybody did, even you," Toby added, looking over at Alex.

Eli felt the need to add his two cents. "He still didn't dance."

"Bad shoulder, here." Alex motioned to his arm.

"How's that shoulder doing?" Toby asked.

"It's healing," Alex answered.

"You're making better progress than I thought you would," Eli added from the backseat of the golf cart. Even though he still couldn't participate in the game, Alex had chosen to join his brothers on the golf course. Their golfing expeditions were rarely about the game, anyway. They were more of a way to catch up with what was going on in each other's lives.

"You ready for the big day?" Toby asked Eli as he parked the golf cart.

"Oh yeah. Wait until you see the place we rented. It's the bomb."

"I can't wait to get out there," Toby said. "I'm going to convince Sienna to recreate the scene from that movie with those two people getting busy in the sand."

"*From Here to Eternity*," Alex supplied. His brothers both looked at him as if he were crazy. "What? It was on television the other night."

Eli shook his head. "You scare me sometimes, Alex. You really, really scare me."

Pulling a four iron out of his golf bag, his brother took a couple of practice swings before sending the golf ball down the fairway.

"Nice shot," Toby said.

"I've been practicing. So, you and Sienna are flying down to St. Martin on Saturday morning, right?"

"Yeah. Keep your fingers crossed that nothing happens with Aria's flight. She's not scheduled to get in until a couple of hours before the wedding."

"It'll only be family there. We can delay the wedding if we have to wait for her."

This would have been a good time to let his brothers know there would be one more person joining them at the wedding, but Alex decided against it. He'd made the decision that he would just have Renee show up at the airport and explain her presence then.

God, he hoped he was doing the right thing. Knowing his family, they would probably embarrass the hell out of him.

Toby took his shot and they climbed in the cart to make their way to the seventh hole.

"Hey, Alex, what exactly did Mama tell you the other day when you asked her about her boyfriend?"

"Her *what*?" Toby turned, jerking the wheel and nearly causing the golf cart to tip over.

"Watch it!" Alex and Eli yelled.

Toby righted the wheel. "What's he talking about?"

"Eli thought Mama had a boyfriend," Alex explained. "But she said she doesn't."

"Monica told me she did," Eli said. "That would explain why she's been acting so strange."

"You calling Mama a liar?" Toby asked.

"No, but why would Monica lie?"

Alex had asked himself that question more than once. It seemed that between the two of them, either Monica or his mother was not being completely truthful. The question was, who would gain the most by lying?

"I think Mama's the one who's lying," Alex said.

"What are we going to do about it?" Toby asked.

"Should we do anything?" Alex was as surprised to hear the words come out of his mouth as his brothers were. Hadn't he just argued this same point with Renee? But Renee had made some valid points, too. What was so wrong with his mother finding someone to make her happy?

"Hell yeah, we need to do something about it," Eli said.

"E's right," Toby agreed.

"Why?" Alex asked them. Neither said anything, so Alex continued. "Have either of you thought about how lonely Mama must be in the house by herself?"

"She's not lonely. She's got her church group," Eli said.

"On Sunday and Thursday nights? Come on, E. Mama is still relatively young. I don't want her to live the rest of her life alone. Maybe it's not a bad idea if she had another man in her life."

"Did you fall and hit your head or something?" Toby asked. "This is Mama we're talking about."

"I know that, but think about it, Toby. She just turned sixty, and she looks good for her age. I'm sure a lot of men Mama's age find her attractive. Let's just hope she's found one who's treating her right."

"I don't like this, Alex. What if they've . . . you know?" Toby shivered.

"I don't even want to think about it," Eli said. "I've convinced myself that Mama only had sex three times in her life."

"Don't say 'Mama' and 'sex' in the same sentence," Toby said.

"You two are acting like children," Alex said.

"Are you telling me you would be okay with her seeing some man?" Toby asked.

"If he made her happy, and treated her right?" Alex shrugged. "Yeah, I think I'd be okay with it."

"Well, I don't like it," Toby huffed, pulling the golf cart up to the edge of the rough.

"That doesn't matter," Alex said. "It's up to Mama. And if she is seeing someone, I think we should support her. Now, can you two get back to the game? You know it's the only time either of you will ever get to say you beat me."

Alex's crack of laughter at the foul language both his brothers shot his way traveled down the fairway.

Alex had decided he and Mama would have a heart-to-heart when he picked up Jasmine, but discovered Mama wasn't home when he arrived at the house. Ebony Collins, the teenage granddaughter of one of his mother's church group members and Jasmine's occasional babysitter, was curled up on the sofa with a sleeping Jasmine snuggled up next to her.

"Hi, Mr. Holmes," Ebony greeted him in a hushed whisper.

"Hey there, Ebony. I didn't realize you would be watching Jasmine."

"Mrs. Margo called me a couple of hours ago and asked if I could come over." She gently extricated herself from Jasmine, laying his baby on the sofa.

Alex took his wallet from his back pocket and fished out a twenty. Ebony waved him off. "Mrs. Margo already paid me," she said.

Alex stuffed the money in her hand. "That's for being honest, and for watching Jasmine on short notice." She shrugged and pocketed the money. Smart girl. "Did Mrs. Holmes say where she was going?"

Ebony shook her head. "She said she'd be back in a couple of hours, but I've been here going on three hours now.
She must have been held up."

"Thanks for coming." Alex walked her to the door. He
pushed the curtain aside and watched while Ebony made
her way to her house down the street. He took out his cell
phone and called Mama's number. She didn't answer.

"Mama, what are you up to?" he whispered into the phone
before shutting it and shoving the cell back into his pocket.

He walked over to the sofa and tried to lift Jasmine, but
he wasn't far enough into his recovery to pull it off. Pain
shot to his shoulder.

"Pumpkin." Alex shook her arm. Jasmine stirred, then
turned over and buried her face into the sofa cushions. Alex
shook her again. "Come on, Jazzy Bean. It's time to head
home."

Jasmine rolled onto her back and stretched her arms up,
yawning. Alex stooped low and tickled her under her arm.

"Stop, Daddy." She squirmed and giggled.

"Maybe I'll stop," he said. "But only if you get up."

Jasmine pushed herself up and into a sitting position. She
kicked out her feet. "Daddy, Ebony painted my toenails.
You like 'em?"

"They're beautiful, just like my Pumpkin Face," Alex said.
"Put on your socks and tennis shoes so we can go home."

"My tennis shoes might mess up my toenails," she complained.

He wasn't up to arguing with a vain six-year-old. Alex
knew which battles to fight, and which to concede. "Go
check in the hall closet; I think you left a pair of sandals here."

Jasmine scooted off the sofa and headed for the closet.
Alex tried calling Mama again, but his call went unanswered.
He left a message asking her to give him a call, then left a
note on the kitchen table just in case Mama still had not
learned how to check her cell phone's voice mail.

Fifteen minutes later, when he pulled into his driveway, Alex's breath caught in his throat at the sight of Renee's car parked in the spot next to where he parked his truck. She was leaning against the driver's-side door, a plastic grocery bag in her hand.

"Daddy, it's Ms. Moore," Jasmine yelled. She was out of the car in a shot.

Alex moved a bit more slowly, using the time to get his body's reaction to seeing Renee under control. She was smiling when he rounded his truck, and his effort to maintain a sense of calm became even more difficult.

"Hi there," she said.

"Hi to you, too," Alex answered. He motioned to the bag. "What's that?"

"Popcorn and Mike and Ike's," she answered. "Movie-watching food. I was hoping I could talk you into checking one out with me," she said.

"Yay!" Jasmine jumped up and down, clapping her hands.

Okay, so he hadn't expected his first date with Renee to include his daughter, but then again, who said this was a date? Alex stared at Renee, and concluded that this was definitely a date. She kept her gaze innocent enough to fly under the radar of a six-year-old, but Alex spotted the hint of desire in her eyes.

"That sounds like a plan," he said.

Alex prepared Jasmine's bath while she and Renee made miniature peanut butter and jelly sandwiches to go along with the other movie-watching food. Jasmine proceeded to take the fastest bath known to mankind while the popcorn popped. Soon, they were all seated on the sofa watching one of Jasmine's favorites, *Lady and the Tramp*, on the fifty-two-inch plasma. Both of the movies Renee rented from the video store had a PG-13 rating, which Alex refused to allow Jasmine to watch.

"I haven't seen this movie in forever," Renee said, holding

a throw pillow to her chest and releasing a contented whimper as the credits rolled.

"I saw it three times last week," Alex said. "Jasmine goes through Disney movie phases."

"Yep." Jasmine nodded. "We can watch *Mulan* next."

"You can watch your dreams next," Alex corrected her. "It's nine o'clock, time for you to head to bed."

"But I thought it was movie night." Jasmine pouted.

"One movie a night is your limit," Alex said. He nudged her. "Scoot."

Jasmine huffed, but that was the extent of her resistance, probably because she couldn't argue through all that yawning. She put her arms up for a hug. Alex wrapped his arm around her and planted a loud, sloppy kiss on her neck.

"Yuck, Daddy," she laughed; then she turned to Renee, her arms outstretched.

Renee's eyes widened as she encased Jasmine in a hug. She looked at Alex over Jasmine's head, a mixture of confusion and relief in her eyes. Alex could not think of a way to accurately describe the sensations that rushed through his blood as he watched Renee and Jasmine together. He had never allowed himself to picture another woman here, helping him raise his daughter. But he could see Renee as Jasmine's stepmother all too clearly.

"Good night, Ms. Moore," Jasmine said. "I'm happy you're coming to Uncle Eli's wedding."

"So am I," Renee answered. "Good night."

"I'll be right back," Alex said, taking Jasmine by the hand.

"I'll be right here," Renee answered.

That sounded really good to him.

Renee settled back on the sofa, taking in her surroundings. She'd been to Alex's house a few times over the past month and a half, but other than the first time when she'd come to see Jasmine's closet, it had only been for a few minutes at a time. The spacious living room was tastefully decorated, just like the rest of the house.

A picture of his wife cradling Jasmine as an infant sat on one of the end tables that flanked the butter-soft leather couch. Renee lifted it and stared at the breathtakingly beautiful woman. She could see how Alex would fall for her.

"You were so stupid to mess up what you had with this man. But thanks," Renee quipped as she placed the framed photo back on the table.

"You weren't lying," Alex said as he reentered the living room.

"Meaning?"

"You're still here." He smiled.

"Told you I would be," Renee said. "Are you up for watching another movie, or are you ready to get to bed as well?"

He stared at her, the wanting in his eyes unmistakable, but there was also a hint of regret. Before he could voice his concern, Renee stopped him.

"Alex, I meant you in your bed down the hall, and me in my cramped little bed in the trailer."

"I want more than that," Alex said. "Just not yet. Not with Jasmine in the next room."

"I understand," she reassured him. "You need time to adjust to the idea almost as much as she does."

"It will happen," he promised, taking her by the hand and pulling her up from the sofa. He pressed a firm kiss to her closed lips, urging them to open.

Renee shook her head and pulled away. "Let's not start that," she said. "We both know what happens between us when there's a sofa near."

"And dusty cardboard boxes," Alex added.

She burst out laughing, but had to agree. "So, another movie? Something with higher than a G-rating? We don't have to watch the ones I brought if you've got something else you feel like watching."

Alex walked over to the wall and pressed the wainscoting. A door popped opened, revealing several shelves lined with DVDs.

Renee gasped. "Look at that, you genius carpenter you."

"I try." Alex grinned. "I'm pretty proud of this one. You have to look really close to see where the break is." He pulled out a DVD case. "Along the lines of *Mulan*, I thought we could stay with the Asian flavor."

"You actually have *Memoirs of a Geisha* on DVD?"

"If you tell my brothers, I'll deny it," Alex said. He slipped in the movie and Renee followed him down on the sofa, snuggling her back onto his broad chest.

"It's too bad they weren't offering an Asian history course in my program," Alex said. "I would have aced it. I love Eastern culture."

"You ever been?" Renee asked, mesmerized by the graceful fan dance the actress performed on the screen.

"No." Alex absently stroked her arm. "I'd love to go one day."

"So would I," she said.

Renee could not hold back the image of trekking along the Great Wall of China with Alex by her side. As her husband.

It scared her, just how much she longed for that. When had she started thinking of this man she'd known for less than two months as husband material? When had she started considering *anyone* as husband material? She had never completely denounced the idea of marriage, but after she'd witnessed the atrocity that was her parents' marriage, it was not high on her list of priorities, either. She was happy right here, single and free to make her own choices.

At least Renee thought she was happy. Until Alex. Being with him had given her a glimpse of what life could be like with someone who knew how to make a woman happy.

"Speaking of school," Alex said, knocking her out of her

blissful daze, "I received some pretty high marks on that paper."

"Really?" Renee turned to look up at him. "Congratulations."

"It would have been impossible without your help," Alex said.

"I wouldn't say that," Renee lied.

"Who are you trying to kid?" he said. "I know that paper was awful; I'm just happy it's behind me. I have just the final to get through before I'm done with that class, and one more semester before I get my degree."

The pride Renee heard in his voice nearly brought tears to her eyes. He didn't need that degree he was working so hard to obtain. He owned a successful business, and probably made more money than 80 percent of Americans who graduated from college, but he'd set it in his head that he would finish the degree he'd given up on.

"You're such an inspiration," Renee said, pressing a kiss to his chest. She heard his swift intake of breath, and felt his chest give. "Oh, sorry. I forgot we weren't going there."

"God," Alex breathed, letting his head fall back on the sofa. "I can't wait until we do."

Chapter Fifteen

As he stared at the people trudging through the airport's security checkpoint, Alex questioned his wisdom in keeping Renee's presence on this trip a secret from the rest of his family. He'd nearly confessed several times over the past few weeks, but could never scrounge up the courage to come clean.

It had been a long time since he'd felt this nervous. Alex

shifted from one foot to the other, the constant opening and closing of the automatic doors adding to his agitation. Of course, he could move away from the doors and solve at least one of his problems, but his head was filled with too many visions of this entire situation going horribly wrong to have something as simple as common sense creep in.

"Daddy, I'm going with Grandma," he heard Jasmine call from where she waited at the airline's check-in counter with his mother.

"Alex, are you coming to the gate?" Mama asked.

"I'll be there in a minute," he said.

"We board in twenty minutes," she reminded him.

The fact that they boarded in twenty minutes was causing an ulcer to form in Alex's stomach. He'd tried calling Renee three times, with no luck. He didn't want to believe it, but Alex was coming to the realization that he was being stood up.

Had he moved too fast? It had been a bold move, asking a woman he'd only known a couple of months to come away with him and his family, but it had not felt too fast at the time. It had felt right. Perfect, even.

"You don't have to wait for them," Mama said. "It's better if we get to the gate now."

"Daddy's not waiting for Uncle Eli," Jasmine said.

Alex shot Jasmine a stern look and shook his head.

"Ooh, sorry, Daddy," she said.

"What's going on?" Mama asked. "Jasmine," she said when they both remained quiet.

"Nothing," Jasmine answered.

"What has Grandma told you about lying?" his mother warned.

"Daddy said it's all right to lie," Jasmine said.

"You told her what?" his mother shot at him.

"Good morning." The sound of the voice behind him could not have been sweeter to Alex's ears. "Sorry I'm late," Renee said.

"Hey, Ms. Moore." Jasmine let go of his mother's hand and wrapped her arms around Renee's waist in a quick but strong hug.

"Hi, Jasmine. Hello, Alex." She turned to his mother. "Hi, you must be Mrs. Holmes." Renee stuck out her hand.

A blanket of confusion shrouded Mama's face. "I am," she answered.

"Mama, this is Renee Moore," Alex said. "You should probably check in," he said to Renee.

"I printed my boarding pass from home," Renee said. "And I checked my bags curbside."

"We're here." Eli came charging through the automatic doors with Monica right behind him. "Why are ya'll standing here? The plane will be boarding in another fifteen minutes," he said. He stopped short when he saw Renee.

Everyone stood in a circle, staring at each other as if they were all on display at a museum.

"I decided to bring a guest," Alex said. "That's okay, isn't it?"

They all agreed at the same time.

"Come on." Alex took the small leather bag from Renee's hand and pulled the strap over his good shoulder. "Let's get to the gate."

"You didn't tell them I was coming?" Renee whispered as they trailed behind the rest of his family.

"They know now," Alex said.

When they arrived at their gate, the plane had already begun boarding. Knowing his mother hated sitting at the back of the plane, Alex had purposely chosen two seats in the rear for him and Renee. Ushering Renee quickly past his mother's row, he deposited Jasmine in the seat next to Mama.

"Alex." His mother grabbed his hand.

"Jasmine will fill you in," he said.

"Alexander Wesley Holmes," his mother hissed.

He decided to give her the quick version. "She's a teacher

at Jasmine's school. I've been helping to fix up her house, and the two of us have been seeing each other."

"But . . . when?" She looked so confused, Alex felt sorry for her.

"Wait until we get to the islands," he said.

Alex knew she'd have a lot of questions once they landed. He'd spent the past few days trying to figure out how he should answer them. It all depended on how he and Renee decided to address their relationship. They had a couple of hours to figure that out.

"I can't believe you," Renee said when he sat down next to her.

"It's easier this way," he said.

"For who?"

"Definitely for me," he said. "This will probably be the most agonizing plane ride my mother has ever had. I give it about five minutes after we take off for her to make her way back here."

"The flight attendants won't allow her to walk until we're at our flying altitude."

Alex settled back in his seat and buckled his seat belt. "You don't know my mother."

"What are you going to tell her about me?" Renee asked.

"What do you want me to tell her?"

"It's up to me?"

"I guess it's up to both of us, but I want you to be comfortable with all of this. What would make you comfortable? Saying you're my girlfriend?"

"I'm okay with that if you are."

He was more than okay with it. Just the thought of claiming her as his girlfriend—his woman—sent a dose of desire shooting through his bloodstream.

"How do you think they will take it?" Renee tipped her chin up toward the front of the airplane.

"They're good people, Renee. A little pushy. A little noisy. Okay, a lot noisy. But they're good people. Just be prepared to have every question under the sun thrown at you."

"Oh, that's comforting."

"Don't worry, I'll be there to run interference. Besides, Jasmine's probably told her everything she knows about you."

To Alex's surprise, the flight attendants were able to keep his mother seated for the first twenty minutes of the flight, but as soon as the light on the seat belt sign went dim, Alex saw her pop up from her seat ten rows ahead of them. She came charging down the aisle like a woman on a mission.

Renee gripped his hand. Alex gave it a reassuring squeeze, relishing the softness of her palm.

"Hi, again," his mother said, reaching over and extending her hand to Renee. "We didn't get much of a chance to talk earlier."

"I know, sorry about that," Renee answered.

"Alex, why don't you join Jasmine for a while?" his mother said.

"Not a chance," he answered. "You've got five days on an island with Renee."

"I just want to chat for a bit," she said.

"It's okay, Alex," Renee said.

Alex shook his head, but rose. "You were warned," he said to Renee.

Mama slapped him on his good arm. "Stop it. You make me sound like a monster."

"You can be a bit scary before breakfast," he said.

Alex found Jasmine watching *Shrek* on the seven-inch portable DVD player Eli had given her for Christmas the year before.

"Grandma took your seat," she said, shaking her head.

"Just for a bit," Alex answered. "What did you tell Grandma about Ms. Moore?" Alex asked, pressing the pause button on the movie.

"I told her that you and Ms. Moore are boyfriend and girlfriend, but that you don't want anybody to know."

"If we agreed that I didn't want anyone to know, why did you tell Grandma?"

She shrugged. "I always tell Grandma stuff. And Grandma's smart. She would have figured it out."

The logic of a six-year-old.

"Grandma said she's happy you have a girlfriend. She said you're too young to be by yourself."

His mother's reaction didn't come as a total shock. She wanted more grandchildren and his seeing Renee was one step closer to achieving that goal. Alex had figured his widowhood had been a free pass to escape his mother's constant badgering and matchmaking, but he knew his reprieve was coming to an end.

"You think I should go and save Ms. Moore from Grandma?"

"Probably," Jasmine said. "Daddy?" She looked up at him, the seat nearly swallowing her.

"Yeah, Pumpkin?"

She motioned for him with her finger, and Alex leaned in closer. Jasmine put her mouth up to his ear. "At Uncle Eli's wedding, please don't dance with Ms. Moore."

"Why?" Alex asked.

"Because if she sees the way you dance, she probably won't like you anymore."

"Thanks a lot, Jazz. You sure know how to make Daddy feel good."

"You're welcome," she said, his sarcasm flying right over her head.

"I'm going back to my seat. I'll see you when we land."

"Daddy? Are you going to marry Ms. Moore?"

The unexpected question gave him pause. Alex's first instinct was to say no. He and Renee had only known each other for a short time, and even though the thought had flitted across his mind for a millisecond, marriage was so far off his radar it wasn't even a blip on the screen. But just because he wasn't about to marry her now didn't mean it wasn't in their future. Who knows where they would be a year from now?

It was also time for him to start being more honest with his daughter. Renee was right, Jasmine was able to handle more than he gave her credit for.

"Maybe after we get to know each other better, and if Ms. Moore wants to get married."

"I think she does," Jasmine said with an all-knowing confidence that brought a smile to Alex's face.

"How are we doing here?" His mother came from the back of the aircraft, the smile on her face a mile wide.

"How *are* we doing here?" Alex threw the question back at her. The fact that he had not heard Renee screaming her head off made him feel marginally better.

"Alex, I love her," Mama said, unable to maintain the cool facade. "She's so sweet. I can't believe you haven't introduced her to the family."

"I told him he should marry Ms. Moore," Jasmine said loud enough for the entire plane to hear now that she'd stuck the DVD player's earbuds in her ears.

"I agree," Eli added from a few rows up.

"I'm going back to my seat," Alex said. When Alex reached his seat, the smile on Renee's face was priceless.

"Sorry about that," Alex said.

"At least I know I've won over the family," she said.

"This isn't an audition," Alex said, realizing how harsh the words sounded as the smile drained from her face. "That came out completely wrong," he said. "I meant that you don't have to prove anything to my family. I hope you don't think that's why I brought you here."

"I hope you brought me here because you wanted my company," Renee said. "But I don't mind getting to know your family, Alex. I want to get to know them better. Do you understand what I'm trying to tell you?"

"I think I do," he said, picking up her hand and placing a kiss on her fingers.

"Alex, it has been a long time since I've felt this way about anyone. If ever." Just like that, she'd put it all out there for him. The ball was in his court. "And since you're looking completely freaked out right now, I'm thinking that was the wrong thing to say," she said.

"No, no. It wasn't."

Damn. He was in uncharted territory.

"Here's the thing, Renee. I'm not even sure what this is I'm feeling. I thought I was in love with my wife, but what I'm starting to feel for you is stronger than what I felt for her even when our marriage was good. I'm not sure I even know what it feels like to truly be in love, but this is as close as I've ever been."

"So, what do we do with this newfound knowledge?"

Alex brought her hand up to his mouth again. "We can see where it takes us."

Renee was able to avoid further interrogation from Alex's family for the remainder of the flight. When they landed at Princess Juliana International Airport on the Dutch side of the island, Alex quickly loaded both Renee and Jasmine into a taxi, leaving Eli and his beautiful fiancée, Monica, to follow them along with their mother. Renee stared in awe as they traveled along the road to the villa Eli had rented on Baie Rouge on the French side of the island.

"Daddy, the water's so blue," Jasmine screeched. "I can't wait to swim."

"You can swim as soon as we settle in. Uncle Eli said the place where we're staying has two swimming pools, and a private beach. But I don't want you going near the water without an adult around, okay, Pumpkin?"

"I promise," she said. "Ms. Moore, do you know how to swim?"

"Yes, I love to swim," Renee answered.

"I have a pink bathing suit with flowers. It's new. I brought my old one with the strawberries, but I don't think I'm gonna wear it."

"I'm sure you're going to look very cute, no matter which bathing suit you wear."

Jasmine nodded. "I'm always cute," she said.

"And extremely humble," Alex chuckled.

"That, too," Jasmine agreed.

Renee couldn't help but laugh. The thought of how easily she could picture both of these people in her life shocked her. She could envision driving Jasmine to school every day, the two of them baking cookies in that enormous, unbelievably beautiful kitchen in Alex's house. She could see herself welcoming Alex home in the evening with a kiss, then treating him to something a lot more intimate once they tucked Jasmine in bed for the night. Not only could she *envision* those things, but she wanted to *experience* them.

Not for the first time since she'd accepted his invitation did Renee wonder if this was a bad idea. Spending time with Alex on this island, known for its intimate coves and romantic, secluded beaches, could only cause her to sink deeper in whatever it was she was starting to feel for him. She knew all too well what could happen when a woman allowed herself to become too emotionally attached to a man. That binding, all-consuming obsession had prevented her own mother from leaving her father, despite everything he'd put her through.

"Renee?"

"Yes," she said, shaking her head of the memories she did not want to stir up while living in paradise.

"We're here," Alex said.

Renee allowed Alex to help her from the taxi. She stared up at the estate before her and nearly stopped breathing.

"Are you kidding me?" Renee said.

"This must be it. I told the driver L'Oasis. He announced

that we were with the Holmes party when we stopped at the gate, and they let us in."

"But this is . . . it's unbelievable."

"That's Eli for you," Alex said. "For what he probably spent to rent this sucker for a week, he could have thrown the big, fancy wedding Mama was hoping he would have back in New Orleans."

"Let's go to the pool," Jasmine said, pulling Alex's hand.

"We need to wait for Uncle Eli," he said. Just as the words left his mouth, another taxi pulled in from the winding road. "Here they are," Alex announced.

The rest of Alex's family alighted from their cab. The two men went for the luggage, but Alex's soon-to-be sister-in-law slapped him on his uninjured arm.

"Don't you dare," she said.

"I was going to use my left hand," Alex argued.

"Get away," she hissed. "You put that down, too, Eli. The cabdriver will bring these in."

"Actually, you have a butler who will bring these in for you," a short, caramel-colored woman with long, braided hair and an island accent said as she came from seemingly out of nowhere. "Welcome to L'Oasis." She spread her hands wide. "Here are your keys. You will have a butler, maid, and the services of our chef from seven a.m. to nine o'clock at night."

"We won't need the chef," Alex's mother piped in.

"Yes, we will," Eli said. "You are not lifting a finger while we're here," he warned her.

She mumbled under her breath, and rolled her eyes at her son. Renee decided she liked Margo Holmes. In a way, she reminded her of her aunt Lorna. From their brief conversation on the plane, Renee could tell Margo had Alex's and her granddaughter's best interests at heart.

"Follow me into the villa, if you please," the hostess encouraged.

Few things literally left her breathless, but Renee acknowledged she would have to add the entryway to L'Oasis to her short list. It was mesmerizing, with a fountain and a high, domed ceiling made of frosted glass.

"Lord, have mercy. Eli, how much did this cost you?" his mother asked.

Renee was dying to know the same thing.

"You'll never know," Eli answered.

"The bedrooms are all ready, with all of your amenities. If you require anything additional, please let me know. Damien, your butler, will put your bags away if you will just let him know which bags belong in which room."

"Monica and I are in the first master bedroom, Mama is in the second. Alex, I had you and Jasmine in another bedroom," Eli continued. "There's one for Toby and Sienna, and another for Nia and Phillip. I figured Aria and Monica's younger sister, Ashley, could share the suite with the twin beds."

"That's where I want to sleep!" Jasmine yelled.

"Well, I guess you can sleep in there, Sunflower," Eli said. "Renee, maybe you can—"

"Renee will be with me," Alex interrupted his brother.

It was as if a giant vacuum had sucked out all the sound in the room. Alex looked across the span of the foyer where she was still standing. "Is that okay with you?" he asked, his voice not nearly as confident as it was just a few seconds ago.

All eyes were on her. Her heart started beating quadruple the normal rate, and Renee was pretty certain she would faint in the next minute. Even though they hadn't discussed it, she had assumed she would be sleeping in the same room with Alex, but now she wondered how it would look to his family—especially his mother, who until mere hours ago had no idea Renee existed.

"Sure. Of course," she answered.

"It's about damn time," Eli said. Monica pinched him on the arm, but she was smiling, too.

Renee chanced a glance at Margo Holmes. The smile on

her face was more inquisitive than anything else. Lord, what must this woman think of her? With his pronouncement that they would share a room, Alex had basically proclaimed to his entire family that they would make love.

She was going to make love to Alex.

The reality hit her like a two-by-four. Renee felt as dense as the pieces of driftwood she'd spotted along the shore of the road they'd taken to this island. Of course they were going to make love, and now all of Alex's family knew it, too. Her skin burned with embarrassment.

Thank you, Alex mouthed. A rare smile lifted the corner of his mouth, and Renee just about melted. She loved making him smile.

"All right, then," Eli said. "Now that the room assignments are taken care of, we can eat and, later on, go swimming. That sound good to you, Rosebud?"

"Yes, yes, yes!" Jasmine jumped up and down.

"Come on, let's check out the rest of this place," Eli said. He crouched down and pulled his niece onto his back, letting her ride piggyback. "What do you want to see first?"

"The pool!" Jasmine screamed, pointing to the pool that was visible through the bank of floor-to-ceiling windows that stretched across the back of what Renee presumed to be the villa's living room.

"Would anyone care for a formal tour of the house and grounds?" the caretaker asked. "There are several features I would like to point out before leaving you to your stay."

"I would," Monica said. "Want to join me, Margo?"

Alex's mother had been quiet since Alex announced that he and Renee would share a room. Renee wasn't sure what to make of her assessing stare. She didn't look upset or offended. Margo Holmes looked almost confused, as if she didn't know what to make of the situation.

"Margo?" Monica prompted.

"Of course," Margo finally answered. "I'd love to see where I'll be sleeping, and I heard there was a nice lanai with a hammock. I brought along a couple of books I've been meaning to read."

"Oh yes, ma'am," the caretaker said. "You'll have ample time to relax at L'Oasis."

The three women took off for rooms unknown, leaving Renee still standing in the massive foyer with Alex.

"Should I apologize for what just happened?" he asked. "I didn't mean to put you on the spot. I just didn't want there to be any doubt about who you are to me."

"Well, judging by the looks of things, this promises to be the most luxurious place I've ever visited. And I get to cuddle up next to the most scrumptious man I've ever known." She reached over and trailed her fingers lightly across his hand, before capturing it and bringing it to her lips. "All joking aside, I came here because I want to spend time with you, Alex. That includes spending the night with you, and everything that entails."

He dipped his head low and captured her lips in a soft, slow kiss. Heaven had to feel like this, Renee thought as she was twisted up into the magic Alex wove around her. She twined her arms around his neck and worked her fingers underneath the collar of his polo shirt. Alex wrapped his arms around her waist, pulling her in until she stood flush against his body.

"We should stop," Renee murmured against his lips.

"Why would I want to stop this?" Alex asked as he deepened their kiss.

She didn't want his mother to walk in on them in a tongue-lock, but Renee decided to keep that to herself until the end of round two. She had one ear trained on listening for others. The rest of her focus was squarely on the man surrounding her with his incredible warmth.

"Maybe we *should* stop," Alex said. "Just in case Jasmine and Eli come back in."

"What do you think Jasmine will think of us sharing a room?" Renee asked.

"I don't know," he said. "Maybe it's time I explain to her that grown-ups who like each other sometimes share a room."

"Are *you* ready for that conversation?"

"No, but she's growing up," he said with a deep sigh. "I need to accept that."

"You don't have to go into the birds and the bees, but be honest with her, Alex. Your little girl is smarter than you think."

"The house is lovely." Monica's elevated voice traveled across the room, and Renee sensed she'd found an ally. Monica probably realized she and Alex might need some warning that they were about to be joined by company.

"This is more than just a house," Alex said to his future sister-in-law as she and Margo reentered the living quarters. The cook announced that lunch would be ready in twenty minutes.

"I still want to know how much this cost the two of you," Margo said. "This big house, a private chef, it's all too much."

"Stop worrying about it. Eli's got the money," Alex said. "You should be happy you don't have to worry about cooking."

"That cook will be gone by tomorrow morning," Margo replied.

"Margo, this is supposed to be a nice, relaxing vacation for you. Hang out on the beach, have a massage—there's a masseuse on call," Monica explained.

"There's also really good shopping," Renee decided to add. "I read up on a few places in the local shopping district on the Internet."

"So, you've known for some time that you would be joining us?" Margo asked. "I mean, you must have if you had time to research the island."

Renee opened her mouth to speak, but Alex stepped in. "I asked Renee to join me a few weeks ago," he said.

"That would have been nice to know beforehand,"

Margo told Alex with a pointed look. She captured Renee's hand. "I know I speak on behalf of our entire family when I say we are so happy to have you here."

Renee hadn't known what to expect, but the unabashed welcome in Margo Holmes's eyes meant more than she had ever thought possible.

"Thank you, Mrs. Holmes."

"It's Margo," she said, patting Renee's hand. "This is a first-name-basis type of family."

"That sounds lovely," Renee said, encouraged by the warmth in Margo's sincere smile. Renee struggled to hold back her bewilderment. Such open kindness within a family was foreign to her. She wasn't used to a family where laughter and teasing were the norm; it made her long to be a part of them all the more.

"I won't lie," Renee said, "I wasn't sure how I would be received."

"I told you you'd have nothing to worry about," Alex said.

"Of course you would have nothing to worry about," Margo said. "Which is why my son should have told us all about you a long time ago. But that's okay." Margo wrapped an arm around Renee's waist and squeezed. "I'm looking forward to getting to know you over the next few days. Any woman who's captured Alex's eye must be very special indeed."

Chapter Sixteen

Alex had done a credible job of avoiding being caught in the same room alone with his mother, but eventually, luck must run out. It had just done so for him.

"Alexander," she called as he passed the door to her bedroom on his way to the villa's private pool. Or at least he thought he was on his way to the pool. This place was so big he wasn't sure where this hallway led.

"Alex, come in here, please," his mother called.

Suddenly, the house didn't seem big enough.

Alex pushed through the partially open door, finding his mother sitting on the plush queen-size bed, her open suitcase next to her.

"What is it, Mama?"

She gave him a look. Playing stupid wasn't the brightest idea. He should just get this over with.

"What do you want to know about Renee?" he asked.

"How long have the two of you been seeing each other?"

"I met her the day I started volunteering at the school."

"Is it serious?" she asked. She patted the bed and Alex took a seat.

"Yeah, Mama. I think it is serious." Alex raised his hands in bewilderment. "It just feels right. When we're together, we have fun. She makes me laugh," he said simply. "Does that mean we're serious? I guess it depends on who you ask."

"I know the type of man you are, Alex. If you thought of her as just a friend, she would be sleeping in another room."

"Don't think badly of her because of that, Mama. We hadn't even discussed sleeping arrangements. I kind of sprang it on her. It probably wasn't very smart of me," Alex admitted.

"It doesn't seem as if she minded very much." Mama smiled. "How does Jasmine feel about her?"

"She loves her," Alex said. "We talked a little about it, and she seems okay with calling Renee my girlfriend, but I don't know if that's because she likes Renee as a teacher. You know what I mean?"

"I think she's at that age where she can accept that you have someone else in your life. She needs to understand that she cannot have you to herself, Alex."

"I'm not sure if I want her to think that, though."

"Alex, you cannot live your life for Jasmine."

"I don't want her to want for anything, Mama, especially my time. I'm convinced that's part of the reason she had those problems at school in the first place."

"I'm not going to let you blame yourself for this, Alex."

"At least Jasmine is getting better," he sighed. "She's not acting up, and we've started talking about things more. I guess that psychologist knew what he was talking about."

He rose from the bed and planted a kiss on the top of Mama's head. "Can I go out to the pool now? The one outside has a much better view than the one at my physical therapist's office. It's a lot bigger, too."

"Alex," she called before he was able to leave the room.

"What is it, Mama?"

"It has been a long time since you've been happy, hasn't it?"

Much longer than she knew.

"It has," he answered. "It feels good."

"I'm happy for you, baby."

"Thanks, Mama." He smiled, before leaving his mother's bedroom.

When Alex finally made it poolside, he found Renee and Monica stretched out on matching dark brown lounge chairs. An open hardback book lay across Monica's stomach, but Alex could tell she hadn't read a word for some time now. By the way her head lolled to the side, she was definitely asleep behind those sunshades.

Renee's eyes were covered with sunshades, too, but the smile that drew across her face as he walked up to her lounger told Alex she was wide awake.

"Hello there," she said.

God, she was beautiful. The understated black one-piece suit fit her body to perfection, and whatever lotion she'd rubbed over her skin made it look as if she'd been covered in sun-kissed honey.

"You look beautiful," Alex said.

"So do you," she answered. She scooted a couple of inches to the right. "Have a seat?" she offered.

He shook his head. "I'm afraid of what might happen if I sit that close to you," he said. Alex lowered himself to the edge of the lounger next to her. He nodded toward Monica. "How long has she been asleep?"

"About five minutes after she sat down. She said she'd worked a double shift before they left New Orleans, which is why they were late getting to the airport."

"That's why she and Eli are such a perfect match. They're both frighteningly dedicated to their jobs."

"She's very nice," Renee said. "Your entire family is wonderful, Alex."

"Spoken like a woman who's only known my family for ten hours," he said. "Let's see how you feel by Tuesday."

"I will still think they are wonderful," Renee said.

"Renee?" he asked after a long moment. "Are you hoping it was already nighttime?"

"Yes," she breathed deeply. "Very much so."

"If you could only see the images running through my head," Alex said.

"Okay, stop," Monica said. A lazy smile curled the corners of her mouth. "As much as I'd love to hear the rest of this conversation, I don't think it's meant for my ears. I'm going to help Eli and Jasmine with their sand castle." She pushed up from the lounger and headed out to the private beach.

"I swear I thought she was sleeping," Renee laughed.

"You know," Alex said, enclosing her delicate wrist in his hand and rubbing his thumb along the sensitive skin. "We can both pretend we're sick when everyone goes out to dinner tonight."

"Oh, sure. Your family would so buy that," Renee said.

"Of course they would. We can say we ate bad fish at lunch."

"The same fish they ate?"

"I'm trying to think off the top of my head here," Alex said. "Cut me some slack."

She scooted up and threw her legs off the side of the lounge chair. "The night will come soon enough, Alex. You know what they say, the anticipation is half the fun."

Renee twisted in front of the mirror and peered over her shoulder, making sure the silky, floral-print fabric draped just right over her rear end. She swept on another swipe of lip gloss and popped her lips.

"I'd do you," she said to her image.

"Renee." There was a slight rap on the door. "We're leaving in five minutes," Alex said through the door.

"I'm done," she returned. Renee took a deep, steadying breath and opened the bathroom door. Alex stood not even a foot in front of her, looking like the most enticing dessert a girl could ask for in his navy slacks and moss-green silk button-down shirt.

"Oh, wow," she said. "That tainted fish story is sounding better to me."

"I told you it would be a good excuse," Alex said. "You look amazing." He held his hand out and she placed her palm inside the warmth of his.

"So do you," Renee said. She tilted her head up to receive his kiss, but before their lips could touch, the door to their bedroom suite burst open.

"Come on, Daddy! The big van is outside." Jasmine ran up to them. She grabbed Alex's hand, then Renee's, and started pulling.

"It's okay, Jazzy. Uncle Eli isn't going to leave us."

"Yes, he will," Jasmine said.

Alex looked over at Renee. "She's probably right," he said.

Margo, Eli and Monica were already sitting in the van. Renee allowed Alex to help her in; then she grabbed Jasmine and sat her next to her in the backseat.

"You had fun building that sand castle?" she asked.

"Yeah, until Uncle Eli pushed me away," Jasmine said.

"You pushed her away?" Margo directed the question to her son.

"I was helping," Eli defended.

"Nah-uh," Jasmine said. "You told me you wanted it to be a fancy sand castle, and made me find seashells to use as the windows. And when I came back, you wouldn't let me touch it."

"Elijah Marcus." His mother's chastising tone said it all.

"I was just trying to give the sand castle a little more depth," he said.

"E, just stop trying," Alex advised his brother.

"The parts you worked on were beautiful," Renee said, pinching Jasmine on the nose.

"Thank you, Ms. Moore."

The driver dropped them off in the heart of Marigot, the capital of St. Martin.

"We have reservations at Le Chanteclair in about an hour," Monica said. "I thought we could walk around the city for a bit before meeting up for dinner."

"Will I want to eat anything at this Le Chan Whatever place?" Alex asked.

"It's French cuisine."

"Again, will I want to eat anything there? Don't the French try to feed you snails?"

"Snails?" Horror washed over Jasmine's face.

"Don't worry about it. Every restaurant has steak and potatoes," Eli said.

"You boys need to broaden your horizons every now and then," Margo said.

Alex and Eli looked at each other over their mother's head. "Steak and potatoes," they both said.

"It's no use," Monica laughed. "The restaurant is in the Marina Port La Royale. What do you say we all meet up in the lobby at about quarter of eight?"

"Sounds like a plan," Alex said. "Jazzy, what do you want to see first?"

"Actually, I was hoping to take Jasmine sightseeing," Margo said. "We can walk through that marketplace over there, and you and Renee can enjoy some time alone in the city."

Renee tried to hide her smile, but couldn't. She'd been so afraid Alex's mother didn't like her. Here she was, trying to buy them time alone.

"That okay with you, Pumpkin?" Alex asked.

"That's fine with her," Margo answered for Jasmine. "She's okay with sharing her daddy's time, right, Jazz?"

Jasmine looked from Alex to her grandmother. "I just want to buy Kayla a T-shirt."

"You see?" Margo smiled triumphantly. "We'll go to some of the shops and check out souvenirs. And you two"—she pointed at Eli and Monica—"and you two," she said to Alex and Renee, "can explore the city. Us girls will see you at dinner," she said, then took Jasmine by the hand and they headed toward the cluster of cafés and shops along the harbor front.

"That woman is a force of nature," Eli said.

"I realized years ago that it's just easier to let her have her way," Alex said. He turned to Renee. "So, you up for a little stroll through . . . where are we?"

"Marigot," Monica supplied. "I'm ready to do a little exploring myself," she said, wrapping her arm around Eli's. "Remember to be in the lobby of the marina in forty minutes," she called as she and Eli went in the opposite direction of where Margo was heading with Jasmine.

"Where does that leave us?" Renee asked.

"I have no idea what there is to do in this city, so I'm not going to be much help."

"I looked it up on the Internet, and there's supposed to be some great French architecture. You mind strolling through one of the neighborhoods for a bit?"

"That's okay with me," Alex said.

They walked along the edge of a cobblestone road. Quaint, colorful cottages sat close upon each other. The salt-tinged sea air blew lightly across her skin.

"Your mother is pretty slick," Renee said. "But in a good way. I can see why you boys are so protective of her."

"She's such a strong woman," Alex said. "My dad died when he was thirty-nine, and Mama hardly missed a step. She worked two jobs to make sure we didn't feel the loss of Pop's salary and she still didn't miss one of Toby's basketball games, or Eli's Quiz Bowl matches. She's amazing."

"And she loves you all so much," Renee said, her heart filling up with sorrow at the thought of her own mother. A mother whose only show of affection came in the form of taking punches from her husband so Renee wouldn't bear the brunt of his rage. Not that it did much good.

If she'd really loved her, she would have gotten them both out of that house.

"What's wrong?" Alex asked. "You're frowning."

"I never had much of a poker face," she said. She didn't want to get into this. The night held too much promise to have it marred by talk of her family's crippled relationship. Yet Renee still found herself saying, "I was just thinking about my mother."

"What about her?" Alex asked.

Renee shook her head. "I know she loved me, Alex, but . . ."

"But what?" he asked.

"He used to beat us," she finally admitted. "My father, he was abusive to both me and my mother."

Renee saw the sympathetic horror that flashed across Alex's face.

"I got out a long time ago, but she's still there. How could she stay with him, Alex?" Renee asked. "If she really loved me the way a mother is supposed to love her child, the way *your* mother loves her children, she would not have stayed with him."

"You'll never know what was going through her head," Alex answered. "Maybe she thought it was for the best."

"How could remaining with someone who takes pleasure in torturing you, in demeaning you, ever be for the best? Even after he became wheelchair-bound and could no longer hurt her physically, she still puts up with the mental abuse. I'll never understand her."

"I'm so sorry, Renee," Alex said, squeezing her hand. It was exactly the support she needed.

"It's all behind me," Renee said, taking a deep breath. "Let's enjoy the rest of the city. We only have twenty minutes before we have to meet everyone back at the marina for dinner."

They strolled, arms intertwined, down the streets of Marigot, but Renee had a hard time concentrating on the quaint homes or the romantic atmosphere. Being around the love that exuded throughout Alex's family had an adverse affect on her. She couldn't help but feel melancholy when comparing Alex's family to her own.

She knew every child did not grow up in fear of feeling their father's wrath on a day-to-day basis, but she truly did not know people could care so much about each other. Until she'd met the Holmeses.

Monica Gardner had better appreciate how lucky she was to have the chance to become a permanent member of this family. Renee tried not to entertain visions of herself joining the Holmeses, but how could she not? After her dismal childhood, being welcomed into this family would be like a fairy tale come true.

"Renee?"

Alex halted his steps, stopping in front of a sand-colored cottage with bright blue shutters. He captured her hands, and pulled her closer to him, until her breasts lightly touched his chest. Renee tipped her head up, instantly drawn into his smoldering gaze.

"Family is more than just the blood flowing through your veins," Alex said. "Even though your family turned their backs on you, you can still have a family that cares for you."

"There's nothing that would make me happier," she said. She stared into Alex's eyes as he dipped his head and settled his lips onto hers.

Just as he'd anticipated, Alex didn't recognize a thing on the menu. Eli had been wrong; they didn't even have steak. The waiter had just taken Monica's order and was making his way around the table. Maybe he should just order a grilled cheese sandwich off the children's menu like Jazzy.

Renee leaned to the side and asked, "Do you need help ordering?"

"I need some help," Eli said from across the table.

"See, when I tried teaching you boys French, you wouldn't listen," Mama said. "It's come back to haunt you."

"That jumbled West Louisiana Creole stuff you grew up speaking isn't French," Eli said.

"I speak Cajun, not Creole, and they are all rooted in French," she clarified. She turned to the waiter, and in flawless French said, "I would like *la filet de thon au beurre Gigondas*." She looked at Eli. "I've also been taking a free course in French at New Hope Baptist Church," she finished with a triumphant nod.

Turned out they did have steak on the menu, except it was written in French, which would make sense. But before his *entrecôte béarnaise*, or whatever the heck Renee had rattled off, could make it out of the kitchen, Alex could feel his appetite waning. His appetite for food, that is.

As the evening drew on, his mind had a hard time focusing on anything but the event he knew would take place once they returned to the villa. After nearly seven long years of meager attempts at pleasuring himself in the shower, of telling himself he didn't need a woman's touch, tonight he would experience what it felt like to make love again. How was he supposed to focus on whatever it was they were talking about around the table?

The waiter offered dessert, but thankfully, the entire table declined. Good thing Toby didn't arrive until tomorrow. He would have ordered first and second dessert.

"Everyone ready to head back to the villa?" Monica asked.

Alex nearly shouted *yes*.

"I've been up since five a.m.," Mama said. "I'm ready to get to bed. Your brother will be here tomorrow, so I'll have to do extra grocery shopping. That chef didn't fix enough food at lunch."

"Mama, you'd better stay out of that kitchen," Eli warned. He pushed away from the table and pulled out Monica's chair. "We'll have to catch separate cabs back to the villa."

Alex offered to pay for the meal, but Eli put up a fight, as he knew his brother would. Alex didn't even want to imagine what this was costing Eli and Monica, but both refused to take him up on his offer to help pay for the villa. It made Alex feel even more justified in buying the all-expenses-paid week in Italy he'd had his assistant, Jennie, purchase for a wedding gift.

They filed out of the restaurant to the waiting taxi stand.

"I'm riding back with Daddy," Jasmine announced.

"If you don't want to ride back with me, I won't be hurt," Eli said, feigning disappointment.

Jasmine heaved a huge sigh and rolled her eyes. "Okay, Uncle Eli. I'll ride with you."

"Actually, E, I'd rather Jazzy ride with me and Renee," Alex said. "We need to talk about a few things."

It didn't take Eli long to get a clue. "Oh yeah. Well, we'll see you all back at the villa," he said as he helped their mother and Monica into the waiting cab, a stupid, knowing grin on his face.

Alex helped Renee into the cab first, sensing the apprehension flowing over her. Jasmine bounded into the car, and Alex followed. The cab took off toward Baie Rouge.

"Jazzy, you know how you said you wanted to sleep in the room with all the games?"

"Yes, I cannot wait. They have the *Shrek 3* game."

"Good," Alex said. Damn, this was uncomfortable. "Well, while we're here, Renee is going to share my room."

"You have bunk beds?"

Okay, yeah. He *so* was not ready for this conversation.

"The room doesn't have bunk beds," Renee said. "But that's okay, isn't it, Jasmine? Shrek and Fiona sleep in the same room because they're adult ogres, and sometimes adults who like each other sleep in the same room."

"You are prettier than Fiona, Ms. Moore."

"Thank you," Renee answered. "But do you understand what your dad and I are trying to explain?"

"Uh-huh." She nodded. "You and Daddy are sleeping together, like Kayla's mommy and her new boyfriend. Kayla's mommy says that women have needs."

"Oh my God," Alex groaned. He was going to strangle Leslie Morgan.

"This isn't about what Kayla's mom was talking about," Renee said. "Your dad and I do like each other, and we want to spend time together since we're on vacation. And when we get back to New Orleans, we'll still want to spend time together, which means I may be over at your house a little more," Renee said.

"She may even spend the night once in a while," Alex added, glancing at Renee. "That would be okay, wouldn't it, Jazz?"

"Yes, Daddy," she said with an exasperated sigh. "We're here." Jasmine clapped her hands together. "Come on. Grandma said once I take a bath and get into my pajamas, I can play *Shrek 3* for thirty minutes."

She climbed over Alex's lap and was out the door as soon

as the cabdriver opened it. Alex paid the driver and took Renee's hand as he walked her to the villa's front door.

"Well, that wasn't so hard, was it?" Renee asked.

"You kidding me? I'm sweating buckshots here," Alex said. "And I'm going to kill Leslie Morgan when we get back home."

"I would think twice before letting Jasmine spend the night at her house again," Renee added.

"Jasmine's not going near that house again."

They walked through the entrance of the house, finding Eli and Monica snuggled up on one of the living room couches, looking out the floor-to-ceiling windows as the inky waves crashed upon the beach. Several small boats bobbed along the water, their tiny lights looking like stray fireflies against the darkened night.

"Where did Jasmine go to so fast?" Alex asked.

"Mama took her in the back. Between the pool and her game room, I think Jazzy's found her own little piece of heaven."

"There's a lot to keep her occupied."

"That's the point," Eli said, lifting his eyebrows, and drawing a laugh from Renee.

"I think it's time everyone goes to bed," Monica said. She pushed up from the sofa and pulled at Eli's arm.

"Yeah, but you really want to sleep," Eli complained.

"As if that ever stops you," Monica snorted. "Good night, you two." She gave them a two-finger wave as she pushed Alex's brother toward the huge master suite.

When Alex turned his attention back to Renee, her face had sobered, and she was rubbing her hands up and down her arms.

"Are you cold?" he asked.

"Not really," she said, still rubbing her arms. She must have realized what she was doing because she stopped. "Alex, I'm a little nervous," she admitted.

"You think I'm not?" he asked. Did she realize how long

it had been since he'd done this? Between excitement over the prospect of finally making love again, and fear that he'd somehow forgotten how to do it, Alex was afraid there would be a reappearance of his expensive French steak in the next five seconds.

"Are you ready to go to the room?" Renee asked.

"You have something else in mind?"

She shrugged her delicate shoulders. "I don't know, maybe we can take a walk on the beach?"

"Did you watch *From Here to Eternity* before you left the States?"

She eyed him for a few moments; then a huge, breath-stealing smile drew across her lips. "I'm not interested in rolling around in the sand, Alex. That would mess up my hair."

"Good, because that doesn't seem sexy to me, especially when there's a big, comfortable bed waiting for us."

She walked the few steps that would bring her to him, and spread her hands over his chest. "Forget the walk on the beach," she said.

"You sure?" Alex asked. Her fingers on his fully clothed skin were driving him crazy. How would he handle it when they were both naked?

"Yes," Renee answered. She linked her hands around his neck and pulled him in for a soft, slow kiss. "Let's go to bed."

Chapter Seventeen

Renee stepped over the threshold of the door leading to their bedroom suite and sensed a charge pulsing through the air. It covered her entire body. Everything was about to change between them. She was ready for it, but she was still nervous to the point of nearly collapsing.

This was silly. It wasn't as if she'd never had sex before. She might not be all that experienced, but she'd done it enough times to know how this worked. There was something about the man she was about to make love to that made all the difference in the world. What she felt for Alex, how he made her feel; it took this experience to an entirely new level.

He stepped up behind her and captured her shoulders in his hands. "Are you okay?" he asked. "Can I get you something to drink?"

Renee took one of his hands and brought it to her lips, kissing the back of his fingers. "I'm perfect, Alex. I don't need anything else. Just you."

He dropped his lips against her neck and pulled in a deep breath before placing a gentle kiss behind her ear. Then he brought his hands down and wrapped them around her waist.

"I am so scared right now," Alex admitted in a soft whisper.

"Don't be," Renee said, though his confession went a long way in easing her own worries. She turned in his arms and captured his face in her palms. "Alex, I feel so lucky to be here with you."

She stood on her tiptoes and kissed him. Alex wrapped his arms around her back and pulled her closer. His arousal, solid, firm, and hot, pressed against her stomach. Renee groaned in a mixture of frustration and anticipation, opening her mouth wider and inviting in Alex's tongue. He accepted the invitation with amazing skill, his tongue invading and retreating in a rhythm so intoxicating Renee could hardly stand it.

"Alex." She heard the word come out in a slow growl, hardly recognizing it as her own voice.

Alex stopped just long enough to guide her to the huge, king-size bed. A white, netted canopy flowed from a hoop hanging above the bed. Alex laid her among the plush bedding, and her body sank into its lushness.

"I can help you get rid of those clothes," he said.

"I can do that on my own," Renee said. She pushed herself up to her knees, captured the hem of her sundress, and pulled it over her head. "Why don't I help you with yours?"

She reached over to help Alex with his shirt, but he stayed her hand. "No, let me just look at you for a little while," he said. The look in his eyes was so intense, it took her breath away. How could a man with so much sexual magnetism go so long without succumbing to his urges? He must have turned away hundreds of women over the years.

Alex took a couple of steps back and lowered himself into one of the wicker chairs in the seating area just to the right of the bed. He sat back and gazed at her with hungry brown eyes.

"You are the most beautiful woman I've ever seen," he said.

Men said those words all the time, but somehow, Renee knew Alex meant them. She could feel it in the way he stared at her. Reverently. Hungrily.

She needed him in this bed. Right now. "Alex, come to bed," she pleaded.

"In a minute," he answered. He started on the buttons of his shirt, methodically releasing them as he continued to stare at her.

"Alex, please," Renee begged.

Alex pushed himself from the chair and sauntered over to the bed. Renee pulled him to her, taking his mouth in a brutal kiss. She pushed the shirt from his shoulders and slid her hands down his chest, running her fingers through the thatch of hair that tapered just above the waistband of his pants.

"Alex, take off the pants. Now."

He flicked open the fly's button and pushed the pants down his thighs, but captured her hand before Renee could help herself to what pulsed under the cover of his black boxers.

Renee glanced up at him. The look on his face was way too ominous for what they were about to do. "What's the matter?"

"I need to warn you," Alex cautioned. "It's been a very long time since I did this."

Renee's shoulders drooped with relief. "I know, Alex."

"No, you . . ." He shook his head. "You don't get it, Renee. The first time is going to be over really fast."

"Alex, I don't care," she reassured him.

"I do," he said, his eyes laden with reservations.

"Alex." Renee held her hand out, beckoning him to join her on the mountain of pillows. He pushed his pants down the rest of the way, and then did the same with his boxer shorts.

Renee crooked her finger. "Come here." She ran her tongue over her lips and smiled at the reaction it caused in Alex. His erection jerked in response. "Tell me you have a condom this time," Renee implored.

"Condoms, with an *s*," Alex assured her. He knelt on the edge of the mattress, balancing one foot on the floor as he reached in the toiletry travel bag he'd left on the nightstand. Renee studied his movements as he retrieved the box of condoms, the way his taut muscles flexed beneath his chocolate-brown skin. Alex didn't need to worry about how long he could last. She would ignite any minute from sheer anticipation.

"Alex, hurry," Renee pleaded.

He grabbed a square foil packet from the box and ripped it open. Renee bit down on her lip, excitement coursing through her bloodstream like electricity through a live wire.

Alex's hands shook as he tried to cover himself with the slippery latex.

Renee couldn't take it anymore. "Gimme that." She knocked his hand away and rolled the condom over his massive erection. "Now come here."

Alex lowered himself on top of her, seizing her lips in a

slow, deliberate kiss. His hands, calloused and work-roughened, worked their way up her legs, traveling over her hips, and settling at her waist. Renee arched into him as he captured her nipple between his teeth, tugging and licking, lapping and sucking. His assault seemed calculated, a strategic battle with her senses, and Renee was no match for the sensual onslaught.

She was incomparably enraptured by this man whose life had been so very different from her own. He'd known love all his life, had known affection and warmth. And he wanted to share that love with her.

Her insides clutched as his erection poised at her entrance. Renee wrapped her arms around his neck and moaned in pleasure as her body welcomed him home.

Alex clenched his eyes tight, his arms trembling, his entire being shuddering at the supple give of Renee's body as he gently pushed his way inside her. Just like that, he'd found paradise. After years of denying himself, of allowing his guilt to rob him of pleasure, he'd discovered his own small piece of heaven on earth hidden in the depths of her wet, warm body.

He moved in deep, burying his full length into the clenching glove cloaking his body. In and out he thrust inside her, urging her to open wider, forcing her leg up and onto his left shoulder.

She gasped, her mouth falling open and remaining that way, as if she didn't have the strength to close it.

"Oh my God, Alex," Renee panted. "This is so good."

"I know," Alex echoed.

But she was wrong. This was *so* past good.

"Hold on," Alex breathed into her open mouth.

He braced himself with his left arm to take pressure off his still-healing right shoulder; then he arched his back and drove into her, pumping up and down, in and out, deeper and higher. Renee captured his right hand and pulled his finger into her mouth, sucking on it as if it contained some kind of life-sustaining serum.

The sight of her taking him into her mouth was so erotic it sent Alex over the edge. He slammed into her, his body convulsing as sparks of pleasure shot through every inch of his bloodstream.

Too weak to hold himself up a second longer, Alex collapsed onto his back and sucked in large gulps of air.

"That lasted longer than I thought it would," Renee said after an exhausted sigh.

"I know. Pretty proud of myself," Alex boasted.

"You should be," Renee laughed.

They lay on top of the covers, the whisper of Renee's soft pants mingling with his harsh, soughing breaths. Alex smoothed his hand across her flat stomach, relishing the softness of her sweat-slicked skin against his palm.

"Oh, damn," he said after a few minutes.

"What's wrong?"

Alex managed to loll his head to the side. He smiled at Renee. "I was supposed to get you to act out my naughty librarian fantasy."

Despite her weakened state, Renee gave him the slap he deserved. Alex caught her hand before she could take it away, and brought it to his chest, tracing the valleys between her slim fingers.

"Alex."

"Yeah?"

"In about a half hour, I'll be ready to do that again."

Alex smiled to himself; then he asked, "Renee?"

"Yes?" she murmured.

"You're really gonna make me wait a half hour?"

Chapter Eighteen

"Mmmmm," came a purr from deep within the covers.

Alex smiled up at the ceiling fan twirling lazily high above the bed, its blades made to look like banana leaves.

"Are you awake?" Renee murmured.

"I am," Alex answered. "But I'm not ready to get out of bed."

"Me, neither." She scooted over to him and draped herself across his chest. "Wait," she said, then bounded out of the bed and headed for the bathroom. A minute later Alex heard the toilet flush, then the faucet running for much longer than he thought necessary for her to wash her hands.

"Renee," he called. "Are you okay?"

"In a minute," he thought he heard.

Alex threw his legs off the side of the bed. He pulled on the pair of boxers that he'd draped across the nightstand and headed for the suite's connecting bathroom.

He widened the slight crack in the bathroom door and found Renee bent over the oval faucet brushing her teeth. She'd wrapped the sheet around her and held it together at her breasts. Her bare feet peeking out of the bottom were so sexy.

She rinsed her mouth and patted her lips dry with a towel. "I hate morning breath," she explained with a smile.

"Does that mean I need to brush my teeth, too?" Alex asked.

"If you expect to kiss me this morning," she answered.

"If I knew it would be this much trouble," Alex mumbled just loud enough for her to hear.

"And just what would you have done?" Renee asked, eyeing him with a keen, knowing look.

"I would have had the mouthwash waiting on the bedside table." Alex grinned.

She threw her head back, the soft lilt of her laughter running over him like a shower of warm honey. She lowered the lid on the toilet, took a seat, and put her chin in her hand as if she were getting ready to catch the Saturday matinee.

"You gonna watch?" Alex asked.

She hunched a bare shoulder. "Why not?"

"I have to warn you, I don't do any tricks. Ten times in a circular motion, rinse, and spit. That's about all you'll see."

"What a sense of humor you have, Mr. Holmes."

"I try." Alex smiled at her in the mirror.

He brushed his teeth, catching her grin in the mirror whenever he raised his head. He'd never felt so at ease with a woman. The entire time he'd been married to Chantal, Alex could not remember a single time they'd shared a morning in the bathroom, just so they could be close to each other.

He rinsed, turned off the faucet, and put his toiletries away. He turned to Renee and crooked his finger.

A slow smile spread across her face. She rose and slowly made her way over to his side of the vast bathroom, resembling some mythological Nubian princess in the flowing sheet. When she reached him, Alex picked her up and sat her on the vanity. He pried away the hand that held the sheet to her breasts and watched as the stark-white material fell from her body, pooling around her atop the vanity. Her naked breasts rose and fell with her deep, deliberate breaths.

"What are you doing, Alex?"

"Making up for lost time," he said before capturing her lips.

Renee wrapped her arms around his neck and locked her legs around his waist. Alex trailed his tongue down her neck, lapping up the salty flavor of her skin. He pushed the boxers down his legs, covered himself with a condom, then lifted Renee from the vanity, and thrust inside her. She cried out, sinking her teeth into his left shoulder to stifle her moans. He turned from the vanity, and carried her toward the shower, but Alex knew within seconds that he wouldn't make it.

Change of plans.

He backed her up against the wall for support. He braced his legs apart, sank his fingers into the plush softness of her behind, and pulling her tighter, pumping in and out in deep, sure strokes.

"Alex," she breathed.

Renee lifted her head and they stared into each other's eyes as he continued to fill her. She took her lower lip between her teeth, but her cry still escaped. Time stood still. There was nothing else in the world, only her body surrounding him, squeezing him, milking him.

His arms trembled. He couldn't let go, but he couldn't hold her any longer, either.

"Renee, I can't hold you up."

"Let go," she said. She braced a hand against the wall and dropped one leg. Alex hooked his arm under her other knee and drove into her, slamming her against the wall, pumping into her with all he was worth. Renee screamed her release, the cry echoing throughout the room.

Her head fell back against the wall. She slid down to the floor and tugged at Alex, inviting him to join her. He did, sitting up against the wall and pulling Renee into his arms.

"That . . . should make up . . . for at least a year," she said between pants.

"At least," Alex struggled to get out.

"I don't have to move, do I?" Renee asked. "I'm way too weak to move."

"I would carry you to the bed if I didn't have a bum shoulder," Alex said.

Once they were back in bed, Alex pulled Renee on top of him. He had no idea how long they lay there completely naked and uncovered. He figured at least a half hour had to have passed when knocking at the door to the suite roused him.

"Daddy?" came Jasmine's voice from the other side of the door.

"Damn," Alex whispered. "Hold on, Pumpkin," he called.

Alex smoothed his hand over Renee's hair. "Renee," he said, "it's Jasmine."

"Hmmm?" she murmured.

"Daddy?"

"Renee." Alex gently nudged her shoulder. "Jasmine's at the door."

Renee bolted upright. She wrapped a sheet around her and escaped to the bathroom.

"I'm coming, Jazz," Alex called.

He scooted from the bed and pulled on his boxers. He grabbed a T-shirt and threw it over his head before opening the door to the suite.

"Hey, baby," he greeted Jasmine. She was dressed in yellow overalls and a white and yellow polka-dot shirt. "Grandma helped you dress this morning?"

"No, I did it by myself," she answered. "Grandma combed my hair, though."

"She did a good job," Alex said, pulling one of her pigtails.

"Grandma said we're going shopping for a present for Uncle Eli and Auntie Monica," Jasmine said. "But it's a surprise," she whispered.

"Oh," he whispered back. "Well, maybe you shouldn't tell anybody else."

"I'm not." Jasmine peered around the partially open door and eyed the bed. "Where's Ms. Moore?" she asked, sneaking past him and running over to the bed.

Instant sweat broke out over his chest. "She's in the bathroom," Alex answered.

"Oooh, your bed is so big, Daddy!" Jasmine climbed on the bed and started jumping up and down in her yellow, lace-trimmed socks. "I'll bet you and Ms. Moore had fun."

Oh Lord.

"Get down, Jazz. I've told you no jumping on the beds."

"Uncle Eli said I could because these are not our beds anyway."

Idiot. "Uncle Eli shouldn't have told you that."

Alex whisked her off the bed, and swung her up into his arms. He spotted a condom wrapper on the floor and nearly had a heart attack. He kicked it under the bed. God, he wasn't cut out for this.

There was another knock on the door to the suite. What was this? Happy hour?

"Jasmine?"

"I'm in here, Grandma."

His mother walked into the room, her eyes darting from corner to corner. "Good morning, Alex," she said. She looked over at the bed. "Is everything okay in here?"

"I came to tell Daddy about the present for Uncle Eli and Auntie Monica," Jasmine said. She'd lowered the tone of her voice, but the volume was as loud as usual.

"That's good, honey, but why don't we leave Daddy so he can get some rest?"

Alex teetered between embarrassment over his mother covering for him and gratefulness that she was there to do it.

"Have fun shopping," he said, helping Jasmine down to the floor.

His mother took Jasmine by the hand. "Eli and Monica are sleeping in, too. Jasmine and I will take a cab. We'll be back around lunchtime."

Alex placed a kiss on her cheek. "Thank you, Mama."

"Make the most of your morning," she said, her mouth tipping up in a grin.

Alex closed the door behind them and hung his head, taking deep breaths to calm his heart. He was not prepared to have the birds and the bees talk yet. Call him old-fashioned, but a six-year-old girl did not need to know what went on behind adults' closed doors.

Alex entered the bathroom and stood stock-still, instantly entranced by the sight before him. Renee stood in the middle of the huge bathroom. She'd twisted herself in the sheet, the linen wrapping around her upper thighs. It fell from her breasts, baring them to his eyes. Dusky pink blemishes marked the places he'd nipped, and licked, and sucked all night long.

"Is the coast clear?" she asked around a yawn. She stretched, arching her back and thrusting her breasts out even more.

If she didn't quit this, he would make up for all six years of celibacy before the morning was over.

"Yes, Jasmine and Mama are both gone. We can go back to sleep."

"Sleep, huh?"

"Among other things." Alex couldn't help but grin. "Or, if you want, you can shower and we can have some breakfast."

"That sounds almost as good as climbing back into bed with you."

"I rank higher than food? That's pretty good," Alex said.

"Unless the chef is making French toast for breakfast. Nothing is better than French toast."

"Seems I have a new goal in life. I'll be damned if I come in second to French toast on your list of favorite things."

"You don't have very far to go," Renee said. "One more session like the one we just had and you own the number-one spot, buddy."

"Then why are we standing here?" Alex said. "Come on."

"No," Renee laughed. "I doubt I can take any more. Until tonight," she was quick to add. She pressed a kiss to his chest, and it burned straight through his T-shirt into his skin. "I'm going to shower. What do you say to taking a walk on the beach to help Jasmine find seashells?"

"She went shopping with Mama, but I'll take you up on the offer. Go and shower, and I'll get breakfast."

"I would ask you to join me, but I doubt we'll ever get out."

Alex closed his eyes. How many times had he fantasized about her in his own shower? He didn't have to imagine what she looked like anymore. The image was forever stamped on his brain. And in his heart.

"Renee," Alex said, "what do you see happening between us when we get back to New Orleans?"

Renee's heartbeat quickened. She'd been thinking about the same thing lately, though she still wasn't sure what she actually felt about it, other than that she wanted them to continue the course they were on. Should they speed up that course? Slow it down? She just didn't know.

She was secure in the knowledge that he was only a few classrooms down the hallway from her. She'd become a pro at making up excuses to pop into Mrs. Overland's classroom just so she could see him and smile. But his days of volunteering at St. Katherine's were rapidly coming to an end. Jasmine's behavior in class had improved.

Alex had a doctor's appointment the day after they returned to New Orleans, and one of the outcomes could be clearance for him to return to desk duty at Holmes Construction. The thought of not seeing him on a daily basis sent a wave of nausea through her stomach.

"What were *you* thinking would happen after we get back home?" Renee asked.

"Things have changed between us, Renee."

She nodded.

"I hadn't anticipated you becoming such a huge part of my life this quickly," he said.

"Alex, I can't imagine not seeing you every day," Renee admitted.

He expelled a huge, relieved breath. "I was hoping you would say that."

"How could you doubt it?" Renee asked.

"I didn't, but it still feels good to hear you say it," he said. "I'm going to talk to Jasmine tonight. I know we touched on it a little, but I want her to understand exactly what's going on between us and explain just what you mean to both our lives."

Renee stared into his eyes. "I want to know that, too," she said.

"What you mean to our lives?" Alex asked.

She nodded.

Alex held her chin lightly with his fingers, tipping her head up. "I'm in love with you, Renee."

Her heart expanded within her chest, so relieved by his words that it nearly burst.

"Is that okay with you?" Alex asked.

"That is absolutely perfect," she said, fusing her lips with his.

When she finally released Alex's lips, Renee's first instinct was to capture them again. He was so delicious. And he was all hers.

"I don't plan on giving that up any time soon," she whispered against his chest.

"That's good to hear." Alex punctuated his words with kisses. "Because I don't plan to give you up, either."

"Any time soon?" she asked, raising her head at the seriousness she heard in his voice.

The playfulness of just a few moments ago had vanished like a whisper in the wind. The look he gave her brooked no argument.

"Anytime. Ever. Not until you say you want out."

"What if I decide I never want out?" Renee couldn't stop herself from asking. Their conversation had taken a drastically more serious turn, but now that they were concentrated on this pivotal point in their relationship, she had to see it through.

"Make no mistake about what I'm saying," Alex said.

"I'm not a little in love with you, Renee. This is real, full-blown stuff I'm feeling. It's stronger than I thought possible, especially for someone I've known for such a short amount of time. But I can't deny it."

She wasn't sure she would be able to speak when she opened her mouth, but Renee didn't have the words to say, anyway. She was afraid to admit she felt the same way, yet she knew in her heart that her feelings for Alex ran just as deep.

Could she allow herself to be so vulnerable?

"Renee, I didn't say the words so you would feel obligated to say them in return," Alex said. "It's okay if it takes you a little longer to fall in love with me." He put his knuckle under her chin and lifted her face so he could stare into her eyes. "But know that making you fall in love with me is exactly what I intend to do."

"Alex, I—"

"No, don't worry about it," he said. "Let's just enjoy the rest of our day together."

"I want you to know I don't take what you've told me lightly, Alex. Thank you for being so honest."

"I'll always be honest with you." He kissed her softly on the lips. "Thank you for coming here, Renee."

A smile broke across her lips. "Thank you for inviting me, Alex."

Renee clutched Alex's hand and swung it back and forth between them. They both held their shoes in their other hand. The wet sand felt good between her toes. Even with all the years she'd lived in Florida, she never took the time to enjoy the beach.

"This island is gorgeous," she said. "It's the perfect place for a wedding."

"It is," Alex agreed. "I'm still surprised Eli didn't go for the big wedding with all the family." He paused, and then chuckled, shaking his head.

"What?" Renee asked.

"Nothing."

"Come on, Alex. What's so funny?"

He shrugged. "I had a big wedding," he said. "Can't really blame E for not wanting to follow in my footsteps, huh?"

Pain tugged at her heart for him, but it was quickly replaced by . . . was that relief? Renee was ashamed to admit it, even to herself, but she would be lying if she could not confess that a small part of her wasn't appreciative that Chantal had been such a bad wife. Renee was certain it had helped to mold Alex into the man he was today.

"That woman did not deserve you, Alex."

"No, she didn't," he said. He bent to pick up a shell, rubbed sand from it, and sent it skipping along the water. "I made every excuse for her," he continued. "I even convinced myself that she had a right to mess around on me because I didn't pay enough attention to her. But that's bull," Alex said. "I gave Chantal everything she could ever want. I'm still paying off the debt she left me in with all her designer clothes and shoes, and that damn Benz she cracked up against that tree. And how did she pay me back?"

Renee squeezed his hand tighter.

"At least she gave me Jazzy," he said. "She put me through so much, Renee, but I'd go through it all again for my little girl. She's the reason I breathe."

If there was any such thing as the perfect man, Alex was the closest Renee had ever encountered. His capacity for love held no bounds when it came to his family, especially his daughter. Renee had never known love like this existed.

The thought gave her pause. Was she really ready for Alex to love her? How could she be sure the kind of love he felt for Jasmine would be the same for her? Love had a way of turning brutal; she'd witnessed that enough times to write a book on it.

Don't be stupid, Renee told herself. She could not picture

Alex turning violent. He didn't have it in him to raise his hand to a woman.

"Your parents did an excellent job raising you," Renee said. "You do realize how lucky you are, don't you?" She stopped walking and turned to face him. "You've gone through some awful times, Alex, but you've been blessed, too."

"I know," he said. He brought his hand up to her hair and pushed a few flyaway strands behind her ear. "I was blessed again when I found you."

She felt the same way. After everything she'd been through as a child and the deadbeats she'd dated as an adult, finding Alex had been a blessing. She trusted him unlike any man that had come before him. She wanted to open up to him. He'd bared his soul about his wife's duplicity, and how much Chantal had hurt him. Renee didn't want there to be any doubt that she was willing to reciprocate that trust.

"Alex?" Renee hesitated for a moment. "I need to tell you something."

Alex stopped their forward progress in the sand. The look in his eyes said he sensed whatever she was about to say would not be good.

"I've told you about my childhood," she started. "And how my father was abusive to both me and my mother. And then how my mother chose to stay with him when I decided to leave."

"Yes," he said, kissing her fingers again.

She kicked at a rock in the sand, then looked up at him. "The abuse was a lot worse than I made it out to be."

"Any amount of abuse is more than you should have to endure."

Renee's throat closed up, but she swallowed the lump of emotion and surged forward. "This wasn't just a few slaps across the face, Alex. My dad tortured me and my mom.

"One day, back when I was a senior in high school, my father came home drunk." She laughed to herself. "Actually, he came home drunk nearly every day from the time I was twelve, but that day, he seemed different, more hostile than usual. He started in on my mom first, threw her head against the wall, kicked her a few times. Then he looked over at me."

Renee shuddered.

"There was just so much evil in him," she said. The image of her father's face sent tremors down her spine despite the years that had passed since she'd last seen it. "I locked myself in my room, but I knew that would only stall him for a few minutes," she said. She focused on a sailboat bobbing in the distance, the gentle waves swaying the vessel to and fro. "He burst through the lock on my door and came after me. I tried to fight him off, but he was so much stronger than I was, even drunk." Her hand went up to her face. "He broke my jaw, my wrist, and cracked two ribs before he was done."

"God." Alex captured her by the back of her neck and pulled her close. He breathed into her hair, and whispered, "Please tell me he served time for what he did to you."

Renee shook her head. "I'm still not sure how he explained his way out of it, but I'm sure my mom corroborated whatever story he told the police. She was *so* afraid of him, Alex. She tried to leave a few times over the years, but she was convinced he would find her.

"Not too long after the day he put me in the hospital, he was hurt in a car accident, and ended up paralyzed from the chest down. It was as if a door had been opened." She took a deep breath. "But my mom just wouldn't walk through it. After everything he'd put her through, she wouldn't leave him. I hated to leave her there, but I couldn't take it anymore, Alex. I don't think I've ever cried as much as I did the day I walked out of that house for the last time."

"Your mother made her own choice," Alex said. "Never regret what you did that day."

"I left her with that man," she said.

"And I'll bet that's something you deal with every day, isn't it?"

She swallowed. "The same way you blame yourself for Chantal's infidelity," she volleyed.

Alex accepted that with a nod of his head. "We both have some things to work through, don't we?"

"Do you think we can get past it?"

"I hope so," he replied.

The compulsion to bare it all overcame her. Renee fought the feeling to stifle the words, admitting in an awed voice, "Alex, I think I'm falling in love with you."

Renee immediately wanted to take the words back. Even if what she was feeling was love, she wasn't sure she wanted Alex to know the depth of her emotions for him just yet.

"I love you, too, Renee. So much so that it scares me," he said. "When I'm not around you, you're all I can think about. Even if you're right in the next room. I want to be with you every second of every day. And you love my little girl. Sometimes, I question whether her own mother loved her, yet you treat her as if she were your own."

"I do love her," Renee said, choking back a sob. "Alex, how did I let this happen?"

"What?"

"Falling in love with the both of you?"

"It's not a bad thing, Renee."

"I know," she said. But a part of her believed it was a very bad thing. Love was a horrifying emotion. Love made you do things no sane person would ever do, like remain in a marriage that could hurt you. She'd vowed to never find herself in the same situation her mother was in. She could not love to the point of losing herself.

"We don't have to act on it any time soon," Alex said. "I'm enjoying what we have here. We still have a few days in St. Martin, and even when we're back in New Orleans, there's no rule that states we have to make drastic changes.

We can take things slow." He captured her chin in his hand and lifted her head until she was looking at him again. "I would love nothing more than to spend time getting to know you better. Both in and out of bed," he said.

Renee smiled despite the stupid tears that continued to well in her eyes. "I would really like that, too, Alex."

"Good." He placed one of his soft kisses on her lips. "Let's see what kind of seashells we can find."

"Grandma, is this one pretty?" Jasmine held up a beautiful mother-of-pearl brooch, though it must have been a fake in order for the shopkeeper to have it just lying around where customers could touch it.

"What do you think?" Margo asked.

"I don't know if it's pretty or not," Jasmine answered. "That's why I asked you."

"Beauty is a matter of opinion, sweetheart. What's beautiful to one person may not be beautiful to another."

Her cell phone vibrated in her pocket. Margo fished out the tiny phone and looked at the screen. A flutter of excitement flitted through her as she recognized the number.

"Enjoying the tropics?" Gerald's deep voice came through the line.

"I am," Margo answered. "But I've missed you."

"I know exactly what you mean."

"How are things back home?" she asked.

"Oh, I suppose everything is okay."

"That case must have you pretty busy."

"Grandma," Jasmine said. She tugged her toward the back wall that held what must have numbered a hundred doll dresses. "I love these," she said.

"They're wonderful, honey," Margo answered. "I took Jasmine shopping this morning. We're just taking a stroll through some of the local shops," she explained to Gerald. "It's hard not to buy everything in the store, but I've been doing a good job holding back."

"You sure about that? Your granddaughter seems to like that pink doll dress she's holding."

"Yeah, but she's not—" Margo's heart stopped when she realized what he'd said. Her eyes darted around the store. She heard Gerald's deep laughter coming through the phone.

"Look to your right," he said. She swung her head around, and there he was, his shoulder propped against a white wooden column just outside the shop's entryway, his sleek cell phone to his ear.

"Gerald," Margo whispered breathlessly into the phone. "What are you doing here?"

She saw him shrug one shoulder. "I had some vacation time."

"No, you didn't. You had an important case."

"Which I left in the care of my very capable partner."

Margo brought her hand up to the bridge of her nose and started to knead. She was torn between wanting to throw the phone at his stubborn head and wanting to run outside and throw her arms around him.

"Are you saying you're not happy to see me?" he asked.

Jasmine tugged on the hem of her shirt. "Grandma, can I please get one doll? I promise not to ask for anything ever again."

"Jasmine, go and pick out a doll," Margo told her, knowing Alex would kill her. They all had strict orders not to buy Jasmine gifts unless she did something to earn them, but she had to get her granddaughter out of her hair for a minute so she could murder Gerald Mitchell.

"Stay where I can see you," Margo called to Jasmine as her granddaughter dashed to the doll display.

Gerald was already walking her way. He was so tall he had to dip under the shop's arched stone entryway.

Margo waited for him, her arms crossed over her chest.

"Why are you giving me that face?" Gerald asked. He bent down and kissed her cheek.

"Because you are not supposed to be here," Margo answered.

"I told you I couldn't stay away."

"Gerald." She shook her head. "Do you honestly think we'll get to spend any time together?"

"Where there is a will there is a way, my darling. You've become pretty savvy at avoiding those sons of yours," he said.

She had, and she wasn't particularly proud of it. In fact, she was downright tired of it. Alex had surprised everyone by bringing Renee here for the wedding; why couldn't she do the same with Gerald?

A weight seemed to lift from her shoulders at just the thought of all the subterfuge finally coming to an end. She could enjoy Gerald out in the open, without the fear of being caught.

"Honey?"

"Where are you staying?" she asked him.

"La Samanna on Baie Longue. It's on the St. Marteen side of the island. It was the closest place available. Damn tax lawyers have a convention in St. Martin." He smiled.

Margo had to laugh. His own practice was filled with tax lawyers. "I'm going to call you this afternoon. Do you have plans?"

"Nothing that won't change as soon as you say the word. I'm just going to hang around the hotel pool with my laptop until you call."

"I still cannot believe you came all the way here," she said.

"I'm not sure why you're so surprised, Margo. Even if I couldn't see you, I just feel better knowing you're close."

Her heart constricted in her chest. Good Lord, this man knew how to make her feel special with his sweet words.

"I'm going to see you tonight," she promised.

"I'll be waiting for you," he said. He gave her a swift kiss and was out the store.

"Grandma, the lady behind the counter said you have to pay for it before I can hold my new doll."

"That's how things work." Margo took Jasmine by the hand and they headed for the counter.

"Grandma? Why did that man kiss you?"

Chapter Nineteen

Alex heard the crush of voices as soon as he stepped through the glass doors that led into the villa's common area. Hearing a familiar voice call out "Isn't there something to eat up in here?" confirmed that Toby had arrived.

"Yeah, where's the food?"

Monica's best friend and sister-in-law, Nia, had arrived as well.

Alex guided Renee into the living room. Toby, his fiancée, Sienna, Eli, and Monica were standing in the entryway, along with Nia, and Monica's siblings, Phillip and Ashley.

"Hello, everybody," Alex called.

"Yo, Alex. What's up?" Toby pointed at him with the phone he was using to text. As soon as he was done, he pocketed his BlackBerry and started toward Alex. "What's been going on, man?" Toby asked, patting Alex on the back. "You taking care of that shoulder?"

"It's nearly healed up," he answered. Alex could tell the exact moment Toby spotted Renee.

"Hi there," Toby said. "You must be a friend of Monica's."

There was a pause.

"Actually—" Monica said.

"This is Renee," Alex said, motioning for her to take the few steps that would bring her smack in the middle of the foyer. He would apologize later for putting her on display like the newest exhibit at a museum.

"Hi," Renee waved.

Alex gestured to Toby. "Renee, this is my youngest brother, Toby, and his fiancée, Cee Cee. I mean Sienna."

"From you, I'll allow Cee Cee," Sienna said, giving him a hug. "Great to meet you, Renee."

Alex continued with the introductions to Nia and Phillip, and Monica introduced everyone to her seventeen-year-old sister, Ashley, who'd flown in from some fancy school for the arts in New York.

"Somebody point me to the bathroom," Phillip said. "Then I'm falling onto the first bed I see."

"He's been up for thirty-six hours straight," Nia explained, shaking her head as her husband retreated down the hallway Monica had directed him.

Alex thought he and Renee could make a clean exit following Phillip's departure, but Toby asked, "So, Renee, you came down from St. Louis?"

"I didn't bring Renee here, Toby," Monica offered, a sneaky smile on her lips.

"I'm here with Alex," Renee said.

"Bullshit," Toby laughed.

"Toby," Alex said in a warning tone.

"Hold up, she's serious?" Toby asked, looking to Eli for confirmation. Eli nodded, grinning.

"Somebody better check the temperature in hell," Toby laughed.

"Why do you always have to be a jackass?" Alex asked.

"That's just how he is," Sienna said.

"Way to stick up for me, baby." Toby grabbed his fiancée by the arm and brought her in for a quick kiss.

One by one, the women filed out of the foyer toward the kitchen.

Pointing in the direction the ladies had just strolled, Toby's expression was a mixture of confusion and satisfaction. "Is this the woman who Eli said you had in your house?" he asked.

Alex nodded. "I've been seeing Renee for a while. Why don't we leave it at that?"

"After all this time playing the monk routine, you finally get around to seeing somebody and I'm sitting here in the dark? Cough it up, man. I want a blow-by-blow of how this all went down." Toby cut accusing eyes at Eli. "You were holding out me."

Eli held his hands up. "I wanted to tell you, but he made me swear not to." Then he put one arm around Toby's neck. "Man, you should have heard him the first night we were here. He sounded like some caveman throwback, 'She sleeps with me.'"

Alex ignored his brothers as he entered the kitchen. The extended marble bar was covered with platters of cold cuts, sliced chicken breast, cheeses, pitas, hard French rolls, and every condiment needed to make a sandwich. A huge salad bowl filled with colorful leafy vegetables sat in the center. Everyone moved to the table that had been set out on the side patio overlooking the ocean.

"Uncle Toby!" Jasmine came racing from the house. Mama followed. She looked like she'd had a rough morning.

Alex pushed away from the table and went to relieve her of the bag she carried. "Why didn't you put this down in the house?" he asked.

Mama's eyes widened at the sight of the bag. "I didn't re-alize I still had it," she said.

"Mama, you okay?" Alex asked.

"I'm fine," she returned.

"Ma!" Toby bounded from the table and came around to greet their mother in a hug. She smiled, but her expression still held a shell-shocked quality that sent a ripple of unease down Alex's spine.

"Why don't you come in and get something to eat?" Alex suggested, but Mama waved him off. With a deep breath, and a nod of her head, she was back to her old self.

At least, that's what she probably wanted everybody to

believe. Alex wasn't buying it. And he was more than ready to get to the bottom of whatever was up with his mother.

Her heart thumped as loudly as the steel drum beats coming from the cab's speakers. By the time they pulled up to the magnificent entryway of the La Samanna, Margo thought she was going into cardiac arrest.

She paid the cabdriver as she exited the vehicle and nearly slipped on the cobblestones. Maybe she shouldn't have lifted these shoes from Monica's closet. It had been way too long since she'd walked in heels this high, and she didn't need to add a broken ankle to her list of problems.

It was a good thing Jasmine would not be around her father or uncles for the rest of the night. Instead of having dinner with the rest of the clan, Monica's little sister had offered to stay in and play video games with Jasmine at the villa. Margo sent up a quick prayer of thanks that her boys seemed to buy her excuse that she was worn out from the sightseeing they'd done today. They had not made much of a fuss at her choosing to stay home, and had warned Jasmine not to bother her while she rested. Margo just had to make sure she was back before everyone returned.

She focused on settling her nerves enough to enjoy the luxury surrounding her. La Samanna resembled a small town on the Greek isles. The Mediterranean architecture, with its white stucco and terra-cotta tile work, was breathtaking. Of course Gerald would stay here. It was probably the most expensive hotel on the island.

Margo walked through the elaborate lobby and asked a young man in a bellman uniform to point her in the direction of the elevators. She was supposed to meet Gerald in the lobby in twenty minutes so they could have dinner, but Margo had other plans. They were not having dinner in a restaurant tonight. If they ate anything at all, it would be from room service because she was not letting him out of his room.

Nervous anticipation skidded down her spine as she pressed the button that would take her to the third floor.

Wesley, please don't be upset, Margo pleaded. It was a silly thing to worry about. Wesley was probably saying it was about time she'd made this step. He would not have wanted her to live the rest of her life alone.

But was she ready to do this?

Just because she'd worn a dress with a low-cut neckline and borrowed her future daughter-in-law's high-heeled shoes, it didn't make her some kind of sex kitten. What if she lost her nerve and made a fool out of herself?

The elevator doors opened. Margo stuck her shoulders back and headed down the hallway in the direction the wall plaque indicated would lead to room 312. When she reached the door, she had to beg her heart to slow down. It's not as if she would fall right into bed with him the moment he opened the door. She still had some time to get used to the thought of being intimate again after nearly two decades. And she could still change her mind. She had not told Gerald of her plans. He wouldn't even know what he was missing.

No. She'd chickened out of telling the family about him; she was not going to chicken out of this, too.

"You are going to do this." She raised her hand to knock on the door, then put it down again. "God, you're pitiful," she murmured.

"Margo?"

"What!" Margo shouted, and turned. Gerald walked toward her, carrying a suit jacket encased in a plastic laundry drape. "Gerald," she breathed with a hand over her chest. She was definitely going to have a heart attack before the night was over.

"I thought you were meeting me downstairs?" he asked. He gave her a swift kiss as he fished a card key out of his pocket and opened the door to the room. "My jacket got messed up on the flight down here. I sent it to the hotel's laundry, but they don't understand the concept of a rush job."

Margo followed him into the room, which she realized, as they walked deeper in, was a suite. Fine wicker and natural wood furnished the room. Soft yellow, cool tan, and copper accents gave it a touch of luxury. An extra-long couch held an open briefcase, overflowing with papers and file folders.

"You want a drink?" Gerald asked, draping the jacket on the back of one of the chairs and heading for the bar. He uncorked a decanter and filled a glass a quarter of the way with what Margo invariably knew was scotch.

"No, thanks," Margo said, then wondered if a little liquor wouldn't do her some good. Probably not. Mixing alcohol with her quaking stomach could be disastrous.

"Did you have trouble sneaking away?" Gerald grinned from behind the bar.

"Everyone left for a night on the town," Margo said.

"And you stayed behind?"

"I told the boys I was tired," she admitted, rubbing her hands up and down her bare arms.

"Are you cold?" Gerald asked. He walked over to where she stood in the middle of the suite's living area. "I turned the AC up because the cleaning lady left it so hot, but I can turn it off."

"No, I'm fine," Margo said, putting her hands down. She'd tried to break herself of that habit, but it tended to come back when she was particularly nervous. She was lucky she hadn't rubbed her skin off her arms as nervous as she was right now.

She looked up to find Gerald staring at her with an odd look.

"What?" Margo asked, smoothing her hand down her hair.

"You look gorgeous," he answered.

An instant blush crept up her cheeks. "Um, thank you," she answered.

He put his drink down and walked the few steps that brought him within inches of her. "Just the chance to look at you across the table tonight will make this entire trip worth it." He trailed his fingers lightly along her shoulder and down her arm.

Margo caught his hand and brought it to her lips. "Gerald?"

"Yeah, sweetheart?"

She swallowed. *You can do this.*

"I don't want to have dinner tonight," she said.

Disappointment washed over his face. "Why not?"

Margo realized how her words sounded. "I mean I don't want to go to a restaurant," she quickly amended. "I'd rather us eat here. In your room. Later," she added.

Gerald arched a brow, and she looked away. She was horribly failing Seduction 101.

Gerald captured her chin in his fingers and raised her head. She closed her eyes. "Margo?" His voice was soft and gentle.

She opened her eyes. Gerald was looking down at her with a look of understanding mixed with anticipation. "Just so I know I'm not reading this wrong, you *are* saying you want to make love?"

Here was her chance to back out. She could laugh it off as a misunderstanding. But as she stared into his kind, sympathetic eyes, Margo realized she wanted nothing more than to finally give herself over to this man who had slowly, expertly stolen her heart.

"Yes," she managed to squeeze past the lump of emotion lodged in her throat.

"Are you sure about this, baby?"

She caressed his slightly stubble-roughened cheek, then took his hand and kissed the soft flesh of his palm.

"Yes," she answered. "Gerald, would you please take me to bed?"

* * *

After the animated conversation at lunch, Renee had surmised the youngest of Margo Holmes's sons possessed the best sense of humor, but watching the three of them together, she found it hard to decide who was the best storyteller.

She'd had an education in what it really meant to be a family. The way Alex and his brothers interacted, one would think they were seconds away from killing each other, but in the next minute they were laughing at the havoc they'd caused while growing up. It was obvious why Alex was so protective of his brothers. He'd helped to raise them, and there was no question both Elijah and Tobias acknowledged and appreciated the sacrifices their older brother had made. During the course of the evening, both had managed to whisper to her how grateful they were that she was dating Alex. Their concern was genuine. And touching.

She never knew families could have such love between them.

"I can't sit here any longer," Toby announced. He grabbed his fiancée by the hand and dragged her onto the dance floor. Nia followed in his footsteps, grabbing Phillip, who didn't put up much resistance.

Eli pushed himself up from the booth they had commandeered at the club Toby had demanded they check out. It was purported to be St. Martin's premier nightspot. "I guess that means I have to dance, too," he said.

"You bet your cute butt it does," Monica said. She allowed him to help her out of the booth, then tapped his butt with a loud pat.

"You know I'm going to make you pay for that," Eli said.

"Why do you think I did it?" Monica laughed as they made their way to the dance floor.

"You want to?" Alex asked with enough hesitancy in his voice to make Renee throw her head back and laugh.

"On a scale of one to ten, how much do you really want to get out there and dance?" she asked.

"A negative one hundred," he answered. "But if you want to, I'll suck it up."

She pushed closer to him in the comfortable booth. "I'm fine right here," she said.

"Thank God. You do not want to see me dance."

"I didn't say I never wanted to dance," Renee laughed. "I'm sure you're much better than you think you are."

"Yeah, I wouldn't bet on it."

"You having fun tonight?" she asked, snuggling closer.

"I'd rather be back in our room at the villa, but if I can't be there, this is a pretty good second."

"This trip is passing way too quickly," she said. "Tomorrow is the wedding, and then we only have one more day before flying home. There's still so much to see."

"You want to come back?"

She looked up at him. "You would bring me back here?"

"If you wanted me to," he said. "I can't promise L'Oasis, but I would love to be somewhere on this island with you. Just the two of us."

Her heart started pounding even faster than the Caribbean techno beat thumping throughout the club. The combination of fear and excitement was heady. How long would she let whatever this was she had going on with Alex continue? She didn't see it ending any time soon. Just the thought of going back to a life he wasn't a part of sent a sharp ache straight to the middle of her chest. When had he become so important to her?

"Are you thinking of an answer?" Alex asked.

"To what?"

"To coming back to this island with me one day?"

She wasn't ready to commit to anything. She still needed to figure out what should come of this relationship. She could easily lose herself in Alex.

She'd told him she loved him.

The thought scared her stiff. She was quickly sinking into a situation she'd vowed to avoid at all costs. Alex had not

shown a single sign that he had a violent bone in his body, but neither had her father in the beginning. It wasn't until he'd lost his job and started drinking that he'd turned into a monster. Who was to say a shocking blow wouldn't cause the same reaction in Alex?

Of course he wouldn't, Renee. Look how he'd reacted when she finally shared the horror of her childhood. He'd opened his arms and offered comfort, and that special sense of understanding that was so Alex.

She did love him. How could she not?

Renee tapped the table and started scooting out of the booth. "You know what? I think I do want to dance," she said.

Alex groaned. "I'm warning you, this is not a good idea."

"Indulge me," she said.

"Fine," he returned. "But when you can't walk because I've stepped on your toes for a solid five minutes, I reserve the right to say 'I told you so.'"

"Agreed," Renee laughed.

How could she even think he would become violent? There was no way this man would put a fist to her. It was unfathomable.

Alex was not exaggerating at his lack of dancing ability, but Renee had to give him credit for trying. After over a half hour on the dance floor, she took pity on him and allowed him to lead her to another table, where they watched his brothers and their fiancées dance for a while longer.

Toby tried to convince them to go to another club, but he got no love from the over-thirty crowd, which included everyone except for him and Sienna. Renee wasn't in the mood for club-hopping. She wanted nothing more than to snuggle up with Alex in that big, comfy bed back at the villa.

"Hey, Toby, make sure you have the camera tomorrow when the dancing starts," Eli said as they all rode in the back of the van that had taken them to the club. "I have

that surprise for Monica, and I want to make sure it's captured on video."

"So, why did you tell me?" Monica hit Eli on the arm.

"I didn't tell you."

"No, you didn't tell me what the surprise is, but you told me you've got one. Now I'm going to spend the entire night trying to figure it out."

"Believe me, baby, that's not how you're going to spend your night."

She hit him again, but her mocha-colored cheeks were already turning a rosy red.

"Hold up," Toby said. "Anybody noticed what just happened? There was sex talk, and Alex didn't tell anybody to shut up."

"Shut up, Toby," Alex said.

"That doesn't count," his brother countered.

"And you were wondering why I felt the need to apologize for my brothers in advance," Alex said to Renee.

"What's wrong with us?" Toby and Eli said in unison.

"Don't worry," Sienna said. "You get used to them. It took me about twenty-eight years, but I did eventually." Toby playfully bit her on the shoulder, and like Monica, Sienna blushed.

When the van pulled up to the villa's entrance, there was a taxi sitting in the drive.

"Aria's not coming in until tomorrow, right?" Eli asked.

Toby nodded. They all exited the van just as Margo emerged from the cab, carrying a killer sequined clutch.

"Oh, I hate to miss this, but I'll burst if I don't get to a bathroom," Nia said, breaking out of the van and running inside.

All three of Margo's sons converged on her before she could make it to the villa's front door.

"Where're you coming from?"

"I thought you were tired?"

"What are you doing in that dress?"

Poor Margo looked like a teenager who'd just been caught sneaking in after curfew, her eyes wide with shock.

Renee stood back with Monica and Sienna on either side of her.

"Oh Lord," Monica said under her breath.

"You know what's going on?" Sienna whispered.

"What are you all doing home so early?" Margo asked. "It's not even eleven o'clock."

"What are you doing getting out of a cab?" Eli asked. "I thought you were tired?"

"I decided to go into the city for something to eat," Margo answered. "Now can we please get in the house?"

Her sons followed her into the villa, but they were far from finished with their interrogation.

"Why didn't you just have the chef fix you something to eat, Mama?" Eli asked. "That's what he's here for."

"The chef leaves at nine," she answered.

"Forget the food. What the heck are you wearing?" Toby asked.

"Yeah, what are you even doing with that kind of a dress?" Alex added.

Margo propped a hand on her hip. "Excuse me, but I thought *I* was the parent here. I didn't know I had to answer to any of you."

"You tell 'em, Margo."

The three sons turned and stared Sienna down with identical blistering glares.

"Please, boys," Margo said, the plea drenched in exhaustion. "I wanted to go out and see the island. That's the end of it."

"I don't believe you," Alex said.

"I don't care what you believe," Margo said, taking off a pair of fierce strappy heels and holding them out to Monica. "I borrowed these," she said.

"No problem," Monica answered with a knowing smile.

"Mama, who were you with tonight?" Alex asked.

"Oh, come on, Alex. Don't start that boyfriend thing again," Toby said. "Mama does not have a boyfriend."

Margo turned, both hands on her hips this time. "And what if I did?" she asked.

The silence that followed was pregnant with tension. The expressions on the faces of the men in the room were so horrified, you would think Margo had asked what they thought of her jumping out of an airplane without a parachute.

"Mama?" Toby said, hurt and disbelief making him sound like a ten-year-old.

"Who is he?" Eli asked, his voice very much the grown-up's. His anger was thick enough to smell.

Margo brought her hands up to rub her temples. "What am I going to do with you boys?"

"Try telling us the truth," Alex said.

"What's the big deal?" Sienna asked, moving to flank Margo's side.

"That's what I want to know," Monica said, moving to Margo's left.

Renee decided to stay right where she had been planted for the past five minutes.

"The big deal is I don't want some guy thinking he can come in and replace Pop, that's what!" Toby said.

"Toby, be real," Sienna shot at him.

"You're just saying that because there's no guy coming in trying to replace your dad," Toby countered.

"I'm not having this conversation tonight," Margo announced. "You're right, Toby, I don't have a boyfriend. I'm going to live the rest of my life in my little house all alone. Is that what you all want to hear?"

Alex reached for her, but Margo jerked her arm away. "No, I'm going to bed. I want to be bright-eyed and refreshed when my middle child starts the rest of his life tomorrow."

She took off down the hallway. Eli went after her, but Monica grabbed the hem of his shirt.

"I can't just let her go off like that," Eli said.

Ignoring him, Monica pushed Eli toward his brothers, then faced the three of them. Pointing to the bedrooms where a door had just slammed, Monica said, "That woman has lived her entire life for you three. *If* she is seeing someone, it's her business. What makes any of you think you have a right to question whether she's chosen to start dating again?"

"You're still new to this family," Toby said. "How you gonna tell us what to do about our mama?"

Eli started to speak, but Monica stopped him. "You want to know just how much I can tell you about your own mother?" she asked Toby. "What did she do last week that she's been waiting to do for the last five years? Huh? Any clue?"

The scuffle of feet-shifting was the only sound in the room.

"Did you know she was up for head deaconess at her church?" Monica continued. "Or that she was recognized by the head of the Neighborhood Watch Association for her work on the board? Well?" Monica asked when Toby remained silent. "Come on, Toby. You've been a part of this family for nearly thirty years, you should know this about your *own* mother, right?

"That's what I thought," she said as Toby looked anywhere but at Monica. "When was the last time your mother confided in you? In any of you," she practically roared at the three men who towered over her.

She walked up to Toby, getting right in his face. Renee felt like cheering.

"I may be new to this family, but Margo feels more comfortable sharing what's going on in her life with me than she does with any of you. And do you know why? Because I treat her like a person, and not somebody who's there to fix dinner, or do my laundry, or be a babysitter," she said, thumping Toby, Eli, and Alex in the chest with her finger.

"Tomorrow is my wedding, and I swear, if there is even an ounce of tension in the air from what happened here tonight, I'm going to kill each one of you. Starting with you." She pointed at Eli.

He held up his hands. "I was about to defend you, baby."

"I don't need you to defend me. I need the three of you to act like men and not a bunch of little boys."

Even with the suffocating unease saturating the air, Renee couldn't help but notice how good Alex looked when he was being chastised.

"If you would just tell us what you know, we wouldn't be in the dark about what's happening with Mama," Alex said.

"If there is anything to tell, it is not my place to tell it," Monica said. "Apparently, your mother doesn't feel comfortable talking to any of you. Maybe you should think about what that says about your relationship with your *own* mother," she threw at Toby. She took a deep breath. "I'm tired, and I don't want bags under my eyes when I get married tomorrow."

Monica turned and headed for the hallway that led to the master suite.

"You see why I love that woman?" Eli said, taking off after her.

Toby claimed all the arguing had worked up his appetite, and he and Sienna headed for the kitchen, leaving Renee with a very weary-looking Alex. She wasn't sure how to approach him. The last time they'd talked about this subject, he had not agreed with her assessment. And since her stance had not changed, she figured he wasn't up for rehashing the conversation.

Renee put her arms round him and placed her head on his chest. "Would it really be so bad if your mother had a boyfriend?"

"I'm starting to suspect it's no longer a question of if, but rather who," Alex answered. "I just want to make sure she's not being taken advantage of," he said.

"Is that it?"

She felt him shrug. "I'd be lying if I say I don't feel a bit of betrayal on behalf of Pop."

"He's been dead for a long time, Alex. From what you've told me about him, your father loved your mother very much. Do you really think he would want her to live the rest of her life alone?"

He sighed deeply, his chest bellowing out underneath her cheek. "If Mama *is* seeing someone it's going to take me a while to come to terms with it," he said.

"But you will eventually, right?"

"Maybe," he said. Renee had to laugh at his stubborn-ness.

"Think of it this way. How would you feel if Jasmine had reacted to the news that we were dating the same way you're reacting to your mother?"

"Actually, this is how I had expected Jasmine to react," he reminded her.

"Yet she was smart enough to accept that you could move on after her mother's death. Don't you think it's a lit-tle ridiculous that a six-year-old can be more open-minded than a thirty-eight-year-old?"

"Which answer will make you more inclined to jump into bed with me?" Alex asked.

"That's going to happen no matter what," she laughed.

"In that case, I defer answering until I'm able to concen-trate on something other than getting you naked," he said. Dipping his head low, he touched his lips to hers and guided her to their room.

Chapter Twenty

"The ceremony was beautiful," Renee said, pulling Alex in and delivering a quick kiss to his lips. "And you, sir, are looking extremely fine in that suit. You almost outshine the groom."

"Almost?" Alex asked.

"That smile Eli had on his face from the moment he saw Monica walking up the aisle is pretty hard to beat," she said.

Alex glanced over to where his brother and new sister-in-law rocked slowly in each other's arms as Aria sang Eli's surprise to Monica, a song Toby had written especially for her. A giant sinkhole could swallow up the rest of the guests; Alex doubted Eli or Monica would notice.

"I just hope their marriage lasts," Alex murmured.

"What makes you think it won't?"

He shrugged. "I was happy on my wedding day, too." Alex felt a pang of regret, and a measure of guilt, for comparing his brother's marriage to his own. It wasn't fair, especially to Monica, who was nothing like his dead wife.

"I haven't had the most ideal model of a strong, loving marriage, either, Alex, but I have to believe it does exist."

"I know it does," he said. "As long as the two people are willing to work hard at it, marriage can be a beautiful thing. I saw it with my own parents."

"Is it something you would consider trying again?" Renee asked.

Alex's first instinct was to shout no since he'd claimed for so long that he would never remarry. But he wasn't as averse to the idea as he had been just a few months ago. Funny how one woman could change his entire perspective.

"I would," Alex finally answered. He reached across the table and trailed his thumb across the rise of her hand. "When the time is right, I want to get married again."

"The time *and* the woman would have to be right, wouldn't it?" Renee asked.

"I'm not worried about finding the right woman," he said. "Not anymore."

Her mouth creased in a smile.

"Daddy!" Jasmine ran up to the small round table he and Renee had occupied for the last half hour.

"Hey, Pumpkin." Alex turned his legs so that he could scoop her up and plant her on his lap.

"Jasmine, you were the cutest flower girl I've ever seen," Renee said.

"I practiced throwing the flowers," Jasmine answered.

"Well, it showed. You were excellent."

"What do we say when someone gives us a compliment?" Alex asked.

Jasmine straightened her back and announced in a prim voice that echoed Margo Holmes, "Thank you. You are too kind."

"You are very welcome," Renee said with a crack of laughter.

"Daddy, can I go swimming?"

"You can't swim in the middle of your uncle's reception."

"But why? Everybody is out here by the pool, anyway."

"Why's my Rosebud frowning?" Eli asked, coming up to their table.

"I want to swim, but Daddy said I can't because you and Auntie Monica are still having the wedding."

"The wedding is over. They're still having their reception," Alex corrected.

"A pool party reception doesn't sound like a bad idea,"

Eli said. "Baby!" he called out in Monica's direction. She left the buffet table where Nia and Phillip stood.

"Yes?" Monica asked, kissing Eli square on the mouth.

"What do you say we ditch these clothes for swimsuits and liven up this party?"

"You want to swim at your wedding reception?" Monica asked with more than a bit of skepticism.

"Why not?" Eli asked. "That sound good to you, Calla Lily?"

"Yeah!" Jasmine cheered, pumping her fist in the air and nearly knocking Alex in the jaw. It was amazing how this little girl still managed to get her way.

"Sounds good to me, too," Monica said. She turned and clapped her hands. "Listen up, everybody. We're changing into our suits and bringing this party into the pool."

Jasmine hopped off Alex's lap and dashed into the house. She was followed by all of the adults, save for himself, Renee, and his mother, who sat just at the edge of the pool area, looking out at the small waves that were crashing onto shore.

Renee must have noticed where his eyes had roamed. She tapped him on the arm. "Why don't you go talk to her?" she encouraged.

"Do I have to?" Alex muttered, knowing he sounded like a coward, but not caring.

"Go on, Alex. I'm going to go in and change."

She rose from the table, but Alex caught her by the wrist and pulled her to him before she took a step. He reined her in for a swift kiss. He tried to let her go, but Renee deepened the kiss, dragging it out for a few seconds longer.

"I really love doing that," she said.

"Not as much as I do," Alex told her.

He let her go, but could not make himself move away from the table until she'd entered through the glass doors. He was falling in love with this woman in a really bad way. After just a couple of days of sleeping next to her, Alex wasn't sure he would be able to sleep alone again. That was really, *really* bad. They had not discussed to any great detail how things between them would change, if at all, once they got back to New Orleans. But it had to change. Alex couldn't go back to the way things were.

Alex tabled thoughts of Renee and the state of their relationship. Looking over at his mother, who was in the same position she'd held since the ceremony ended, Alex swallowed the lump of guilt that had settled in his throat. He bore a share of the blame for the sadness on Mama's face. She had not enjoyed Eli's wedding day the way she should have. She'd pretended well enough. Anyone who didn't know her would have thought Mama the epitome of the proud mother of the groom. But Alex knew better. Last night's argument had cast a pall over her day, and because of him and his brothers, Mama would never get a chance to bask in the joy she should have been feeling as her middle son walked down the aisle.

Alex strode up to where his mother stood and leaned his elbows on the white, waist-high stone wall that separated the pool area from the private beach.

"What's his name, Mama?" Alex opened, figuring it best to get straight to the point.

She paused for a moment, then on a tiny breath said, "Gerald."

Alex acknowledged the shot of betrayal that came with the confirmation that she had, indeed, found a man to replace Pop.

"How long have you been seeing him?" he asked.

"Seven months," she answered.

"That long?" Alex couldn't keep the shock from seeping out of his voice. His mother had been lying to them for all those months. "You thought you couldn't tell us about him?"

She turned, the level of animosity in her eyes topping anything Alex had ever witnessed. "You have the nerve to ask me that after last night?"

"That's not fair, Mama," Alex said. "You said you were staying in because you were tired. You lied to us."

"What's not fair is the way I've been treating Gerald, all because I was too afraid of how the other people in my life would react to the thought of me dating again. Well, you know what, Alex, I don't care anymore. I. Don't. Care. I'm in love with Gerald, and I'm not hiding it anymore."

"Hold on." Alex put his hand up, as if it could halt the words his mother had just spoken, because he surely had not just heard her say she was in love with some man no one in the family had yet to meet. "You're moving too fast," Alex said.

"I'm sixty years old," she said. "I think I've lived long enough to know how to pace myself."

"You don't want to jump into anything too soon with this guy."

"How do you feel about Renee?" she threw at him, catching Alex completely off guard.

"What does that have to do with you and this Gerald guy?"

"You're in love with her," his mother said with a certainty that made it hard for Alex to deny. "Even if you're not ready to acknowledge it yet doesn't mean it's not true. I see it in the way you act around her, Alex. If you can be in love with Renee after only knowing her a few months, what makes you think my feelings for Gerald are any less real?

"I'm tired of sneaking around," she continued. "If you boys can't deal with the fact that I've found someone else to love, then that's your problem, not mine."

"What about Pop?" Alex asked.

She threw her hands up and sighed. "He's dead, Alex." She reached over and patted his forearm, giving it a reassuring squeeze. "I loved Wesley so much that after all these years all I have to do is say his name and my world just lights up. I will never love another man as much as I loved your father." She put her palm against his cheek and nudged his head so she could look him in the eye. "But I still have my own life to live. I don't plan on going anywhere for a very long time, and I don't want to spend the rest of my days on this earth alone.

"And before you say it, having you three boys and your families is not enough. I deserve to find my own happiness. And I have. With Gerald."

Alex was about to speak when the glass door opened and Toby and Sienna came out of the house dressed in their swim-suits. They were quickly followed by Jasmine, Nia, Ashley, Monica, Eli, and Aria. Phillip came out in cargo shorts and a T-shirt.

"Alex?"

He turned back to face his mother, and for the first time in a very long while saw her as something other than Mama. She was Margo Holmes, a healthy, outgoing woman, who Alex prayed to God had many years left with her family.

"I hope you and your brothers can be happy for me," Mama continued. "But whether you are or not, you will have to accept Gerald in my life," she said.

The thought caused a sour taste to form in Alex's mouth, but those words had not been a threat. This man was a part of their new reality.

"I guess we don't have a choice," Alex said.

"Yes, you do," she answered.

"If it's a question of being a part of your life or not, then no, there is no choice. If this Gerald makes you happy, we're all going to learn to accept him," he said, feeling no compunc-tion at answering for his brothers. Even if he had to force them into compliance the way he did when they were kids, Alex would make sure Toby and Eli supported their mother.

"Thank you," she said, pulling him down and kissing his cheek. "I didn't need your blessing, but I wanted it."

Alex nodded, even though a part of him wanted to take it all back. It was that part of him that wished things could go back to the way they were when Pop was still alive. But they couldn't go there. Things change. Life goes on.

"I'm going to make an effort to accept Gerald, Mama. A true effort."

"I know you will," she said, her face lighting up with the first genuine smile Alex had seen from her today. "Are you getting in the water?"

"Nah, I'll just sit on the sidelines and watch, as usual," he answered.

"Are you sure? I would rethink that if I were you," she said, motioning with her chin.

Alex turned fully and noticed what had caught his mother's eye. Renee had just come out of the house, dressed in a chocolate and cream one-piece bathing suit that was sexier on her than the skimpiest bikini on your average supermodel.

It took him a moment to catch his breath.

Mama laughed. "She's so good for you, Alex."

"I know." He nodded.

"I'm going inside to make a phone call," Mama said. "I think you should come in and change into your swim trunks. It's supposed to be a party, remember?"

"Only if you join in the party, too," Alex said.

"Give me about a half hour," Mama said. "I think I'll be in more of a party mood."

Renee snuggled up even closer to Alex. She needed to feel his warmth, despite the heat from the whirlpool. He pulled her into his body, running his hand up and down her arm.

"Where are you from?" Nia asked. She signaled for the waiter and held up her empty margarita glass.

"Most recently Florida," Renee answered.

"What area? I love the Keys," Nia said. "I told Phillip we have to retire there, if we don't buy a house in New Orleans, that is. I fall more in love with that city with every visit."

"Monica would love it if you moved to New Orleans," Alex said.

"But my waistline wouldn't," Nia laughed. "Speaking of my waistline, I think there's still room for some of those conch fritters."

Nia climbed out of the hot tub and headed in the direction of the buffet table that the staff replenished at regular intervals throughout the afternoon, leaving Alex and Renee alone in the semisecluded hot tub.

"Nia must work out five hours a day to maintain that figure," Renee said. "I don't think she's stopped eating since she's been here."

"Don't ask her to choose between you and a pork chop," Alex said. "You'll lose every time."

Renee smiled up at him. "So, did everything go okay with your mom?" She tilted her head up to catch his expression. It was as sour as she'd expected.

"I'm still trying to decide," Alex said. He recounted the conversation.

She patted his chest. "It'll be okay, Alex. I'm sure he's a nice guy."

"He'd better treat her like a queen," Alex said.

Relishing the smooth skin underneath her fingers, Renee drew tiny circles on his chest. "Your mom would not willingly date a man who didn't treat her right. You should trust her judgment."

"Says you and my common sense," Alex snorted. "Another part of me wants to find this guy once we get back to New Orleans and pay him to get the heck out of the city and never come back."

"Have I ever told you how cute you are when you're being overprotective?" she asked, pulling herself up to give him a kiss on his lips. They kissed in the shadow of a wide banana leaf that partially obscured them from the rest of the crowd enjoying the poolside comfort.

When Alex finally released her lips, Renee twisted around, leaning her back against his chest, soaking in the decadent softness of his skin.

"Uh-oh," she sang.

"What's wrong?" Alex asked.

"I think you're about to meet your mother's new boyfriend."

Chapter Twenty-one

Margo clasped the strong hand Gerald held at his side, squeezing it in an attempt to soak in a bit of his strength. She had nothing to be afraid of anymore. The cat was already out of the bag.

She'd hoped she would feel a bit more confident now that she had finally admitted to one of her sons that she was seeing someone for the first time since their father's death. Margo was happy it was Alex she'd finally come clean with. She knew her eldest son would be the most understanding, and he would be a staunch ally when she encountered Eli's and Toby's animosity toward Gerald. And there would be animosity. Margo knew her boys well enough to anticipate their impending reaction.

Gerald stopped just before the doors that led to the pool area, the light shining through the glass bathing them in its warmth. "I know you've feared this moment for a long time."

She only nodded.

Enclosing her hands in his, Gerald stooped to her eye level. "Whatever happens out there, I want you to know that I'm not giving you up without a fight," he said.

"You don't have to worry about losing me." Margo smiled.

"You say that now, but children can be very persuasive," he said. "Remember, I'm a father. My girls gave me hell over the first woman I dated after their mother's death, but they learned to deal with it. Your sons will have to do the same," he said.

"If they care at all about my feelings, they're going to treat you with kindness and respect. And I have to believe that I've raised them to do that," she said. "Let's just hope I'm not fooling myself," she muttered under her breath.

"Are you ready?" Gerald asked.

"I'm ready." Margo gave his hand a solid shake.

Gerald slid the door open and they entered the pool deck where the reception was still going strong. Eli, Monica, Toby, Sienna, Nia, and Aria were playing pool volleyball. Ashley seemed to be giving Jasmine backstroke lessons in the shallow end of the pool. Phillip had fallen asleep with a copy of the *New Yorker* opened on his chest. She didn't see Alex and Renee.

"Can I get everyone's attention?" Margo called above the music coming out of the speakers mounted to the house's outside back wall. The activity in the pool came to an abrupt halt. Margo noticed Alex and Renee coming from the area where the hot tub was located.

"Everyone, this is Gerald Mitchell."

Eli wiped water from his face, which held a look that seemed both astonished and agitated. The look on Toby's face wasn't much better.

Blessedly, Alex's expression was more neutral when he approached Gerald with his hand outstretched.

"Mr. Mitchell," he said.

"Hello, Alex," Gerald replied, returning his handshake.

"I guess you've known about me a little longer than I've known about you," Alex said.

"I have. It's nice to finally meet you."

Toby approached, patting his arms dry with a towel. "Who's this?" he asked.

"Gerald Mitchell," Gerald answered.

"I heard your name, I want to know who you are," Toby said, ignoring Gerald's outstretched hand.

A fist of anxiety knotted in her stomach, but Margo curbed it by sheer will. She would not allow her family to make Gerald feel unwelcome, no matter how they actually felt about him.

"Gerald and I have been seeing each other for the past seven months," Margo said. There. It was out for all the world to hear. Her shoulders sagged with relief at the realization that the lying and sneaking around were officially behind her.

Sienna's shocked gasp was followed by a choking sound from Toby. Monica stood to the side, smiling, and Margo instantly regretted not taking her daughter-in-law's advice to come clean about her relationship with Gerald months ago.

"I can't believe this," Toby said.

"Gerald, do you mind coming into the house with me and my brothers?" Alex asked.

"Not at all," Gerald answered.

"Come on," Alex called to Toby and Eli, who had yet to say anything.

When she tried to follow them, Alex and Gerald both halted her steps.

"I think I should talk to your boys alone, baby," Gerald said.

"Did this man just call my mama 'baby'?" Toby asked with his usual incredulousness at something he didn't like.

"Toby!" Sienna warned, pinching his arm.

With a petulant frown clouding his face, Toby reluctantly led the way into the house. As soon as Alex slid the glass door shut behind them, Margo collapsed into a chair. She was instantly surrounded by Monica, Sienna, Nia, and Renee, who all gushed about Gerald's distinguished good looks and his air of protectiveness. Margo answered their questions about Gerald's business, his daughters, and everything else they wanted to know.

Despite the bevy of inquiries from the women, Margo's mind remained on the conversation that must be taking place inside the villa. Were the boys bombarding Gerald with hostile questions? Toby could be as obnoxious as a four-year-old when he put his mind to it.

Gerald could handle himself. He faced hostile witnesses

and obnoxious judges on a daily basis. Though Margo doubted anyone Gerald encountered in a courtroom could raise more opposition than her three sons.

When the door slid open her entire being stood still in breathless anticipation. *Please let there be no bloody noses or bruises.*

All four men returned with the same serious expressions they'd held when they'd first entered the house, but as soon as Gerald spotted her his face softened.

Margo stood as they approached. They formed a semicircle around her.

"Well?" she asked.

Eli shrugged. "We're going to play a foursome at English Turn when we get back home. If he lets us beat him on the golf course, he can stay."

Relief melted into her bones. Margo threw her arms around Gerald, and kissed him on the mouth.

Toby pulled her out of Gerald's arms and tucked her next to his side. "Yeah, dude, I'm not ready to see that."

"Grow up, Toby," Alex said.

"Bite me," Toby returned.

"Boys, please," Margo said. She turned to Gerald. "They're not usually like this."

"Yes, we are," all three of her sons answered.

"That's fine with me," Gerald said. He eased her out of Toby's hold and wrapped his arms around her waist. "Young man, you may want to close your eyes," Gerald told Toby as he nuzzled her neck and placed a gentle kiss on the top of her head.

"I'm really going to miss this place," Renee said as she burrowed more snugly under the covers, wrapping her leg around Alex's.

"I'll buy a lottery ticket when we get back home," Alex said. "If it hits, the villa is yours."

"I'm really going to miss this place," she repeated, laughing.

"Don't lose hope. Maybe Mama's new boyfriend will buy it for her," Alex snorted.

"I can't believe he's *that* Gerald Mitchell," Renee said. "I've only lived in New Orleans for a little while, but even I've heard of him."

"His law firm has to be the biggest in the city," Alex acknowledged.

Which made it even more unbelievable that Margo had been able to keep their relationship out of the public eye, Renee concluded. Gerald Mitchell's face was constantly plastered on the news, connected to all types of high-profile cases. They must have been supersecretive.

"It looks as if he really cares for your mom. He's going to take good care of her."

"Not that she needs anyone else to take care of her, but I think you're right," Alex agreed. "Mama looked really happy today, once she brought Gerald over. I hadn't realized how long it had been since I'd seen that look on her face." He nuzzled her neck. "You look really happy, too."

"What do you expect?" Renee asked. "After the last hour, I'll probably smile for the rest of the week."

"My aim is always to please," Alex said. He lowered his hands to grip her butt and pulled her into contact with his unmistakable arousal.

"You're pretty good at pleasing," Renee moaned, astounded at just how much she wanted him again.

By the time they collapsed onto each other in panting contentment, Renee's entire being throbbed with satisfaction. Alex's deep breathing was instantaneous, but Renee knew it would be a lot longer before she was able to drift to sleep, despite her complete exhaustion. The thoughts running through her mind were too intense to allow anything as paltry as rest to put a stop to them.

She couldn't help but wonder what the future would bring. Was it this man, and his huge, wonderful family? Could she even dare dream of having the sense of belonging that embodied the Holmeses? Their love for each other was evident in all facets of their lives. Even when things seemed dire, as they had during the intense moments when Margo had first introduced Gerald this afternoon, there were underlying currents of affection and understanding.

How would she even function in such a family? She didn't know love, not the way these people expressed the emotion. Renee wasn't even sure she could learn it this late in the game. Maybe it was something that must be taught from early on in order to truly grasp the concept of loving another human being with your whole heart.

The only love she knew was warped by a fist that soon followed.

"You are so messed up," she whispered to herself. Alex stirred under her, and Renee looked up at him from where she rested on his chest. It was possible that if she allowed it, this man could help her to heal.

If only she allowed it.

Chapter Twenty-two

"Daddy, don't you think we should move here?" Jasmine asked as she tied her pink and white tennis shoes.

"What about our house back in New Orleans?" Alex asked.

"We could sell it."

"You would leave your princess suite that easily?"

"No." She shook her head. "Let's just come back to visit. Oooh, Daddy, I know." Her eyes lit up. "I can have my next birthday party at the pool! You can fly my class out here."

"You must think Daddy is made of money," Alex laughed. He held out the towel he used to carry their loot. "Is this enough seashells?"

Jasmine scrunched up her nose. "No, not yet. I have to

bring one for Kayla and Mrs. Leslie, one for Mrs. Overton. Oh, and one for everybody in my class."

"You're going to need an extra suitcase just to bring all of these shells back home, Jazzy."

"Uncle Eli said I could bring my dirty clothes home in a pillowcase," she said.

Idiot. "Don't listen to your uncle Eli anymore," Alex said. He spotted the tip of a pinkish seashell and dug it out of the sand. "We'll pick up a few more; then we need to get back to the house so we can start packing up. We have to leave really early for the airport tomorrow, and I know you want to swim one more time before you pack your swimsuit."

"I don't need any more seashells," she said. "Let's go swim."

"What about all your friends?"

"I can give them rocks from Grandma's yard," she said, and Alex had to bite back his laughter.

"It won't take too long," he said. "We'll get just a couple more."

They walked a few yards more along the stretch of white sand. They ran across a collection of shells that had washed upon the shore. Alex crouched in the sand next to Jasmine and picked out a few.

"Do you miss Mommy?" Jasmine asked.

Alex's head shot up. Where had that come from?

"Of course I miss her," Alex lied. "Why?"

"I dunno." She shrugged.

"You miss her, too, don't you?"

"Kinda," she answered, staring intently at the sand.

"Kinda? What do you mean by that, Pumpkin?"

Another shrug.

"Jasmine." Alex tipped her chin up so he could look into her eyes. "Talk to me."

She picked up a seashell and placed it in the pouch she'd made by curling up the edge of her shirt. "I miss Mommy, but sometimes I don't miss her," she said. "Mommy used to fuss at me if I got mud on my shoes. But, Daddy, it's hard to play outside and not get mud on your shoes, especially in the back of Grandma's yard."

"I know," he said.

"And when Uncle Kenneth would come to the house, Mommy used to make me go to my room. She told me I didn't have to sleep, but that I couldn't come out of my room, even if I had to pee." She whispered the last part.

Uncle Kenneth. The bastard Chantal had been screwing. She'd brought him to the house Alex had worked day and night to buy. She'd banished his child to her room so she and her lover could roam free around his house.

Until this moment, Alex had never experienced true hate. If Chantal were alive, Alex wasn't sure he would be able to abstain from putting his hands around her neck and relishing the rush of seeing the life drain out of her.

"I'm sorry Mommy did those things, Jazzy," Alex said.

"I don't think Ms. Moore would care if I got mud on my shoes," Jasmine said.

"No, Ms. Moore wouldn't."

"I want you to marry Ms. Moore," she said. "Just ask her, Daddy."

"When I ask Ms. Moore to marry me, you will be the first one to know," he said, dusting sand from the tip of her nose. "In fact, I want you to be there when I do ask her."

"Let's go ask her now!"

"Jazzy, no!" Alex said, reining her in with a tug to the back of her shirt. "I'm not ready to ask Ms. Moore to marry me yet."

"Why not?"

"Because getting married is a big step, and Ms. Moore and I need to get to know each other better."

"But she's pretty and she don't fuss. And Grandma said that Ms. Moore likes you. If you don't ask her to marry you, she might marry somebody else."

"I don't think Ms. Moore would do that," Alex said.

"And if she did, that means God doesn't think we should be together."

The thought of that actually happening set a sickening acid burning within Alex's gut. He could not stomach the though of Renee standing at an altar with another man, pledging the same vows Eli and Monica had recited yesterday. Lying in bed with another man, doing the same things she had done with him last night.

Maybe he should just put it out there and ask her to marry him. What was the worst that could happen? Other than her thinking him a lunatic for proposing after knowing each other for only a few months?

But the fact that he was even considering marriage again after his vow not to even date was a testament to just how close they had become in this short span of time. The idea of popping the question didn't seem like a bout with lunacy anymore.

By the time they arrived back at the villa, it was nearly time for dinner. Alex allowed Jasmine to swim since he'd promised her she could do so before packing. Toby and Sienna were hugged up together on one of the poolside lounge chairs.

"You mind watching her while she swims?" Alex asked.

"What if I said I did mind?" Toby asked.

"I'd tell you to do it anyway," Alex replied. "Where is everybody?"

"Mama and her new boyfriend went to some fancy restaurant," Toby scoffed.

Sienna slapped his arm. "Monica, Eli, Nia, and Phillip went to Marigot before going to the airport to drop Nia and Phillip off," she said.

"What time does your flight leave tomorrow?" Alex asked.

"Not until seven p.m." Toby smiled. "Me and my baby get this place all to ourselves for a good eight hours."

"Of which I'll probably sleep seven and a half hours," Sienna said, closing her eyes.

"Dang, I'm happy you suggested it first," Toby said. "I was afraid you'd want to fool around. I need the rest," he said.

Living the life of a high-powered music mogul seemed to be taking its toll, Alex thought as he stared down at his brother.

"What about Renee?" Alex asked. "Have you seen her around?"

"Not for a while," Toby said. "Go on. We'll watch out for Jazzy."

"Don't let her go past that first marker," Alex said, pointing to the area that marked the change in pool depth.

He entered the villa through the side door that led directly to the wing with the first and second master bedroom suites. When he went into their room, Alex found Renee lying atop the bed, cocooned in the fluffy covers. He didn't want to disturb her, but he was dying to crawl in that bed and wrap his arms around her. He wanted to feel her against him.

She stirred, turned over, and opened her eyes. She smiled. It was one of those lazy, not-all-the-way-awake kinds of smiles, and it was so sexy his body was instantly gripped by arousal.

"Hello there," she murmured. She patted the bed. "Care to join me?"

He shook his head. "That's a dangerous invitation."

"Haven't you guessed by now? I'm a thrill seeker."

"This may be more than you can handle," Alex said.

"I doubt that," she laughed.

"It's probably more than I can handle," he said. Alex sat on the edge of the bed, but maintained his distance.

"What's wrong?" Renee asked.

"Nothing," he said with a deep sigh; then he shook his head. "It's just . . . Jasmine has been opening up to me over the past weeks since Mr. Powell has been working with her, and . . ." Alex fisted his hand in the cover. "Every time I hear about some crap Chantal did, I just . . . I want to hurt her, Renee. She's been dead for two years, but I find myself wishing I could kill her with my bare hands. Does that sound demented to you?"

She shook her head, running her hand up and down his thigh. "No one can fault you for how you feel toward Chantal, Alex, but you have to forgive her. It's the only way to stop these thoughts from invading your life. Believe me, I know how that feels. She's robbing you of your happiness."

"Forgiveness is not an easy thing," he said.

Renee nodded. "I know, but the relief it brings is worth it."

Alex trailed a hand down her arm, settling it at her waist. "Have you really forgiven your parents for what they did to you?"

"Not fully," she admitted. "But I'm gradually letting go of the hate." She held him captive with her meaningful, understanding gaze. "It makes room for love to take its place."

"I love you, too," he said. Taking her hand and planting a light kiss on her knuckles, Alex asked, "Are you hungry at all? I thought there would be a farewell dinner, but looks like it's every man for himself. We can go out to eat."

"I'd rather stay here," Renee said, pulling him on top of her despite his protest. She was treading in dangerous waters, but he had warned her. Alex refused to be responsible for what happened next.

"We can do that, too," he said, following her as she leaned back into the mound of pillows and wrapped her hands around his neck.

Chapter Twenty-three

A faint, salt-tinged breeze blew across her skin, lightly fanning the wet wisps of hair that framed her face. The sun, ducking in and out of the high clouds, warmed her entire body.

"The recess period is over."

Renee jumped so high she nearly fell off the side of the bench. She opened her eyes to find Penelope staring down at her, partially blocking the bright sun that peeked through the branches of the massive oak that grew in the middle of St. Katherine's Episcopal's schoolyard.

"It's a good thing no one got hurt on the slides today, because your mind obviously hasn't been on supervising the kids on the playground."

"My mind isn't even in New Orleans," Renee admitted.

"You should have taken the day off. Better yet, you should just take off another week and bring me down there to St. Martin. If that island can put the kind of smile you've been walking around with on my face, I definitely need to head down there."

"It was wonderful, Penelope," Renee crooned, grabbing her water bottle from where she'd set it on the ground next to the bench. They walked under the covered walkway that led to the main building.

"Was it the island, or the company?" Penelope asked with a wide smile.

"A little of both," Renee answered.

"Yeah, right," Penelope snorted. "As if you'd be grinning like a hyena if Alex hadn't been in St. Martin."

"He's just so . . . God, I don't even know how to describe him," Renee said.

"Gorgeous, gorgeous, and really gorgeous?" Penelope suggested.

"That's just an added bonus," Renee said. "He's a lot more than his looks."

"I'm sure he is, but you won't tell me about that part," Penelope complained, holding the door open for her.

"It's more than just *that*, too. Though that's better than I ever imagined," Renee couldn't help but add; partially to get a rise out of Penelope, but partially because it was the undeniable truth. Alex Holmes could teach a class on how to please a woman.

"I so don't like you right now," was Penelope's answer.

"That *was* pretty mean on my part," Renee agreed.

"Try evil," Penelope said. "You know how long it's been since I went on a date?"

They arrived at Penelope's empty classroom. "I've got to prep for my next couple of classes, but if you want to fill me in on more of the details, feel free to stick around," Penelope said.

"Can't." Renee shrugged apologetically. "I have to pick up Mrs. Luke's third grade class for library skills."

"Have fun," Penelope said.

"Actually, that comes later tonight when I see Alex," Renee said before she closed the door.

She heard Penelope shout "evil!" through the closed door.

When Renee returned her final group of students to their teacher's classroom, she was tempted to sneak out of the side door and leave early. She was going to Alex's for dinner tonight. Kayla was coming over so Renee could help her and Jasmine practice softball; then they were having hamburgers. But she wasn't expected at Alex's until five o'clock, so leaving school early would only mean more time for her sit at the trailer and watch the clock. She spent her final minutes at school reshelving books the students had left on the tables.

When Renee parked at the curb in front of her aunt's home, she sat behind the wheel of her car for a few moments, staring absently at the nearly renovated house. She'd attempted to keep memories of today's morbid anniversary at bay, but they crept up on her all the same. It had been eighteen years, but seemed like nearly a lifetime ago. Her father had stumbled into the house, drowning in more liquor than a single human being should be able to consume without dying of alcohol poisoning. He'd started in on her mother; then he'd come after Renee.

Her chest tightened, the fear as real today as it had been eighteen years ago. She could feel the crack of his palm against her jaw, his elbow crashing into her ribs. Renee absently ran her hand over the wrist he'd broken in his drunken rage.

Suppressing the dark memories, Renee focused on the scene before her, marveling at the amount of work that had been accomplished while they were away. Alex's reaction to the progress his crew had made had not been nearly as enthusiastic as Renee's. He thought they would be finished, but two days of heavy rains while they were in St. Martin had lengthened the timetable. Despite the delay, they would be in the house by next week.

She locked up her car and made her way to the trailer.

"I thought you were going to Alex's," Aunt Lorna greeted her, opening the door to the FEMA trailer, which—thank God—would be picked up next week. Renee had been tempted to take FEMA up on their offer to sell the trailer just so she and Aunt Lorna could burn the thing in effigy.

"I'm going over there in a bit," she said, following her aunt inside. "Do you have dinner plans?"

"I've got left over hot and sour soup."

"Do you want to come over to Alex's? I doubt he'd mind."

"No, indeed." Her aunt waved off the idea. "This is the first time in about a month that I haven't had some place to be. I'm going to lay my butt across this lumpy couch and fall asleep watching the evening news."

"Uh-huh," Renee said. "I'll leave the light under the stove on so you can see when you come in tonight."

"Thanks, honey." Aunt Lorna winked. "I'm about to change right now. Have a good time at dinner. And after dinner, if you're lucky." Her aunt grinned.

Renee laughed as Lorna retreated to the tiny bathroom. A few minutes later she came out dressed in a peasant skirt and frilly blouse.

"I'll be back later, honey," Aunt Lorna said, giving her a kiss on the cheek. She took a step back and looked Renee in the eye, concern etched across her face. "Are you okay, Renee?"

Renee knew what she was referring to. "I'm good," she answered.

"I didn't want to bring it up—"

Renee stopped her. "It's fine, Aunt Lorna. Have fun tonight."

"I always do." She shot Renee a grin before closing the door behind her.

Renee ruminated on just how different her aunt was from her mother. Lorna, outgoing, spontaneous, full of spunk, would never allow a man to treat her the way her mother allowed herself to be treated.

If only she would leave that man. . . .

"That's not going to happen," Renee said under her breath. Why she even bothered to entertain such thoughts after all these years continued to baffle her. It was a dream that would never happen, and even if it did, how could she mend the chasm that stretched between her and her mother? Doreen Moore had made her choice years ago.

Renee willed herself to push aside all thoughts of that night. She changed into a pair of jeans and an old sweatshirt. Like Florida, the mild Louisiana autumn weather didn't allow for anything heavier than a sweatshirt. She drove the fifteen minutes to Alex's house, and was hit by the aroma of charcoal wafting from the backyard. Renee passed through the side gate, and rounded the side of the house. She spotted Jasmine and Kayla playing catch, and they quickly spotted her, running up to her and screaming, "Ms. Moore!"

Alex stepped from behind the huge stainless-steel grill. The grin that lifted the corner of his mouth made Renee think instantly of kissing him.

"Hello, Ms. Moore," he said, looking down at her from the edge of the wooden deck. "I hope you're hungry."

"If I'm not, I'm sure these two will help me work up an appetite," Renee said for the benefit of the two little girls following her up the steps. She hung her purse on the edge of one of the patio chairs and walked over to Alex, unable to refrain from reaching up for him and placing a brief kiss on his lips.

"How was school?" he asked.

"It's just not the same now that a certain volunteer has left," she answered.

"I miss being there, too," he admitted.

"Ms. Moore, you ready?" Jasmine called.

"Time to get to work," she said, stealing another quick kiss before joining Jasmine and Kayla.

Renee brought them through a few practice drills, changing up her pitch and teaching the fundamentals of catching fly balls.

By the time Alex shouted that the burgers were done, Renee was done, too. She considered herself pretty athletic, but she was no match for a couple of six-year-olds. They sat around the glass-topped patio table that held the platter of grilled burgers, an array of condiments, lettuce, tomatoes, and pickle spears.

"Daddy, can I have a piece of cheese?" Jasmine asked.

"Sure, baby," he answered.

"Me, too," Kayla added, squeezing out of the chair without bothering to push it back from the table and following Jasmine into the house.

"Those two wore me out," Renee said.

"They are pretty determined to say they only have one game left," Alex said.

"But it's the biggest game of the season," Renee reminded him. "The other team has a third grader."

"I forgot about that. You may have to stay longer to make sure they're extra prepared. And maybe," he said, leaning toward her, his lips a few inches from her. "Once Jasmine goes to bed." He inched closer. "You can stay just a little bit longer."

"Just a little?"

"I'm up for whatever you are," he said.

Jasmine and Kayla came barreling through the back door

onto the deck before Renee could make the dirty remark that was on the tip of her tongue. She'd tuck it in the corner of her mind until later tonight.

They all proceeded to stuff themselves with hamburgers, corn on the cob, and green salad as Jasmine and Kayla talked about Saturday's upcoming game.

"Anybody want strawberry shortcake?" Alex asked once they were done with the burgers.

"Oooh, that sounds good," Renee said. "But I couldn't eat it if I tried."

"Can me and Kayla go practice some more, Daddy?" Jasmine asked.

"Kayla's mom will be here in a few minutes," Alex said.

"Well, can we practice till she gets here?"

"Go on," Alex relented, and the girls bounded from the table, grabbing the bat, softball, and glove from where they'd deposited them on the edge of the deck.

"I used to be that way," Renee said. "Now the first thing I think about after eating a meal like that involves a comfy couch and a solid hour of nap time."

"I'm sure you can think of something better to do on a couch than nap," Alex said.

"Not at the moment," Renee teased.

"Well, let me give you a couple of clues," he said as he came in for another kiss.

"Mr. Holmes!"

Kayla's scream caused instant panic to race down Renee's spine. She turned and looked toward the far back corner of the yard where the girls had gone to practice, and spotted Jasmine sprawled on the ground. Alex was down the steps of the deck before Renee could push her chair back from the table. She rushed after him, stopping to grab Kayla by the hand and drag her to where Jasmine lay on the ground.

"What happened?" Alex asked.

"I—" Kayla hiccupped. "I—"

"Kayla, what happened?" Alex shouted, picking Jasmine up from the ground. The child was limp in his arms. Blood seeped out of a nasty gash just above Jasmine's left ear.

"The ball hit her," Kayla cried. "I'm sorry."

"It's okay, honey," Renee said, putting her hand around the little girl's shoulders. "Is she breathing?" Renee asked, her chest tightening with fear.

Alex put his head to her mouth. "Yes," he answered. "Wake up, Jasmine," he said, tapping her chest. "Jasmine, wake up!" Alex shouted.

Jasmine began to stir. "Daddy," she said in a weak voice.

"Thank God," Renee sighed.

"I'm here, baby," Alex said. He looked to Renee. "I'm still taking her to the hospital."

"Of course. I'll follow in my car," she said.

Alex carried Jasmine close to his chest, making his way quickly out of the backyard and to his truck. Renee ushered Kayla to her car and gave the little girl her cell phone so she could call her mother and have her pick Kayla up at the hospital. But before Renee could pull out of Alex's driveway, Leslie Morgan pulled in behind her. Renee relayed what had happened, leaving out as much detail as possible. Kayla was distraught enough.

Once she reached the hospital, she parked and hurried through the emergency room's double doors. She grabbed the arm of the first person in hospital attire she spotted.

"A little girl was just brought in with a head injury."

"Are you a relative?"

"Yes," Renee lied.

"You'll need to go to the nurses' station, and—"

"Eli!" Renee ran over to the elevator bay where Eli had just exited. She caught him by the arm.

"Hey, Renee. What are you doing here?" he asked.

"Alex just brought Jasmine in. She was hit in the head by a softball," Renee explained.

"Shit," Eli whispered under his breath. He took Renee's

hand, practically dragging her as his long legs ate up the white-tiled floor with quick strides.

"Patty, did you see my niece come in?" he asked a nurse who was carrying two IV bags.

"Room five." The nurse nodded toward a door.

The exam room was filled with activity. Monica was in charge, which allowed Renee to take at least a small breath of relief as she hurried to Alex's side. He stood a few feet from the bed, his arms crossed over his chest, his Adam's apple working itself up and down, as if he were having trouble swallowing.

"How's she doing?" Renee asked.

"Monica says she's okay," he answered.

Renee pulled at his elbow, just enough to make room for her to slip her arm through. Several interminable minutes later, Monica said, "Take her to CT so we can run a full scan." Shucking the gloves from her hands, she started toward them.

The crew wheeled Jasmine out of the room, but Monica stopped Alex from following with a hand to his chest. "She's on her way to radiology," she said.

"Be straight with me, Monica. How serious is it?" The emotion clogging his already deep voice made it barely audible.

"She is going to be fine. She's got a pretty nasty cut that will require a few stitches, but other than that, she's going to be *just fine*," Monica stressed.

"Are you sure?"

Monica took a frustrated breath. "Are you seriously this hardheaded? I swear, you and your brother are two of a kind."

"Hey," Eli said with an affronted snort.

Monica rolled her eyes at her husband, then turned back to Alex. "They're going to X-ray her head just to make sure everything's okay—"

Alex cut her off. "I thought you said she's going to be fine."

"It's customary with a head injury," Renee provided. "It doesn't mean there's anything serious."

"Thank you," Monica said. "At least I've got one voice of reason here."

Eli cleared his throat, but Monica ignored him. "Are we clear?" she asked Alex.

"Yeah," he said with a relieved sigh. "So, what am I supposed to do now?"

"Look, if you really want to help, go to the blood bank on the third floor and donate blood," Monica suggested.

The door flew open.

"Dr. Gardner-Holmes, we have an MVA pulling in," a nurse called.

Monica turned back to them. "I have to go. After you're done at the blood bank, come back down to the ER waiting room. I'll give you an update on Jasmine as soon as I can." She looked directly at Renee. "Will you be here for a while?"

Renee nodded. "I'm not leaving until Alex does," she said.

"Good. Keep him away from radiology. They don't need him pestering them."

After Monica had left and they were alone, Renee tugged on Alex's arm. His face was devoid of emotion, though his apprehension was so thick it was practically another occupant in the room.

"Alex, they're going to need this room. We have to go," Renee urged.

He looked down at her, the pain in his eyes causing her chest to ache in sympathy.

"I'm sorry about overreacting." Alex's voice broke. "It's just that . . . she's everything, Renee. She's the reason I breathe."

"I know, Alex, but Jasmine is going to be fine." Renee tugged at his arm. "Come on. Let's go down to the blood bank."

"You know you can go home if you want to."

"I don't want to," Renee said. "Not until you do."

Alex cupped her face in his palm and stared into her eyes. "Thank you for standing by my side."

She covered his hand with her own. "There's no other place I'd rather be."

Alex could hardly recall the trek from the ER to the blood blank, then back to the ER waiting room. His mind was still clouded by a fog of uncertainty too thick for the surrounding environment to penetrate. All he could think about was his baby lying on the ground, not making a sound. That trail of blood trickling from her ear.

For a moment, before she'd awakened in his arms, his mind had jumped to the most horrific of conclusions.

There was no such thing as life without Jasmine. She had been the center of his universe from the moment she was conceived. He could not remember his life's purpose before she was born. Any personal dreams or goals he'd held instantly dissipated the moment he laid eyes on that tiny, precious baby sucking her fingers in the hospital's nursery ward.

Now his little girl was stretched out on an X-ray table with a two-inch gash on her head.

"I can't take this," Alex whispered. "I need to know what's going on." He pushed up from the chair, but Renee caught his arm.

"Alex." Her calm, sensible voice reined him in again. The doctors of Methodist Memorial had Renee to thank for him not barging in on them a half dozen times. She had been a rock at his side, offering support in the way she lightly squeezed his hand or rubbed the small of his back when he leaned over with his head bowed to pray.

Alex settled back into his seat. He hunched his back, placed his head in his hands, and tried to stave off the tears that had been threatening to fall. Other than the one he'd allowed to escape back in the emergency room, he'd been pretty successful at it. Renee started rubbing his back in sure, soothing circles.

"Do you need anything?" she asked.

He shook his head. He wanted to say he was okay. But

that lie was too far from the truth for him to pull it off. He wouldn't truly be okay until he held his baby girl in his arms.

Alex stopped her with a hand to her shoulder. "Renee, you know you don't have to stay here. You have work tomorrow."

"Alex, if you tell me to go home one more time, I'm going to punch you. I told you I'm not leaving until you do."

"But you don't have to st—"

She pressed two fingers to his lips. "I want to stay," she said. "If I went home, I would have you on the phone every five minutes for an update. I'd rather just stick around so I can get the news firsthand."

Alex brought her into his arms and squeezed. "Thank you," he said, pressing a kiss to the crown of her head.

"You're welcome," she answered, pulling him even closer to her body. She raised her head from his chest and looked up at him. "Now, are you sure I can't get you anything? Some chips from the vending machine, maybe?"

"I can't eat," Alex admitted.

"Promise you'll let me know if you need anything."

Several minutes later, Monica came through the door. Alex stood. The relieved smile that broke across her face caused Alex's heart to catch in his throat.

"Her X-ray came back negative," Monica said. "They're stitching her up right now."

Relief rushed through his veins at a startling rate, turning his muscles into mush. Alex sank down, grateful there was a chair to catch him.

Alex turned to Renee. "I want you to go home," he told her.

She punched his arm. "I warned you I would do that if you said those words again," she said with a laugh.

For the first time since he had seen Jasmine lying on the ground with a trail of blood flowing down her face, Alex allowed himself to feel something other than pure misery.

Renee was the only one who could elicit a smile from him at this moment.

"Sorry," he said.

"How long before we can see her?" Renee asked Monica.

"It shouldn't be too long."

"I just need to see her with my own eyes," Alex said. He had to know for himself that his baby really was okay.

Monica was paged to the ER.

Alex put his arm around Renee's shoulder and pulled her closer into his body. "Would it be inappropriate to kiss you in the middle of a hospital waiting room?" he asked.

"Probably," Renee said, "but I doubt we'd be the first to do so. Receiving good news tends to put people in the mood," she said.

Alex lowered his mouth to hers and eased into a slow, thorough kiss. He had been alone for over two years, had handled his share of scrapes and bug bites, but Alex sent up a special prayer of thanks that he had not had to face this by himself. Just being in the same space he occupied, Renee had offered a sense of comfort and strength Alex hadn't realized he'd been missing.

"Thank you for not listening all those times I told you to go on home," he said.

"You're welcome," she answered.

She wrapped her arm around his waist and cradled her head against his chest. They sat that way for a long time. Now that Jasmine was out of the woods, he could finally relax.

The waiting room door opened. Alex looked up from where he rested his jaw on Renee's head. Dread shot up his spine at the cautious look on Monica's face.

"What happened?" Alex asked, bounding from the chair.

Monica looked from Renee to Alex. "Uh, Alex, can I speak to you in the hallway?" she asked.

Instant fear held his gut in a Vise-Grip, tightening with each nanosecond that passed.

"What is it?" he asked.

"Alex—"

"What's happened to my little girl?"

"No, she's fine," Monica said, and Alex shuddered with relief once again. "I'm sorry. I didn't mean to scare you. Jasmine is still being stitched up."

"Then what's wrong?" Alex asked.

"Alex, please just step into the hallway with me."

"I'm going to tell Renee whatever you tell me, so just say it," he said.

Monica wiped her palms on the sides of her white lab coat. "It's about the blood you donated to the blood bank," she said.

"What about it? Is there something wrong with me?"

"No, no," Monica said. "Lord, how am I supposed to do this?"

"Monica, what in the hell is going on?" Alex yelled.

"Your blood type is AB-positive."

"I know that."

"Jasmine is O-positive," Monica said. She looked at Renee, who'd squeezed his fingers with one hand and covered her mouth with the other.

Alex shook his head. "So? What the hell does that matter?"

Monica's eyes were filled with sympathy. "Those blood types don't match up, Alex. It's medically impossible that Jasmine is your biological daughter."

Chapter Twenty-four

Renee felt the jolt that seemed to shoot through Alex's body at Monica's announcement. He dropped her hand.

"You'll need to take a DNA test to be sure," Monica continued.

"That's . . . no . . . something got mixed up," Alex said,

backing up, as if he could physically distance himself from his sister-in-law's words.

"Alex." Renee went for his hand, but he shook her off.

"That's bullshit," he said.

Monica held her hands out, pleading. "Alex, don't you think I checked and rechecked before coming to see you?"

"You got something wrong," he said. "Somebody's got something wrong."

"Alex, please," Monica implored.

He brushed past her and burst out the door. Renee went after him, but Monica caught her arm.

"Maybe he should be alone for a bit," Monica said.

"I don't think so," Renee said, and took off after Alex. She saw him turn the corner, and she ran down the corridor after him.

"Alex!" Renee called, but he ignored her. "Alex!"

He entered a door at the end of the hallway. Renee was there in a matter of seconds, pushing through what she realized was the entryway to the stairwell. She heard Alex as he bounded down the stairs.

"Alex!" she called.

By the time she got to the bottom of the stairwell, Renee knew there was no way she would find him. But when she pushed through the door that led to an alley, she found Alex facing the hospital's exterior wall, his head resting on his arms as he leaned against the brick.

"Alex?"

"Just leave." The words were barely audible.

Renee took a cautious step forward. "Alex, please talk to me."

He whipped around, his handsome face contorted in anger and heartbreaking anguish. "What the hell do you expect me to say?" he asked, bearing down on her. "You were there. You heard Monica," he said, his voice rising with every word. "My baby girl isn't really mine. The child I've raised for six years—who is my *life*—isn't my daughter. What the hell do you want me to say to that?"

He picked up an empty crate and slammed it on the ground, the wood splintering into a dozen pieces.

Renee jumped back. Shock and fear stalked through her at the aggression radiating from Alex. It pulsed through the air surrounding them. She'd witnessed the look in Alex's eyes before, years ago, on an almost daily basis. Memories of the violence she'd been subjected to at her father's hand pummeled her.

"What's the matter, Renee? You can't think of anything to say, either, can you?" Alex asked.

"Alex, don't do this," she said.

He took another step forward. "What? I'm just looking for a little help here. You want to help, right?"

He backed her up against the wall, his large body framing hers.

"Help me out, Renee. What's a guy supposed to do when he finds out his whore of a wife had another man's baby? There's not really a book on how to deal with this situation, is there?" he yelled, slapping the building next to her head.

Renee jumped. She brought her fist to her mouth, fighting back a scream. She would not cave to fear. Not again. Never again.

But she couldn't fight this.

Ducking under Alex's arm, Renee escaped his hold. And ran.

Alex covered his face with his hands and sank to his knees, the fight draining from his body in a rush, leaving in its wake a sense of emptiness that filled every chamber of his heart.

Was he really expected to function after this? Was he supposed to walk and talk? Breathe? Exist? How could anybody expect him to behave like a normal human being after having his world shattered?

His baby girl.

How could his baby girl not be his? How could he not know?

God, he would give anything to have the chance to face Chantal right now. He wanted to feel his hands wrapped around her throat. He wanted to look into her eyes as he slowly drained the life out of her.

"Alex?"

His back stiffened at the sound of his brother's voice.

"Just leave me alone, E."

"Alex, you can't sit out here all night." This from Monica.

He was not dealing with the two of them right now. "I told you to leave me alone," he said.

Alex flinched when a hand gripped his shoulder, but he didn't have the strength to knock it away. "Alex, come on," Eli said. "We can go to my office if you want to."

"I don't know what I want to do," he answered. Except possibly die. Maybe then the pain would go away. But Alex doubted even death could ease the ache coursing through him.

"Come on," Eli encouraged.

At his brother's urging, Alex finally stood. He stared at Eli and was nearly brought back to his knees by the understanding on his brother's face.

Eli opened his arms. "I'm so sorry, man," he said.

He couldn't shoulder this on his own a second longer. Alex fell into his brother's arms and sobbed like a child.

Chapter Twenty-five

Renee swiped viciously at the tears that continued to stream down her face. She looked in the rearview and snorted at the vision that stared back at her. Eyes red and puffy. Nose the color of a bing cherry. Cheeks soaked with an onslaught of tears that would not stop.

She stopped at a red light and leaned her head back against the headrest. She shut her eyes, but quickly opened them when Alex's enraged face popped into her mind's eye. Cold fear raced down Renee's spine at the thought of the hostility she'd witnessed; violence she didn't think Alex was capable of.

She'd been on the receiving end of what happened when that type of rage was released. Her fingers trembled as they traveled idly along the scar behind her ear. It was her reminder, her one true anchor that kept her grounded in the harsh reality of what people who supposedly loved you could do when they turned violent.

Behind her, a car horn blew.

Renee pressed on the accelerator and told herself to put Alex out of her mind before she cracked her car against a tree.

Just like Alex's wife had done. But not before she'd lied to her husband about who had fathered her child.

"Oh God, Alex."

He had every right to rage. It was the ultimate betrayal. To discover the child he'd raised and loved as his own was a product of one of his wife's affairs. Even though she'd seen it in his eyes, Renee knew she would never comprehend the pure anguish Alex must be feeling at this moment. For a second, he thought he would lose Jasmine tonight. In a way, he had.

"And I left him to deal with it on his own," Renee whispered. After everything Alex had done for her, when it had come time for her to be there for him, she'd left. And what was her excuse? He'd shattered a crate on the ground? He was justified in doing that and more. But there was no excuse for her cowardice. She'd allowed her past demons to rule her decisions, and in doing so, had allowed her father to win yet again.

"Not this time," Renee said. She turned into a gas station and pulled back onto the street she'd been traveling, heading in the opposite direction back to the hospital.

Ten minutes later, Renee pulled into the hospital's covered parking garage. She didn't have a clue as to where to find Alex, but knew of at least one person who could help. She walked past the room labeled TRIAGE and spotted Monica coming from behind a curtain.

"Monica," Renee called.

Monica came out of the room. "Renee—"

Renee grabbed her wrist. "Where's Alex?"

"He's with Eli," Monica answered. "His office is on the fourth floor."

Renee took off for the elevators. She fidgeted as she watched the numbers illuminate one by one above the door. It dinged at the fourth floor, and Renee ran to the large nurses' station that sat in the middle of the massive space.

"Can you point me to Dr. Elijah Holmes's office?" she asked the woman behind the desk.

"I'm not sure he's here," the nurse said. "Dr. Holmes's shift ended a half hour ago."

"His wife said he's still here."

"His office is down the hall and to the right. Room 426."

"Thank you," Renee threw over her shoulder as she headed in the direction the nurse had pointed. She turned the corner, and nearly ran into Eli's chest.

"Whoa, hold up there."

"Eli, is he in your office?" She gestured down the hall.

Eli shook his head. "Probably in Jasmine's room. They decided to keep her overnight for observation. It's not unusual with a head injury. I'm headed up to Pediatrics right now." He took her hand and they walked to the elevators. As soon as the doors closed, Eli turned to her. "You know the whole story?" he asked.

Renee nodded. "Eli, how is he?"

The doors opened to the sixth floor. Eli held it open and gestured for her to go ahead of him.

"Heartbroken," he finally answered.

Her own heart constricted even more. She followed Eli

into the room that was divided by smaller rooms with glass walls. JASMINE HOLMES was printed in bold letters in the slot next to the fifth door on the right.

Renee entered the room after Eli, but when she walked in, the only other occupant was a sleeping Jasmine, a square gauze bandage taped to the left side of her head.

Renee's chest tightened as she watched Eli lean over his niece and whisper, "Hey, Sunflower," before placing a kiss on Jasmine's forehead. This child was so loved.

The door creaked opened, but it was only a nurse.

"Hello, Dr. Holmes," she said. She nodded at Renee.

"Hey there, Cheryl," Eli returned. "Have you seen my brother?"

"The chapel," the nurse answered. She read one of the machines and made a note on the clipboard that hung on the bottom rail of Jasmine's bed, then left the room.

"It's on the bottom floor," Eli said. "Take a left once you get off the elevators."

Without another word, Renee left the room. She wasn't sure what reception she would get from Alex when she encountered him. She'd left him at the precise time that he'd needed her the most. She wouldn't be surprised if Alex refused to speak to her. It would be no less than she deserved.

When she arrived at the bottom floor, she debated turning right, toward the hospital entrance.

Stop being a coward, she told herself. Whatever Alex's reaction, she would accept it, and they would move on, but she would help him get through this whether he wanted her to or not.

The door to the chapel was closed. Renee laid hands on the smooth wood and pushed. The room was small. It held about a dozen folding chairs, arranged in two rows of three on each side of an aisle.

Alex sat facing the tiny altar, his elbows on his thighs, face in his hands. His broad shoulders heaved, and his back shook. Renee covered her mouth, her heart breaking as she watched the silent sobs that racked his body.

She walked over and put a hand on his shoulder. He jerked up, his body instantly stiffening. He looked up at her with reddened, tear-soaked eyes.

The ache in her chest was almost more than she could bear. The pain coming through Alex's eyes was so profound, it touched the very depths of her soul.

Renee crossed her leg over his and lowered herself onto his lap. She wrapped her arms around him, and buried her face in the crook of Alex's neck, fitting perfectly in the hollow between his jaw and shoulder. After a moment's hesitation, Alex's arms circled her, his uneven breathing making his chest rise and fall.

She wanted to reassure him that everything would be okay, but it was an assurance she could not guarantee. There were too many unknowns, the span of uncertainty so vast she could hardly wrap her head around it. The only thing Renee was sure of was her vow to remain by his side through whatever he faced.

Cocooned in his embrace, she offered the only gift she could, the silent promise that she would never leave him again.

Locking her arms around him, Renee swallowed her own sobs as Alex cried in her arms.

Alex didn't know how much time had passed. He only knew he wasn't ready to leave. He wasn't ready to cope with the world outside the walls of this tiny chapel. A world where his daughter had been conceived by another man.

Pain and disbelief slammed through him once again.

He couldn't stay hidden in this chapel, despite his body's insistence to remain wrapped in Renee's soothing embrace.

"Renee?" Alex whispered in her ear.

"I'm here," she said.

"I know. Thank you," he answered.

She lifted her head, the streaks down her cheeks some-how adding to her beauty; maybe because they had been shed for him?

"I'm sorry I left," she said.

Alex shook his head. "You're not the one who's supposed to apologize."

"Yes, I am," Renee countered. "I won't do that again," she said.

"Those are supposed to be my words." He ran a hand down her back. "I'm sorry for what happened outside. I've never lost it like that before."

"Who could blame you, Alex? After everything you've been through in the last few hours? Who could blame you for wanting to beat up the entire world?"

"I never would have touched you," he said, needing her to know that. "I may have smashed every car window in the parking lot, and punched every wall within striking dis-tance, but I would never raise my hand to you or any other woman."

"I know," she reassured him. "I knew it seconds after I left." She ran her hands up and down his arms. "The mem-ories just bombarded me. In that instant, all I could see was my father's fist coming toward me."

Alex shut his eyes, a sick feeling gripping his stomach at the thought of her facing those memories once again. "I am *so* sorry for scaring you, baby."

Renee leaned forward and rested her forehead on his. "It's over," she whispered.

Alex's chest tightened. He was humbled and over-whelmed by her swift forgiveness.

"What are you going to do?" Renee asked. She was talk-ing about Jasmine. The question had entered his mind, but the thought had been fleeting, because Alex knew there was only one thing he could do.

He took a deep, lung-cleansing breath. "I'm going to sit by Jazzy's bed and hold her hand," he answered. "When she wakes up, I'm going to tell her how much I love her, and that she's a princess. Same as always."

Alex wiped the tear that ran down Renee's cheek.

"She's my little girl," he said. "She will always be my little girl. I don't care about the man who fathered her. God created her for me. From the minute she was born, I knew my sole purpose in life was to love that little girl. No blood test is going to change that."

"She is so lucky to have you for a father, Alex." It wasn't the first time Renee had uttered those words to him.

"I'm just as lucky to have her as a daughter," Alex said. He cradled Renee's cheeks in his palms and pressed a delicate kiss to her trembling lips. "I'm lucky to have you as the woman I love, too," he said.

Tears ran down her cheeks in earnest. Alex used his thumbs to wipe them away, but the trail continued to flow.

"Alex, I love you so much," Renee choked on a sob.

He couldn't contain his smile. "I told Jasmine she could be there when I asked you to marry me."

"Then let's go to her room," Renee said. "Right now."

"Does that mean I'll get a yes?"

"Oh yes," she said, holding his face in her hands and placing another kiss on his lips. "I'm dying to say yes to you."

Chapter Twenty-six

"That is the ugliest bunch of flowers I've ever seen," Toby said.

"Leave it alone." Eli punched Toby on the arm before strolling over to Jasmine's hospital bed. "I told the florist to give me one of every type of flower they had in the place. I wanted to make sure my little Petunia, Rosebud, Water

Lily, Bird-of-Paradise had a lot of color in her room," Eli said, pinching Jasmine's nose.

"You're silly, Uncle Eli," Jasmine laughed.

"But you love your uncle Eli, no matter how silly, right?"

"Yes," Jasmine answered. She stretched her arms out and enveloped Eli in a hug, plopping a sloppy kiss on his cheek.

"Does this mean I have to get you a bunch of flowers to get some of that sugar?" Toby asked.

"No, you can have a kiss, too," Jasmine said.

"Not before I have mine," Alex said. He pushed from the wall next to Jasmine's bed and leaned in for a kiss. "The doctors are going to take one last look to make sure everything is okay up there." Alex pointed to her head. "Then we get to head home. Uncle Eli and Uncle Toby will come over to the house to see you later tonight, right?"

"Oh yeah. I'm bringing back something special," Toby said. "And it'll be a lot better than a bunch of mismatched flowers."

Alex didn't bother to remind Toby about the no-gift-giving rule. He'd already accepted the fact that Jasmine was destined to be spoiled rotten by the entire family for the rest of her natural-born life.

After a rapid DNA test confirmed his baby girl was, in fact, not his biological daughter, Alex broke the news to Mama and Toby. They were both devastated, but quickly agreed that nothing would change where Jasmine was concerned. She was born a Holmes and would always be a Holmes.

Alex still had the tough decision to make regarding whether he would tell Jasmine about the circumstances surrounding her birth, but even if he did, it would be years from now. If ever. She was his, and always would be. It was as simple as that.

The nurse wheeled Jasmine out, leaving Alex, Renee, Toby, and Eli in the room.

"Hey," Toby said. "I forgot to ask if I should start looking for a flight back to St. Martin."

Alex draped an arm around Renee's shoulder and pulled her in close.

"We haven't gotten that far yet," she answered.

"Well, ya'll need to figure something out quick. I'm ready to go back."

"What about you and Sienna?" Eli asked. "The two of you can get married out there."

A smile drew across Toby's face. "Actually, Sienna and I were married in Vegas last week."

"What!" Alex and Eli both yelled.

"Don't tell me you got married at one of those cheesy Elvis chapels," Alex said.

"Boy, are you crazy? Mama is going to kill you," Eli said.

"Yeah, well, it was either that or have Sienna walk down the aisle in a maternity wedding dress. We figured a quick wedding was better."

Silence reigned, until Alex and Eli swamped him, grabbing Toby in a three-person bear hug.

Eli's grin was huge. "You're going to be a daddy?"

"Wait until Mama hears this," Alex said.

"Don't say anything," Toby warned them. "Sienna and I want to tell Mama together."

Renee walked up to Toby and wrapped her arms around him. "Congratulations." She kissed his cheek.

Eli's BlackBerry went off. "That's my cue," he said. He held his hand out to Toby. "Congratulations again, man," Eli said, pulling Toby in again for a one-arm hug.

"I need to head out, too," Toby said.

Alex brought his brother in for another hug. Knuckle-headed Toby was going to be a father. It was hard to believe, but then again, Toby had grown by leaps and bounds this past year. In a way, all three of them had. "You're going to make a good dad," Alex told him.

"I had good examples." Toby grinned. "I'm just following in yours and Pop's footsteps. See you later, man. Tell Jazzy I'll see her tonight."

As Alex watched his younger brother walk out of the hospital room, pride filled every chamber of his heart. Yeah, Toby was going to do just fine. His Jazzy would soon have a cousin to play with, and Mama would finally have another grandbaby.

"That's some exciting news, huh?" Renee said, sidling up to him and wrapping her arms around his waist.

"Toby'll be a good dad," Alex said again.

"I can tell just by the way he interacts with Jasmine."

Alex dipped his head and planted a kiss on her lips. God, he loved these lips. He wanted to spend the rest of this lifetime kissing them.

"Jasmine's been the only grandchild for such a long time, I wonder how she'll react to the news that there will be another kid around."

"I think she'll do just fine," Renee said. "She's adjusted pretty well to sharing her daddy. Actually, I thought as soon as we were married we could start working on giving Jasmine a little brother or sister. You think you're up to that challenge?"

"I think I can handle that."

Renee ran her hand up his chest. "Well, we'll probably need a few practice runs before we get it right."

"Just tell me the start time." He lowered his mouth for another kiss. "I'm there."

Epilogue

The rose petals Jasmine dropped from the white wicker basket floated on the wind and into the ocean a few feet away. Monica motioned for her to hurry, but Jazzy took her sweet time strolling up the aisle.

Alex leaned over and whispered to Eli, "You sure you're ready to deal with that?"

Eli switched the baby girl cradled in his arms from one side to the other. "Little late to ask that question, isn't it?" he said, tugging the lace-trimmed bonnet around his niece's face. Zenobia, Toby and Sienna's eight-week-old daughter, punched her tiny fist in the air. "Besides, if you and Toby can handle a baby, I sure as hell can."

"It's not as easy as it looks," Alex said.

Toby turned. "Would ya'll be quiet? I can't hear what's going on." He reached back for his daughter, an instant smile breaking out over his face. "I missed Mama's first wedding, I'd like to actually hear the second one."

Monica caught their attention and raked her finger across her neck, making a "cut it out" gesture. With two short months from delivering her and Eli's baby girl, the maid-of-honor dress flowed over her protruding belly like a peach waterfall.

"I don't want to have to answer to her," Eli said.

"Me, neither," Alex agreed. They sat for the rest of the short ceremony and watched as their mother was united in holy matrimony with Gerald Mitchell in the same spot Eli had married Monica a year ago.

After the ceremony, Alex sat poolside at L'Oasis with Renee on his lap. He let his gaze roam over the people gathered at the reception. Gerald had enough dough in the bank to fly the eight members of Morning Star Baptist Church's deaconess board, along with about a dozen of his and Mama's mutual friends.

"Your mother made a beautiful bride," Renee said, dipping her head low and nuzzling the spot behind his ear.

"Almost as beautiful as you were the day we were married," Alex said. He pressed his lips to her smooth jaw, consuming the unique fragrance that was solely Renee. Earlier, as she'd walked down the aisle as one of his mother's bridal attendants, his breath had caught in his throat at the sight of her. As he looked down on his wife's stunning face, Alex experienced that same breath-robbing sensation.

"Look at your brother." Renee nodded toward where Toby cradled Zenobia, staring at his daughter as if she were an exquisite piece of art.

"Oh yeah, that boy's in love," Alex laughed. "Little girls do that to their daddies. I was just as in awe of my princess the day she was born." Alex sought out Jasmine, who swam laps in the villa's pool. She still took his breath away.

"This family is overflowing with princesses," Renee said. "I think your mom was hoping Eli and Monica's sonogram would show that she was having a boy."

"It is funny after having three sons we all would have girls."

Renee shrugged. She took his hand and placed it on her flat stomach, and covered it with both of hers. "Who knows?" Renee mused. "Maybe we're the ones meant to have the first boy."

"Maybe," Alex said. Then he stopped, catching the grin at the edge of Renee's lips. Alex captured her chin in his hand and turned her to face him. He questioned her with his eyes. Renee's grin widened and she nodded.

"Oh my God," he breathed into her kiss. "I love you so much, baby."

"I love you, too, Alex." Renee kissed him back, fierce and strong. "So much more than I can ever put into words."

"I don't need words," he said. "You show me every single day. I didn't know how precious love could be before you, Renee."

"I'm happy I could help you find love again."

"You did more than that. You rescued me."

☐ **YES!**

Sign me up for the Love Spell Book Club and send my FREE BOOKS! If I choose to stay in the club, I will pay only $8.50* each month, a savings of $6.48!

NAME: _____

ADDRESS: _____

TELEPHONE: _____

EMAIL: _____

☐ I want to pay by credit card.

☐   ☐ MasterCard   ☐ DISCOVER

ACCOUNT #: _____

EXPIRATION DATE: _____

SIGNATURE: _____

Mail this page along with $2.00 shipping and handling to:
Love Spell Book Club
PO Box 6640
Wayne, PA 19087
Or fax (must include credit card information) to:
610-995-9274
You can also sign up online at **www.dorchesterpub.com**.
*Plus $2.00 for shipping. Offer open to residents of the U.S. and Canada only.
Canadian residents please call 1-800-481-9191 for pricing information.
If under 18, a parent or guardian must sign. Terms, prices and conditions subject to change. Subscription subject to acceptance. Dorchester Publishing reserves the right to reject any order or cancel any subscription.

GET FREE BOOK8!

You can have the best romance delivered to your door for less than what you'd pay in a bookstore or online. Sign up for one of our book clubs today, and we'll send you *FREE* BOOKS* just for trying it out.. **with no obligation to buy, ever!**

Bring a little magic into your life with the romance of Love Spell—fun contemporaries, paranormals, time-travels, futuristics, and more. Your shipments will include authors such as **MARJORIE LIU, JADE LEE, NINA BANGS, GEMMA HALLIDAY**, and many more.

As a book club member you also receive the following special benefits:
- 30% off all orders!
- Exclusive access to special discounts!
- Convenient home delivery and 10 days to return any books you don't want to keep.

Visit www.dorchesterpub.com or call 1-800-481-9191

There is no minimum number of books to buy, and you may cancel membership at any time. *Please include $2.00 for shipping and handling.